AN UNFINISHED LIFE

a novel by

MARY A. WASOWSKI

First Edition: March 2016
Library of Congress Cataloging-in-Publication Data

http://authormaryawasowski.com/

Wasowski, Mary A.
An Unfinished Life / 1st ed
ISBN-13: 978-0-9969605-1-9

This book is for the readers. Thank you, from my heart.

Note from the Author

Thank you, readers, for taking the time to read *An Unfinished Life*. Please consider leaving an honest review.

A true Thank You would not be complete until I thank the angels that live in my life every day…

Henry: thank you for loving me. It's been an amazing 26 years sharing my life with you. You are a forever romantic, and not a day goes by that you don't make me smile or laugh. I love you, husband.

Our boys: You are my world. I love you three with all of my heart. You raise me up when I am feeling down. Your support is amazing for my ego. You call me a rock star. You treat me like a hero. At the end of the day, I am just a mom.

Mindy: thank you for taking the time to read my words. Your feedback is instrumental. I'm never worried when I receive your critiques. I trust you completely, and I am so lucky to have your support when it comes to my writing, and even more in friendship. I love you more. You wear many hats my friend. You not only are my number one beta reader, but an amazing cover designer. You designed an outrageous cover for this book. You rock my world.

Joe: the other guy in my life. You are not only my editor, but my very dear friend. Thank you for inspiring me and listening to all my crazy book ideas. You. Get. Me. And I love you for it.

JT Formatting: thank you, Julie, for all you do. This is book number six for us. I have fond memories of our first interactions with each other, and smile when I think of them. You must have thought I was crazy with all of my questions, but you answered each one and helped me understand how everything works. You give

100% to every client you work with. I am honored to be one of them. I have the utmost respect for you and honored to call you friend. Your creativity astounds me with every book you format for me. You are a rock star.

For the bloggers: thank you to Kylie McDermott of Give Me Books. You did an amazing job spreading the word for *An Unfinished Life* to the blogging community. Everyone who participated has been so supportive, sharing my cover and spreading the word.

Lastly, to you, my readers: I hope you enjoyed reading Jack and Jacob's story. These two men grabbed hold of my heart and did not let go. This was the book I never intended to write, but it was the support from my readers who asked for more. I am thankful that I listened.

XOXO

Mary

PART One

Jacob

CHAPTER One

COMING UP FOR AIR...

I rubbed my face with my hands as the morning light invaded my hotel room. My eyes were calling for more sleep, and my body was calling for...*her*.

I gave my body a stretch and rolled onto my side, taking in the now empty bed. It was cold with only a faint smell of the missing beauty who rocked my dick repeatedly until I fell into a deep slumber. Or as I called it...passing out. However, I would definitely welcome a bender like that again if given the chance.

Whoa, where did that come from? No! Don't go there, Jacob. It will only bring more hurt, and I've had enough to last me a lifetime.

Then again, this woman from last night not only awakened my deadened senses, but with the bat of an eyelash and a sexy shake of her ass, I actually felt like I came back to life—back from an existence where I was closed off and feeling dead inside. I started to think that maybe she could be...someone special.

But I knew better than anyone not to believe in and cling onto moments like the one we shared last night. It was just sex, very hot sex between two consenting adults, a hook-up after the wedding of a mutual friend.

Nevertheless, a small part of me continued to romanticize what happened last night. What is it with weddings that give people hope? Last night was only all about sex, right? Nothing more? *Whatever!* I couldn't spend any more time pondering the what ifs.

I had something real once, but she was taken from me in a senseless tragedy. She took a bullet for me and died in my arms, but not before telling me one last time how much she loved me. It didn't get more real than that.

I covered my eyes with my palms to hold back the tears that would surely fall. As I closed my eyes, there she was…*Minela, my beautiful girl. Her big, bright, brown eyes were glazed over with tears as she accepted my marriage proposal. I slid the ring on her finger, and I knew then that she would be mine forever.*

Fate had other plans for us, though. I never saw it coming. The moment I heard the firing of the gun and felt the wetness of her blood on my hands, I knew Minela was dying in my arms. The happily ever after we dreamed of was never going to be a reality.

"Why did you leave me!?" I screamed out into thin air in my empty hotel room.

Parts of my heart had closed off after I witnessed her coffin lower down into the ground. Her father, a police captain for the Boston Police Department, along with her four brothers—all Boston police officers—were dressed in their finest blues. All the LaRocha men were standing tall with no signs of falling apart. They were being strong for Julia, Minela's mother, who had to be repeatedly held back from throwing herself on the coffin.

The loud shrieking cries from Julia resonated throughout the cemetery. She was inconsolable and screaming at God to take her too. Her husband, Captain Joseph LaRocha, wrapped his arms around his wife protectively. She finally settled down and fell against his chest, and they grieved together.

I had my own share of support rallying around me. My parents, all three of my brothers, Andrew, Cameron, and Simon, along with his wife, Nicolette, were my lifeline. I wanted to scream like Minela's

2

mother was doing, but I held my tongue and remained numb. I was as still as a statue, and my heart felt like it had turned to stone.

My family took it all for me: my cries, my anger, and my grief. They vowed to get me through the darkest time of my life. Although my heart was completely broken, the Paulson Family was close and would never allow me to shut them out.

"Why do you torture yourself!?" I once again screamed out for no one to hear me. Fuck! This is what happens when I allowed myself to feel. Why now, after all this time, was this even happening?

Minela was my sun. Her shimmering rays of light made me see everything so clearly. I wanted a life with her. We talked every night about our hopes and dreams. How many kids we would have. We argued constantly over paint samples and china patterns. She frustrated me to no end, but I always gave in just to see her smile and claim another victory over me. She used to call it "foreplay," a warm-up to the great sex that always followed. I wanted it, all of it…with her.

Now, after all this time mourning her loss, feeling the dull ache pounding in my heart, I've come up for air for the first time in over two years. Again, I asked myself: *How is this possible?*

It's not possible, that's why. Nothing will become of this one-night stand. I can never allow myself to get that close to anyone again. This was a hook-up…nothing more.

I was done with memory lane and dragged my hungover ass out of bed. I stepped out of the bathroom freshly showered with the cobwebs of memory lane now gone. I'd decided that I'm never drinking Tequila again. My eyes scanned the room, and that's when I saw the Starbucks coffee cup sitting on the side table, along with two Advil, a bottle of water, and a note:

J,

Take these.

Drink this.

Enjoy your coffee. I have a feeling you'll need it. And on a hunch, I went with chocolate croissants. I'll be seeing you soon.

Z

Wow! That girl Zoey was something unexpected and certainly not a figment of my imagination. She was real and very unforgettable. My head was still spinning at the fact that a few stolen moments with a stranger and the night we shared—oh, what a night, spent wrapped around her—could make me feel again. I truly didn't think it was possible.

I saw how happy my brother Simon was with Nicolette. Their love story was magical. I was jealous of my kid brother. I wanted what they had. I had it once, and then it was taken from me without warning.

And after getting dressed, my memory from last night was becoming clearer. I remembered my friend and colleague Tenley, who was Zoey's best friend, tell me all about her. She described Zoey as a bolt of lightning, a human force of sparkle that can't be denied. She was sexy as hell. Her intelligence was off the charts, and she was one of the finest New York attorneys around. But Zoey also spent a night in my bed and showed me her wild side. I remember every curve of her body as it connected with mine. She clawed my chest as I made her come, and she screamed out my name from the pleasure I was giving her.

A hook-up…that's all this was…two consenting adults letting go and having a great time. My brain is rationalizing what my heart will not believe.

My heart? Oh my God! It actually was racing. My heart was telling me to take a chance. Zoey could be the game changer for me: the one that would allow me to feel again, to welcome human touch without wanting to punch something.

Was this what my father meant when he told me that when I was ready, I would find love again? I couldn't entertain that thought back then, but why now for some reason? This girl made me want to.

I was never drinking Tequila again! The joke was on me, because my head didn't hurt from my hangover; it was from overanalyzing my night with Zoey.

My phone beeped with an incoming alert. My car was here to take me to the airport. Saved by the bell. No point thinking about this any longer. It wouldn't work anyway to entertain such thoughts about Zoey. Her life was here in New York, and the case that brought me here was now closed. Our mutual friend Tenley was off living her happily ever after with her cowboy, and I needed to get to California for my next assignment.

I grabbed my bags and took one last look at the bed, with its tangled sheets that Zoey and I had wrapped ourselves in.

Enough, Paulson! I needed to remember that it was just a hook-up and nothing more. *Now walk out of that door and forget about the very enchanting Zoey Steele.* I placed my forehead against the door and took in some deep breaths to calm my racing heart and overactive mind.

It was no use.

All I thought was: *Yeah right! Good luck with that.*

CHAPTER Two

BRIEFING...

E ven with nearly a six-hour flight to Los Angeles, my thoughts were still running uncontrollably through my mind. My past and present were fighting against each other, and all I wanted was to find some peace before meeting with my boss to discuss the case that has brought me to California.

A car was waiting to bring me to the FBI Field Office in downtown Los Angeles. I caught up on the dozens of e-mails I missed while working the Bornarelli case with Tenley. I hadn't had the opportunity to call my family to tell them I was in town yet, so maybe I'd just surprise them.

"Sir, we should be there in twenty minutes. We seem to be caught up in some late morning traffic."

"Thank you, Adam. I have plenty of work to keep me busy until then," I replied and then raised the privacy screen.

My headache wasn't getting any better, and I had a long day to still get through. Any time spent with Captain Duffy was sure to be a very long day. I closed my eyes for a few minutes until my cell phone was ringing. I smiled when I saw who was calling me.

"Hey, you! Aren't you supposed to be on your honeymoon?

You don't want to make your new husband jealous and make him think you should have married me instead," I joked with my friend.

"No worries there, Jacob. I married the right guy. I am on my honeymoon. And if there was any doubt in your mind, my cowboy is a very jealous one."

"Thank you for the reminder. So? Why the call then?"

"My husband is out for a run, and I had a few minutes to talk. I wanted to check in with you."

"What about? I believe we said all we had to say at your wedding."

"Jacob Paulson! Why are you being so cross with me? This is just a friendly call from one friend to another."

I could hear the hurt in Tenley's voice. I was being a jerk and taking it out on her. I already regretted my harsh tone with her.

"I'm sorry, Tenley. I had a rough night with hardly any sleep and a horrendous flight today. I'm kind of beat. Forgive me?"

"You're forgiven, but I think you might be tired for another reason, right? Come on, Jake…give me all the naughty details."

"Um…I think you've been misinformed, counselor. I'm just tired."

"Oh, you jerk! I saw you leave the wedding with Zoey! I can't believe you are making me work this hard for information. And, before you ask, she's not saying too much either."

"Maybe that's for the best."

"No, it's not. You two looked great together. She's my best friend, and obviously, you know that I trust you with my life, so I want this to happen! If you have some sparks between you two, then I say…go for it."

"I appreciate the support, but my work comes first and my life has no room for romance right now."

"Are you sure about that, Jacob?"

"I'm sure. Now, please…leave it alone."

"Oh, Paulson, you are the cliché onion. Every time we talk, layer by layer, I still don't know you completely."

"There was a time I could say the same thing about you, Ms. Fairchild. Kettle meet black."

"Fair point taken. And it's *Mrs. Parrish* now. I guess I'm just high on love right now, and I want my friends to be just as happy. Sorry for being so intrusive. Forgive me?"

"You're forgiven, but I don't believe you're really sorry, counselor. Still, I appreciate the apology just the same. Hang up with me, and go back to your honeymoon."

"Okay, I will, but Jacob, can I ask a favor first?"

"Of course, anything."

"Try to let people in, into your heart, my friend. Take it from one who lived life behind a wall of loneliness for far too long."

Loneliness? If she only knew how much I lived my life in the dark! I couldn't go back there. I knew Tenley was trying to help me, but she had no idea what I'd been through, and it was not a subject I could easily talk about.

"I'll take it under advisement. I have to go, Tenley. I'm just about to pull up to my office."

"Okay, partner. Keep in touch?"

"I will. Goodbye, my friend."

Oh, the tenacious Tenley Fairchild. She can go twelve rounds with me and not break a sweat. She was digging for info about Zoey and me, but I wasn't sure what to say because I didn't know myself. I was going with the conclusion that my time with Zoey Steele was a hook-up and nothing more.

"Mr. Paulson, we're here."

"Thank you, Adam."

I closed my laptop and gathered my things. I was here for work and nothing more. No more re-visiting the past or last night's encounter with Zoey. I took in a few deep breaths and entered the building, where I was greeted by staff to bring me upstairs for my briefing.

"Sir, here are your credentials while you're here in LA. Use both forms of ID when entering the building. You will have to go through several more security checks upstairs before meeting with Director Wade."

"Fine. Lead the way," I said.

The very efficient agent practically escorted me right to the door.

"Has my captain arrived yet? Captain Duffy? I was told he would be joining me here."

"He called, Mr. Paulson, sir, but unfortunately he has been delayed back in New York."

"I see. I guess I'm on my own then."

"Agent Paulson, you can wait for the director in the conference room. Shall I get you anything? Coffee?"

"No, thank you."

My head was pounding. I was in no shape for this meeting today. I just wanted to crawl under a rock and remain there until my mood changed, but work always comes first. My phone beeped with an incoming voicemail. I hit the button and listened to the message.

"Jacob, this is Duffy. Keep your head clear today and your eyes focused on the bigger picture. When I can, I will be in touch."

It wasn't like my captain to be vague with me, but knowing him, there was a hidden meaning behind his words. He was very much like my father. Maybe that was why we got along so well. The door opened and closed behind me. I pocketed my phone and turned to meet the director.

"Hello, Agent Paulson, I'm Director Timothy Wade. Happy to have you join us here in California."

"Thank you, sir. The pleasure is all mine. Shall we get down to why I've been called here?"

"Well, you certainly live up to your reputation."

"Pardon me, Director Wade, but I'm not sure what you are referring to."

"Don't you, Paulson? You're all about business. Cut and dry, black and white."

"It's worked for me so far."

"I'm sure it has, but I prefer my team to behave as such…a team. You've been the lone ranger for far too long now, and it's time to change what has worked so far."

"Excuse me, Director, but what is this? I do not need a lesson on how to behave on a team. If you know anything about me at all, then you know my background. I have successfully led my task force team to solve more cases than any other agent you have on staff and just recently wrapped up the Bornarelli case in New York. If that's being a 'lone ranger' as you call me, then so be it, but don't ever question my work ethic again."

"Fair enough, Paulson. I was testing the waters, and you passed with excellence. Keep that temperament of yours in check, especially here while we work together. Any other agent who takes that tone and speaks to me like you just did would have been thrown out on their ass, but I will make this one exception for you."

"Why, sir? What makes me different from the rest?"

"I'll answer that for you," said a man who had just entered the room.

I questioned, "And you are?"

Wade responded, "Settle down, Paulson, this is not the Spanish Inquisition. This is Director Dante Marino, from the Criminal, Cyber, Response and Services Branch."

"Sir, pleasure to meet you."

"The pleasure is all mine, Agent Paulson. Your captain speaks very highly of you. I've been looking forward to speaking with you and getting to know you better."

I guessed that this was what Duffy was referring to in his voicemail. This guy reeked of trouble, and for some reason, I interested him. He walked over to Wade and shook his hand.

"Thank you, Director Wade, for this opportunity."

"It was no trouble at all. I'll leave you two to get to know one another better, and we will resume in the briefing room in one hour with the team."

"Thank you, sir," Marino responded.

Director Wade exited the conference room, and I was left with Director Marino, who I still knew nothing about nor why I was here. He walked over, opened a cabinet containing a hidden bar, and fixed himself a drink. He turned to me and raised his glass.

"Pick your poison, Paulson: scotch, vodka? What will it be?"

"It's a bit early for me, thank you, and I have a feeling that I will need to remain clear-headed around you."

"Blunt, I'll give you that. Fine. Have it your way, Paulson."

"Director Marino, you say I'm blunt—well, that's a fair assessment. Therefore, I won't mince words with you. I feel like this is some sort of cat and mouse game, and I'm the bait. What is this? Why don't you just say what you have to say, and be done with it?"

"Eager as ever for information, Agent Paulson…" He smirked at me as he took the last gulp of his drink, quickly filling his glass with another. "It's too bad you weren't this eager to solve your fiancée's murder."

What the fuck!? The mention of Minela made me see red. I don't know what came over me, but I leaped out from where I was sitting and charged at Marino, like my old football days when I ran the field and took out my opponents with little effort.

"Who are you? What the hell do you want from me?" I screamed.

Instantly, my hands were wrapped around his neck as if any moment I could snap it in half. He gritted his teeth as he spat obscenities to me.

"Get your fucking hands off of me, Paulson, or I will have your shield quicker than your head will spin."

I dropped Marino, and he fell to the floor like a rag doll.

"Fuck you, Marino. What kind of game are you playing here?"

"No game, Paulson. This is as real as it gets. Now that I have your undivided attention, how about that drink?"

"I'd rather not."

"Fine, have it your way," Marino said as he got back up and rubbed his neck.

He paced the room as he said, "I've been reading your file. Quite impressive. You graduated at the top of your class at Northwestern. Then from college, straight to the NFL, even claiming all the glory with being the MVP in your one and only Super Bowl. Too bad, it all ended. You showed such promise for an amazing and lasting career. But your brothers are still in the game and doing quite well."

He continued, "Then, instead of staying in the limelight and reaping the benefits of all those flashy endorsements, you just simply walked away and became a good ol' cop, NYPD to be exact. Wow! Paulson, that even impressed me. You worked the streets for no more than a year, and you made detective in the Intelligence Unit soon after that. Again, wow! I'm not a man that easily gets impressed, but you, Paulson, kept surprising me with every page I read."

"I'm happy to serve as entertainment value for you, sir, but I have more important things to deal with than listen to you go down memory lane about my career."

"I can assure you, Agent Paulson, I was entertained. You're not just any cop; you are a highly accomplished one, and one that proves useful to me."

"Director Marino, I work for the United States Government, not you. You've wasted enough of my time, and now I am needed in the briefing room. If you will excuse me."

"Oh, I assure you, Paulson, you will be working for me very soon. Director Wade will explain everything to you, and then we will talk again. Next time? Keep your hands off my neck; I rather like it."

I left the conference room and the smug sonofabitch that was smirking at me. This was the most bizarre morning of my life. Why the mention of Minela? He was baiting me, and I took it: hook, line, and sinker.

The career I worked so hard for could have ended the minute I put my hands on Marino. But he didn't flinch. It was as if he knew exactly what I would do. I showed him my one Achilles heel, and this asshole would stop at nothing to use it against me, but why?

I splashed some cold water on my face and composed myself. I couldn't be going off unhinged again and attacking my superiors. I'd never crossed the line for as long as I'd been a cop, but this guy pushed all my buttons. I had no connection to him whatsoever, so what did he want with me? I was called here by my boss to meet with Director Wade on a mystery case, which I've yet to hear about, and it was not sitting well with me at all.

No time like the present, I thought, as I walked into that briefing room like I'd done hundreds of times before and tried to begin this day over. The briefing room was busy with agents giving statuses to their current cases. Director Wade was front and center commanding the room. He took notice of me immediately, and then went back to addressing the room. I took a seat in the back and listened in.

"Come to order now. Let's get to it. We have a lot to go over. We have visiting guests here from New York, so please welcome Director Dante Marino, and Special Agent Jacob Paulson. Please welcome them both to our team. Their individual talents will serve useful as I brief you to why you are all here. Please direct your attention to the screen. The body of Michael St. Clair was found in the laundry room of the California State Prison, Los Angeles County. He was determined deceased by a single stab wound to his heart."

"Now this name may seem familiar to you. Michael St. Clair is the son of former Paramount Studio President, Clayton St. Clair. It wasn't national news, but young Mr. St. Clair was found guilty of the rape and sexual assault of Nicolette Vanelle. He was sentenced to serve a maximum sentence of five years. Too bad he didn't make it. Both parties chose to keep this case off the national wire and it probably wouldn't be on ours, but the game changed when *he* arrived in town. Gentlemen, meet Jack Vanelle. He's evaded our agency for years, claiming to be a simple restaurant and bar owner in Chicago, when the truth is it's just a front to hide who he really is."

"And who is he?" an agent questioned.

"He is the one and only Jack Vanelli, former enforcer to the Carlucci family of Chicago. He made a name for himself back in the day when the local streets were overrun by the mob. We have never been able to place him in any connection to the Carlucci's on paper, but word on the street is different. This guy Vanelli, now Vanelle, discreetly hides in the shadows and strikes when the right time serves.

"And you think this guy, Vanelle, is involved with St. Clair's murder?" the same agent questioned.

"That's what we are here to find out, and with the help of Director Marino, we will get our answers. That's it for now, gentlemen. You are dismissed."

I sat there with a sinking feeling in my stomach. I wanted out of this room, but Marino had his eyes trained on me as he talked with Director Wade. My first impression of this guy was spot-on. There was something about Marino that I didn't trust, and after he mentioned Minela, I knew he wasn't someone I cared to work with. But I feared my hands were tied.

They looked engaged in their conversation, so I took the opportunity to step out and make a call, but I heard Director Wade call out for me.

"I'm sorry, sir," I responded. "I was just about to make a call. Could you give me a few minutes?" I asked in the hopes that he would.

"Jacob, before you do, would you mind coming back with me to my office? We need to talk, and it will not wait."

"Of course, sir," I dutifully agreed, and we walked over.

"Have a seat, son. I'm sure by now you understand why you're here."

"I think I do, sir. It's a major conflict of interest, and not just one or two, but many."

"I'm sure you see it that way, but I can assure you that this office will conduct a proper investigation. We don't cut corners here."

"You may not, sir, but what about Marino? Is he willing to play

by the same code of ethics? Because from what I have already en-
countered, I do not trust him, and I work with no one I don't trust."

"I admire that quality in my agents, but you do well to remember to whom you are speaking to. I am your superior, and you will
work with whomever I choose. You have a personal connection to
the Vanelle's via your youngest brother Simon, who is married to
Jack Vanelle's niece, Nicolette. An opportunity like this doesn't always come along, and I will certainly take advantage of what we
have."

"You mean *me*? Use my relationship with the Vanelle Family to
get to Jack? I hardly know the man. I've met him only a handful of
times. This certainly doesn't constitute a relationship with the man."

"But you do know Nicolette, your sister-in-law, and right there
is the in that you will need to get to Jack. This man is guilty, I know
it. We just have to connect the dots, and we will prove our case and
nail his ass to the wall."

CHAPTER Three

BACKED AGAINST THE WALL...

I couldn't believe what I was hearing. This man—Wade, a man with an impeccable service record, a man I had respected for many years—was bulldozing me, and if I didn't comply, I'd be the one that got burned.

Fuck that! I didn't play this way, never have and never will.

"So what do you say, Paulson? Do we have a deal?"

"No, sir, we do not have a deal. I will not work under the umbrella of your threat or anyone else's. Find another scapegoat to do your dirty work."

"Paulson, this is not a request. This is an order. You don't seem to understand what's going on here. You don't negotiate the terms. I do, and I am telling you that you will be the lead agent on this case—our case—against Jack Vanelle. Michael St. Clair savagely raped your sister-in-law. On the books, justice may have been served, but in the world of a wise guy like Jack, that act of brutality only gets avenged with an equal one. I'm telling you, son, Jack Vanelle avenged his niece by seeking out his own brand of justice with one single stab wound to the heart of her rapist. So, you tell me, Paulson...was justice avenged? Go ask Nicolette. See what she thinks. I'm sure she's heard the troubling news by now."

I practically shouted at Wade, "This is my family we are talking about! You can't expect me to just bring back all the pain my brother and his wife endured just so you can add another win to your list of accomplishments. I won't hurt them like this."

He remained steadfast while I aired my grievances about this case. He never even flinched.

"I'll tell you what I'm going to do for you, son. You get settled in and take the night to think about what we've discussed here today. Sleep on it if you have to, but I expect to see you here in my office at nine with your full intent and cooperation. Is that understood?"

As he waited for my answer, he retrieved a glass from his hidden bar and poured himself a drink of amber liquid. I stood and fastened my suit jacket, making my way to the door.

"Are we clear, son, on the matters discussed?" Wade asked.

"We are, sir. Crystal clear. And don't ever call me 'son' again. That honor is for my father, and my father only. Are we clear?"

My hands were in my pockets with my fists balled up in fury.

"Crystal," he replied with a satisfied look in his eyes.

Wade won this round with me easily showing him my hand. I couldn't make that mistake again with Wade or Marino, not with the threat looming over my family.

As for my father...so much for surprising my family with a long overdue visit. I needed him more than ever. I only hoped he could help me. Hurting Nicolette and Simon was the last thing I wanted to do, and going after her uncle would do just that.

Getting in to see my father was no easy task without alerting his staff of my presence. I could have just called him, but I wasn't ready for anyone else knowing I was in town, especially my mother or Simon.

The only thing my father has changed through the years I've been away is the location of his office, which is now in downtown Los Angeles. Without traffic, I could be there in about twenty-five minutes. I hadn't had time to rent a car yet, so I had a taxi drive me over.

Gee, dad! It doesn't get any more grandiose than the Aon Center, I said to myself as I took in the huge skyscraper before me.

Since two of my brothers shared my face, keeping my anonymity was difficult at times. The only distinguishing factor that separated us was our hair. Andrew had a beard, and Cameron wore his hair very short. He had taken a fall a few years ago and needed stitches. Once his wound was healed, he never grew his hair out, preferring the shorter look. I miss those guys so much, but I've also kept them at a safe distance. And although I'm not playing football anymore, I've managed to remain in athletic ready shape and still look exactly like them.

My NFL career ended going into my second season playing for the Denver Broncos, my team from my home state. I was in my glory. How many players can say they get to be part of their dream team, play in their first Super Bowl, and actually win leaving with a ring? Not too many, but I can.

This was my moment, a dream of mine and my twin brothers, who were also playing in the NFL. Our father couldn't have been more proud of us. This was the dream we chased since beginning college at Northwestern University. We had a lot of things going for ourselves. One: we were triplets, and you don't see that too often. Two: we were huge and could take out many opponents with a strong block or hit. Three: we loved the game.

Having been scouted in our senior year of high school back in Boulder, Colorado, my father knew we would make it. We all showed promise and the drive to someday make it all the way to the NFL.

For me, my dream ended with a career ending injury that would cost me more than football, but my eyesight. I had taken some tough hits throughout my college playing days and the first year in my professional career, but true to form, I was stronger in mind and could take the body hits.

Then came the game changer...the one hit that changed my life. The force behind the attack was fierce, coming out of nowhere, and he was unforgiving. I had just made the game winning touch-down, and before I could even celebrate my victory, I was hit, and hit hard. My body skipped across the end zone as easily as a stone skipping across a pond. My head snapped back and hit the ground at full speed, and then there was just darkness.

Whispering voices were all around me. I heard the beeping sound of machines and the door opening and closing. Someone was holding my hand, and then I felt her tears. I knew it had to be my mother; no time for a girlfriend back then since my life was all about football.

Marina Paulson begged me to open my eyes, and when I finally managed to do so, I was surrounded by darkness. I had never been so scared in all of my life. I gripped my mother's hand to the point of pain. She shrieked, and I instinctively let go. My father was by my side and telling me to calm down, saying that I would be alright. But how could I be alright if I couldn't see?

A neurologist had been flown in from Johns Hopkins. He was said to be the best in his field. Dr. Samuel Briggs was flashing a light into my eyes, and I began to slowly see it as he examined me. He told me that what I was experiencing was just temporary on account of the blunt force trauma I took to my head. Concussions were part of the package of playing, and most of the time I dealt with it and nothing ever happened...until now.

Over the span of twelve long hours, my vision slowly returned. I had to stay for a few days for observation while more scans were being performed on me. The day Dr. Briggs entered the room with my films was when I knew my NFL career was over. His expression said it all, and if it wasn't him, I saw it on my father and my two brothers, Andrew and Cameron, who left their teams to be with me after my accident. My coach and agent were also there and wearing the same sullen look. Whatever happened to wearing a poker face? Their expressions were all the same, and for a brief second, I wished I was still in the dark.

"Come on now, what is this, a funeral?" I said to lighten the

mood, but my joke fell on deaf ears.

"It's good that you are in lighter spirits, Jacob. It will help with what I have to tell you." Dr. Briggs said. "I'm so sorry, Jacob, but the scans show what I expected. You suffered another hematoma surrounding the occipital nerve. The swelling has gone down, and you have no bleeds, which is a positive sign, but you do have scar tissue from previous injuries, which is not so good."

"But I'm okay now, right? I see just fine, and my head is fine. When can I be released? I'm playing in New York this weekend," I asked with hope in my voice. It was all I had to hang onto.

Their faces had fallen again, especially my father's. Dr. Briggs placed the scan on the light to show me what he was trying to explain.

"You see this right here, Jacob? This is where your now healed hematoma presented, and here and here are patches of healed scar tissue. Your brain simply cannot take another hit like the one you just went through. I'm sorry, son, but your days of playing professional football—or any other physical sport—are over. Another harsh trauma like this and you will surely go blind."

The room was silent after that. Dr. Briggs again gave me his apologies, shook my father's and coach's hands and made his way out of the room. My brothers were looking at me with dumb as fuck expressions. I wanted to scream at them, but they took the hint and left with my sobbing mother.

My father stayed, and it was back to business. He was not only my father, but my lawyer as well. I still had two years on my multi-million dollar contract. I would be paid out on that contract, millions of dollars to be banked.

I had just received the worst news of my life, and there was my agent in the room still working deals for me. I would still have my endorsements, and although I wasn't playing, I could still be part of the game. I could coach, broadcast, the choice was mine.

But I respectively declined it all and declared that I was done. The hit I took ended my football career, but I still had options, and with a Super Bowl ring on my finger, I already got the brass ring—no pun intended.

I felt it was time to move on. I went through the stages of grief when it came to my football career, but I fortunately still had my sight and plenty of money and I wasn't even twenty-five yet. I had my charity work through the United Way, and I also ran a football camp for kids who couldn't afford to go on their own. I'll never forget the high I felt when I was playing the game, but I also knew I was given a miracle from God himself. I still had my sight, and I wasn't going to take anything for granted.

One thing that was tougher than walking away from a success-ful football career was finding and having someone so perfect for so short a time, only to have her taken away just as quick. I grieved for so long for Minela. Hell, I'm still grieving! I lived in my own private hell, and I never wanted my hurt to touch my family, so I stayed away and concentrated on my work.

That same work has brought me here today. That same work has the potential of hurting the people I loved and vowed to protect. It was all too calculated, though. Wade and Marino's plan felt off from the very beginning. This was why I needed my father. He had con-tacts all over the world, and I knew there was more to this Marino guy than meets the eye.

I walked in through the vast lobby where a team of security per-sonnel awaited me. I presented my official FBI wallet and was granted a visitor's badge. One of the guards recognized me immedi-ately from my playing days. I wasn't that guy anymore and almost resented anything to do with my old life, but I indulged the guard for about a minute.

"No, I don't wear my Super Bowl ring. Who knows—maybe if New England or New York win next year's big game, then perhaps you can view one on the hand of either one my brothers."

"I hope so, man. I have followed the famous Paulson trio for years now. This game misses you," the guard said as he smiled through his pleasantries.

"Again, thank you, but I do need to get upstairs. If you please, can you keep my arrival here private? I really can't afford to be stopped again."

"Of course, sir. Sorry to have taken so much of your time. Like I said, I'm a fan."

I shook his hand and said, "You didn't. I just need to visit with my father."

He escorted me to the bay of elevators, and I took it directly up to my father's fortieth floor office. I was greeted by a floor manager, who led me to my father's office. His assistant, Claudia, was waiting for me.

"Do my eyes deceive me, or is the great Jacob Paulson actually standing before me?"

She winked, and then I took his longtime right hand gal into my arms.

"Oh, you bear of a man! The famous Paulson welcome. Put me down! I usually have to fight off your brothers with a stick, but now you too?"

"You look wonderful, Claudia. How have you been?"

"I'm good, love. Really good. How are you? It's been a long time. I guess the last time I saw you was at...oh my goodness! I'm so sorry, Jacob."

"My fiancée's funeral? Was that what you were going to say? It's okay, my friend, don't be sorry. That was a long time ago, and it only proves how long I've been away."

"Your father misses you. He's going to freak when he sees you. I'm sorry, Jacob, but he's out right now at a meeting but should return within the next half hour," Claudia said as she looked down to her watch.

"That's fine. Would it be alright if I waited for him in his office? And please don't tell anyone including my father that I'm here. I prefer to surprise him."

"Okay, just please don't give him a heart attack. He's a great boss, and we love him."

"I love him too, and I promise I'll go easy on the old man."

"Don't let your mother hear you say that, son."

"My lips are sealed."

I gave her one more hug and made my way into dad's office. For an office being located in one of the most prestigious buildings in California, it had a sense of home to it. It was modestly decorated with years of awards, family pictures, and I even noticed a painting by my late Aunt Grace. Pangs of guilt pounded in my heart, as I continued to take in my dad's lifetime of memories and achievements. He was a man of honor, a respected and natural born leader with unmeasurable amount of integrity. He had many humanitarian awards in his name, as he dedicated his life to public service. I'm sure I was making him sound like an anointed saint, but that was how he raised us.

When it came to his sons, he wanted us to obtain a different type of glory...football. To have his triplet sons all make it to the NFL was any father's dream come true. I thought my father would be disappointed in my choice not to remain in the game after my injury, but he never was. He supported my decision and all that followed. I was a grown man, and I was the only one responsible for my happiness.

Living this life as a rogue FBI agent was not in my plan, but it was what kept me going for all of these years. Maybe it was the adrenaline rush. Sure, it was different from how I felt when I was playing football, but the rush nonetheless was the same. When a target was in sight, I set my aim and fired. There was nothing more satisfying than when I opened and closed a case successfully.

I only wished that were true for Minela. We never found her killer or the reason behind it. There's a proverbial saying: "Vengeance is more satisfying when exacted in cold blood." There was a time when I wanted just that, but it nearly destroyed me.

And now, after all of this time, this guy Marino attacks all of my vulnerabilities with the mere mention of her name. Wade said that I passed his test, but I failed Marino's miserably. I don't show that side to anyone, especially colleagues and superiors. What the hell was I thinking going after Marino the way I did? It was reckless and very careless on my part.

I didn't lose myself in booze, drugs, or any other recreational vice to ease my pain. I just went numb and remained this empty vessel for too many years to count…until I met Zoey. She awakened my senses, all of them. A part of me wanted to find her, tie her to my bed, and show her how much she excited me. To love on her. To own her sexy body, and to make her scream my name and tell me that she was mine, and mine alone.

Why this girl?

Why now?

Professionally speaking, I was on top. As for my personal life… I thought I was doing a great job living under the radar, not giving too much away. Tenley unsuccessfully tried to get me to open up about my life when we were in New York, but I evaded her questions. I had that down to a science by now. And now I was in this fucking city with these corrupt agents that wanted me to be a pawn in their chess game to take down Jack.

The road to revenge was paved with many potholes, and what lies ahead still remained to be seen. I tried with every fiber of my being not to travel down that road, but this case seemed to be pulling me in.

Confucius said it best: "Before you embark on a journey of revenge, dig two graves."

CHAPTER Four

THE DEVIL BEHIND THE SHIELD...

A light tap on the door and Claudia walked through.

"Jacob, I just wanted to let you know that your father has arrived and is making his way up here. Do you still intend on surprising him?"

"You can just tell him that his next appointment is waiting in his office, and I'll take it from there."

"Very well. Are you okay, Jacob?" Claudia asked me with concerning eyes.

"I'm not and haven't been for a very long time. This is one of the reasons why I'm here. I need my father."

"Jacob!?!"

We both turned to see my father standing in the threshold of his office, looking like he's seen a ghost. I might as well have been considering the length of time I'd been away. He had tears in his eyes but none that fell. He just dropped his briefcase to the floor and made quick strides over to me.

"Is it really you, son? I'm not being punk'd right now by one of your brothers?"

His remark made me laugh, because that is something that Cam or Andrew would do. I didn't have to say anything. I just took my father into one of our bear hugs, and he knew it was me. Claudia made a discreet exit and closed the door behind her.

"I'm afraid to let you go, son, out of fear that I'm dreaming."

"Dad, you can lighten the hold you have on me. I can assure you that I'm real, and I'm not going anywhere."

And with that, he punched me in my arm for safe measure.

"Ow! Old man, me standing in front of you is not proof enough?"

"Watch your mouth and choice of words," my father retorted. "I am not old—far from it, son. And you deserved that punch and so much more. Do you even know how long it's been since these eyes have seen yours in the flesh?"

He gestured to his face, and his elation over seeing me had shifted into anger. I couldn't blame him, it had been a long time.

"Dad, please? I need you."

"So you've said. Excuse me for a moment," my father said as he walked around his desk and pressed the intercom. "Claudia, please cancel the rest of my day. I do not wish to be interrupted."

"Yes, sir. Already taken care of, and I've ordered lunch for you and Jacob."

"Thank you, Claudia."

"My pleasure, sir."

I watched my father remove his jacket and loosen his tie. He was a fair man, and I knew he would listen to what I had to say, but there was hurt behind his eyes—a hurt I put there with my absence. The Paulson family never minced words with each other, nor turned their backs on one who needed our love, support, or help. And now I'm here, asking for all of those things and so much more.

"Look, dad, I know my sudden arrival has probably left you in a state of shock, but I really need your advice. You may be the only one I can turn to."

"Jacob, our door has never been closed to you or to your broth-ers. First off, you need to stop beating the hell out of your conscience and just forgive yourself."

"That's not the advice I came here asking for, and that's easier said than done."

"It is easy, son. You just have to allow yourself to do it. Put one foot in front of the other, and just forgive. I'm not going to pretend to truly understand what you've been through. I don't think anyone can unless they have faced it themselves. Grief knows no bounds, and if you still feel it, then feel it, but also lean on the people who love you. Minela—oh, that sweet girl—would not want you to be living like you've been."

"And how have I been living, dad? You weren't there! She died in my arms, and I could do nothing to save her. She took a fucking bullet for me, and I still don't know who's responsible for it. Her death is on my hands, because that bullet was meant for me, I know it. I had everything going for me and didn't have to prove a goddamn thing to anybody. But I took risks, worked the hardest cases, and for what, dad? A better title? A pay grade I don't need? It all seems so fucking futile now."

"Jacob, please talk to me. I can't help you unless you allow me."

"I'm here, aren't I?"

"You are, but you still haven't told me the reason behind your visit. Or is this just a drop-by, where you state your business and skulk out the door without letting anyone else know you're here? What about your brothers? Your mother!?! Did you think of her when you were working the streets of New York taking out the bad guys? Oh yes, I've read the papers. Another notch on the belt, taking down not one, but two Bornarelli's and dismantling a major New York crime family."

"Are you finished? Because I've already had one reminder today on my career record. I don't wish to hear it again from my father. Dad, this is my job, and it's what I have to keep me going. It's practically all I had when I lost Minela."

"That's bullshit, and you damn well know it. You have your family! We are right here; we've always been. It was you who shut us out. Why son? Why?"

"I'm sorry, dad. When my football career ended, I didn't know what was going to become of me. And then you gave me advice and guidance like you always did, and I picked myself up and moved on. When I decided to change course and pursue law enforcement, you supported me one hundred percent and never once questioned my choices. So why ask why now? I never meant to hurt you or mother, but when Minela died, she took a piece of me with her. And believe me dad, I wasn't the only one who shut down and slowly retreated from the rest of the world."

I continued, "Minela's family is no better off. Her father is now retired after taking an extended leave of absence. Her mother had a complete breakdown, then a stroke followed shortly after. Her brothers went about their lives, still fighting the good fight, but they were not the same men anymore. That's what grief does, dad. Believe me, I wasn't the only one that checked out, but I'm here now, and if you give me a chance, I will tell you the reason."

"I'm sorry, Jacob. I certainly did not want our reunion to begin like this. I'm just happy to see you and so damn angry at you all at the same time."

"I get where the anger is coming from, and I will apologize a thousand times until I can earn your forgiveness and trust again."

"You never lost it, son. I can assure you of that."

"I love you, dad."

"And I you, son. Now, let's get some food in us and knock back a few cold ones."

"I think I might need something stronger than beer."

"No worries, son. I'm fully stocked."

We ate mammoth-sized steak burgers and chatted about the easier subjects, football always the best subject to drink beers over.

"Okay, son, you've had enough time avoiding the reason why you're here. Spill it!"

I wiped my mouth on the linen napkin and placed it back on the table. Looking at my father with eyes that matched his, I felt like I was about to be scolded for breaking the neighbors window with my baseball. His gaze never broke, and this look told me that he was done with waiting. He wanted answers. *Where do I begin?* I let out a deep breath and just blurted it out.

"Dad, I'm here in California for work. When I received the call that my next assignment was going to be out here, I was excited at the fact that I would have an opportunity to see all of you again. There will never be enough apologies I could say that would erase all the time I've shut you out, but I also know that I have an amazing family who will forgive me without question. Is that still true?" I asked my father.

"You know it is, son, and we understand why you needed your space to grieve over Minela and find your way again. I'm not sure if you've done that yet, but we've always been here. What your brother went through with Nicolette should show you that we Paulsons always stick together, no matter how serious the problem. This is who we are. This is who you are."

"Thank you, dad. I'm still the son you raised. I've just been so lost without her that I didn't want to pass all the pain I was going through onto you. And before you say that's bullshit, it's how I felt and still do. I'm technically your first born, and I've always handled my problems on my own, knowing I could come to you if necessary. And today is one of those times. Have you seen today's paper?"

"As a matter of fact, I haven't. I was out the door early this morning and haven't had the opportunity to peruse any of my usual papers."

"What about the news? Dad, I know you wake up to the morning headlines, so I can't believe you don't know what I'm talking about here!" I practically shouted at my father while balling my fists at my side.

This case had me in knots, and it's hardly begun yet.

"Jacob, why don't you just tell me what I don't know, and we will take it from there."

He sounded irritated with my dancing around it, but I just

couldn't bring myself to say it. I took the newspaper from my messenger bag and handed it to him. He took the paper, and I saw his eyes go from irritation to shock.

"Oh, holy hell! Murdered in prison? I guess this only means one thing…" my father muttered under his breath.

"Excuse me? Why would you say that? It's now *your* turn to tell me what I don't know. Talk to me, dad."

"I say this because his revenge has finally been carried out. I never believed he would allow Michael to just walk away clean and have the opportunity to live his life freely one day, knowing what he did to her."

"Dad! What the hell? You're talking in circles. To whom are your referring?"

"Jacob, have you been so far away from your family that you sit here and act like you don't know to whom I am referring? Wake up, son! If you don't know, then you damn well should know who I'm talking about. Jack Vanelle, Nicolette's Uncle, who turns out is really her biological father! Come on, you really didn't know?"

My father looked beside himself as I was completely stunned, but now the pieces were beginning to fit.

"No, I did not. How do you know all of this?"

"Simon told me. Years ago, after the rape, many truths came out about Nicolette's family history. She shared it all with Simon after discovering it herself. She was protected from the truth until her parents felt it was the right time to tell her, and then the rape happened. Her Uncle Jack is her biological father, but Mason Vanelle is her father in all the ways that matter."

"Wait…did her mother have an affair with the brother?"

"No, nothing like that. Mason could not give his wife a child, so Jack helped make their dream come true, and it was agreed that Jack would always be known as her uncle and nothing more. Jack was extremely protective of Nicolette, and when he discovered she had been attacked, he became enraged and immediately flew out to be by her side. She knew none of it, but one day while she was in the hospital, she overheard her parents and Jack arguing, and that's when the truth of her parentage came out. On top of everything else that sweet girl was going through, learning this information divided her family even more."

"Simon was there for her throughout it all, and even when he thought he lost her, he never gave up hope on being with Nicolette again. Then you know what happened next. They did reunite, the trial happened, and then Michael St. Clair began his sentence for what he did to her."

"Tell me more about Jack. Why did you instantly come to the conclusion that he must be responsible for St. Clair's death?"

"Jacob, I'm sorry I ever mentioned it. I really thought that Simon shared this with you and your brothers."

"Well, he didn't, dad, so now you tell me. I would rather hear it from you rather than reading it in a file."

My father deeply sighed while looking at the newspaper again but continued to tell me the story.

"Jacob, your brother once told me that Jack may have been connected to the mafia back in his younger years in Chicago. The argument that Nicolette heard was about just that: how Jack provided for his family and took care of things his parents could not provide. They were immigrants from Italy with little money to their name. They worked endless hours to provide for their family, but Jack couldn't bear to see his parents work and work and not have much to show for it. The Vanelli parents lived a simple life, whereas Jack's life was not, at least not in the beginning. He did some things he wasn't proud of but justified them as a means to an end, because it was about survival. That was his past. To my knowledge, he runs a legal business in Chicago and lives his life out in the open with his wife, Sara. They run their business and are pillars in their community. But..."

"But what?"

"I also know that Jack had threatened Michael when he was in the hospital, and he vowed to see him dead for what he did to his daughter. His words…not mine. I guess when it was all over, he confided in Nicolette about his anger and what he could have done, but he told her that he didn't because of promises made to his wife and brother. Ultimately, anything Jack would have done to that boy would inevitably hurt Nicolette, and he would never do that."

I interrupted, "But then again, dad, the minute you saw the paper, that's exactly what you thought. And I'm afraid if your initial reaction is correct, then Nicolette will be hurt by this in more ways than one. And that's why I'm here, dad. I'm here in LA to prove the FBI's suspicions that, in fact, Jack Vanelle is responsible for the death of Michael St. Clair, and it is my job to bring him to justice."

My father turned ashen, and then he walked over to his cabinet to fix himself a drink. He poured me one too and gestured to me to sit beside him on the couch. I took my drink and gulped it down, debating if I wanted another one. I had no reason to return to the field office today, so I decided that I might as well drink with my father and hope he could help me out of this fucking mess.

We remained quiet while both of us drank our second shot of scotch, and then my father turned to me.

"Jacob, have you told me everything?"

"No, sir, not by a long shot. I'm not only being pressured by my reporting director, but there's this guy from New York who is also on the case. His name is Dante Marino, and he is hell bent on making Jack burn for this. He was defiant from the moment he introduced himself to me. And then we were left alone, and he showed me his true colors. He was trying to get a rise out of me for some reason, feeling me out, and then he mentioned Minela, and I just about lost it and choked him to death. Dad, his eyes were laughing at me. It was like he knew something I didn't. If I don't take on this case, then I will never know what he knows."

"Do you think he knows what happened with Minela?"

"I do, and if not, then he's a really good actor to make me think that he does."

"I have connections all over the world, Jacob, and I could probably obtain some intel on Marino, probably just as effective, if not more, as your fancy computers."

"I have no doubt about that, dad, and yes, I want your help, but no one can know about this case or my involvement."

"That's going to be a little difficult, son. As soon as Simon learns about Michael, he's going to fly into protection mode for the sake of his wife and unborn child."

"What?"

"You heard me right. After years of trying, Nicolette is pregnant, and Simon is on top of the world with this news. They have been through so much and have come out stronger than ever before."

"Dad, I swear I will make this right and no harm will come to Nicolette. My hands are tied, dad. I have to take this case. If I don't, then I'll lose my shield and Marino will go after anyone that leads him to Jack, regardless of who he hurts. They are using my connection to get to Jack, which as you say…leaves me in an impossible situation. It is my duty to bring the bad guys to justice, but how can I do that and not hurt my brother and his wife at the same time?"

"I don't have the answers this time for you, Jacob. I wish I did. As for Simon and Nicolette, they are away right now. They left a few days ago and will not return until next week."

"Where are they?" I questioned.

"Simon and Nicolette are out on discovery. He's doing some diving off the coast. He said at times they would be out of reach, but they have their satellite phones to keep in contact if an emergency would arise."

"Is that safe for Nicolette? I mean, with her condition and her past history with the miscarriages?"

I only mentioned that painful fact because even though she was assured by her doctors that she could have a child again after the rape, that wasn't how it turned out. Nicolette did suffer two more miscarriages after her near fatal one. My brother was devastated but remained confident that they would have a family someday, and now that day is coming soon. It just gives me all the more reason to protect them from harm.

"She's doing great. She's just beginning her second trimester and was cleared by her doctors. The ship is fully equipped with a trained staff. They love the ocean, and she wanted to go with Simon. She was so excited, he couldn't stop her."

"So then they don't know about Michael?"

"I don't believe so. If yes, then Simon would have phoned me the minute he did."

"This is good news, better than I expected. With Simon and Nicolette away, their absence buys me some time to figure things out."

"What about your mother? Please, Jacob, promise me you'll find some time to visit her."

"I will, dad, I promise, but I need to get back to my hotel and begin working on things. Please do what you can here, and I will be in touch."

I quickly gathered my things and made my way to the door with a better resolve than before I walked in. He stopped me before I could leave.

"Jacob," he said in his most stern voice, "please be careful."

"Always!" I bear hugged him and then headed out.

There was no fucking way a guy like Marino was going to back me into a corner without me trying everything in my power to claw my way out of it. He played dirty, this I knew from the minute I met him. He was cold and calculating. But Marino had a weakness just like everyone else. I just had to find it and use it to my advantage.

No way would I ever allow anyone to hurt my family. I guess that's the one thing I shared with Jack Vanelle. He protected what was most important to him, as did I. This life I led was not easy. It claimed the love of my life. I would not allow it to claim anyone else I loved, especially my future niece or nephew. Simon and Nicolette would keep having their happily ever after, and damn it to hell to anyone who tried to prevent them from it.

CHAPTER Five

THE BEAUTY RETURNS...

I replayed the conversation with my father over and over again until my head pounded. I gauged his expression when he mentioned Jack for the first time. It was as if Jack was the obvious wrongdoer.

My father was no saint. He played hardball when he had to and had his share of favors to call on when needed. If he could dig up anything on Marino to help me with this case, I could gain some leverage on him. The fact that Marino mentioned Minela is still weighing heavily on my mind. He could have easily pulled my file and used what he read to his advantage and elicit the right reaction from me. He definitely succeeded when I nearly choked him.

I swallowed two Advil, followed by two bottles of water. I shouldn't have had that scotch back in my father's office, especially after the hangover I was still battling, but today had been a day of revelations. I needed something to take the edge off.

My mind retreated back to my night with Zoey. She was incredibly beautiful. Her cerulean eyes were so bright, I could almost see my reflection in them. That vixen could easily turn my head in any direction, hypnotize me with her eyes, and use my body for any pleasure she desired. Just thinking about her had my dick hard and pressed up against my jeans to the point of pain.

I could have pulled one off in the shower to get some relief. *Yeah, right!* That would give me pleasure for about a minute, and then I would be lost in my fantasy again, thinking about Zoey and how I was deep inside her all night long. She rode my dick and took all of me into her small frame. I don't remember exactly when we finally passed out, but I remember her and how she made me feel. I also felt her loss when I woke up alone. These were all feelings I hadn't felt in a very long time, feelings I wasn't even sure I wanted to have again. I was really confused, convincing myself that it was just a hook-up and nothing more. *Ugh! I can't even go there right now.* A cold shower was looking promising, but a knock on the door dragged me out of my thoughts.

I opened the door and blinked back a few times. *Whoa, is this a dream?* I was just thinking about her, and she appeared! In California! Zoey was standing on the other side of the doorway, looking like a hungry, vamped up tigress. She winked at me sexually. I was clearly her prey of choice. Again, my dick hardened against the inside of my jeans.

"Fuck me!" I whispered out loud.

"That's the plan," she said and smiled as she moved past me and made her way to my bedroom.

Oh holy hell! I closed the door and followed the beautiful Zoey into the bedroom.

"You sure do have a way of disappearing and reappearing into my life, don't you, Zoey?"

"Oh, you sexy man! Disappearing is not my intention at all. And clearly by the looks of you, you're happy to see me again. Am I wrong?"

I swear I could feel my face flush with heat, and I was seconds away from blowing my load. She wasn't wrong. She's all I'd been thinking about since the moment I woke this morning in New York to an empty bed. It's clear that she wanted me just as much as I wanted her. I was done overthinking for today.

I watched Zoey slowly remove her trench coat. What was underneath took my breath away and left little to the imagination. Her petite frame was covered in leather and lace. Purple lace intricately ran down her spine in fine ribbons that tied at the base of her spine. She looked like a perfectly wrapped Christmas present about to be ripped open or a succulent piece of candy for me to unwrap and devour. Either way, I was going to taste her very soon, but not before peeling off her silk stockings that covered her sexy legs.

She seductively put on a private show for me. The bed in my suite was a king-sized poster frame, giving Zoey exactly what she needed to bring me to my knees. Climbing onto the bed, I loved how she left her shoes on, wrapped her legs around the pole, and sexily spun her body on it.

"Like what you see?" she asked as she worked the pole again.

"I do, very much. But I think we've had enough show and tell, don't you agree? Lie down and place your hands above your head, interlocking your fingers together."

Once again, her beautiful, oceanic colored eyes brightened and was ready to play.

"Have I been bad? Am I under arrest? Will handcuffs be involved?"

She smiled through her questions as I quickly got undressed. My arousal was evident. I wanted her more than anything else in the world right now. I was completely hers for the taking, but I wanted to play first.

"You are so beautiful, Zoey. And yes, there will be handcuffs to ensure you don't run this time. I want to wake up tomorrow morning with you underneath me."

It was just my luck that when I returned from seeing my father, I deposited my stuff conveniently in the same drawer. I opened the side drawer and retrieved the handcuffs and condoms. Dropping them onto the bed, Zoey was squirming with excitement. The way she was looking at me was making me so hard for her. It looked like

I was expecting her all along, but her sudden arrival was a very welcomed surprise for me.

I took her into my arms and hungrily kissed her. I needed to taste her, roll my tongue with hers. She let out whimpers of pleasure as I gently leaned her back onto the bed. My knee parted hers, and I could feel the wetness between her legs.

"Stop teasing me, Jacob, and fuck me."

"In due time, Ms. Steele. I need to get you ready for what I plan to do."

"And what exactly are your plans?"

"So many questions, Ms. Steele. You can't help yourself from always being a lawyer now, can you?"

"I guess not, just like the cop in you. We love the questions, but I see no need for negotiating right now. We both already know what we want, so why the questions?"

"I have many for you, but I'll save them for later," I said.

She smiled and pulled me down onto her. I loved what she was wearing, and it took all my control not to rip it off of her. I flipped her to her stomach and began untying the laces. Once they were undone, her flawless back was exposed. I held her shoulders down and kissed the back of her neck and worked my way down to her sexy ass. It was so inviting for me to take, but not tonight. I turned her over and removed her from her lingerie. Her delicate thong panties did not survive. One hook of my finger, and they were shredded. I plunged my tongue into her dripping folds, causing her to buck her pelvis up to me. My one hand held her two, as I continued to feast on her delicious pussy.

"Are you ready for me?" I asked as she rode out her orgasms, the evidence of which were all over my face.

It was so freaking hot, I wanted more of her. I quickly placed the condom on my ready to explode dick and entered her body. I was praying I could hold out for more than a few minutes, but Zoey wasn't making it easy for me.

I took her deeper and deeper as she wrapped her legs around me like a snake. Her heels were digging into my bare ass, causing me to wince in pain, but it was a pain I would take from her. I wanted to take her from behind, but I knew it would be rough and tonight was not the time for that kind of play. I just wanted to feel her, hold onto the connection I felt the first time we met, to lose myself with her touch and quench my hunger for more. This is what I wanted from Zoey Steele, and I had full intentions of taking it all.

I rolled us over with her now on top. We were both panting. The way she looked at me enticed me in more ways than ever before. My heart was beating rapidly like I'd just run a marathon. My hands gripped hers as she rode me, bouncing up and down.

"I'm so close, baby, I can't hold on much longer," I whispered.

"I'm right there with you, come with me."

She screamed out as I joined her. My insides were on fire. I'd never been so turned on in all of my life. My dick was still pulsating inside of her while still semi-hard. I didn't want to lose this connection: Zoey lying across me and our sweaty bodies still wrapped around each other.

Her breathing was slowly returning to normal. I lifted her off of me and placed her beside me. I removed the condom and tied it off, tossing it into the wastebasket near the bed. She let out some sexy moans, and then she was out cold.

All I could do was to stare at her. Her long, blonde hair draped down her sexy backside. I imagined her hair tied back into a ponytail and wrapped around my wrist as I took her from behind. I couldn't control all of the naughty thoughts running through my mind. This was what she did to me. How I ever thought our first encounter was just a meaningless fuck was now so irrefutable.

I left the sexy Zoey asleep while I made my way to the bathroom. It was fully stocked with essential bath salts and oils. Normally I would never entertain using these girly products, but I so wanted to share a bath with her, and I would soon, but I settled for a warm washcloth with some jasmine on it. I filled a bowl with warm water and oil, carrying it back to the bedroom. I dipped the soft cloth into the warm scented water and began washing her from head to toe. She only stirred a bit when I reached her entrance, almost an invitation for me to be there again, but I left her to sleep and finished up with her sponge bath. I quickly washed up and joined her back in bed.

She fit perfectly next to me as if she was made solely for me. I hadn't felt this way in a very long time. I had nearly forgotten what it was like to have a woman make you come to life, but Zoey accomplished just that. I'd grieved for so long over Minela and never thought I would ever feel this way again. It comforted me and also scared the shit out of me too. How, after all this time of not feeling, can I just switch over to exactly that?

Back in New York, I was there for work, never knowing that meeting the beautiful Zoey Steele would change my life. Now I'm here in Los Angeles, again for work, and she's here with me. Of all the times fate stepped in and knocked you on your ass, this would be one of those times. My head was spinning with all sorts of crazy scenarios, but I shrugged them off and just concentrated on the now.

I wouldn't waste one more valuable second with her. She was here with me now, and that was all that mattered. Tomorrow was a new day, a new day to take on the corrupt Marino and to figure out what this was with Zoey. Did she see it as just a hook-up, or something more happening between us? I couldn't wait to find out what her answer was.

And what surprised me was that I would do just about anything for her to be mine. *Damn! It felt good to say that.* I pulled her naked body closer to mine, and for the first time in a long time...I slept soundly.

CHAPTER Six

Game on...

I t surprised me how well I slept and with Zoey in my arms. I had awakened a few times to make sure she was still with me, and to my surprise, she was. I wanted to be inside of her again, but I also wanted to experience what it was like to hold a woman in my arms again and to appreciate the simple act of intimacy.

I knew I was to report to Director Wade's office by nine to give him my answer. With Zoey arriving unexpectedly, I didn't even think about the case...I only saw her. I needed a run to clear my head, and the hotel gym would not do it for me. My eyes opened at five, and I quickly changed into my running clothes. I made my way out as quietly as I could, but not before securing Zoey in her place. *Now where are those handcuffs?*

Seven miles wasn't nearly enough to get me prepared for what today would bring, but it was a start. I entered my suite, which was very quiet. Maybe Zoey was still asleep and I could slip back into bed with her.

What are you saying, Paulson? I'm acting like a lovesick fool right about now, but I don't really give a fuck. I felt alive again with Zoey here and in my bed.

I walked as quiet as I could into the bedroom and that's where I found Zoey awake and just like I left her...bound to my bed with her mane of sex hair.

"Good morning. I trust you slept well?" I said with a hint of sarcasm to my voice.

She looked incredible, naked and cuffed to the bed posts where she performed an exotic dance for me last night.

"Did you not believe me when I said I would be here in the morning?" She gestured to her bound wrists.

"I wasn't taking any chances this time around, so to answer your question, no, I didn't believe you."

"You should have. I wouldn't have followed you across the country to mess with your mind. I'm here to stay for as long as you want."

Stay forever. I wanted to say that, but I just smiled and remained silent. I felt like I'd known Zoey for years. My head was all messed up right now, and starting something with Zoey should have been the lowest thing on my priority list. I was here for work...that was all.

"Let me get you out of those cuffs."

I pulled the key from my pocket to free her, but that's not what she wanted.

"Jacob, how about we keep the cuffs on, and you do what you intended to do with me last night? Hmm? What do you say?"

"Tempting, but I can't. I have to get to work, and you have to..."

"I have to what? Leave? Go back to my life in New York and forget you? I don't think so, lover, and I don't think you want me to either. If you can honestly tell me that you want me to leave, then take these cuffs off so I can go."

Hearing her make a bold statement like that actually made my heart sink.

"I don't want you to go. I don't even understand what is happening here between us, but having you leave is the last thing I want you to do," I told her.

She immediately softened under my words, making me want her more. I leaned in closer to kiss her swollen lips, and she took mine into her mouth. The things I could do to her right now with Zoey all trussed up was making me so hard.

"Jake, just fuck me, and we will work the rest out later."

I grabbed a condom from the drawer and quickly placed it onto my dick. I didn't give myself time to think. I entered Zoey with an intense wanton desire. I felt like I was going out of my mind.

"This is going to be quick, baby, so wrap your legs around my waist as tight as you can."

Oh, she didn't disappoint. She screamed for me to go faster, harder, deeper. I was hitting her to the tilt with my thumb pressing hard against her clit. Zoey was screaming my name. I was so close, but I wanted her hands on me. I unlocked the cuffs and flipped her on top.

"Touch me, please?" I practically whimpered as she ran her long nails up and down my chest.

I held her in place as she continued to ride me and leaned down onto my legs. I could feel my balls tightening. I was going to come hard. Zoey sat straight up. It took all my strength to sit up and hold her as we came together. She wrapped her arms around me, bit down onto my shoulder, and rode out her orgasm.

She was once again on top of me with our bodies still connected. I couldn't move as we tried to get our breathing under control.

"That was amazing," she said.

I couldn't disagree if my life depended on it. I held her to me and raised my head from the pillow to kiss her.

"I agree," I said.

And then I kissed her again. I could have done this all day long if time allowed me to.

"You agree?"

"I do," I said. "Not only was what we just did amazing, but you were amazing. Let's wash up."

I didn't give her a chance to agree or disagree, and I carried her into the bathroom.

"You know, Jake, I'm perfectly capable of walking. This carrying me around is very chivalrous but not necessary. I'm a sure thing, in case you haven't figured it out yet."

"What's wrong with a man giving a woman some special attention? I rather like you in my arms."

"And I rather like you inside of me," she said with a wink. "So what will it be? Shower or bath?"

Damn, she was so sexy, and I didn't want to rush my time with her. I enjoyed just soaking in a hot bath with her in my arms.

I was having this overwhelming need to take care of her for some reason. Something told me that she had no clue as to how a real man loves his woman. *His woman? Wow, I need to get control over these crazy emotions. I haven't felt this strong about anyone since Minela.*

"Penny for your thoughts?" she asked as I was lost in thought in our warm bath.

"Too many to count, and I'm out of time. Let's get you out of this tub before you freeze and get sick on me."

I left Zoey on her own while I got dressed in the other room.

I can't do this now with Zoey, I just can't. I let my guard down with her, behaving like a fool in love as if I didn't have a care in the world. In love...a feeling I never thought was possible to experience again, and now after a couple of nights shared with Zoey, it's all I think about.

My cell phone was buzzing. Director Wade. Talking to him was the last thing I wanted to do, but I was due in his office at nine and it looks like I've missed my meeting.

"Paulson." I curtly answered, wishing I could send it right to voicemail.

"My office in one hour, and don't even think about not showing up."

Fuck! I mumbled, but it was loud enough for Zoey to hear.

"Now that sounds promising, but you did say that you have to go to work."

She hugged me from behind, and I held her hands, bringing them up to my lips.

"Zoey, I..."

"It's okay, Jake. You don't have to say anything. We had a good time—more than once—but you don't owe me anything. I'll get out of here in a few minutes, and you can be on your way."

She raised herself on her tiptoes and kissed my cheek. *What the hell? Be on my way?* She turned away from me and closed the bathroom door behind her, clearly dismissing me and this conversation. I knocked on the door asking for entrance. I waited a beat, and then she opened the door allowing me to come in. She kept her back turned to me, but I wasn't going to allow her to shut me out after what we shared.

"Zoey, please look at me."

When she wouldn't turn to face me, I put my hands on her shoulders to make her look at me. She had tears in her eyes, which was slowly slicing my heart. There was nothing worse than seeing a woman cry and to know you're responsible for it in some way.

She was confusing the hell out of me, but I needed her to talk to me. First, she's this seductress rocking my world. We shared an incredible night of hot sex, and then she's gone but with a promise of returning. I thought it was crazy at the time since I was heading across the country, but then I opened my hotel room door to see her standing on the other side of it, once again completely blindsiding me and turning me inside out. I'd never felt this confused in all of my life. I was wrong before. Zoey was so much more than a hookup.

"Zoey, I can't begin to understand why you are crying, but somehow I feel responsible. We shared an incredible night together, and I can't have you leaving and thinking it was less than that. I have to go, I really have to, but can I please see you tonight?" I asked, hoping that she would say yes.

I wiped her tears and held her in my arms. She remained quiet, but at least allowed me to hold her. She felt incredible against me, but I had to go.

"Please be here when I return tonight? I really have to go, Zoey."

Did she not know how much her silence was gutting me right now? I hoped my pleas were enough to convince her to stay. I could only hope that she would. The internal struggle to not just take her back to bed was the ultimate test of my will power. I kissed her forehead so gently, I could barely feel her skin on my lips. I turned to leave with uncertainty flooding my mind. *Fuck my life!*

My car was waiting for me downstairs. Wade wasn't putting anything to chance, so he had Adam waiting for me in the lobby.

"I don't need a watchdog. I can find my own way downtown, Adam."

"I'm sorry sir, but I have my orders."

"It's alright, Adam. Don't we all?"

I raised the privacy screen and phoned my father.

"Hi, dad, it's me."

"Good morning, son, and of course I can recognize my own son's voice. How are you this morning?"

"I'm good, dad, better than yesterday. Wade is flipping out and threatening to pull my shield. I didn't show up to his office as scheduled, so now I'm in the back of his car on my way to the office."

"Why, son? This is not the way to go about things with your superiors. First, you physically attack one boss, and then antagonize the other with your tardiness. What gives, Jacob?"

"Dad, I didn't call you to be chastised. I need to know if you've heard from your contacts yet regarding Marino."

"Jacob, I only just put out feelers late last night. I need some time to gather the intel."

"Dad, I only have a few days before Simon and Nicolette return from their trip. I need to gain the upper hand on Marino and Wade before I get any deeper into this case."

"Keep your head about you, son. Do not show them your hand

again. Get through the meeting today, and then call me back. Hopefully I will have something for you soon."

I hung up with my father, not feeling any more secure about today. His advice was the same as the words Duffy said to me. I called him next.

"What have I gotten myself into, Patrick? You need to tell me why I'm really out here."

"Jacob, I've told you all I can."

"You've told me nothing. This guy knew about Minela. Duffy, why does this guy know about my fiancée?" I shouted into the receiver.

"Calm the hell down, Paulson. Please listen to me. Meet with them today, and for Christ's sake, keep yourself in check and your hands off of Marino! I'll be on the red eye flight to Los Angeles, and I'll meet up with you tomorrow, okay?"

"Fine."

I was beyond livid. I threw my phone against the privacy screen, resulting in shattering the glass screen on my phone.

"We're here, sir," Adam spoke through the intercom.

I made my way into the building, flashing my badge and taking the stairs instead of the elevators. This was crazy, with Wade's office being nearly on the top floor, but I needed to clear my head. I was at war with myself. I just wanted to bring on the pain, and my target would be Marino.

I took a minute to catch my breath, grabbed a water, and then his secretary showed me in to his office. No sign of Marino, just Wade sitting behind his desk on the phone and gesturing me to take a seat. I reluctantly sat, crossing my leg over my ankle in defiance. I hated being here, and for the first time in my life, I hated being a cop, but I knew I needed to be one now if I was going to help my brother and his wife.

Wade ended his call and then leaned back in his chair, not taking his eyes off of me. Neither of us spoke. It was a war of wills, but I would not break. He did.

"Paulson, let me make myself perfectly clear, because I will not repeat myself again. You not keeping our agreed time this morning was not a wise decision on your part, but I will overlook it this time. A lot was thrown at you yesterday, so I understand you needed time to process all of it, but I'm not sure how much thinking you did with the lovely Ms. Steele showing up."

Breathe Jacob…just breathe.

"Keeping tabs on me, huh? Who knew the FBI could afford such resources?"

"When it comes to you, I pulled out all the stops."

"Why, Wade? Why me? What's your take on the death of Michael St. Clair? Of all the cases that pass through this office on a daily basis, your main concern is a former rich boy that got shanked in prison?"

"Paulson, do you realize in the past fifteen years, homicides in California state prisons are considered to be common? Over one hundred-sixty deaths in that time. Many of them you never hear about, but the death of Michael St. Clair is at the top of the newsfeed because of the person who murdered him. This wasn't just a random three knee deep hit, this was a fatal strike right through the heart, a clear message that justice has been served."

"And beyond a reasonable doubt, you, Marino, and this entire office is convinced that Jack Vanelle is responsible for the hit?"

"That's where you come in, Paulson. You will prove our case by infiltrating Vanelle's very tight circle of trust and bringing me the proof to convict him."

"And how exactly am I to do that? I just show up in Chicago and grab a burger in his restaurant? Shoot the shit over beers? And while I'm at it, just ask him if he had St. Clair murdered in prison?"

"Well, not exactly like that, Paulson, but you're on the right track," said Marino, as he entered Wade's office.

The fucker returns! He made his way into Wade's office and walked over to his desk. The two men exchanged pleasantries, and Marino took a seat beside me. Wade was eyeing me down. I knew I had to address him, so I just nodded with the gesture of my chin. My mouth was as dry as a desert. Anger was boiling deep inside of me, and it was taking all of my discipline not to walk out and never look back.

"Dante, I need a minute with Agent Paulson. Will you please wait for me down in the conference room?"

"Of course, sir. Paulson, I'll see you soon," he said with a smirk. *Jackass.*

"Jacob, I'm not sure what is running through your mind right now, but I can assure you that this investigation will be run clean. I can only imagine how I probably came off to you, but I run a solid unit here, and my record speaks for itself."

"That may be, sir, but what about Agent Marino? He seems pretty determined for me to be his partner, and I'm not sure why. I've never met the man until yesterday, but he appears to know a lot about me and not just my obvious connection to Jack."

"All I know is that when it came time to choose our best agents for this case, your name was at the top of the list. You have an inside knowledge of the mob. Taking down Bornarelli was no easy task, but you did it, and now it's time to do it again with Vanelle."

"Director Wade…"

"Please call me Tim. I think it will lighten some of the tension here in the room."

"I prefer to go by protocol, but if you insist, then Tim it is. As I was beginning to say, Tim, I had help on taking down Bornarelli. It was a team effort, a very successful one at that. Yes, it all turned out good in the end, but what this office is asking me now is just wrong. You say you run a clean office? Well, how can that be when you spy on me and my hotel guests? Then you expect me to just blindside my family, using deception to bring down an 'alleged' suspect? You're all convinced that Jack is the one, but there's no real proof here. You have Jack Vanelle in California during the same timeframe surrounding St. Clair's murder, but that's all you have. He has family here, and I can guarantee he has a solid alibi to back him up. If anything, you have circumstantial evidence, but nothing that can connect him to the murder. You must know this already, or you wouldn't have called me at all. Any number of agents could have worked on this case, but you have nothing on Vanelle. Now, Tim, am I wrong?"

"You're not wrong. You've never been more right. But the truth remains, we have a murder to solve, and the trail begins with Vanelle. So what will it be? Are you in? Or are you out? But know this, Jacob: if you walk away from this case, then the family you are trying to safeguard will truly be unprotected. Any other agent will not be so delicate when it comes to their feelings. As for Marino, he has years of experience with cases such as this one, and he only works with the best. His request for you went through all the proper channels. And him knowing intimate details about you…well, he probably read it in a file. He comes off crass, but he has a solid service record."

"Jacob, I've read your file as well, and I am truly sorry for your loss. She was a great cop and came from a long line of police officers that were and still are much respected in the Boston community. I only hope one day that her killer will be brought to justice. Your backstory is very unique, Paulson. You go from the NFL to law enforcement and excel in both. I'm confident you will stay within the bounds of the law here and do your very best to prove this case. Not every case guarantees a win, but I'm hoping all will work out with this one."

I sat there for a moment and processed all we discussed. He was right. If I choose to walk, then I can't protect my family. Another agent or agents will not show the same compassion and concern that I would. It's a risk, but I have no choice in the matter. I have to see this through to the end.

He waited for my answer. I gave it to him with a handshake and a warning.

"Director Wade, I will take the lead on this assignment, but I will do it alone. I don't trust Marino, and I don't think my opinion will change. He can consult when needed, but I will be the lead. Do you agree?"

"Agreed. I expect weekly reports, and although he won't like it, you will be the lead."

"Very good, sir. Thank you. One more thing?"

"Yes?"

"I do not wish to be monitored. Please remove the surveillance you have on me. My personal life is my own, and I will not share it with the FBI."

"Understood, as long as you understand where your priorities lie."

"Always."

Wade left me on my own to peruse all the intel our office had on Vanelle. I wasn't 100% sure that I could trust Wade completely, but he was as fair as he could be with me today, so I gave him a very guarded benefit of the doubt.

My stomach began to rumble, giving me a clear sign that I was hungry. I had chosen sex with Zoey over having breakfast. I'd been in this office for hours combing through a mountain of paperwork. Vanelle's arrest record was minor at best, a few misdemeanors that never resulted in anything substantial. If he did commit any hard crimes, he certainly covered his tracks because there was nothing here to tie him to anything we had on the books.

There had to be something more, something not in this file. Only one person could answer my questions, and that was Jack Vanelle himself. I guess I was going to Chicago. But there was Zoey to think about. I hadn't heard from her all day, not even a text. What if she left again? I was about to phone her when Marino entered the conference room carrying a bag of food.

"Even tough guys have to eat. Join me for a sandwich? LA is filled with fluff type restaurants, food you can't even pronounce, but I found a deli outside of town that has some pretty good sandwiches. I have roast beef and Swiss or pastrami on rye? What will it be?"

"Neither. I'm a vegetarian."

"Bullshit! Don't worry, Paulson. I didn't poison them."

He laughed as he threw me the roast beef. I accepted it against my better judgment. We ate in silence for a few minutes, with me constantly eyeing the door for my escape. I didn't have the energy to go another round with him, but he didn't look like he was going anywhere. I downed the sandwich in four bites, and then tossed the wrapper into the wastebasket.

"We need to talk, Paulson. Are you ready to?" he asked as he wiped his mouth with his napkin.

"I can't imagine what about? I'm the lead on this case. What else is there to discuss?"

"Boy, you are one arrogant sonofabitch. How about we begin with how you will get to Jack Vanelle? I assume your flight is already booked for Chicago?"

"You don't need to be concerned with my itinerary. I'll get to Chicago on my own time. I'm still going through the files."

"All work and no play, that's what I've heard about you. It will serve to your advantage as you delve deeper into the investigation. Just don't lead with your dick. Can't have any distractions now, can we?"

"What the fuck are you talking about?"

"Oh, you know, no need for discretion. She's quite lovely, but I'm not really into blondes. I prefer lovely brunettes…like your dead fiancée…now, she was breathtaking."

Fuck! Not again. I nearly jumped from where I was sitting, but he saw me coming this time. He put his hands up, stopping me before I beat the living shit out of him. I was so done playing this game.

"Don't even think about it, Paulson, because you will surely lose your shield if you do. Boy, you have quite the temper. I would have thought with all of your years of training and discipline, you would be more reserved."

"I have all those things, and so much more, but you seem to know exactly what button to press. Now, I don't know what your plan here is, but I do not play games and certainly not with the likes of you. I really don't care about your service record, and according to Wade, your outstanding reputation. You play dirty, Marino, and it's probably under the guise that you actually play by the book, but I know better. Now you've mentioned my fiancée more than once. If you've read my file like you say you have, then you know that she was murdered and died in my arms. A bullet meant for me. You also are trying to make me believe that you know something about her murder, so if you do, then be the honorable man they say you are and just tell me. If you're just trying to bait me, I would suggest you not do it again."

"I'm shaking in my boots. Your size doesn't intimidate me, Paulson, so pull back the threat. I come from the streets, boy, and the bigger they are, the harder they fall. You want to test that theory, be my guest. Let me ask you a question: how you can be so sure that bullet was meant for you? Are you sure you know everything about the family you were going to marry into?"

"What are you saying? Again with the sly innuendo. You don't give up, do you?"

"No, I don't, and you don't either. Now, if you want to know what I know, then sit the hell down, shut the hell up, and just listen."

"And if I don't?"

"You can't be that stupid. You're challenging me? Here I thought you were smarter than that."

"Fuck you, Marino. I'm far from stupid. I'm dangerous. And if you were smart, I would think twice before trying to bait me again. On the day I watched her coffin get lowered down into the ground, I made a vow to her father that I would bring her killer to justice. I keep my promises, Marino, and I don't want nor need any help from you."

"Have it your way, Paulson, but this conversation is far from over. We have much to discuss, and I have a feeling you will want to know what I know. And maybe next time the info will not be freely offered. We'll talk again. I'm sure of it. Have a safe flight to Chicago. Watch your back with Vanelle, especially around sharp objects," he said as he walked out.

"Damn it!"

I was so enraged that I trashed the desk I was working on, papers flying everywhere. My breathing was heavy, my chest felt like it was on fire, and my head felt like it would split in two. What does this man know? I'm going crazy here. Once again he's planted more questions for me to obsess over.

I was knee deep in hell back then. I worked those streets like the back of my hand, and I knew I made some enemies along the way. For endless months, I combed through every case file I ever worked on, and I turned up nothing. The trail for her killer went cold. I had nothing to go on. I sunk deeper down into my despair and lost myself to the job. Now this fucker just appeared out of nowhere and was playing me at every turn.

I had to get the hell out of here. I gathered all the strewn papers from the floor and stuffed them into my bag. I phoned my father next.

"Dad!"

"Jacob, are you alright?"

"No, I'm not alright, dad. I'm so fucked right now, and I don't know what to do. Please tell me you have something for me? Anything on Marino? This guy needs to be shut down, and I mean like yesterday. He's playing with my mind dad, like no one has ever done before. He knows something about Minela's death. He's connected somehow, but I just don't have any proof of it. All I have is my gut, and it's telling me to watch my back. And not from Jack Vanelle, but from Dante Marino."

CHAPTER Seven

More than meets the eye...

My phone call with my father didn't put me in a better mood. If anything, I felt worse. He did his best to calm my nerves, but I was heated and needed to find a way to let off some steam. *Zoey Steele would be exactly what I need to accomplish that. Please let her be waiting for me.*

My suite was dimly lit when I entered. Hopefully this was a good sign that Zoey was still here. I called out for her, but there was no reply. My heart sunk deeper down into my chest. She left again, probably leaving just a note with a few lines of her sassy attitude. *Fuck!*

I stomped into the bedroom, throwing my suit jacket onto the bed.

"Hey, what gives?"

What? I turned the light on and there she was half asleep on my bed.

"Zoey! You're here!?!" I exclaimed.

"You seem so surprised! Why is that? Isn't my word good enough, Agent Paulson, or do you need more assurance?"

Fuck me, she was sexy, and mine for the taking. I didn't answer her question...I showed her. She gave me the naughtiest striptease ever last night, so why not return the favor? I removed the rest of my clothing, but she sprang up when I went for my tie.

"Leave the tie. Take off the rest."

"Do you want to play?"

"Hasn't it been a great game so far?"

She was now on her knees with one hand on my tie, pulling me closer to her.

"Is that what this is, a game to you?" I asked, but I was beginning to get angry.

I wasn't some guy that just bedded women, took what I needed, and discarded them without a second thought. And Zoey was different, not like anyone I'd known before, and I hoped to get to know her better.

There was no answer in return, just her lips on mine. I let our bodies speak for us, and for now, the conversation was over.

I ended up taking off my tie and using it on Zoey's wrists. She didn't complain and just played the naughty submissive. Everything in me was screaming to take her, own her, and possess every inch of her. She screamed out rather loudly when I took her nipple into my mouth, biting down just enough without causing her pain, but pure pleasure. I repeated the attention on the other, and it was the same reaction, which only excited me more.

"I want you so much," I said.

"You have me, Jake. I'm right here."

I left her wrists tethered together but wrapped her arms around my neck as I entered her wet folds. I never had sex bare with anyone other than Minela, but I was clean, and Zoey told me she was too. Another strong emotion I easily felt when I was with her: trust. I had given it to her so easily, never once questioning it. After we were both sated, I finally untied her and just held her in my arms.

"Where did you come from, Zoey Steele?" I asked.

Her naked back was facing me. As I ran my fingers down her spine, I could see faint goosebumps rising on her soft skin. She turned to face me and smiled.

"I could ask you the same question. Maybe when the stars aligned for Tenley and Jagger, the universe had a few to spare for us. Don't get me wrong, I'm not a silly, starry-eyed blonde that wishes for her prince before she goes to sleep at night. I'm a realist and pretty much take things at face value, but you, Agent Paulson, proved that theory wrong for me. From the moment I met you, I felt this intense attraction towards you, and I was drawn to get to know you better. At first I didn't think you even liked me, but then Tenley explained your tough exterior."

"Oh yeah? How so?"

"Keep your testosterone down, Paulson. She only meant tough because of your profession and how you have to be because of it."

"I guess so when you summarize it like that, but Zoey, it's so much more than just coming off like a tough guy. This job requires one hundred percent focus, discipline, and no margin of error, not ever. It can be very rewarding, but it can also destroy all that's good in your life and replace it with feelings no person should ever have to experience."

The expressive look in Zoey's eyes just about made my heart split in two. This was the same look that everyone in my life had shown me since Minela died. *What is it with me? Do I just naturally put out this vibe: feel sorry for me? Well, fuck that, not anymore. I can't do this with Zoey after she's the one that has finally made me come back to life.*

"Don't pull away, not now," she said.

Her hands cupped my face. I leaned up to kiss her.

"I wasn't going to, even though I should. This life that I lead is just too ugly for you, beautiful girl, and I can't have it taint you."

"What if I don't care? You are worth taking the risk."

"Oh, Zoey, you don't know how much I want to, but I just can't right now. Please understand that these last few days spent with you have meant the world to me. I will always cherish them."

"Sounds like you're saying goodbye. Is that what you're doing?"

Fuck my life! Now tears were forming in her eyes. I had hurt her. I wiped them away with my thumbs and kissed each one of her cheeks.

"Please don't cry. I'm sorry."

I repeated it over and over again until she was down to a quiet sniffle. I held her in my arms until she fell asleep. She felt so good next to me, I didn't want to let her go, but I knew I had to. I finally managed to dislodge myself from her enveloped arms. I already felt the loss of her warmth.

My heart was so conflicted with my two lives: professional and personal. I was here for work. I had to get my head back into the game and not let any distractions affect my ability to do my job.

I left her sleeping while I closed the door behind me to do some work. I hadn't heard anything from my father yet on Marino. I then phoned Duffy. He was not only my boss but my trusted friend. I had to get some answers. I phoned his private line and allowed it to ring several times before it went to voicemail. I simply just told him to call me back.

I leaned back in my chair to close my eyes for a few minutes, and once again Minela came back to life in my dreams. I dreamt about the first time I met the very feisty Detective Minela LaRocha, back when we were NYPD.

"Are you serious, Duff? I'm getting a partner? I don't want a partner, especially a female. Just what I need: a damsel in distress that I have to look out for. I work alone, and I do it very well."

"Don't let the equal opportunity crazies hear you say that. You will be deemed a sexist pig and will probably be tied up by your balls."

Duff was now laughing at me. I guess I did sound like a dick, but in some way I meant what I said. My last partner turned out to be a waste of space, and I wasn't in the mood to break another one in, male or female.

"I know what you're thinking, Jake, and I will tell you right now

that you are wrong about this one. She comes from a law enforcement family. Her father is currently the chief of police for the Boston PD, and she has four brothers who are also police officers. Imagine her father's surprise when his little girl told him that she wanted to follow in her family's footsteps. I've met her, Jake, and I've had some very enlightening conversations with her. She's smart, tough, and can do the job as well as any man I've ever met, maybe even you."

"Gee, thanks, Duff. You're all heart."

"I'm just trying to make the introductions a little easier for you. Her record is flawless. She has a high arrest record and has solved and closed seventeen out of twenty cases. Not bad for a young detective just transferred in. I think she will be a good match for you, but..."

"But what? What were you going to say?"

"Just don't fall in love with her. This job has no room for it."

"Thanks for the advice, Duff, but I have no intentions of falling in love with Detective LaRocha."

"Duly noted, Detective Paulson. How about we introduce ourselves first before we plan our nuptials?"

Heat was rising in my cheeks and my manhood was making its presence known when the exotic Minela LaRocha walked through my captain's office. No freaking way was this woman a cop. She's too gorgeous not to be a model. God! I hated sounding like this chauvinistic guy, but how could I not notice her face too? She was the most beautiful woman I had ever seen.

"It's a pleasure to meet you, detective. You already know who I am, so how about we grab a cup of coffee and get to know one another a little better?" she said.

Her hand was extended, waiting for me to shake it, but I was a goner. Duffy slapped my back to get my attention. What was I, a awkward prepubescent boy who could not speak around girls? Finally coming back down to earth, I greeted her with the standard pleasantries I would use with any cop. But she was the first one I had ever wanted to kiss—and by that I mean fucking devour.

"After you," was all I said while following her out the door.

I almost put my hand on the small of her back, but I pulled back quickly before I was cited for sexual harassment. Thank God she was a few steps in front of me when I looked over my shoulder to the laughing Duffy.

"Yeah, Paulson. Good luck not falling in love with her," he said.

I would gladly take his abuse for the next few days. I knew I was acting like a lovesick fool. What could I say? She made it easy.

Fall was upon us, and it was the perfect time to walk in Central Park. The leaves were beginning to change color, and there was still a hint of summer before the brisk nights would follow. Minela and I grabbed some coffee and walked around the lake.

"So tell me about yourself, tough guy. Who is Jacob Paulson? And why do I want to be his partner?"

I laughed at her easy way of breaking the ice with me. I stopped and sat on a nearby park bench overlooking the water with the New York skyline serving as our backdrop for the perfect picture.

I turned to face her. She was waiting for me to talk. She was patient, I'll give her that. I tried to hide my smile, but I was failing miserably.

"What would you like to know that you haven't already read in a file or found on Google?"

"Fair enough. Why did you become a cop?" she asked and then finished her coffee, tossing it into the trash can. "Score! Two points," she screamed.

Damn! Can this beauty actually like sports too?

"After my injury made the decision for me to leave the game, I wanted more from my life. I had already earned my degree and just needed to enter the academy to make it official. No one understood my decision to leave the game behind me, especially my brothers who were playing alongside with me. It was our dream to play in the NFL from the moment we could throw the ball, and one third of the

trio was leaving the band."

"I guess it all worked out in the end for you. You seem to have taken the career change quite well."

"And only knowing me an hour tells you that?"

"No, but your record is impressive. You found success early on in your career and have moved up the chain of command rather quickly than others, so that tells me that you are one hell of a cop. Maybe playing football was just an appeasement for your father, not really for yourself. Am I close?"

"No, you're not. I've always loved the game. For years, football was all I knew, all I had, and then one day it just was gone. I needed to find fulfillment again in my life, and that's where the law came in."

"A natural star on the beat, then Intelligence, and finally detective. You're my hero."

"Okay, Miss Nosey Pants, you got me all figured out. What about you? How did the apple of her daddy's eye become a cop? What are you, a rebel? That's it. Probably treated like a princess from daddy and your brothers, so becoming a cop might shake up the family tree a bit. Now tell me, Minela, am I close?"

"I'm hungry. How about a dog with the works, my treat."

"Way to go avoiding answering my question detective, and yes...you can pay."

The rest of our afternoon was filled with more questions about each other. She was easy to talk to, but not so easy answering my questions. She simply told me that she wanted to be a cop probably as long as I wanted to be a football player. Playing with dolls and tea parties wasn't her thing, not when she had four older brothers in the house to grow up around. She loved all sports and played them too. I had never met anyone like her and definitely wanted to know her better.

Of course I was right about her father. He was adamantly against her decision to join the force, but her mind was made up. She wouldn't change her mind, not for anyone. Eventually they came around, she said, and her graduation picture in her blues was placed on her living room wall that joined her brothers'. She said her father had never been more proud of her, but he secretly wished she would occupy a desk job and not the streets. I guess if I had a daughter, I may have wanted the same thing.

The days and months that followed our meeting were probably the happiest days of my life. I didn't think I could feel that happy again since my days playing ball, but Minela sure kept things interesting. She was tough, kind of a badass, with legs that went on for days. We teased each other constantly. I called her Minela Vanilla once, and she basically told me that she would cut my balls off and feed them to me on a platter if I ever used that nickname again. I laughed at first, and then I stopped because of the way she was looking at me. I wasn't the only one that called her that, and I promised I wouldn't do it again. She had a tough skin when it came to being a cop, harassed by her brothers, but she always said she wanted things easy with me.

I was a goner from the minute I met her. How could I not fall in love with Minela? She was everything I could want, and one day I grew a set of balls and came clean with her.

She was leaning over her desk reading through some files with her glorious ass pointed right at me. Fuck my life! I have to just tell her. Minela, I love you. I've loved you from the first moment we met. We practically spend every waking minute together anyway. You're not seeing anyone. I'm not seeing anyone, so why don't we just see each other? What do you think?

"Earth to Detective Paulson. Hey! Are you with me?"

I felt a flick to my cheek and came back to the reason I was standing behind her.

"What?" I questioned.

"You are a million miles away. Can you come back to earth? I need some help."

I saw her in front of me, and I heard everything she said, but no words would come out of my mouth. I was frozen to the spot, be-

cause I just didn't know how to tell her that I had fallen in love with her.

"Good chatting with you, Jake."

She patted my shoulders and walked away. What was wrong with me? When I was in high school and college, I had girls all over me all the time, and when it came to Minela, I went mute.

Duffy stuck his head out from his office and called me in, "Paulson, my office."

"Yes, sir."

"Cut the formalities, Jake. You look like your about to drool all over yourself."

"Sorry, Duff, but I can't help it. I become an adolescent anytime I'm around her. How I've done the job with her this long without screwing up is a miracle. I need to tell her, or I'm fucking transferring to Alaska."

"Oh, I love it when I'm right, but you're also right. You have to talk to her. You're lucky I love you like a son, because if you were any other one of my guys, I would have kicked their ass already. I told you not to fall in love with her, and that's exactly what you did, son."

"I guess it had to happen eventually. I'm my parents' first born son, and my kid brother gets married first. I'm sorry, Duff, but she's the one. If she doesn't return my feelings, I give you my word that I will walk away clean, but I have to know one way or another."

"Fine, go be stupid, but don't marry her."

"Yeah, okay, boss. If she tells me that she loves me, I am so putting a ring on that finger. I will make it known to the world that she is mine. Knocking her up will be at the top of my priority list, and lastly..."

"Oh please! There's more? I can't wait to hear this."

I held my stomach I was laughing so hard. Duff was just so easy to talk to. He had become a good friend over the years, and I did respect his opinion on my life. My parents were in California, and I was on my own here in New York. Duff was like a second father to me.

I turned away, and before I left the room, I said to him, "I plan on making Minela LaRocha the happiest woman in the world. It will be my vow to make her smile and laugh every single day. She's the next Mrs. Paulson. I just know it, Captain."

I left his office with a new sense of purpose. Yup! Tonight would be the night I made her mine.

CHAPTER *Eight*

BAD TIMING...

I'd never forget the sound of that gunshot. The feel of blood on my hands. The feel of a higher than life physical form was now lifeless in my arms.

"No baby, please don't leave me. Please baby, help is on the way. You stay with me, baby. Don't you fucking die on me. Not here, not now, not in the middle of the street. Come on, baby! Where's my tough Boston girl who took on her brothers in a hockey game? They had nothing on you. You scored three goals. I'll never forget the look on your brothers faces. Come on, baby. We have another game in our future. Please Minela, please? Don't leave me!" I screamed as loud as I could and prayed for a response back. *"Our life is just beginning. Don't you know that, baby? You have to stay with me, please. I hear the sirens getting nearer. You're going to be okay. Just hang on."*

"Ja..." was all she could push from her lips. Her voice was so faint, I could barely hear her say my name.

I was internally struggling with what I wanted to believe and what I knew was actually happening. She tried to say my name, so I convinced myself that if she could do that, she would be okay. I *didn't want to believe the alternative. I tried to pull myself together to show her that I actually believed she would make it through this, but I knew better. The bullet nearly hit directly into her chest and didn't go through to the other side, so I knew it shredded her chest wall on account of the blood she was losing. I tried to calm her, but she was determined to talk. I couldn't believe this was happening to us. Just a mere hour ago, we had everything: love, life...a future.*

"Shhh, don't try to talk. Help is on the way."

She was struggling to breathe, struggling to stay alive. My thumb was on her pulse. I knew I only had seconds left with her, but that didn't stop me from begging her to live and to stay with me.

"I love you Minela, so much. I love you. I love you."

In her last moment of clarity, she looked right into my soul and whispered her last words to me, "I...love you too...Paulson...I'm so happy...you didn't listen...to Duff...and fell in love with me...anyway."

I was crying, screaming, shaking her, but she was gone. She half smiled at me, then closed her eyes, and her hand slipped from mine.

The ambulance arrived with the two EMT's trying to separate me from her, but no matter how vehemently they tried to save her, she was dead in my arms.

The t-shirt I was wearing was no longer white. It was red from Minela bleeding out. I brushed the hair away from her forehead and placed my lips down to kiss her. Her skin was already beginning to go cold. Why? Why did this happen to her? And to us?

"Jacob, wake up. Please open your eyes and look at me."

"Minela?" I called out.

"No, Jake. It's Zoey. You were having a nightmare. Please open your eyes."

I felt her soft hands glide down my jaw. I opened my eyes and took in Zoey's bright blues staring back at me. They were beautiful pools of the ocean, but I also saw fear in them. God knows how loud I was and how it must have frightened her. I could never predict when the PTSD will strike again, but when I succumbed to the nightmares, I was just pulled down deeper and deeper into a bottomless abyss until I came up for air. This time it was Zoey who breathed life into my heart.

I wasn't ready to talk to her, certainly not about my past. I took Zoey into my arms and kissed her passionately.

"Are you okay?" she breathlessly asked.

She was completely taken off guard with my assault on her mouth. What an inviting mouth it was, and one I never wanted to stop tasting.

I let out a breath, and then placed my forehead to hers.

"I need to make love to you, Zoey. Please let me love on you and help me forget. Can you do that for me? Help me forget?"

I heard the words slip from my mouth, a raw vulnerability I had no control over. The dam had been breached, with my soul just gutted wide open.

I was ashamed with how broken I sounded, so weak and lost, and here I was asking a woman to comfort me with her body. This was not who I am. This man was not the same man my father raised me to be. I couldn't undo the past no matter how much I fought it. Minela was gone, and I had to free myself of this loss, or I would never truly be able to experience the joy I had with her, with anyone else. *My God!* Zoey's beauty just brought me to my knees. She was absolutely perfect, and my nightmare was nearly forgotten just focusing on the beauty before me.

"Yes, please make love to me," she responded.

She held my face and kissed me. I carried her back to the bedroom and made love to this beautiful woman who in just a few short days had managed to break down my walls and make me want more out of life.

After I knew Zoey was asleep, I leaned on my elbow to watch her. She looked so peaceful, which left me wanting that same feeling. I couldn't pretend like time spent with her hadn't been amazing, but the fact remained that I was here for work, and by all accounts Zoey was here for me.

I had breakfast ordered up. Not knowing what she would like, I ordered everything on the breakfast selection list. I was just putting my suit jacket on when she walked out from the shower wearing only a towel.

"Good morning. How did you sleep?" I asked her as she toyed with her towel.

Any other time, I would be game to playing, but I needed to get downtown. *Please, you tease...do not drop that towel.* Thank goodness she didn't and just walked up to me standing on her toes to kiss me.

"Good morning to you too. How are you? Did you manage to get any sleep?" *There were those concerned eyes again.*

"I think you know the answer to that one. You wore me out. Were you a gymnast or dancer back in school?" I teased her, earning a smile in return.

"Pilates, baby. It's addicting."

"Well, I may have to send a thank you note to your instructor, because you are an A student."

She had beads of water still lingering on her shoulders, making me want to lap them all up with my tongue.

"I know you have to be going, so I won't keep you, Jake. I'll just get dressed and get out of your hair."

What? I don't want her to leave, and where to, back to New York? Since she has arrived, all we've done is have sex, with her helping me through my nightmare last night. I needed to say something without making myself sound desperate or needy.

"Um, Zoey, when you say 'leaving,' what does that mean exactly?" I asked her the question, nearly biting the inside of my mouth.

She stepped out of my embrace and grabbed a croissant off the breakfast tray. She took a small bite and turned back to me.

"What do *you* think it means? I'm curious to know."

She continued to nibble on her food while teasing the shit out of me with that sexy mouth of hers.

"I'm not sure, so that's why I asked. Are you leaving LA and returning to New York? Will I see you again?"

She dropped her food and walked back over to me. I wanted to take her up against the wall for making me wait for her answer. She looked at me. No words, just touched. She pulled me down to her lips and pushed her tongue inside of my mouth. *Fuck my life!* Now I was hard.

"I'm not going anywhere, Jake. My father has a condo here, not too far from this hotel. I'm going to go back there and get some much needed sleep. You see, some ex-football player who is built like a brick wall really worked me over last night. He could go all night like a freaking sex machine. He says I'm very bendy, but it was he who was the physical phenomenon."

I couldn't help but smile at this beautiful girl.

"I would rather have you wait in my place, in my bed, but I guess we can both take today to do what we have to do. I'm not sure when I will return tonight, but can I call you when I do?"

"Of course you can. My number is programmed in your phone. And Jake, do me a favor today?"

"What would that be?"

She kissed me again, this time biting my bottom lip, leaving it slightly swollen. I fucking loved it. She almost ran back to the bathroom but first turned to say, "Don't drive yourself too crazy today with all those unanswered questions spinning around in your mind. When you're ready, we will have that conversation. Okay?"

I just nodded back while she blew me a kiss and closed the door behind her.

I had declined the car service today. I needed to definitely think and clear my head. Zoey already knew me too well, and I liked it. I called Tenley and hoped she would be able to give me some more info about her best friend.

"Hey, Jake, how are you?" asked my very happy friend.

"I'm good. I hope I didn't interrupt anything?" My fingers were crossed behind my back. "Are you still in New York?"

"No, we're back in Wyoming. Jagger is already out somewhere

on the property. I'm just staring at my new, huge home and trying to figure out where to put everything."

"I thought you had a furnished home already to move into?"

"I do, but my things arrived today from my apartment in New York, so I'm surrounded by boxes. No worries, I'll manage. So how are you doing, and how's the current case? Can I help you with anything?"

"The case is complicated, and I'm just beginning to get into it, but that's not why I called. It's about Zoey. She followed me out here, and other than the obvious, and I'm so confused to why."

"Oh, Jake! Now it all makes sense."

"What makes sense? Because I'm completely in the fucking dark."

Tenley sighed on the line, and then began explaining, "Jake, on the day I packed up my office, Zoey said goodbye to her father and to me. She said she was going to take a leave of absence from the firm and head west. I was completely caught off guard by her announcement. I had so many questions, but she made it clear that she wasn't ready to answer them. She promised me and her dad that she would be in touch when she could, and that was it. Her father was just as confused as I was, but he hugged her back and let her go. I haven't heard from her since, but I guess I will soon."

She continued, "Since I've known you, Paulson, you've been closed up and all about the job and nothing else. If Zoey, my very sparkly friend, has changed that, then all I ask of you is to not hurt her. She obviously has feelings for you. I have never known her to behave like this, not ever. Her work is just as important, and she won't stand for one night stands. I can't even remember the last time she told me about any guy, and now she's left her job, home, and family to follow you across the country! You could be the game changer for her, Jake. But if she's not the one for you, then please be honest with her before she gets in too deep. Okay?"

Fuck my life! If Tenley only knew I was the one that was in over my head. I ended our call and made my way to the office to once again meet with Marino.

I reached out to my own sources in regards to Jack Vanelle. He'd been seen at his restaurant and all around town, not keeping a low profile by any means. He was making his presence known anywhere a camera was in sight. He wasn't stupid and has played this game before. If he was responsible for the death of Michael St. Clair, he covered his tracks with a well-devised plan, leaving no room for mistakes.

I stepped off the elevator and made my way to the office Director Wade allowed me to use. He even gave me an assistant to fetch my coffee, but I didn't need a puppy dog to follow me around, not when I had a pit bull like Marino breathing down my neck.

I did accept the coffee and the breakfast that was offered. Earlier, I had made sure that Zoey had everything she needed to eat, but I declined to take care of myself. It was so easy to take care of her, and I would do it again and again if she asked me to.

Where is this coming from? Focus, Paulson, and get your head in the game, for Christ's sake!

My dutiful assistant, I think her name is Chloe, knocked on the door. She was so perky that she should be sitting on top of a cheerleader pyramid.

"Yes, what is it?"

"Um, Mr. Paulson, sir, you, um, have a call on line three."

"And? You don't know how to use the intercom?"

"Um, no. It's, like, new, and I'm still learning the system."

Oh. My. God! She was actually twirling her hair, and what the fuck was that? A giggle?

"That will be all, Chloe. I'll be fine here on my own. You can just run off and do what you normally do around here, far away from me."

She gave another toothy smile and nearly skipped out of the room. I shook it off and took my call.

"Paulson. Hello?" I repeated myself several times and then hung up. I guess whoever it was got tired of waiting for me, or she didn't connect the call correctly.

I went through all of my notes and files again. I hoped my father was successful on finding info I could use against Marino. Director Wade would surely want a status report and expect me to have my flight set to Chicago.

"Paulson, what do you have for me?" Director Wade questioned as he entered my office.

"I wish I could give you better news, but there is not much to go on. But I'm guessing you already knew that."

"Very perceptive of you, Paulson."

He took a seat and crossed his leg over his ankle.

"Again, this is why you are here. No evidence? Find the evidence. Build a case. Nail his ass against the wall. It seems pretty easy to me, wouldn't you agree?"

"You seem to have it all worked out, sir."

"I do, Paulson. The question is: do you?"

"I know my job, sir."

"Good. Go do it then. Report to me when you have something."

He got up to leave my office and turned to tell me that Duffy had finally arrived in LA and that I could use all the help I could get. *Asshole.*

My phone buzzed in my pocket, and sure enough, it was Duff. He asked me to meet him downstairs. I grabbed what I needed and quickly took the elevators down. We met off-site, away from the building. I knew what he had to tell me was big and didn't want any ears listening in.

"It's about fucking time you got here. I've been drowning out here since you put me on this fucked up assignment."

"I'm glad to see you too, son," he said and then brought me close for a hug, where he slipped several files into my hands. "Let's walk and talk. We have much to discuss. Your father called me and brought me up to speed with everything. His contacts found nothing, so I did some searching on my own. Now, what I am about to tell you could probably end my career, but certain players have made this game very personal for you, Jake, and I love you like a son, so let's roll the dice and play roulette with both our careers."

He continued, "I was skeptical from the moment you were requested, first by Wade, and then Marino was also assigned. This is highly irregular. Why are two directors from two coasts suddenly interested in a rich kid's murder? And then it hit me. This Wade guy is on deck for a big promotion. As in Washington, DC. As in presidential status. You see where I'm going with this? If his office solves this murder case, his shield looks shinier than ever, and it pretty much secures his spot working closely with the Director of the FBI."

"Okay, so that's Wade's story. What about Marino?"

"Revenge. It all comes down to revenge. This guy doesn't care who he has to go through to get it. Michael St. Clair's murder was just what he needed to finally get what he has wanted for years, and that's Jack Vanelle. This guy is running on purely personal reasons, and that's the only thing driving him to push you to where he needs you to be. You said he's acting like he knows something about Minela, and well, son, that's probably true. Marino has worked the streets since the beginning of his career in Chicago and then moved on to Boston. He's connected both with the force and behind the scenes. His pockets are lined with paper, not coins. He's going to keep coming at you until you give him Jack, and he won't just be using your dead fiancée to light a fire under you. He will pick off your family one by one."

"Jake, he had a brother, his youngest, who he loved very much. They were extremely close, but when Dante left, that's when his brother got into trouble. He did some stupid things and crossed the wrong people. Dante tried to reason with him, get him off the streets, but his brother was in too deep."

"Duff, you said Chicago? Did Marino have ties to Jack years ago?"

"Not directly. But his brother, Michael, did. He was known around the streets as Mikey. He ran game for some mob guy named

Johnny Carlucci. It seems Mikey was skimming from the till in not one bar, but several Johnny had owned. A message had to be delivered, and that's where Jack came in. No one fucked with Jack Vanelle, and if you saw him coming, you better be sure to run the other way. Jack broke Mikey's spine, and he never walked again. Mikey was a criminal and in too deep. There was no way he was getting out. He was later convicted and sent off to prison where he only served about six months before slicing his wrists. He bled out and was dead for many hours before he was found in his cell the next morning."

Duff gave me a minute to process all he had told me. It all made sense now. Marino could give two shits about St. Clair's death. He wanted Jack, and this was the way to finally get him, by using me.

"Duff, if Marino is connected like Jack, then why not take matters in his own hands and avenge his brother's death?"

"I don't have the answer to that, Jake. That's a question only Marino can answer. His record is clean on paper, but old guys like myself just believe what we believe. He's had a good career with many merits, but you can't get what he has solely on a cop's salary, and his salary in the FBI is not that much better. He has a house out in Westchester County. A summer house over in the Hamptons, of course in his wife's name. Two kids in college, and not in a state school. Do you get what I'm saying, Jake?"

"Yeah, I get it. So what do I do, Duff? How do I do my job without hurting my family? Am I just supposed to walk into Jack's bar and slap the cuffs on him? He's too smart to fuck up."

"Jake, I don't even know how to advise you on this one. You're caught between the job and your family. All I can say is to stay ahead of him—not just by one or two steps, but many steps. You're a good cop, Jake, probably one of the best I ever had the honor to train, but only you can decide what happens next. Sometimes we have to look the other way to protect what's most important."

"You can't be serious, Duff. Being a cop is all I know, all I have. I can't just not pursue this, especially if Jack is guilty."

"You can't, Jake, or you won't? Marino is going to keep coming at you, and once Jack finds out that he's on the FBI's radar, it won't be pretty. Please consider all your options, son. You are surrounded by sharks out here and on your own. I've given you everything I have. I have to walk from here."

"Please, Duff, I need your help. Please stay in LA. We can work the case together."

"Jake, don't you see what's happening here? It's all been carefully formulated from the beginning, the perfect plan. From the minute you were assigned to this case, we've all been played by the bigger player in the game. With knowing what you know now, you have to go back to Marino and deal. You need to use what you have to gain some leverage. If my suspicions are correct, and most of the time, they are dead-on balls accurate, then he will use what he knows about Minela to get what he needs from you. You just have to have the better hand. Be careful, son. Watch your back with this guy."

"Okay, I will."

I said goodbye to Duff as his car pulled away to take him back to the airport. How I wish I was getting on a plane too, leaving for parts unknown with Zoey by my side. *That's just a fantasy I can't entertain right now.* I needed a meeting with Marino.

We met a short time later down on the Santa Monica Pier. The sun was beginning to set, and the pier was filled with tourists. He was waiting for me at the entrance of the pier and led me down to the beach where less people were.

We walked in silence for a few moments until he turned and stopped. He had a serious look on his face, but as he was attempting to stare me down, I did the same. He spoke first.

"So, I gather you know, don't you?"

"What do you think I know? I know many things. Please be more specific."

"Play time is over, Paulson, so don't fuck with me. I know Duffy hand-delivered confidential files to you today, and don't you want to know why those files became available for him to easily access? Because I was the one that led him there. You are not stupid! So don't fucking pretend to be. It's all a shell game, Paulson, and I just made sure he picked the right one. Now that you know my past, go ahead and ask me. You know you want to. What's going through your mind right about now? *What does he know? And how does he know it? Is he just trying to play me again? Or this time, can I actually believe him?* Hmm?"

He was so asking for it, but I held my own against his taunting me. This was the game, and I would play, but no more giving Marino the expected reaction.

I said, "Let's get it all out then, shall we? Two brothers: One good and the other...bad. From where I'm standing, I'm not sure what side you were ever on, but you want me to believe good. You just have a hard-on for Jack Vanelle, because you hold him responsible for your kid brother's death. But Jack wasn't the one that took a blade to his wrist and ended his life—a life built around crime that he chose all on his own. Sorry, man, but the decision to live that life and to end that life was on your brother. You can't blame Jack or even yourself. Your brother owns his death and the way he chose to live his life."

"You don't know shit!" Marino screamed at me. "It was Jack who drove him to take his own life. He would have never done that if not pushed against the wall with no way out. My family was never the same again after my brother died, and I swore on Mikey's grave that I would get justice for him. Today is that day."

"And then what? No matter what you do will never bring your brother back to you. You want to pin Jack Vanelle for a murder he probably didn't commit, with no evidence by the way, solely to satisfy your personal vendetta. And then where will you be? Your career will be over. You will lose everything, and at the end of the day, your brother will still be gone. He was of age, and he knew what he was doing. You have to know that, Dante. You don't go up against mob figures, fuck them over, and expect your crimes to be forgiven. Your brother fucked up by crossing someone he shouldn't have, and that ultimately led him to Jack's front door. They each knew what they were getting themselves into, and that has to be on them. You've been carrying this around with you for years when you should have been living your life. Let this go, Marino. If Jack Vanelle is found guilty of murdering Michael St. Clair, then justice will be served. But we need to find hard evidence first."

"Wow, Paulson, I didn't peg you for being so forgiving when it comes to matters like your family! You are one to talk. *Me* not living *my* life? That's a fucking joke. What about *you*, big shot? You're all preaching about how the past is the past, all is forgotten and forgiven, and what, are you such a happy guy? You don't actually believe that bullshit you're peddling, do you? You're a fucking liar, that's what you are. I don't doubt for a second that if you knew who was responsible for your girl's death, then you wouldn't stop at making them pay. Come on, man! We've both worked the streets long enough to know what you would do: put a fucking bullet in his brain and not think twice about it. Or maybe through his heart, exactly the same way she died."

"You motherfucker!"

I had never been so enraged in all of my life. I charged at him like a fucking bull, knocking him on his ass. I delivered punch after punch to his gut until I lost my footing, and he pulled his service weapon on me.

"Back the fuck off! You know that what I'm saying is true. You fucking help me take down Vanelle, and I promise you on my brother's eyes that I will tell you who is responsible for killing your girl. I swear it."

"Tell me now, or no deal."

"No way, Paulson, so you can fuck me over later on? You do exactly what I say, and then we have a deal."

My breath was ragged. All I saw was red when I looked at him.

"See you around, Marino. I want to get off of this ride."

I played a hand that I never thought I would have the courage to do, but I called his bluff and walked. He had his gun still pointed at me as I made my way to the pier. He was screaming about how much of a fool I was, and maybe that was true. No matter what I would agree to, he would never tell me the truth, only use it over my head to get what he needed.

Minela was a great cop, loyal to the shield. Her killer was out there somewhere, and I would keep my promise to bring that person to justice. I just won't be manipulated to do it, though. As I walked back to my car and drove back to the hotel, a new plan was formed. There was another player in this game that could help me. I just needed to figure some things out, and then I would reach out to him.

Once again my hotel room was dark. I was hoping that Zoey would be here, but this time I was alone. The room had been cleaned and the linens changed, leaving no remnants behind of the night we shared. I was caught between two women: my past with Minela and believing I may have a future with Zoey Steele.

It was just bad timing. I couldn't risk another woman in my life getting hurt. I'd never survive it. I had to let her go…for now.

CHAPTER Nine

HELLO...GOODBYE

After my meeting with Marino, I needed a hot shower to wash the disgust off of me. He wasn't a man to be reasoned with, although I tried. But he wasn't having it. He was a fucking coward, and I believe deep down he knew it. He just wanted a scapegoat to do the dirty work for him, and he was using his position to get me to do it.

As for Wade, he was just clueless as to what was really in front of him. I decided that it wasn't my job to school him on how to be a cop. He was basically a pencil pusher with a badge, climbing the ladder to kiss more ass than to actually get some. I was done with him and his office.

Before leaving my suite, I looked around for any note Zoey may have left for me, but I didn't find anything. Maybe she changed her mind after all? I didn't have time to find out. I had one more stop and needed to see someone before I caught my flight to Chicago.

My brother Simon was closest to our aunt, so it made all the sense in the world that he would ultimately live in the home she loved so much. They shared a special bond between them, and she was the only one that truly understood his passion for the ocean and all of God's beauty that lied beneath the waves.

I spent many summers here with my Aunt Grace. She would sit on the shoreline and watch us surf and do tricks on our boards. She would paint and cheer us on. Flowers lined the long path leading up to the staircase. The beach house was set high above, where you would have to look down to see the beach. It was just breathtaking. It was just like I remembered.

My father texted me that Simon had returned home earlier than expected. Simon wasn't a news junkie, and I didn't think he would immediately check all he had missed when they were gone. I told my father that I would be the one to break the news to them.

On the drive over, I filled my father in on all that happened to-day. He wanted to see me, but I declined his invitation. I still hadn't seen my mother, and I was sorry for that. He understood where I needed to be, so he chose not to even tell her that I was in California. What was the point of hurting her feelings?

The one person I wished I could avoid would be Nicolette and the look she was sure to give me when I told her about Michael. After the trial, she never mentioned his name again, and now I feared I would bring all of her pain back. She had to know and so did my brother.

I took the stairs two at a time and rapped on the double French doors. Their cars were here, and I saw lights coming off the kitchen that led to the back deck. I waited another beat, then walked around. I didn't want to frighten them, or heaven forbid walk in on them in a compromising position. Yeah, they do that with the shades open. Living out here gives them lots of privacy.

Where the heck are they? I thought as I continued to look around the house. I couldn't access anything else without a key, so I just took a minute to take in the amazing view. The sun had set for the night, leaving hues of beautiful colors bouncing off the waves. I'm not all that religious, but taking in all of this beauty, I almost felt God's presence here. It was no wonder why Simon was so passionate about what he did. He worked so hard preserving what most of us took for granted.

Just then I heard laughter coming up the stairs and a loud thud to the deck.

"Those waves were spectacular, Simon, but I'm still afraid of the sharks. Next time, *you* can do the night surfing, while *I* just watch safely from the shore," I heard Nicolette tell my brother.

"Baby, how many times do I have to tell you? It's perfectly safe out there. I've taken on the waters of Australia and South Africa, and nothing has ever happened," Simon reassured her.

"Yeah, yeah, husband, but our children are not going out there anytime soon."

"Wrong again, baby. Our babies *were* just out there, because my baby mama was out there, so your statement is squashed."

"Oh, Simon! I wasn't really surfing. It was more like sitting."

"You stood up once, and you glided in, so that counts my love. I'm starving! Let's put the steaks on."

I was tucked in the corner, and just as they passed me—hand in hand, of course—I popped out and said, "I'll take mine medium well."

"Oh my God! Jacob!?! What are you doing here?" Nicolette asked after the shock wore off.

She immediately let go of Simon's hand and jumped into my arms. It felt so good at this moment to be with her and my brother, who was staring at me as if he was looking at a ghost. My fault, this I know. It just reaffirmed once again that I'd been away from my family for more time than I ever expected to.

"It is so good to see you, Nicolette. You look beautiful. And congratulations to you, Mommy-to-be. I can't wait to meet my nephew or niece."

"Oh, thank you, Jacob. I'm sure that…" Nicolette hesitated and turned to look over to Simon. "Can we tell him, honey?"

Simon, who still was not talking, simply nodded and smiled back to his wife. Nicolette's cheeks reddened. She was glowing.

"Like I was about to say, I'm sure that our children will love their Uncle Jacob."

"Children? Plural? Twins? That's amazing news! Does the family know?"

"No, not yet. We wanted to wait to make sure I could even hold the pregnancy, and so far everything is going great. I'm in my second trimester now, and my doctor says there is no reason why I shouldn't be able to carry our twins to nearly full-term. They hope for me to make it to 36 weeks with my health history."

"Sorry for asking, sis, but should you really be surfing in your condition? I hate to sound sexist, but is it safe?"

"You're not being sexist. You're being the concerned big brother who we love very much. I wasn't really doing anything physical out there. I've been through a lot, but I'm healthy and strong, and I know our babies will be too."

"I'm so happy for you both. I can't wait to meet them."

I hugged her again and didn't miss my brother scowling at me. Nicolette excused herself to go tend to dinner, giving me some time with Simon.

After she was a safe distance away, I started to say something to him, but he walked by me and said, "Not here. Follow me down to the beach."

I could do nothing but follow. He was angry at me, and I really couldn't blame him. We were always very close, and then I simply just checked out and fell off the grid. My father certainly told me how he felt about my non-presence in our family, so now I was ready to hear it from Simon.

We walked a bit with Simon not saying anything, and I continued to follow until he turned around to look at me.

"You asshole!" he screamed, and then I was stunned and knocked on my ass with a punch to my jaw.

What the hell! I knew he was mad at me and had every right to be, but to hit me? I never saw that coming, and that blow fucking hurt. How did my scrawny kid brother deliver such a powerhouse punch to a guy like me? It was almost humorous, but I didn't want to tell him that and risk getting punched again.

Simon was standing over me, almost breathing fire. The only time I have ever seen him look like this was when Nicolette left him years ago, and he thought he lost her forever. It took me and our two brothers to hold him tightly in our hold. He was completely devastated.

"Can I get up now? Or are you going to hit me again?"

I wiped the blood from my lip and slowly stood up.

"That depends on you, big brother. Why are you here after all of this time? Where were you all the times I needed you? You weren't the only one going through a tough time. Yes, I had Andrew and Cameron when time allowed them to come out here, but it was you who I really needed. Where was my big brother to talk me down, tell me that everything is going to be okay? You weren't here, not for me, not for anyone. So why are you here now? Why are you back?"

Every word Simon said was absolutely spot on. I could do nothing to defend myself. I abandoned my family and chose to hide behind my shield while grieving for Minela. I shut all my friends out and just walked away. I turned to look at Simon, who was still clearly upset with me just showing up here without warning. This was not how I saw our reunion playing out.

"Simon, you will never know how sorry I am for not being here for you. Dad told me about the miscarriages. I can't even begin to understand what you and Nicolette have been through. All I'm asking is that you take a second to also understand what I've been through. These last few years have been the hardest ones in my life, and after all this time, I'm finally coming up for air."

"I tried to be there for you Jake, but you shut me out. How many times did I fly out to New York, Washington, or wherever you were working to be there for you? Huh? And you turned away from me at every turn. It was like you exiled yourself to your own private island. An army of one, yeah…that's you."

"I'm sorry, bro. I am so sorry that I hurt you."

"Yeah, so you say."

"Simon, look at me, dammit! Now, I love you, so don't stand here and pretend that all our years as brothers have meant nothing to you, because that is simply not true. People make mistakes, little brother. I made mistakes, but I'm here now and am asking you to forgive me for them, please?"

I took a step back to give him space. I saw his hurt, and then his lip quivered and I knew I was forgiven. He charged at me like a bull —apparently, that's what we Paulsons do—and I opened my arms to catch him. He hit my back with his fist a few times, never loosening the grip he had on me. He cried and told me how much he missed me, but he wasn't sorry for punching me. I accepted that, and when he calmed down, we finally talked.

"How's your hand?" I asked.

"It hurts. How's your face?"

"It hurts, but I'll live."

"You can't do this again, Jake."

"Do what?"

"Leave. No matter what, we are a family. We are stronger together than apart, and we need you in our lives. It's time to come home, and I don't mean to California, but back to our family. You can't just check out for months at a time, or years like you've been doing. I'm about to become a father…do you even know how scared I am? Every time my beautiful girl up there even sneezes, my heart constricts. We've lost two babies already, and she's never made it this far. I can't go through that again. It nearly destroyed us. We just went numb and drifted away from each other for a while, and then one day, we had hope again."

"I'm sorry, Simon. I had no idea things were that rough for you and Nicolette. I should have been here. Maybe you should hit me again?"

He smiled, and the easygoing flow we always had as brothers slowly returned. Simon continued to bring me up to speed.

"Nicolette had asked me to meet her down to the beach. It was our special place, on the same dune I found her at when she had taken off from her parents' house. That day I vowed to never to leave her, to love her forever, and always take care of her. I begged her not to run and to trust me with her heart. We were drowning in our grief over the loss of our babies, and the thought of us not making it was just incomprehensible. Nicolette had immediately put together a nursery, and she practically slept in that room. She was happier than I had ever seen her, even topping our wedding day. We were picking out names and baby carriages, and then one day, our baby was gone. It was devastating."

My brother wiped some tears away from his eyes, and then continued with his story.

"We went to therapy and tried to come to terms with what the doctors were telling us. 'Some babies were just not meant to be born.' I heard that before when Nicolette lost her first child and nearly her life. Fuck! Just talking about it still makes my stomach sick. We got through it, Jake. And after some time, she handed me another white pee stick with two lines on it. We were here again with new hope in our hearts, but also fear. And then that baby went away. Another loss we endured, and it nearly destroyed us. Jake, when I showed up at our spot, I didn't know what Nicolette would say to me. My heart was bleeding out from our losses, and at the end of the day, all I wanted was my wife. I walked up to the dune, and there she was waiting for me on a blanket, candles lit, and wearing a smile that would bring the toughest men to their knees."

Simon talks about his heart bleeding out? How did I not know all of this? Simon wore his heart and feelings on his sleeve for the world to see, where in my case, I hid and shut down. We had a few spaces between us. I could see the anguish on his face as he relived the past. I still hadn't told him why I was here, and a part of me wanted to never tell him, but I knew I couldn't do that.

"Hey Simon, we don't have to talk about this anymore. Again, I'm just so sorry for not being here when you needed me to."

"No, it's okay Jake. I want to tell you the happy part. It's good, so listen. So back to the beach. I was completely blown away by her romantic gesture, but then I shouldn't have been surprised. We knew our love could conquer anything that challenged it, so in the end we put our trust not only in each other, but to God himself. We made love under the moonlight in our special place, where we sealed our love for each other all those years ago back in high school. I had my Nicolette back, and we promised nothing would ever come between us again. And now here we are, big brother. I'm going to be a father to twins. It is truly a miracle. And yes, it's going to be a surprise. We don't want to know the sex of the babies."

"That's amazing, Simon. Thank you for sharing that with me. I'm so sorry for your loss."

"Thank you. And I'm sorry for yours. We loved Minela, you know that."

"I do, and she felt the same way about all of us Paulsons."

"Are you okay, Jake? I get that there is no timetable on grief, but have you finally been able to accept her death? Are you seeing anyone? Are you happy?"

"Yes. Maybe. And I'm getting there. I won't lie, Simon, my personal life has been a shit storm for the past few years, but I'm fighting my way back to the land of the living, and I promise I will never stray too far away again from our family. I can't believe I'm going to be an uncle."

We talked for what seemed like hours. How did I think I would be able to just quickly stop by and be on my way? I had re-scheduled my flight for first thing in the morning. I still hadn't told them about Michael, and once dinner was over, I had to find the courage to do so.

Simon started a fire in the massive pit they had in the corner of the deck. Over the years, they added some upgrades to this amazing beach house. It was going to be a great place to raise their family. We chatted some more about our brothers and how well they were doing on their teams.

Simon was so animated when he talked about his work and their recent trip on the discovery. He was diving off the reefs and collecting samples for his latest research. Nicolette just smiled with pride at her husband. They were so much in love, which made it hard for me to say what I needed to say.

Hearing Simon relive parts of his past that caused him so much pain was difficult to listen to, but now time had run out and I had no choice. My face had fallen a bit, and I knew they could tell that something was weighing heavily on my mind.

"What's on your mind, Jake?"

Simon leaned down onto his knees and looked at me with seriousness in his eyes. None of us Paulsons ever could hide anything from the other. It was our connection as brothers.

I needed a little liquid courage to get through this conversation. I cleared my throat and took the last gulp of my drink. Simon was still staring at me, and then Nicolette rubbed her hand on her belly. *Fuck!* This was going to be hard.

"I'm actually out here for work. After I wrapped up my case in New York, I was excited to know that my next assignment was here in California. The thought of seeing my family made me very happy. It was my intention to surprise all of you, and to make amends for time lost, but then plans changed. Next to you, I've only seen dad, and I'm asking you both not to tell mom that I was here. I've already delayed my flight, and I have to leave in the morning. I have no time to see her, unfortunately."

"What's going on, Jake? Why did your plans change with this assignment?"

"This case is different from anything else I've ever taken on. Typically, I can keep my personal feelings out of my work life. It's how I'm able to do what I do so well and stay focused. But this case...it's very complicated and personal. This case involves someone directly connected to you, Nicolette, and I've been asked to take the lead on this investigation—well, more like it's being forced onto me with no out clauses."

"Who, Jake? I can't imagine anyone I know could be in trouble," she asked, and then her eyes shifted and her hold tightened in Simon's hand. "No! It can't be."

She began to cry, as if she already knew what I was going to say.

Simon jumped in, "Baby, calm down right now. You don't even know what's going on, and you getting excited is not good for our babies. Take a deep breath, and focus on your breathing."

After a few moments, she was calmer, and then Simon turned back to me and asked me to explain.

"Simon, Nicolette, there is no easy way to say this, and I am sorry for any pain it will cause you…Michael St. Clair is dead."

I watched Simon and then Nicolette for some kind of sign, but they just remained silent where they sat and stared blankly back at me. There was nothing…absolutely no reaction. Were they in shock? Did they even care?

"Did you hear what I said? Michael St. Clair is dead."

"Oh for fuck sakes, Jacob! We heard you the first time. You don't have to say it again," Nicolette screamed out, taking me by surprise. "I'm sorry, but what do you expect me to say? I would never wish this on anyone, and I'm sure his father is grieving over the loss of his son, but believe me, Jake, I have had my share of grief and I am so over it. I put him and what he did to me away and buried them deep into my past. I will not allow him to hurt me again, not even from the grave."

Simon took Nicolette into his arms and just held her as she cried, calming her the best way he knew how, while I just sat here with many questions.

"Nicolette, I'm not here to hurt you, although I knew the news would. Your reaction to the news surprised me, as well as the outburst that followed. I can understand that this is painful, but this case involves someone else connected to you."

"Back off, Jake. I'm warning you."

Simon gritted his teeth, but I wasn't a brother right now. I had to be a cop if I was going to protect them, and right now I needed information.

"Nicolette, because this crime was committed in prison, it has caught the attention of the FBI, and they have a suspect in mind. It's your Uncle Jack. Although they don't have anything on him yet, they do have a timeline—one that matches up to when Michael was murdered. Jack was here in California at the time of the murder."

She stepped out of my brother's protective embrace and walked over to the railing, looking out to the ocean.

"What are you saying, Jacob? Because my uncle was here in California, he had to be the one who killed Michael? His entire family lives out here, so he has a perfectly good reason to visit. How could he have known that Michael would be killed at the same time he was here?"

"That may be true, but I still have to investigate it."

"He didn't do it, Jake!" she shouted at me.

"And what makes you so sure, Nicolette?" I countered.

"He promised me, that's how I know. God! I can't believe this is happening."

I watched her pace the room. Something in her eyes shifted from confidence to doubt. *Does she know more?* She covered her mouth to stifle her cries. I looked back to Simon, who wasn't doing a great job at hiding his contempt for me at the moment. His fists were balled at his sides, and he looked ready to pounce if necessary to protect his wife.

I chose my life when I became a cop and accepted that sometimes I would have to do what was necessary to seek the truth, but I never wanted this right here, seeing my family hurt by my profession. Although she was a cop and fully aware of the risks of the job, Minela became collateral damage with a bullet that was meant for me, and I could do nothing to save her. Here I was again, putting my family in a precarious position because of my job, and hurting my brother and his wife. Nicolette looked pained, and Simon wasn't calming down. He and I already went one round tonight. I didn't want a repeat of what happened between us on the beach.

Nicolette wiped her eyes and reached for my hands as she said, "Jacob, you must understand that after Michael raped me, Uncle Jack nearly killed him by slicing his throat when we were both in the hospital. But he stopped himself because of me, my aunt, and my father."

Her voice dropped low and more tears were falling. God! My heart couldn't take much more.

"So I know he didn't do this. He promised he wouldn't. He promised me, Jacob."

I wanted to comfort her, but she flinched when I went to touch her.

"Nicolette, you don't have to do this," Simon said as he walked over to her and made Nicolette look at him.

"Simon, what's the point of hiding it? Uncle Jack is already a suspect, and the truth always comes out eventually."

"And what truth might that be?" I asked.

"I swear to God, Jake, shut the hell up or I will punch you again."

"It's okay, Simon," she said, now calmer and wiping away the last of her tears.

"No, it's not. He comes here pretending to want to make amends with his family, but all the while he's really here as a cop? What the fuck, man! This is not cool, and I want you to leave before you upset my wife any more than you already have."

"Simon, you know I can't do that. And you are wrong. I came here to reconnect with you, and everything I said was the truth. Dammit! You have to believe me that I would give my life for any-one in this family. I am more than just a cop. I am your brother, and you damn well are going to trust me."

They both looked lost but knew deep down that I would never intentionally hurt them, so they walked over to me, and we just embraced, reveling in the fact that our family is stronger together than apart.

Nicolette finished telling me that she vaguely knew about Jack's mafia connection back in Chicago. While she was recovering, Jack visited and swore that he would never hurt Michael, because it would ultimately hurt his own family. She explained to him that she only thought that because who else would be connected to a crime but Uncle Jack? She felt horrible for even second guessing their trust with each other, but it was understandable.

I didn't go into any more details with Nicolette. She was exhausted, and Simon put her to bed.

"Is she asleep?" I asked.

"Yeah, down for the count. How did we get here, Jake? Why are we still being haunted by fucking Michael St. Clair! We survived him, Jake, and came out stronger than ever before. I can't even process how I feel about his death, but Nicolette was right about one thing: he will not hurt us again, not even from the grave. Dammit! We are so happy and about to become parents. Why is this happening now?"

"I don't know, bro, but there's more."

"Yeah, I figured that. Tell me everything."

"It's not just any case, this is complicated for many reasons. The two higher ups in charge have a hidden agenda. If we get a conviction, then one gets a step up in his career, and the other...revenge. You see, back in the day when Jack ran with a crew out of Chicago —little Italy to be exact—he was known as an enforcer. To our knowledge, he never killed anyone...more like he served as a messenger. He was the one that was sent out when something needed to be explained, and it wasn't with words, get what I'm saying?"

Simon shifted in his seat and downed his beer. He quickly grabbed another one for himself and one for me too.

"There was this boy who ran parcels for the big guy that was in charge. I really know no other way to explain it. The kid was skimming from the top and enjoying a pretty good side business. Anyway…all good things come to an end because the big guy, Johnny, finds out and is pissed. He sends Jack in, and what we have left is a kid with a broken back, never able to walk again."

"Holy shit! I don't even know what to say to this. I can't believe what I am hearing about Jack. Yeah, he's a scary fucker, but he's undoubtedly devoted to his family. I can't even begin to comprehend him hurting Nicolette in any way…well, other than that one time. Um…anyway."

"You mean about him hiding that he was Nicolette's bio dad?" I said, earning a surprised look from my brother.

"You know? How?"

"Dad told me. It slipped out when we were talking the other day. He didn't mean to betray your confidence, and he thought I knew. Which brings me to my next question: why didn't you tell me? Dad was kind of surprised when he discovered I didn't know."

"What can I say, Jake? You weren't here. You had checked out. I'm sorry."

"No, it's alright. I guess I deserve that."

"It's in the past, bro. But just tell me more about Jack."

"So this kid with the broken back, Mikey, was sent away to do some time, and he couldn't hack it. He was already confined to a wheelchair, and to be in prison without the use of your legs…well, do I have to paint a picture for you? He concocted a makeshift shiv and sliced his wrists during the night. He was found the next morning dead in his cell."

"Unbelievable! So what does this have to do with the other guy and revenge? Who is he, and what does he have to do with this?"

"Mikey had an older brother, who vowed his revenge on Jack someday. Well, that day has come, because the older brother became a cop…and not just any cop. He's a big shot in the New York FBI field office. He plays hardball and is out for blood, Jack's blood on a silver platter, and…"

"And? What is it?"

"He's using me to get to Jack. This is why I am on this case in the first place…because of my family connection to Jack. They figure I could use my personal relationship with Jack to get close with him from the inside while working the case. I gather what I need. Jack goes down for the murder of St. Clair, and the FBI gains a big win. As for Marino, he puts his vendetta to rest with knowing that Jack will probably die in prison just like his brother."

And that was when I heard her. We didn't know how much she heard, but Nicolette was crying behind the door. She was repeating over and over again that he didn't do it, he promised. Simon comforted her and brought her back up to their room. I felt sick to my stomach that I was bringing this to their doorstep, but they had a right to know.

"I'm sorry about that. She's just exhausted. Jake, she loves her uncle very much. What does this mean for our family, bro? I can't let this ugliness touch us. I just can't."

"It doesn't have to, Simon, and it won't. You have my promise that I will see this through and make it right."

"How, Jake? From what you've already told me about this Marino guy, he won't stop until Jack gets the fucking gas chamber."

"There's more Simon."

"Oh, come on! I don't think I can take it."

"Yeah, I didn't think I could either, but I have no choice now. Marino knows something about Minela's murder, and if I don't work with him to bring Jack down, then I will never know what he knows."

"Fuck that, Jake! Beat it out of him if you have to."

Oh, how I loved my brother.

"I almost did, several times actually, but I believe I have another way of getting to the truth about Minela. Trust me on this."

"I guess I have no choice but to trust you like I always have. Just promise me that you will be careful no matter what road this case takes you down on."

"You have my word, bro. I will make this right, I promise. I'm not going to stay tonight after all. Please give my love to Nicolette, and tell her I'm sorry for making her cry."

"No worries, it's the hormones." Leave it to Simon for making a fucked up situation better. "Where to next, Jake?"

"The only place that makes sense…Chicago. I need to talk to Jack."

CHAPTER

Ten

Don't believe everything you hear...

After leaving the beach house, I had nothing but time to replay all that happened tonight with Simon and Nicolette. My head was spinning with all we talked about. Simon was angry, happy, and angry again, and then sad to see me leave. His feelings were justified, and he mostly behaved the way I thought he would. His wife was his entire world, and now with the babies on the way, he would do everything in his power to protect them.

I parked my rental by the beach and sat while the sun began to rise. A new day was about to begin just over the horizon, I had no idea what today would bring once I met with Jack. Simon and Nicolette would meet with her parents today and stand united no matter what happens with Jack. The death of Michael St. Clair was nationwide news now. Simon worried that Nicolette would be hounded by press, so they were going to leave later this morning to an undisclosed location. They would have to be near a hospital for Nicolette, but Simon had worked everything out and texted me the details.

Speaking of texts, I heard nothing from Zoey. It was as if she just disappeared from my bed and my life. I didn't think I was alone in my feelings. She had a physical reaction to me as strong as mine.

It couldn't have just been about sex, a hook-up like I had first played it out to be. No, Zoey was more—my more—and once this case was over, I was going to find her. I would happily remind her what a mistake she made by walking away from me and what we could have together.

I cleaned myself up and made my way to the airport, just barely making my flight. I had no choice but to tell Wade where I was headed. He was still my superior, and he hadn't kicked me off the case yet. Marino dropped off the grid. Wade suspected he went back to New York. I couldn't worry about him at the moment. I made it perfectly clear to him that I would never go along with his plan and that I was on my own.

I declined riding on the dime of the FBI, so I bought my own plane ticket to Chicago. I could easily afford it, so I went with first class. I needed some TLC and the much needed rest before speaking with Jack. Hopefully the four-hour flight would do the trick, but when I closed my eyes my thoughts went back to the first of the two women taking up space in my heart.

"When are you going to tell your father that we're living together? It's been three months since we announced our engagement. Don't you think they should know that we were serious about getting married?"

"I will, Jake, but I'm their only daughter. My father probably thinks I'm still a virgin and I'm saving myself for you. Come on, now. I don't want to give the old man a stroke by shattering his perfect image of me."

"Babe, he's not stupid and neither are your brothers. Don't you think it's time that they cut the apron strings and allow you to live your life, your way?"

"You would think that after I became a cop, they would have, but not the LaRochas. We're tight, and we live in each other's lives. They can't help themselves. It really shouldn't come as a surprise to you. You Paulsons are close. I've seen how you are with your brothers. Can you imagine what it's going to be like at Christmas? Oh, I

love just the thought of it. Don't you, Jake? Just picture all of us, surrounded by this huge dinner table, and then a kid table! It's just a matter of time until I get pregnant, and then mine and your brothers have babies. Oh my goodness! We're going to have to rent a banquet hall!"

I loved this woman. I loved this woman with all of my heart and soul. How did I get so lucky to have found her?

"Hey, Jake! Are you listening to me?" Minela asked as she finished unpacking another box. She threw crumpled paper at me to get my attention. She was adorable. I just couldn't tell her that. Minela wasn't one for labels. She knew she had the looks but never wanted to be defined by them. Being taken seriously as a cop was the most important thing to her.

"Yes. I am listening, and stop throwing paper at me. As much as I love our apartment, you know I'm loaded right? I have my ranch back in Colorado with a huge house built on the property. We can live anywhere we want, so why do you want to live here, a brownstone in Staten Island?"

"Because it's ours. Our first place as a couple, a newly engaged couple that will be married very soon, if I have anything to say about it. Every couple needs a first place, and this is where I want to be with you. Do you understand?"

"I do, and I love you for making our first place a home. Wherever you are is where I want to be, beautiful girl. I love you baby... so much."

"I love you too! I want ice cream."

"Yeah, and I want you. Bed...now!"

I tackled her to the couch and began kissing her neck. She opened up for me and kissed me with all she had.

"Jake..." she enunciated very slowly. "I will let you have me anyway you want to, but first, I want my ice cream."

In one swift move, she leaped from the couch and ran for the door, grabbing her purse on the way out.

"Last one to the shop gets handcuffed to the bed!"

"That's okay, you go right ahead. I will be happy to bind you anyway I can," I said.

"Good to know, baby, because wearing this gorgeous diamond on my finger binds me to you for life. I can't wait to be Mrs. Jacob Paulson."

"I love you."

"I love you too! Now get your butt up, and let's go."

"Right behind you."

We walked hand in hand down the overcrowded street. This time at night, all the commuters were just getting home from work. You had the dog walkers in the park, the joggers out running the lake. Our shoulders were being bumped as we continued to walk. I led Minela down a side street to avoid the crowd. I couldn't help pinning her against the wall to kiss her. We lingered for a few minutes and then continued our walk to the ice cream shop. This place sold cupcakes and flavored coffee too.

We sat inside with a large cup of Neapolitan to share. Of course it was covered in hot fudge, walnuts, and whipped cream. It was sugar overload, but my girl said we had earned it from all of our morning exercise. I laughed, because she wasn't referring to the gym.

"What are you thinking about?" she asked me as we walked home.

"You. How can I not when I'm engaged to the most beautiful woman in the world? How big of a wedding do you want to have? With our combined families, that's probably one full side of the church, and then it's friends from the force, my football buddies, coaches. Wow! We may need to have it outside on the football field just to hold everybody."

"Whatever you want, Jake. I just want to be your wife."

"It's all I want too."

I held her in my arms where I crushed my lips down onto hers, sealing our commitment to one another. She came up for air and smiled at me.

I never saw it coming. I only had her in my eyesight until it was too late. The tires screeched. The shot rang out. A single shot to the chest. And then I was on the ground over her bloodied body. Minela's face had fallen from happiness to sadness as she knew what was next to come. My world was shattering. How could this have happened to us?

My eyes blinked opened. I had a flight attendant standing over me, asking me if I was alright. I said a silent prayer in hopes that I wasn't screaming again. She placed her hand over mine and asked me in her quiet voice if she could get me anything. She saw my badge sticking out from my pocket. She addressed me as Agent Paulson.

I didn't like to be fussed over, and I still wasn't sure if anyone had heard me. Only three other passengers were in first class and not paying attention to me, so that was comforting to know. I declined food but asked for water. She poured it over ice for me with a wedge of lemon. I saw the concern written all over her face, but I told her that I was fine. I accepted the hot cloth to wipe my face and neck. I was soaked through my shirt. This was a bad one, but anytime you relive the love of your life getting gunned down in your arms, how could you not break a sweat?

My flight landed at O'Hare around one. I took advantage of the first class lounge and cleaned up in their bathroom suite. I had new shirts with me, tossing the soaked one back into my bag.

I looked as good as I was going to get. My beard was a few days old. I needed a haircut, and I was running on no sleep. I wasn't going on a job interview, just confronting an "alleged" former mob enforcer who possibly murdered the guy who raped my sister-in-law. Yeah…good times.

With the lunch crowd now gone back to work, Jack's restaurant, The Neighborhood, was quiet. I made my way inside. This place was huge, with two full sized bars on each side of the restaurant. It had a second floor reserved for private parties. It sure didn't look like a front for mob business. It looked to be a casual, good feeling pub to have a beer in and shoot the shit with friends.

I was still looking around when I was tapped on my shoulder. I turned around to see a guy that matched my height but needed to work on his personality.

"You need something, pal?" he asked, holding his bar rag in one hand while balling up his fist in the other.

"I'm not your pal, so let's get that straight, first off. I'm here to see Jack Vanelle."

"And what do want with Jack?" he asked as he took in my badge.

"What's your name?"

"Tommy. I'm in charge, and no one gets in to see the boss without me knowing about it first, especially cops, the feds, anybody."

This guy matched me almost in size. He would be a workout to take down, unless I capped him in the knee, and then he would fall easily. Not too sure I wanted to wage war on Tommy the giant and in an open bar, so I tried a more tactful approach.

"Um, Tommy, I know Jack personally, and I would like to speak with him. So if you please, go get him for me, and thank you."

"Fuck you. Try again. I'm not blind, pig. I see the badge, and you are not seeing the boss today."

"Pig? They still use that word when referencing members of the law enforcement? Good to know, Tommy, but I am not just a cop, I'm Federal Agent Jacob Paulson, and usually when I ask for something, I get it. Now you have two choices. One: turn around and locate your boss for me. Two: I knock you on your ass and arrest you for not complying with my request. I've asked you nicely, and still you say no. So what's it going to be?"

Fuck my life! What made me think this was going to be easy? And here I thought this was a friendly place.

"Fuck you."

As I expected him to say. He crossed his arms over his chest and used his large frame as a blocker to keep me from passing. I stepped off to the other side, and he blocked me again. My patience was done. Time for the big guy to fall. I swept my leg under him, catching him off balance, and then I landed a punch down to his knee, causing him to cry out in pain.

"You sonofabitch! I think you broke my knee!"

"Yeah, I probably did. Now you can go fucking crawl to get your boss. I'll fix myself a drink while you do that."

Fucker! I flipped the divider that separated the bar from its patrons, and hit the tap on the Coors. As I poured myself a beer, his guy was still yelping in pain on the floor.

In walked the man of the hour. He was confident in his stride. The few patrons that were in the bar who witnessed me taking down Tommy looked up to Jack with nothing but respect. He shook one guy's hand and announced a free round for everyone, signaling the waitresses over. He whispered in one's ear, and she nodded in agreement. Jack took notice of me still behind his bar. I wasn't too sure if he appreciated me being there. Then he called over his shoulder to his two guys who were silently waiting off to the side.

"Take Tommy to the ER, and get him fixed up."

His guys just nodded and left.

"Help yourself, Jacob. We are family, after all. What's mine is yours."

I shut the tap off and walked back around the bar to take a seat beside Jack.

"Really, Jack? Does your guy Tommy know that? With the warm reception I received, I can't be sure if he received the memo on that."

"You never can be too careful nowadays…So Jacob, welcome to Chicago. It's been a long time. What can I do for you?" he asked while lighting up a cigar, never taking his eyes off of me.

"I think you know, Jack. I hear you have eyes and ears everywhere."

"Nothing wrong with that, son. I protect what's mine, that's no crime."

"Answer me this, Jack. What lengths would you go to *protect* what you say is yours?"

He blew out a few puffs of his cigar and tapped the ashes into the ashtray.

His brown eyes turned cold as he replied, "What wouldn't I do? Ask any family man that same question, and I would bet everything I own that the answer would be the same. There's no greater thing on this earth than family. I love mine more than anything else in this world, and from what I know of yours, we are cut from the same cloth."

"I don't think so, Jack. You and I are miles apart."

"Do you have something to say to me, Jacob, or are we going to continue this dance?"

I finished off my beer, slamming the mug down onto the bar. His eyes widened.

Not backing down, I stood tall, stared Jack directly in the eye, and simply replied, "Michael St. Clair."

PART

Two

Jack

CHAPTER
Eleven

THE MAN BEHIND THE MASK...

If you had the power to turn back the clock, would you? Hit the rewind button on your life and just start over? A man can dream, can't he? Yeah, I would definitely do it if I could. I would pick certain parts...the harder ones I wished I could erase from my mind and never think of again.

As I descended the stairs to the main bar area on the first floor, I saw most of Chicago watching our Bears destroy the Cardinals and sending them back to Arizona in tears. You could feel the energy in the bar, as the game went on to a winning victory.

I loved this bar. I loved that Sara, my wife, the love of my life, convinced me to open it and give back to the neighborhood that always had my back. This was why our bar was called The Neighborhood Bar and Grille. It was a place to have a laugh with a friend, to blow off steam after a hard day's work, and it was a place that kept me honest, whereas in my younger days, I wasn't always. I hated to admit that I did some things that I wasn't proud of, things no matter how hard I tried to forget, would always be present in my memory.

"Jack, you need to do me a favor, and I don't mean picking up a few packages for me. This is something of a different nature, and one

that requires a different approach. Do you think you can help me out here?"

Johnny leaned back in his chair and blew out puffs of smoke from his Cuban cigar. I didn't hesitate at all with the request. Johnny had paid me well, and I was in his debt. I agreed immediately without knowing what he wanted me to do.

"That's what I wanted to hear my friend. You are exactly what I need for this job. Go see Carmine. He will give you the details, and once the job is done, you come back here. Understand?"

He took another deep inhale on his cigar, and he waited for my answer.

"Yes, sir. I won't let you down."

"That's good, Jack. I was hoping you would say that. I'm counting on the right message being sent, so our other associates understand what it means to fall in line and never fuck with my business. You make sure they know that crossing Johnny Carlucci is a grave error in judgment, one they will regret."

After Carmine gave me my instructions, I left to find Mikey. He was holed up in some shitty motel on the east side. As Carmine kicked down the door, Mikey made a run for it. He didn't know I would be waiting for him on the fire escape. He was trapped with nowhere to run. I shoved him back through the window as Carmine pulled him up from his shoulders. He was scared, just a kid who didn't know any better, but he should have, working for Johnny Carlucci.

Carmine punched him in the gut, making him fall down to his knees. He was crying and begging for his life. I wasn't there to end his life, just to send a message. Johnny had told me to make it hurt, a pain he soon would not forget. Carmine taped his mouth, and with my height and weight compared to his small skinny frame, I must have looked like a giant to him. He tried to struggle and fight me back, but I was too strong to be knocked down.

I picked him up with all my strength and smashed his back against my raised up knee. He shrieked in pain, and I dropped him back to the floor. I instantly knew what the force of my attack had accomplished. I felt sick. I needed to get out of there. We just left him there crying in this rat infested motel room.

Carmine pulled the tape from his mouth and whispered into his ear, "You get to live, Mikey. If you're stupid enough to cross the line again, I'll come for you and finish what my boy Jackie started."

His voice was cold, scary as fuck, and downright vicious. We made it outside, and I bent over and vomited all over the sidewalk. Carmine wasn't fazed by this at all. He hit me on my back and assured me that I would get used to this real quick.

"It's the life, Jackie."

I returned that night to Johnny's office, and he was pleased with me. He handed me an envelope and took me in his arms like a father would do with a son. I felt sick and disloyal to my own father.

"You did good, Jack. Really good."

I didn't say anything in return and walked out of his office feeling sicker than I ever had before.

Once upon a time I didn't think I had a choice, so I took a different road and made my peace with it. I convinced myself that my actions were justified for the betterment of my family. If mama and papa were taken care of, then that meant they didn't have to work the usual fourteen hour-plus work days that sadly was their life. The only day they didn't work was Sunday. They spent half of it in church, and then mama would spend the rest of the day cooking over a hot stove so we could have one dinner together that week. We would bow our heads while holding hands and reciting the Lord's Prayer.

This was important to my parents, so although I was the one at our table committing sin after sin, I silently prayed that I would be forgiven for them. Again, if what I did benefitted my family, then I could live with that.

I'll never forget when the truck pulled up in front of the brownstone we lived in, and out came a second hand piano. Papa nearly knocked my head in for that one. He didn't believe the story I told him that it was tossed on the side of the road and free to anyone who wanted it. I just happened to know some guys that could get it to me. This was one lie that I didn't feel bad about telling. My kid brother, Massimo, was a musical prodigy and needed this piano to show the world his gift. The look on his face was priceless, one I will never forget.

Although they didn't like it, my parents allowed my brother to keep the piano. Of course the first song he played was "Ava Maria." My parents wouldn't say it, but they loved hearing music resonating through our small home. It made them smile, convincing me once again that what I did was justified.

My parents tried with all of their heart and soul to live the American dream. They worked from sun up to sun down and never complained about it. I was the one that had a problem with it and did what I had to do to make things better.

This was how I lived every day of my life. I worked the streets—some say I owned them—but whatever. I did what I had to do to survive and make things better for my family, no matter how much my soul suffered for it. If someone needed my help, I would give everything I could and hope it was enough. I would still fight the good fight and give you the shirt off my back, but I'd like to think that I'm a better man today, someone that papa could be proud of.

No one's life is perfect—hell I knew that better than anyone—but the life I was now living came pretty close to perfection. It was clean with no ugliness in it. I was blessed with two gifts: one being my beautiful Sara, my miracle, and the other was my daughter, Nicolette.

Nicolette was my entire world, my sole reason for waking up every day. She made me smile, and Sara made me want to be a better man who was deserving of her love. With all the sins of my past, I probably didn't deserve either one of them, but I was blessed anyway with their goodness and love.

The dream of becoming a father ended on the day my wife was diagnosed with cancer. I nearly lost her and begged God I would try to be a better man if he would spare her life. Sara beat her cancer and thankfully was still in remission and doing well. From then on, I would not live by past sins that used to define me. I would simply move forward with Sara and live happily and thankful for what I'd been given…another chance to make it right.

I maintained to keep that promise, and when my only brother was struggling, I found a way to give back. Family was everything to me. All he and I had was each other after our parents passed away almost back to back. I gave him and his wife…a life. They were childless and were not able to conceive on their own. It was probably the only unselfish act I ever did in my life. I never claimed her as my own, because she was never meant to be mine. It was an act so pure and beautiful, knowing I was part of a living miracle that blessed our family, erasing the ugly parts that I longed to forget.

I never felt I was deserving of anything good, but Sara proved me wrong by just loving me unconditionally. When Nicolette was born she would forever be my niece. You would have to be blind not to notice the strong physical resemblance we shared. But again, I shared the same likeness with my brother, so no one ever questioned it. I nicknamed her Nickel, because the day she came into the world, I said she was shiny and new like a brand new coin. It always stuck, and she loved the term of endearment, as our beautiful girl grew into her own.

Nicolette and I were very close, almost inseparable at times. There wasn't a single moment or milestone in her life that we didn't share. My brother never reneged on our agreement. I would always play a role in her life as long as we understood our roles. Biological-ly, I was her father, but only one man would claim her as his, and that was my brother, Massimo.

Our given names were Vanelli, but our parents changed it to Vanelle. They thought it would be easier on us if we lost the vowel sound at the end, and this way we sounded more American. I resent-ed them for that, and for the first time in my life, I was disappointed in my own parents. They took that choice away from me, but even though I promised to accept our new name, I always used Vanelli. Another lie they didn't need to know about.

After they died, my brother changed his name to Mason. You couldn't get more preppy than that, but he was building a life for himself, and it was separate from the life we knew. I never liked it and most of the time called him the name our parents had given him. He would get angry with me and accuse me of being stubborn and unwilling to change my ways. Oh, if he only knew how much I changed to be the man he knew me to be today.

I was at peace with the decision we made about Nicolette's parentage. I also knew that if Nicolette ever questioned it, then we would all explain how she became our entire world. So you can imagine how I felt on the day my brother announced a relocation from our home in Chicago to California, taking our girl with him. I of course fought him on every talking point he made. I already felt disconnected from them, and they hadn't even left. Mason explained that they were given an opportunity of a lifetime, one he and his wife could not refuse. I knew deep down how talented they both were, and I was proud of his accomplishments, but that didn't give me peace at night knowing our life as a family was about to change.

No matter what assurance Mason had promised me, my heart was breaking with the thought of not seeing Nicolette daily and listening for hours to all the great things that she was experiencing as a teenager.

I waged a war against my brother and his wife. I said no. I wouldn't allow them to take her away from me. Then, in what was probably the most vicious argument I had ever had with him, my brother painfully reminded me who she belonged to. Nicolette was their daughter, and I was just Uncle Jack. She was theirs, this is what we agreed, but tell that to my heart that always believed she was mine. My gift from God. My miracle. My redemption.

Mason and Christina promised me that I would always have her in my life. I tried to believe his words, but I was still angry deep inside. I promised Sara that I would not react and take it out on my brother. Once his family was secure in the car, he patted my back and tried to once again reassure me while trying to mask his doubts on what I already believed to be true. Our lives would change, but Mason being Mason, he said, "The only thing that will change is our address, and everything else will be the same."

I watched her tears fall as Nicolette waved goodbye from the backseat of their car as they headed to the airport to begin their new life, a life I was so sure I wouldn't be a part of. I knew this was madness on my part, but it was my heart that was hurting and I needed my brain to catch up.

My brother was wrong. The picturesque life I was living with Sara, owning my bar, and being a staple in Nicolette's life changed the day she left. Then it was shattered and forever changed with one phone call...and three words.

NICOLETTE WAS RAPED.

It was as if time had just stopped. I was back there again, pulled deeply into a dark and ugly world, a world that was ruthless, cold, and unforgiving. I was all those things once upon a time, and for a little while, I actually believed that I wasn't anymore. One phone call destroyed that belief.

I wanted vengeance against the animal that hurt my girl. I couldn't believe I was back there again. Did I really ever leave? My blood had run cold. I felt no warmth on my skin. I saw red...blood red, and I thirsted to destroy the monster who hurt her. I had to be the one to do it. She was my daughter! Fuck! It was my job to protect her, and I had failed her.

God, forgive me for what I wanted to do. I'd hurt and killed that bastard in my mind so many times.

The day after the Bears versus Cardinals game, I had errands to run outside. Winters in Chicago were brutal. The temps never reached above thirty-two degrees. I should know, I'd lived here all of my life. I loved walking through Little Italy on a Sunday morning. You could smell the fresh baked bread and pastries for several blocks. I always picked up my papers, cannoli were my weakness, and then I would have an espresso with Gino and the rest of the guys from the barbershop before I made my way home to Sara.

I didn't deserve my beautiful wife, but she loved me anyway despite what I'd put her through these last years. A dark period in our lives that I wish I could forget, but still a very present memory that I think of every single day.

How was he still breathing? He shouldn't be, and if I had my way back then, his corpse would be a pile of dust by now.

My heart still felt the heavy burden of the promises I made to my brother, my wife, and my Nickel. Massimo knew better than anyone that once I found out what happened to her, I would want to seek vengeance, act before thinking, and not feel a bit of guilt when it was over. I knew I could live with my choices, but Massimo threw all my past sins in my face that day in the hospital, and my hand was forced by the love I felt for my family.

I'd never forget that day...

"How could you let this happen to my girl? How could you?" I screamed. My voice was menacing, while still clutching my brother's throat.

"Jack, get your hands off of him!" my brother's wife screamed at me.

Security officers rushed toward us. I didn't care and kept my hands on his throat. Christina kept repeating the "misunderstanding" to the security guards, and we were allowed to remain in the hospital. My brother fell to the floor gasping for air, as I tightened my fists. Standing back on his feet and supported by his wife, Mason continued to let out some calming breaths. Trying to keep her voice down from the now curious onlookers that were in the hall, Christina tried to reason with me, but I didn't want to hear her excuses.

"Jack, I didn't call and tell you about Nicolette just so you could fly out here to beat the hell out of your brother. What the hell is wrong with you?" Christina asked and then slapped my chest.

"How did you expect me to be, Christina? You all avoid my calls for days, and then when you finally do call me, I'm told that my

beautiful girl has been raped by some animal. How the hell did you think I was going to react? You should know me better than that."

"I didn't think you would act this way, Jack," Christina answered.

"If you thought I was going to be anything else, then you don't know me at all, woman. I love that girl more than my own life!"

After our hallway brawl, all three of us left the hospital to speak in private. We had already put on a large enough show, and we didn't want to call any more attention to ourselves.

"Mason, I need to see Nicolette. She needs to know that I'm here."

"Jack, after the way you just behaved up in there, you are in no shape to see her. You need to calm down, and let us take care of our daughter."

"No, Mason, that's where you're wrong, Nickel is as much my daughter as she is yours. I have played it your way all these years, and today we are going to do it my way. You failed her, but I will not. I never should have agreed to let you take her here to this place! She would have been fine had she stayed with me and Sara. You insisted that she would be okay out here and that you would always protect her."

"Jack, she has been protected from the minute I held her in my arms. What happened to Nicolette was beyond my control. I had only now just found out what was going on the night she was raped."

"That is bullshit, Mason! Where the hell were you? How could you be so oblivious to what was going on in Nicolette's life? Beyond your control...my ass! You're her father, for God sakes, and yet you did nothing! Why, Mason? Explain it to me! Why didn't you protect our girl? Was it because you were too busy with your career!?! I should take her back to Chicago, with her real family!" I taunted him with a vileness in my tone.

"Please, Jack, stop this," Christina was pleading with me. "Blaming Mason will not change what happened to Nicolette. Please don't reveal the truth to her. She has been put through hell. I don't

know if she has the strength to take another shock to her system. Jack, I am begging for you to wait and give us time to explain it to her."

I ran my hands through my hair and sighed.

"Christina, you have had nothing but time—eighteen years to be exact—and I will not wait any longer. I will seek justice for Nicolette, my way."

"No, Jack. Please don't go after Michael. How will that help her if you're in jail?"

"Don't worry about me, Christina. I will do whatever it takes to right this wrong for my daughter. You sure as hell can count on that."

"That's your answer for everything, right Jack? Hit first, think later. The police are taking care of Michael, so you need to stay out of it." Mason screamed at me and pounded his fists to the wall beside my head.

That took balls, but I would not be deterred to why I was really there. I then leaned into Mason and quietly spoke to him so his wife could not hear what I was about to say. There was nothing more important than family, and it painfully hurt me to remind my brother of that fact.

"Remember who you are, brother. Papa may have changed our names, but that doesn't change who we are and where we come from. You, Massimo Anthony Vanelli, remember who you are. Stop hiding! Stop running! Remember who you are!"

Stepping back from me with a calm expression on his chiseled features, he turned to Christina. She was trembling in his arms.

"Honey, will you please give me a moment alone with my brother?"

"Are you sure that is a good idea?" she questioned.

"I'm sure. Please go sit with our daughter, and I'll be along soon."

"Come with me, please?" she pleaded, pulling at his arm to make him follow.

She was afraid, and I couldn't blame her for fearing me. I knew how I sounded, and I could only imagine how I looked to her.

"Christina, go to Nicolette, now! You were the one that called him here, and now I have to deal with this."

I watched my brother change before me. I knew he already regretted his harsh tone with his wife. He watched her turn away from him with tears in her eyes. Once she was out of sight, he turned back to me.

"Jack..."

"I don't want to hear it, Mason. There is nothing you can say to me right now that will change my mind. That fucker has to die!"

"Jack, I get that your first instinct is to want justice for Nicolette by causing harm to her rapist, but you are not thinking clearly right now. Remember who you are, Jack. The man that is standing before me right now is not Johnny's guy anymore. This hit-first-and-ask-later approach may have been your way in the past, but you let that go a long time ago. Don't let this bring you back to a world that you never belonged in."

I hit the wall and then turned to slide down it. I looked up at my brother.

"What do you know about my old life? You were just a kid who followed me around like a lost puppy."

"I know enough, Jack, and I know you got caught up in a life that you didn't want, but you lived it until you had a chance to break free from it."

"I couldn't stand how hard mama and papa worked. They always kept saying that they worked this way for us and we will understand one day. I never did, and then Johnny asked me to do him a favor. All I had to do was make some deliveries for him when he asked me to. I would get paid, and paid well, he said. How could I refuse the money? He said, 'No one would get hurt. Just make the deliveries and report back to me.' I did it with no questions asked, and Johnny always kept his word."

"It wasn't just deliveries, Jack, was it? They always wanted

more from you, and you had no choice but to do what they asked of you."

"Mason, you make it sound like I was a hired gun. I think your imagination is running wild."

"You can play it off as much as you want, Jack, but I know you were their muscle when they needed someone to be taught a lesson. Don't lie to me, Jack...I saw you."

"What the hell are you talking about?"

"You know exactly what I'm talking about. It was the night that I had my concert at school. Mama was sick, and papa was working late. You promised them that you would take me and be there while I performed my solo piece, but you never showed up, because Johnny had yet another 'errand' for you to run. When you finally got home, I saw your bloodied knuckles, and as much as you tried to hide it from mama and papa...they knew, Jack. I knew, Jack! I hated you at that moment, because I know what you did to Mikey Marino. That poor kid never walked again, Jack, because you did Johnny a favor."

"I'm so sorry, Mason. I didn't know any better back then. I never meant to have you disappointed in me, but I was just trying to make a better life for our family. I knew I was in over my head after that, and I went to Johnny and asked to be let go. He laughed at first and said no, but then I stood there with no fear and asked again. He said...no man ever asked him this and lived to tell about it, but I was different and he always knew this day would come. He did let me go but always promised to have my back, and if I ever needed anything, I could come to him or any one of the guys in the crew."

"Jack, you are a better man now, and maybe I didn't always see it growing up, but I do now. You are my brother, and I love you. Please don't let what happened to Nicolette bring you back to those dark days. Think of Sara, who loves you, and think of how she makes you better every day."

"That's a low blow, Mason, even for you."

"Jack, I'm not trying to hurt you, but you need to see that as *much as you're angry about what happened to her, you can't let this insanity become your life again. I want to rip that boy apart with my bare hands, but it won't change anything and will cause more hurt for Nicolette. We need to be here for her now and not let this separate us. Please, Jack...I'm begging you. Let the police handle this, and stay out of it. Can you do that? If not for me, then for Nicolette and Sara?"*

Walking away from my brother that day was the hardest thing I ever did in my life. He broke me down piece by piece and wasn't even sorry for it. I knew he would say just about anything to protect his family and keep me from hurting them even more, but I didn't start this...that animal did. And I couldn't harness the overwhelming feeling that I needed to finish it.

"Hey, you're back," I heard her call out from behind the bar.

My angel. My moral compass. That's what she was. Goodness radiated off of her, and anyone who met her could see what I have known all of my time loving her: Sara was light. I didn't deserve her, this I knew, but she was here with me and never once left my side.

I was the one always leaving her. I ran from our life when I heard about Nicolette. I shut her out and didn't allow her to console me, but I lost that battle and she came to me anyway. She wouldn't allow me to fall and lose myself to the pain that I was feeling. She knew who she married but also trusted that I would never hurt her. Her faith in me was astounding. I tried every day to live up to my vows and be an honorable man who was worthy of her.

I placed the bags down onto the bar and removed my hat, coat, and gloves. Sara practically leaped into my arms, and kissed my cold cheeks. "Wow! How long were you out there? Jack, you left hours ago. You must be frozen down to your bones."

God! I loved this woman.

I kissed her passionately and held her close to me. "How about we go upstairs, and you warm me up?" I asked her with a hope that she would agree.

"I was thinking more on the lines of a brandy. Don't tempt me,

Jack! There's a big game on today, and you know this place is going to be packed to the seams with customers. We have to prep and get ready to open."

"Let the staff take care of the prep today. I need you, Sara. Please let me make love to you."

I know how desperate I sounded, but I needed my wife to bring me back to the light. For days now, my mind had been retreating to a place I didn't want to be, but no matter what I did, the nightmare was always there.

She never took her eyes off of mine. What was she looking for? I hope when she looked at me, she saw the love I had for her.

"Okay, take me upstairs."

Sara led me from the main bar area to our private apartment upstairs. Our restaurant was two floors, but we had added a third floor to get away to. We practically lived here. Sara was our head chef, and my presence was always required out in the open. I had a great staff that took care of everything when we couldn't be here, but it was to the point that we liked to be here. We were surrounded by our friends and customers who had been coming here since we opened. This was home, the only thing that was missing was Nicolette.

I was lost in my thoughts. Sara knew it but did everything to please me. She held my face in her small, delicate hands and said she would help me forget, if only for a little while. There were moments when I almost didn't trust myself with Sara, afraid I may hurt her. She never denied me her touch. We made love for hours, and then we showered and went back to our bed, where I held her.

"Talk to me Jack, please. What can I do to help you?"

I didn't answer her. I just tightened my hold on her and breathed her in. Just having her here with me was all I needed and forever wanted.

"We have to get up," she said.

"Five more minutes."

"Jack, I need to get back to my kitchen. Do you really trust the guys to make Sara's famous Roof Top Burger?"

She buried her face to my chest and giggled.

"I love you, Sara. Please don't you ever forget it."

"I won't, Jack, not ever."

Her words put my restless mind at ease. We dressed and made our way down to our restaurant. Sure enough, it was a full house. Both sides were filled, and the pool area was lined with college kids knocking back beers and having a great time. I kissed Sara, and she made her way into the kitchen. Then I heard someone call out for me.

It was my longtime friend, Max, the one person who knew all my sins and then some. He stood up as I got closer and asked if we could speak privately. I checked in with Tommy, who was behind the bar and managing the crowd.

Everything seemed to be under control, and I led Max to my office. You couldn't get more private than what I had built downstairs in the basement. It wasn't convenient, but when I needed space, this was where I retreated to.

"You look good, my friend," he said before lighting up a cigar.

I declined one and instead poured myself a drink.

"I have news for you, Jack, and it isn't good."

CHAPTER Twelve

WHAT DO YOU WANT TO DO...?

"I figured as much. You don't have a great poker face, Max."

I turned in my chair and opened the bottom door to my wall credenza, finding exactly what I needed to get through this conversation with Max.

"You don't even know what I'm going to say, and you go for the hard stuff? Damn, Jack, that must have set you back at least a grand."

"More like $1800 a bottle, but I didn't buy this one. My brother sent it to me for Christmas."

Bourbon wasn't Max's drink. I offered him something else from my bar, while I poured myself a glass of the 16 year aged A.H. Hirsch Reserve bourbon I kept for my private collection.

I readied myself for what Max was about to tell me. I had sent him to California to get me some intel on Michael. I didn't like what I was hearing the last few months, so I sent Max to go directly to our sources. I'd kept tabs on St. Clair from the minute he was incarcerated for raping my daughter. His stay in prison had been monitored by me from the very beginning of his incarceration. I had dreamt up ways to make him suffer, but then I decided a different approach by keeping tabs on him. He should suffer—he deserves nothing, least of all protection—but judging by the way Max was looking at me, that might soon change. I was fortunate enough to have men on the inside who would do anything I asked of them.

"What do we know, Max?" I asked as I twirled the amber liquid in my glass.

"Like I said, Jack, it's not good. It looks like our boy may be getting released early for good behavior. Word on the block is that he's been shooting his mouth off about how money buys you everything, even out of prison. He met with his lawyers a few times last week, and he's wrapped up a few of his side businesses he has going on up in there. What do you think? Sounds like he's getting ready to pack up?"

I finished my drink, then shattered the glass against the desk. I had little jagged pieces embedded into my palm with droplets of blood trickling down to my wrist. Max went to hand me his handkerchief, but I declined it. Feeling pain was better than being numb. I needed this to remind me of all the pain that animal had caused our family. The promises I made to the ones I loved had broken me down over the years, piece by piece, to the point that I didn't recognize myself anymore. Michael St. Clair should have never been allowed to live…it's that simple.

Max was silent and gauging what I would say next. I finally snapped back from my dark place and cleaned up my hand. He poured me another drink and handed it to me.

Clearing my throat, I said, "Max, everything we don't know, we need to know, and I mean yesterday. Gather me all that we have on the warden and his close knit circle. I need the layouts of the inside and outside perimeters of the prison. He's not in maximum security, and from I already knew about the wing that he is housed in, it seems pretty easy to come and go."

"Hey, Jack, what are you really asking me here? Come on, man! It's not like we can just walk into a state prison and take this guy out."

"And why not?" I heard the words spill from my mouth and wasn't shocked by them at all.

Max appeared to be puzzled by what I was asking of him. This was a first, even for Max.

"Jack, if you want this guy taken out, then we can arrange it from the inside. It can happen in any place he has access to. Just say the word, and I will take care of this for you."

"No! If anyone is going to take this piece of shit out, it's going to be me. I need this, Max, more than you know."

"I do know, my friend, but you don't know what you're asking. We all wondered why you didn't take action back then, but it wasn't our place to counsel you. We just needed to have your back. We will always be on your side for anything you need, but the family can't allow you to do this. It's too dangerous, and we can't risk having the family compromised if anything were to go wrong. I'm sorry, Jack, but I can't do what you are asking of me."

"Max, what you seem to not realize is that I'm not asking the family for anything, nor do I want your help. I was simply asking for some information. If that is too much for you, then I will get it my-self. Anything I decide when it comes to Michael St. Clair is on me, not the family. Do I make myself clear?"

"Jack...come on. You are not on your own here. You're talking crazy right now."

"No, my friend, I've never been clearer on anything in my life than at this moment. I've waited my time out. These years have not been easy to get through, but I did it with one vow on my mind. I will have my revenge on Michael St. Clair, and only then will justice be served. It doesn't matter how long he has spent in prison. It will never be enough. He's not remorseful; he never was. He said all the right things to the judge and has maintained to be the perfect inmate, but we know better Max, don't we? This guy has quite the enterprise going on behind those walls, sides that we have created for him. He's so fucking dense and arrogant that he never even figured it out. A pretty white boy from Beverly Hills goes in to a state prison for sexual assault…and doesn't get touched? He should have been somebody's bitch by now, if not just one, but many. And yet, he's lived under the illusion that he's untouchable and soon will be free."

"Why, Jack? Why this guy? He should have been taken out the minute he laid his hands on your girl. No one is allowed to even breathe in his direction, because you gave an order for us not to. This is what we don't understand," Max said as he gestured over to my bar and fixed himself a drink.

"I had my reasons, Max."

"Care to share them with me? I'm on your side, Jack. I just need to understand where your head is at right now? I mean this guy could be walking any day now. Once he's out, you know his daddy is probably going to ship him off to parts unknown, and then we will lose any opportunity we once had to get to him."

"Show me what you gathered from his cell."

Max shifted in his seat as he retrieved the envelope that was in his bag. He took a deep breath and handed me the envelope. I braced myself for what I would find: pictures of Nicolette, dozens of them. I recognized some of them almost immediately. Pictures from her eighteenth birthday party, when she was smiling and looking just beautiful as she was surrounded by her friends. I became more enraged as I flipped through them all. Michael had been keeping tabs on her life all the time he's been in prison. Newspaper clippings of Nicolette opening up the CALI center, picture after picture. All of these appeared to be from public search engines. Her parents were famous, and anyone with a computer had access to their life. Then there were authentic photos that had to be taken by someone. A recent photo from a local breakfast shop where my daughter was having coffee and was engaged in a conversation. Another with Simon, walking hand in hand. I nearly flipped my desk when I picked up the last one.

"What the fuck! This was taken only three days ago by the timestamp on the back. How the hell did he get his hands on a picture of my daughter coming out of what appears to be a medical building?"

I nearly lunged at Max, as I slammed the photo down to the desk. He kept his tone quiet and guarded.

"From what we know, she's been under surveillance. We don't have any leads yet on the photographer, but feelers have been put out. I'm just waiting to hear from my guys out in LA." There haven't been any recent photos to surface until now."

"Yeah, Max, like three fucking days ago. He's still stalking her…and from fucking prison! How did I not see this? He's coming after my girl. I need to find this photographer for hire and shut him down before anyone else finds out. I can't have Nicolette's safety compromised. She's pregnant, Max! After years of trying, her dream of becoming a mother is going to come true. I will not let anyone come between that, especially that pig, Michael St. Clair."

"Say the word, man, and Michael St. Clair will be silenced to-night."

"No, I have something else in mind for our friend, and he won't see it coming."

We sat in my office in silence as I continued to study each photo of Nicolette. Every image was the same. She looked happy, carefree, and beautiful. Her innocence beguiled me, and then my heart was pained at that fact that that monster was waiting for her outside of her happy life. She tried to be so brave in thinking that she was strong enough to handle this on her own, but he was stronger. I battled within myself for so long that she didn't come to me for help. She hid it all from her parents and me. She left herself open to this predator, and I could do nothing to stop it because she didn't tell me.

I blamed my brother for all of it. I trusted him to take care of her and keep her safe. If he hadn't taken her from her home to live in California, miles away from me, then this wouldn't have happened. I convinced myself what I was saying was true, but Sara never agreed. She was my anchor and told me that what happened to Nicolette could have happened in Chicago or anywhere, for that matter. It was easier to blame Massimo than to believe anything else. Eventually I worked out my feelings about it and took back all of my hurtful words. He was my brother, my kid brother who I loved very much. I would do anything for him, and I did when I agreed to help him become a father.

I knew deep down it wasn't his fault, nor was it Nicolette's. It was Michael's. He was just sick with his delusions and created a fantasy in his mind, an imaginary life that would not be realized with my daughter, so he decided to take it instead.

After some long pauses, my intent was clear.

"This is what we're going to do: I need his complete routine from the minute he wakes up until they call lights out for the night. I'll take care of securing the blueprints of the layout and handling the warden, if that makes you uneasy. You just check with your guys, and get me his breakdown, I'll do everything else. Clear?"

"Jack, I've never questioned you in all the years I've known you, but this is crazy. It will never work. Please reconsider another way. We have you covered, but we just can't risk exposure. Times have changed, my friend. There are eyes everywhere, and we can't be on anyone's watch list."

"Max, you have been my friend for more years than anyone else in my life, but don't ever question me again. It will only break down the trust we have, and it will not be good for either one of us. I told you I have my reasons for why he is still breathing, but now that has changed with this new development. I will not be working under the guise of the family. I know and understand that I am on my own here, so don't worry about blurred lines. I've got it covered."

"I mean no disrespect, but I'm just worried for you. You've been out of the game for a long time, my friend, or maybe that's what you want us all to believe. You are one scary motherfucker Jack. The streets still fear you, and Michael St. Clair should too. Just think about what I said, please. And Jack, don't fool yourself into thinking that you are on your own, because that's simply not true. Being concerned for you is not cutting you loose. There is a difference."

"I'll see you around, Max."

I stood with my hands firmly in my pocket and my jaw clenched so tightly that I thought my molars would snap. I couldn't be angry with Max for advising me. He's been here with me for years, but I meant what I said when I was on my own. I'd struggled with my demons for too many years to count, being pulled in multiple directions. I was torn between good and evil, never too sure which side I would end up on. To look into Sara's eyes and lie to her is abhorrent to me, and that goes for Nicolette as well.

Max left everything with me and took his leave. My friend looked defeated, but I couldn't worry about that right now. My palms were placed against the door, and then I leaned my head against it, thinking about that monster and my Nickel. I couldn't let him hurt her. Not again. Never again. I'd never survive it if his hands touched her again. She'd been through so much, and now when she truly has everything, he resurfaced to taint her light with his darkness. No! I was willing to do everything in my power to stop him, even if cost me all that I had.

After Max left, I had spent hours in my office just studying all the surveillance pictures of Nicolette. I was disgusted, but yet I couldn't tear my eyes away from the images. This was my daughter, and she had been through so much at the hands of this predator. And he is still stalking her even behind the confines of his prison walls. What is he after? Does he have a plan after he gets released? Is he that confident in his father's abilities to use his money and resources as his ticket to freedom? I scrubbed my face down with my hands in frustration and uncertainty.

I was so lost in my mania that I didn't even hear her enter my office. I only felt the chills that coursed through my body whenever she was near. It was a need, one that was carnal and fierce, that any man with a pulse would want what I had. Sara was my weakness, and there was nothing I wouldn't do for her. I already proved that fact when I laid my heart at her feet and promised what she needed to hear. I could only pray that I would not lose her after making this decision to break my vow.

I didn't want to look up at her. I knew I was about to be scolded for abandoning the restaurant today, and during its busiest time. Being the angel she was, she held back and looked at me with love in her eyes instead of anger. I opened up my arms as her invitation to walk toward me, which she did with no hesitation. I once again closed my eyes, this time relishing in the fact that my Sara was here, and she was mine.

She combed her delicate fingers through my hair, scratching my scalp as she always did. Her touch once again left me with chills. We had privacy here. I could easily take her across my desk and claim every part of her just to remind myself that I still had a touch of humanity somewhere in my soul, but that wouldn't be fair to my wife. I was angry and repulsed at what I had seen in the photos and was looking for a quick release to sate that anger. That would not be something I would do with Sara.

"Talk to me Jack. Aside from this morning, I haven't seen you all day. Do you even know what time it is?"

"I'm sorry, babe, but I don't."

She pulled her phone from her pocket and showed me the screen. Holy shit! I had been down here for over six hours.

"I'm sorry, Sara. I lost track of time. I'll come up and help with the closing prep."

"Don't bother. It's already done," she said, now leaving my arms to pace my office. "What's going on with you? Or do I even have to ask? I'm tired of this emotional merry-go-round carnival ride that we've been on. It's time to get off and move on. Don't sit there with a scowl on your face, because you know exactly what I'm talking about."

"What do you want from me, woman?" Instantly regretting my tone, I kept going. "So I skipped out on the dinner rush, big fucking deal. We employ an arsenal of employees that I pay very well to take care of things. I doubt I was even missed."

"You can sit there and believe that I'm actually upset with you because you didn't work today? Oh, Jack, I wish that was the case, but we know it's not. I'm not blind. I saw Max enter the restaurant today. I also saw the grim expression he wore on his face, not to mention the thick envelope he was carrying, kind of like this one on your desk. May I?"

She gestured to the papers and turned upside down photos, but slamming my hand down stopped her curiosity.

"Don't...please."

My voice sounded so small. I couldn't allow this part of my life to touch her. The hurt in her eyes sent me a clear message. I tried to go to her, but she refused me.

"Keep your secrets, Jack. I don't want to know. Don't the wise guys believe that a crime is never a crime if no one was there to witness it? Right?"

And with the sound of her voice and look on her face, I might have lost all the faith she ever had in me. Just for good measure, she slammed the door on her way out, leaving me feeling more alone and lost than ever before.

Days later, Sara was still giving me the silent treatment layered with a side of coldness. I wasn't even needed when our weekly vendors stopped in with our deliveries. She was phasing me out, and I didn't like it one bit. But nothing would prepare me for the confrontation that I would have with her when I walked into our bedroom to see her packing a bag. Now it was my turn to slam the door.

"Care to explain where the fuck you are going?"

I hated how I lost my temper with Sara, but she was decimating me with her silence, and now her actions would destroy me if I didn't do everything in my power to stop her from leaving. She maintained her composure and ignored me. I finally had to walk over to her and grab her by her shoulders to force her to look at me.

"Please," I drew out, "don't leave me, Sara. I won't be able to live without you."

I held her to me until she finally broke down and placed her arms around my back.

"Jack…"

I cut her off by crushing my mouth down to hers. I coaxed her mouth until she opened for me finally allowing me to kiss her, taste her, and show her how much I loved her. She had stripped me bare with the sight of the suitcase. I couldn't lose her. I was in a daze, had been since our fight. I wasn't sleeping, nor eating much. Max had come through and got me everything I needed to get to Michael, if I desired to do so. He was still secure, and for now I didn't need to make any decisions on what my next move would be. I was waiting for one more piece of the puzzle to connect, but that would have to wait until I settled things with Sara. She finally disengaged from me, putting more distance between us.

"Please don't leave me," I asked again.

The tone of my voice was barely above a whisper. She was taking a sledgehammer to my heart. I stroked her soft skin, making my way up to her eyes, where they would meet mine.

"Please, baby, don't go."

Another quiet plea to make her stay. I struggled to say the words and fought against my unadulterated desire for her. The desperation in my voice made me feel defenseless against her. She had made her mind up, and I could do nothing to change it.

"I'm not leaving you, Jack, but I am taking a break. I need some time to myself to think some things through, and I can't do that here with you. I'm sorry."

"If you were so sorry, then you would stay and talk to me."

"And say what? You are an island, Jack, tucked away somewhere off the coast of nowhere, and I'm not invited to visit. I have tried, but you stop me at every turn. So I'm going to go to my own island for a while and take a long vacation from our life—or at least what it used to be before Nicolette was raped."

I had lost all ability to speak after Sara's bold statement. How could she have been so cold? I didn't even believe it was possible…not ever. My only choice was to walk away from Sara, because if I were to stay, I probably would say or do something that I know I could never take back.

Sara continued to pack her things, and I allowed her to do it. I made a fast retreat out of our home and down to the bar, picking a bottle as I went down to my office. Tommy came down about an hour later using caution as he asked for entrance into my private hell.

"Did she leave?" I asked him.

"Yeah, boss, about a half hour ago. She asked me to give you this."

Tommy handed me an envelope with Sara's initials on it. It was the matching envelope to the stationary I had given her. Every anniversary we shared, we would write a love letter to each other, and then read them out loud. It was always a beautiful ending to another year gone by spent loving each other, and then we would make love and make more promises for the next year to come. And now I'm about to read what, a goodbye letter? 'Thanks for the memories, Jack?' "

"Can I do anything for you, boss?" Tommy asked, always having my back, but all I wanted was to be alone.

"I'm fine. Just take care of everything upstairs for me. Have Marco and the girls help you with the closing prep, and then lock up on your way out."

He nodded and then left my office. Tommy knew better not to push me. Hell, he had seen my worst when Christina called me with the news of Nicolette's attack.

I couldn't read this letter. I wasn't ready to have my heart tormented any more than it already was. So I poured myself a whiskey and didn't stop until I drained the bottle. My cell had gone off a few times, and I ignored whoever was trying to get a hold of me. It wasn't Sara, this I knew. She was off on her own fucking island or whatever she said when she walked out on me. What the fuck does that even mean? I have shared everything with her, even the ugly parts that should never have been repeated, but I did it with my wife. And this was how she repaid my trust, by leaving me?

Her letter was laughing at me. The thin envelope was just sitting there on my desk, taunting me. I could shred it without ever knowing what it said, or I could man up and just read it. I took a deep breath and fought against my better judgment.

My Dearest Jack,

I know you're angry with me, so let's begin there. I'm angry too, but with myself for hurting you. I should have never said something so hurtful to remind you of what has pained you all of these years.

It was cruel on my part, and I am very sorry for doing that to you. In my defense, I was out of options. You say you endeavor to always be honest with me, but do you? You tell me what you think I could handle, and then you hide the rest and keep me sheltered from other parts of your life. I thought I was your life? Isn't that what you always led me to believe? I don't trust you anymore, Jack, because I fear you are about to embark on something that you will not come back from.

I won't be there to see you fall. I'm just not strong enough to go through that again. I love you, Jack...always. But sooner or later, one of us had to get off the ride. I need time, and I am hoping you will allow me to have it. When I'm ready, I will call you, but for now, please let me go.

Yours,
Sara

Crumbling her letter in my hands, I tossed it into the trash. *How the fuck did I get here? And what will become of me if I have lost Sara, forever?* Not giving any more attention to my liquor cabinet, I grabbed my keys and took a walk. It probably wasn't the smartest thing to do in the middle of winter during probably one of the coldest weeks Chicago had ever seen, but I was numb anyway, so to hell with it.

Not even knowing how long I was walking, I found myself in front of the old brownstone I grew up in. These buildings dated back to the early 1900's. They were now protected and cared for by a

foundation that fought to preserve the authenticity of the Italian immigrants who arrived in America to make a better life for themselves. Ellis Island had their own piece of history, and we had ours
here in this neighborhood. I learned many lessons on these streets,
some good and some bad, but ones that stayed with me all of my life.
These streets were lined with the blood, sweat, and tears of all who
lived here, including my family. If I closed my eyes, I could still see
mama sweeping the front stoop to our doorway. We didn't even have
a yard for a garden, but mama made do with what she had. She had a
few planter boxes that she grew fresh herbs in, and when she cooked,
you could smell the fruits of her labor down the row of houses on
our block. In a moment of clarity, a pang of guilt pounded through
my heart as I continued to stare at the decrepit buildings before me.

"Forgive me, mama and papa. I tried to be a good son. All I
wanted was more for you." All of these years after their passing, I
never really allowed myself to grieve for them. I had to be strong for
Massimo. He grieved and mourned them for a long time. I never
rushed him. I just stepped in and took care of him like I had always
done. He was their pride. He had their respect, whereas I had their
disappointment because of the choices I made. Too late to change
now, right? With Sara walking out on me, what else did I have to
lose? I shrugged off all the pity I was spouting out and began walking again. By the time I got back to my bar, I was frozen down to my
bones, but at least I wasn't drunk anymore. The walk did me some
good clearing my head. If only my heart would feel better too.

Walking the old neighborhood put things in perspective. It
served as a reminder to who I was, where I come from, and quite
possibly where I was going. For me, I didn't get too far as to location, but that's just logistics. As long as I had Sara, my home was
where she was. I could have made some calls and find her by morning, but if she wasn't willing to talk to me, then I would have only
made matters worse between us.

Even when we think we are protecting the ones we love with
our intentions, sometimes they get hurt anyway. Back then, I al-

lowed my brother and the love I had for my wife manipulate me into going against everything I believed in. They knew what it had cost me but convinced me to follow their path. I believed I had honored their wishes up until now, but how could I ignore an open threat of intent? I was angry beyond reason when Nicolette hid her secret from me, refusing my help. My heart ached for Sara to come back to me, but for now, I would give her the space she asked for.

CHAPTER Thirteen

TIME TO SHATTER THE ILLUSION...

A s I began to unlock my bar, in the corner of my eye a dark figure was stepping out of a car and walking toward me. With my alarms raised, I was thankful for the piece that I always carried. With my hand on my gun, I was ready to take down whoever was attempting to rob me.

"Jackie, it's Max."

"What the fuck, Max? It's past two am. What are you doing here at this hour?"

"Looking for you, my friend, and not really looking forward to a bullet in my head for my efforts." I let out my breath and secured my gun back into its holster.

"I haven't seen you since we last talked. You've been off the grid for the past few days, and now I come here to find you like this."

"And what did you find, Max? Coming home from a walk is not national news."

"Okay, sorry for being concerned. Can I come in before my balls freeze off?"

Leave it to Max for keeping it real.

We made our way into the bar and warmed ourselves with a brandy.

"You have something for me? Pretty late for a social call."

Max handed me another envelope, this time containing something that surprised me.

"Is this what I think it is?"

"You got that right. We found him, Jack. The mysterious photographer that's been working for St. Clair. He's based out of LA, some ex-con now redeemed. He's small time. Does weddings and shit like that. We tracked him to his studio after we noticed a mark on one of the photos. It's like his personal signature to let people know his work, and he's up for hire."

"How did you guys find that mark, and I didn't? I've been staring at the photos for days."

"We didn't see it either Jack. We called in a favor."

"And that might be?"

"No worries, Jack. No one lost a limb over this intel. One of the captains from Petey's crew helped us out. His boy is like some freaking genius out of MIT, and he was here for the weekend visiting. We showed him the photos, and he found the mark. He then did some shit on his computer, and voila! We have the photographer."

"Where is this guy now?"

"Like I said, in LA."

"And?"

"Let's just say…he's secured."

I was too tired for this back and forth volley with Max. I owed him a lot for all he had done for me. I downed another shot, and then Max told me the rest.

After a hot shower, I managed to get a few hours of sleep and then booked myself on the next flight out of O'Hare to LAX. I needed a meet-and-greet with the neighborhood photographer.

A car was waiting for Max and me when we walked out into the bright California sunshine. Max was whooping, hollering, and reveling at the temps, but we weren't here for a vacation. We drove for about an hour until we reached the house where this guy Eddie Valdez was being held.

"So what's the plan, Jack?" Max asked before we walked into the ranch-styled house with a manicured lawn.

"Who owns this house?"

"No worries, Jack. I've got your back. This is on loan from someone who owed me a favor. I only had to promise to replace the carpet if there were any mishaps."

I raised my eyebrows at my friend, but he busted out in laughter.

"Relax, Jack. We go in, get what we need, and then we let him go."

My head was beginning to throb with Max's antics. He wasn't a heavy hitter anymore, but if he needed to step up, he would with no hesitation.

We entered the house with Max taking the lead. He knew these guys out here better than I did. I was beginning to feel disconnected, almost second guessing my decision to come out here at all, until two guys walked up to greet me. They both introduced themselves and shook my hand. One was rambling on with useless small talk until the other elbowed him to shut up. He made his apologies for his talkative partner. I nodded and wanted to get on with everything.

I was led downstairs into the basement where one Eddie Valdez was bound to a chair. Clearly he was roughed up a bit before my arrival. His swollen, black and blue eyes widened at my appearance. I saw the fear, but I wasn't here to hurt him. All I needed was information, but he didn't need to know that. Max remained stoic and off to the side while I unfastened my jacket and took a seat in front of Eddie.

"Do you know who I am?" I asked him.

He nodded his head yes, and then I spoke again.

"I'm going to remove the tape from your mouth. If you decide to scream, that will be a mistake on your part as no one will hear you. Do you see the man standing behind me? Nod again so I know you understand." He did without hesitation. "Okay then. Anyway, the man standing behind me is prepared to put a bullet in your head if you disregard my warning, so don't be stupid and you won't get hurt. Do you understand?"

He nodded rather nervously, convincing me that he got what this meeting was about. I ripped off the tape like a Band-Aid, and he let out a small shriek. Couldn't say that I blamed him, though, since some of his beard hair came off with it.

"Now that we've been introduced, let me tell you the reason behind my visit. You've been really busy taking photographs of someone that is very special to me, and I want to know why that is?"

"I didn't mean any harm, man. All I had to do was follow her around and snap a few pictures."

"A few pictures? I think you took more than a *few* pictures, Eddie! Looks more like stalking. Tell me…what do you get out of this? Fast money, perhaps? And when the job is over, where will you be? Let me tell you…nowhere. Now, you may think this is harmless, and once again, it's just you taking a few pictures, but I see it differently. Do you have an end date? When do the pictures stop?"

"He never said when. I get an envelope filled with cash in my mailbox once a month, and then after I develop them, I send the prints to a post office box. I swear that's it, man."

I got up and gestured over to Max to join me in the other room.

"What did we find at his studio?"

"We flipped it inside and out and found nothing leading back to St. Clair."

"Then tell me something, Max, who the fuck is Eddie Valdez? And how the hell did he become St. Clair's lackey?"

I grabbed a chair and threw it against the wall, smashing it to pieces. You tell me this guy is small time and just out to make some easy money? But that doesn't tell me how he got this job in the first place. Who's the courier that delivers the money? Where's this PO box located? I need to know this shit, Max, and I will beat it out of him to get it. Let's go back in and get what we came for."

Eddie looked to be shaking, unsure of his fate. I sat back down in front of him to question him once more.

"Now, Mr. Valdez, let's start at the beginning. Who hired you? It's a pretty simple question, and one that I will not ask twice."

"Michael St. Clair."

"And how did your path cross with his?"

"I was doing time when he waltzed his preppy ass into the block where I was being housed. It was too good to be true. He didn't look like he belonged there. He was too pretty to be deemed a criminal. We saw him as an easy target that we could shake down right from the start, but then we were told to keep our hands off of him. The order came from Big Spike, and what he says goes. No one crosses him."

I looked over to Max, and he already knew what I was thinking by my expression. Big Spike was one of our guys on the inside. Max gestured to his hair because apparently Big Spike's hair was shaped into a mohawk, then divided into what looked like spikes. I shook my head and went back to listening to Valdez.

"St. Clair was on kitchen detail with me for a while, and then I talked to him a few times out in the yard. This guy was smooth, but there was something about him that at times made the hair rise on my neck. His eyes would go cold, and then he would just shoot his mouth off about being wronged and how everything will change when he gets out. I only had a few months left on my sentence, and in that timeframe we got to know each other better."

"I don't care to hear the details about how you got to know each other better, Mr. Valdez. Get on with it."

"No man, you don't understand. No prison booty. I don't play for that team, and I had a wife to get back to. I just told him about needing money when I got out. I was good with a camera and hoped I would find a job on the outside. A few days later, he asked me to join him in his cell, and that's when he showed me a picture of this girl…his girl, he said. He told me all about her and asked me to follow her around, take the pictures, and then send them to a PO box. He said that as long as I delivered what he requested, I would still get paid until he no longer needed my services. I didn't see any harm in it, man, and the money helped my family. I was set-up in a small studio where I developed the pictures and took other jobs. I had already fucked up big time by doing something stupid that landed me in that hole, so this was my way out. I had left my wife and kids with nothing, so taking pictures of some girl for cash didn't seem like a bad deal. I swear, man, I never touched her. She didn't even know I was there. Please, you have to believe me! I got a sick kid, and this money pays for his care. I'll stop and won't take anymore pictures, but please let me go back to my family. I did it for them!"

He began shaking again and then crying like a baby. I gestured to Max to gag him again. I walked out to compose myself.

"What do you think?" Max asked me.

My mind was reeling at the fact that with all I had in place to protect my daughter and track Michael, he still managed to get around me. This was not sitting well with me, the realization that I had fucked up somehow.

"Look, Jack, his story matches up. His cell was right next to St. Clair's. We have photos of them talking on the block and more accounts from our guys on the inside."

"And his family? Does he truly have a sick child? Or is he playing us?"

Max handed me some papers. They contained medical statements and a picture of his son, a ten-year-old diagnosed with kidney disease who's currently waiting for a transplant. *Fuck!*

"Let's go back in and talk to him again."

Once again, Max removed the tape from his mouth, and this time he remained silent.

"You are shut-down, Mr. Valdez. You will no longer take any more photos of this young woman. Your relationship with Michael St. Clair is over. You are not to have any further contact with either of them. Do you understand?"

"Yes, sir."

"Am I assured that my associates here have all the remaining prints, memory cards, and everything that ties you to St. Clair?"

"Yes, sir."

"You wouldn't lie to me, would you?"

"No, sir."

"Fair enough, because if you even dare to disobey my orders, then Mr. Valdez, you will find yourself at the bottom of the ocean with blocks around your throat. And then where will that leave your son?"

"I swear, you have my word. I will never take another picture. I'm done, man. I swear it on the life of my son."

I leaned down into his ear and whispered, "Mr. Valdez, if I were you, I would promise on something else and not disgrace your son with your sins. Hasn't he suffered enough already with you as his father? You get to live today because of him. Don't take my gift for granted."

After leaving the house, I was lost in thought. This guy meant nothing to me, but there was a child involved who needed him more than my first instinct to make him pay for stalking Nicolette. He got another chance to do the right thing, whereas that was lost on St. Clair, who did not appreciate the incredible gift of penance he was given by my girl.

"Where to next, boss?"

"I need to take care of some things on my own. I will see you back in Chicago."

"I can stay, Jack. Whatever you need."

"Thank you for that. I just need to be on my own for a while."

I found myself driving around for hours with no destination in sight. Had I stepped so far out of bounds that I was willing to risk losing Sara and possibly my freedom to avenge my daughter?

I'd never forget when she told us her unexpected news. She was so happy, probably the happiest I had ever seen her. It was Thanksgiving, our first holiday together in Chicago since they left for California. I had been over the moon when Nicolette phoned me and asked if I would host the holiday at our restaurant. The Paulson clan would also be joining us, minus Jacob and Cameron. Cameron had a game that weekend, and their oldest son, Jacob, hadn't been in touch for a while. I was told not to add them to the list. I didn't care, though. All I wanted was my girl back in her home...back with me.

I closed the restaurant down the entire week of the holiday. My customers weren't happy with my decision, but this was a time to celebrate my girl's homecoming. Sara worked tirelessly along with our other chef to create the perfect menu including all of Nicolette's favorites. Simon's brothers were known to eat second and third portions, so we made sure we had plenty of food on hand. Only Andrew would be joining us. His team was the New England Patriots, and AFC teams had off for the holiday. Cameron was a New York Giant, so I knew that either during dinner or after, my bar would be booming with cheers for him playing on TV. He was a brilliant running back and a showstopper at every game he played in.

With the preparations all in place, all we needed were our guests to arrive. Nicolette wanted to be here before Wednesday, but her husband couldn't get away and didn't want her flying without him. I loved that boy—or should I say young man. He had been devoted to my girl since the first day they met. He was there from the darkest days to the brightest of days when they finally got their happily ever after and were married. They defied the odds and made it to the other side. And now after all of this time, we are all going to be together as two families celebrated Thanksgiving as one. What better holiday to appreciate all you had been given than Thanksgiving!

"What time is it, Sara? They should be here by now. Are you sure we checked the right flight number?"

"Yes and yes. Mason called from the car. They are just caught in some traffic, but nothing to worry about. What has you so nervous?"

"I know I sound crazy. I'm just excited to see my girl."

"Honey, you know not to speak that way in front of Mason and Christina, right?"

"And why not? She's my daughter, Sara, and I really don't give a rat's ass on how it affects my dear brother."

"Okay, honey, this is not the greatest time to bring this very sensitive subject up, but you should care about how you speak of Nicolette, because it pains her deeply when you and Mason butt heads. She's not traveling all the way here with her entire family so that she could referee you two. It's certainly not fair to our guests and to me. I planned every last detail down to the place cards for this holiday, and I'm asking you, my love—more like telling you—to behave yourself."

"Come here, so I can kiss you madly. God! Woman, I love you."

"And I love you too, Jack, but I was being serious. No one knows better than I do where this stems from, but now is not the time to go there. Better yet, please let it go."

"How can you say this to me after everything this family has endured to get to this moment? When the truth came out about her paternity, I was elated at the fact that I didn't have to hide it anymore from her. And before you go on with another lecture, I know she belongs to Mason, but hell, she's mine too. She's this family's miracle. Don't you see that, Sara? When you survived your cancer, it was an awakening for me. I took nothing for granted, and all I wanted to do was please you and make you smile."

"You do that, Jack, and so much more. I am so lucky to have you as my husband."

"And I am blessed to have you too, but I also want to be a father. I've been there for that girl every day of her life, maybe even more than Mason has. And when she got..."

I choked up with just saying the words until Sara knew—of course, she knew—and took me into her arms to comfort me.

"Okay, please, honey, let's not discuss any of that on this day. Your daughter will be here any minute."

"Thank you," I whispered as I hugged my wife.

"Hey! You have one of those for me?" the voice of my angel called out to me.

She looked beautiful, on top of the world, sparkling with a smile that lit up my heart. I kissed my wife's forehead and rushed over to my girl. My Nickel had returned home. She hurried over to me and jumped into my arms. I wrapped my arms around her and spun her until she begged me to put her down. I couldn't help myself, I had missed her so much. It had been months since our last visit, and it was never enough time to share with one another. Her husband followed close behind her, and then my brother, his wife, and the Paulson family.

Still in my arms, she reached up to kiss my cheeks.

"Uncle Jack, I missed you so much! Happy Thanksgiving!"

"Happy Thanksgiving, Nickel."

I kissed her and then made my way over to my brother.

"Massimo, it's been a long time. Welcome home."

I could tell he was already not pleased with me on account of how I addressed him, but too bad. I called him by his given name out of respect for our parents. I hated how our last name was changed, and then he went and changed his first name to Mason. No. I just couldn't call him that. Call me stubborn, but that's how I felt.

After all the greetings were made, we all went upstairs to the private dining room for dinner and what I hoped would be hours of conversation and catching up. Simon placed his hand on the small of Nicolette's back and led her up the stairs. He was so gentle with her, as she deserved to be treated. I hated the distance between our homes, but as long as I knew she was being cared for, I didn't worry as much as I used to.

Tonight's reunion was just a warm-up to what tomorrow would bring. I had planned to join Nicolette, Simon, and the others to watch the Thanksgiving Parade along downtown's historic State Street. Crowds of over 400,000 were always in attendance for this tradition. We never missed it when Nicolette lived here. It was a rite of passage for us to share, and I couldn't wait to have it again tomorrow.

Clink, clink. I tapped on my glass several times to get every-

one's attention.

"On behalf of Sara and me, thank you so much for joining us here in our home for Thanksgiving. It means so much to us to have you all here, especially Nicolette. Thank you, sweet girl for giving me the best day that I've had in a long while. I love you. Okay! Back to eating."

The look on Sara's face didn't go unnoticed by me, or my brother for that fact. We had our share of disagreements these past years, but now that he had returned home, I was hoping to make a fresh start.

"I'm proud of you, Jack. I know that was hard for you," my voice of reason said as she hugged me from behind.

If Sara only knew how much it hurt to hold my tongue out of respect for Nicolette's feelings. I raised her hands to my lips, and then we joined the others back in conversation.

An hour later, the party was coming to an end. I could see the exhaustion on my girl's face, but by the way she carried herself, you wouldn't know it. She saw me staring and walked over to me.

"Thank you, Uncle Jack. Everything was out of this world amazing."

"You are most welcome, Nickel, but Sara did all the work."

"So that's your story? Why can't you ever just accept a thank you? You know you're my hero."

"Oh, darling, as much as I would love to believe that, you have Simon now, and from what I can see, he's all you need."

"There's room in my heart for more than one hero, Uncle Jack. Can we take a walk?"

Her eyes were hopeful as she knew I would agree to anything she asked of me.

"Of course, but it's cold out there. Are you sure your thin California skin can handle it?"

"You never forget where you come from, Uncle Jack. I'm a Chicagoan through and through."

I love this girl. She told Simon that we wouldn't be long. Mason and Christina worried over her, telling her to reconsider going out and that it was cold. She wasn't 12, and she was perfectly safe with me. And Sara thinks that I had control issues!?! Mason never ceased to remind me of our roles in her life. My only saving grace was that Nickel never chose one over the other and loved us both.

We walked a few city blocks with her arm wrapped around me. She loved walking through Little Italy while I pointed out all of the historic buildings. We passed a few establishments where I was well-known, and friends would shout out hellos to us as we passed by.

"Is everything okay, sweetheart?"

I loved our time together, but I also knew her well enough to sense she had something weighing on her mind.

"I'm fantastic, better than ever."

We stopped at our favorite spot in the park, grabbing two hot chocolates before we found our bench. This was our place, where most of our heavy conversations took place. It was a good feeling to know that she never forgot it.

"What's on your mind, Nickel?"

"Am I that obvious?"

"Yes, but you know you can tell me anything."

"I know, Uncle Jack."

She dropped her chin and sipped her hot chocolate. Damn it! I didn't mean to phrase my words in that way. I knew where her mind had just retreated to. I lifted her chin and made her look at me.

"I'm sorry, baby, I didn't mean to upset you."

"You didn't. It's just old scars." She effectively talked right over her statement and continued, "Anyway, that's not why we're here. I have some news to share with you, and before the rest of the family finds out tomorrow, I wanted to tell you first."

She smiled the widest of smiles and took my large hands into her delicate ones.

"Uncle Jack, I'm pregnant. I'm pregnant with Simon's child, and this time I know the heartache is finally behind us. The universe won't be so cruel to us again and take another child from me."

She could no longer hold back her tears and immediately placed her cheek to my hands, where more tears fell. It pained me to see her in this state. I knew they were happy tears but some had to be sad ones remembering the past. She had to endure three miscarriages, so I wasn't so sure she would survive another one without losing hope. I wasn't going to go there, not when she just was positively glowing.

"Look at me, sweet girl. You are going to make a wonderful mother to this child you are carrying, and Simon is going to be one hell of a dad. No more tears, love. You have a miracle growing inside of you, and I want you to smile and be happy."

"Oh, I am, Uncle Jack. I've never been happier."

"Thank you for sharing this with me."

"You're welcome."

No words needed to be said after that. This was my girl giving me yet another gift for us to share. We always shared a special bond with one another, and it had never been stronger. To give me this news in person, with no one else present, just made me the happiest father in the world. She never minded if I slipped once in a while. Maybe she knew that this was what I needed. I wasn't going to tempt fate. I gave her one last hug, and then we made our way back to the bar.

All eyes were on us when we walked through the door. I could see the relief on Simon's face when he greeted Nicolette, taking her in his arms. She whispered something in his ear, and now it was his smile that lit up the room. I left them on their own and poured myself a drink when my brother joined me.

"You look good, Jack. The restaurant looks great, and Sara seems well. I'm happy for you, brother."

Was he really? Or was his blatant hostility leaning toward another statement?

"Thank you, Massimo. And how is your perfect, compartmentalized life going out in sunny California? Your tan looks fabulous."

Yeah, I was being an ass.

"Couldn't be better, Jack. Our songwriting keeps us busy with

established and new artists that sign with our record company. Vanelle Records is in the mainstream, growing every day. By the way, let up on the 'Massimo.' How many times do I have to tell you not to address me by that name?"

"I don't know, Massimo. Maybe I'll quit when it stops bugging the shit out of you. You are some piece of work, little bro. After all I have done for you, you show me no respect and in my own fucking home. Drain the vein and have another drink. You are too uptight for me, and I've had a pretty good night, so don't fuck with me."

I downed my drink and poured myself another one. It was either that or punch him in his "holier than thou" face.

"Careful, Jack. Nicolette is watching. You don't want to shatter your God-like status in front of her now, would you?"

"That's what this attitude is really about, isn't it? You just can't stand the fact that she loves me and looks to me like a daughter would with her father. Am I close, MASON?" I drew out his name to the point where he seethed with anger.

"Keep telling yourself that, brother, if it helps you sleep better at night. I don't have to play games when it comes to my daughter. We are here for her, and only her, so keep yourself in check until after tomorrow. Then I will leave, and I will take my daughter with me."

"Fuck you, Massimo."

The words were out of my mouth before I could stop myself. I looked over his shoulder and hoped no one had heard me.

"No, Giovanni, fuck you. That is your name, right? But yet, you prefer good old Jack. You never let me forget how I disgraced our family by changing my name, but why give me grief when you are the biggest hypocrite walking. I bet no one from the streets even knows your real name. Tell me something, JACK...was Giovanni too Italian for you to use on the streets? I guess that's why the wise guys keep it simple. Tony, Vic...you get what I'm saying?"

I inhaled a deep breath as if my life depended on it. From where we were standing, the hope of us finding middle ground looked grim at this point. He was fueled with animosity toward me, and I wasn't going to have him use my relationship with Nicolette to get to me.

"We are going to table this conversation for now, but make no mistake, little brother, we are not finished discussing what has crawled up your ass. You give me tomorrow with our daughter, and then you can come at me with all that you've got."

"I look forward to taking you down a few pegs."

I knew Mason was trying to get a rise from me, but there was no way in hell I was going to lose it, especially in front of Nicolette.

"Good luck trying," I replied with my best "go fuck yourself" face.

We plastered the fakest smiles on our faces and walked back into the main room. Nicolette was being helped into her coat by Simon. The Paulsons bid their farewells to us and took a separate car to their hotel. Massimo grabbed hold of Christina, and she just waved to me with a sad look to her face. She loved her husband, and me too for that matter, but hated to high heaven that we were at odds with one another. Christina and Sara...bless these women who put up with our crap.

Nicolette and Simon stayed behind and waited for everyone to file out. "Thank you, Uncle Jack. It's okay to hug Simon. He knew I was telling you tonight."

"Congratulations, son. I can't even begin to express how happy I am for you both. You are a good man, Simon. I'm a little biased, but next to what I have with Sara, I've never seen a perfectly matched couple like you two. Your life is blessed."

I took Simon into an embrace and kissed each side of his face, reciting an Italian blessing, "Un vero uomo si prende cura della sua famiglia. Sii buono con tua moglie e tuo figlio. Che Dio vi benedica."

I laughed out loud on account of the bewildered look on his face. He turned back to Nicolette, who was laughing at her husband, knowing he didn't speak Italian.

"Let me translate for you, baby." Uncle Jack said, "A true man

takes care of his family. Be good to your wife and your child. God Bless."

"Thank you, Jack. That means a lot to us both."

"No need to thank me, son. Just continue to take care of my princess, and we will never have a problem."

"This has been the perfect day, Uncle Jack. Thank you for always being there for me. Io ti amo."

"I love you too, my sweet Nickel. See you tomorrow."

I locked up the bar and left the rest of the clean up for the staff. Sara walked into my arms and kissed me soundly.

"I'm exhausted. Thank goodness we have help for tomorrow. Uh oh...what is it?"

Leave it to my wife to pick up the slightest change in my demeanor.

"Nothing. I'm fine."

She raised her eyebrows, not believing me for one minute.

"I saw you with Mason earlier. Care to talk about it?"

"No, I don't. The only talking I care to do is to get into bed with you. I hope you have a little energy left for me."

"Always," she said with a wink.

Her answer calmed me, while the desire in her eyes aroused me. I carried my Sara into my arms and placed her gently down on our bed, forgetting about the bullshit that waited for me the next day with my brother.

CHAPTER
Fourteen

TORN...

W e couldn't have asked for a better day with Chicago's weather cooperating with us. There was very little wind and a temperature of thirty degrees. Our Thanksgiving tradition: three hours of bliss watching the annual parade that marks the beginning of the holiday season.

This was the Paulson's first time ever witnessing the time honored event that brought so many people together. They were familiar with Illinois and had visited the city of Chicago many times but never took the time to enjoy this spectacular parade. Simon was in conversation with his brother and father, while I stayed close to Nicolette and Sara. My brother and his wife had joined us too but kept their distance. In between enjoying the performers and enjoying the delicious eats of Chicago, Simon's brother Andrew was signing autographs. He was smiling and even posed with fans for pictures.

Nickel's cheeks were rosy red, and her eyes were sparkling with happiness. She was wearing a smile that could launch a thousand ships. This was my girl as I had always remembered before her life changing attack. I have only thanked God for a small number of miracles he has bestowed on me, and my daughter returning home to us was one of them. We feared we lost her when she left, but once again she surprised us with her strength and courage. I only had today with her before she returned to her home in California. I pulled her into a warm hug, feeling the glare of disgust from my brother, who hadn't taken his eyes off of me.

What was his problem? She was normally thousands of miles away from me, and now that I had some time with her and was expressing my affection, he looked like he wanted to rip my head off! I'd maintained my control out of respect for Sara, Nicolette, and her family, but I'd had enough. I needed to set some things straight with my brother.

We went our separate ways after the parade. Nicolette and Simon went back to their hotel to rest and said they would join us in a few hours. The Paulsons decided to do a little sightseeing before dinner. Everything had been already prepped at the restaurant, so I encouraged Sara to join them and serve as their guide. She loved this city as much as I did, and she didn't mind. It took some coaxing to get Christina to join them, but I gave my sister-in-law a hug and assured her that we would be okay in their absence. She gave me a distrustful look, but reluctantly agreed. I gave her a small hug, kissed her forehead, and whispered "Thank you," which caused her to smile.

My brother looked as if he was about to spit fire, but I wasn't going to allow him to erupt in the middle of my bar. I led him downstairs to my office, where we would not be interrupted and certainly not heard.

He bypassed me with a shove with his shoulder. I ignored his action and closed the door behind me. He didn't take a seat and instead fixed himself a drink, not offering me the same courtesy.

"What the fuck is your problem, Massimo? What have I done that has you so enraged with me? You have done nothing but brood since your arrival. This is a happy time, for fuck sakes! And you're walking around with a stick up your ass. What is it?"

"You, Jack, you are the problem! My problem for years now!

It's always about you. I'm exhausted, and I can't do this with you anymore."

I took a hard swallow, making my throat muscles tighten up.

"Me? I'm the one to blame for all of your problems? I think you need to explain yourself, my brother."

"Why? You never listen to me. It always comes down to you, and I'm done with it. Think about it, Jack. When we were younger, you took care of me. You took care of our family and never yourself first. Mama and papa tried to reason with you. They tried to get you to attend church with us, be home more for dinner, and not be out there in the city on your own. You were my hero at one time. I loved you so much and idolized the ground you walked on. Here was my big brother who always protected me. No one even looked cross-eyed in my direction out of fear that you would rip their head off."

He continued, "And as for my piano…I loved that piano, as you well know. I held onto that musical instrument for years until I could afford to buy myself a new one, one that I would create my music on with Christina. Do you want to know why I still have that piano? Why it has been restored and proudly sits in our home in California? Because I could never ever part with it, knowing what you sacrificed in order to give it to me."

With every word my brother was saying, his anger softened and turned into sadness. The only times he ever spoke to me with such purpose in his tone was when we were at odds with each other, like now.

"I never knew that, Massimo. I'm sorry."

"Because you never asked! This went on for years, Jack, because the more you gave us, the more you lost in the end. Pieces of you—and your sold-out soul—were laid all over the streets of our neighborhood, and you just went on being someone's bitch to justify the means that you were providing for us."

"That's not true, Massimo, and you damn well know it. Are you trying to piss me off? Because you don't want to go there with me."

"Why, Jack? What are you going to do? Shoot me? Beat me up?

I don't give a fuck what you threaten me with. It's never going to change how much I love you."

What did he just say? He rested his head against the wall and looked defeated while I was in shock. He had been behaving as if he hated me. He reminded me of all my sins with his self-righteous atti-tude, and then went and said that he loves me?

He slowly turned around to look over at me and said, "You are my brother Giovanni, and I love you. I will always be thankful to you for what you gave to me and Christina, but over the years our rela-tionship has been strained. And from where I'm standing, it doesn't look like we will ever reach a reconciliation, not even for Nicolette. This is why we are here to spend the holiday with you. You forced her hand, because you are constantly making her choose between us, and that is not fair to Nicolette."

"You have blamed me and Christina for taking Nicolette to Cal-ifornia all those years ago, and then when that animal hurt her, that was the beginning of the end of our relationship as brothers. You were enraged and blamed me for our girl getting hurt. You nearly choked me to death on sight. If I could, I would do anything to turn back the clock to prevent what happened to Nicolette, but we know that's not possible. He left her broken, and we nearly lost her, but she came back to all of us and faced her fears head-on that day in the courtroom. I begged you not to go after him, and I know what that cost you. It's still costing you, Jack, still consuming you. I see it every time I look into your eyes, and I don't know if I will ever be able to see anything else."

"Jack, I never understood your life back then, the choices you made, and the consequences of what you had to live with. I can't im-agine the stories you have deep in your soul. We are two different men. I know that, and I'm okay with it. What I'm not okay with is your hungered desire for revenge. You never forgave me for forcing your hand, changing who you are. Tell me that I'm wrong. Just tell me the truth!"

I responded, "And then what? What happens to us after I share *my feelings with you, brother? As usual, you will not like what I have to say and then use it against me, further driving a wedge between me and Nicolette. I will tell you this: that is not going to happen. Over my dead body will I allow you to come between us. I'm so tired of your superior attitude and you rubbing your nose down at me like I'm trash. Yeah, Massimo, I have a past, and it was fucked up from the very beginning, but I survived it, and Nicolette has survived hers. I will never forget for as long as I breathe what that animal did to her. He marked her and scarred her with his manipulations and then his touch. I wanted him dead, that's no fucking secret. But is he? No! Because I kept my promise to you and to my wife. As long as he is not a threat to her, I told you I would honor that promise. So fuck you for ever doubting my word. Fuck you for reminding me of the worst memory my brain and heart will never allow me to forget. Fuck you for constantly reminding me of what I gave you, but yet never allowing me to cherish what I gave you freely. You, Massimo, are always pushing me out, and I have to force myself back in."*

"You want to judge me for my past, Massimo? You do that then. You want to sever ties with your only brother, because you are not willing to move past our differences? Go right ahead. I don't give a fuck any more. My world turned right yesterday when she walked through the door. My heart nearly burst with knowing that my beautiful Nickel is going to be a mother, a dream we didn't think would ever be possible for her after all she has gone through. But God has blessed her, and I am going to be there for her, whether you like it or not."

"Jack, I never pushed you out. You did that on your own with your desire for revenge. I know what you promised, but that doesn't make me rest easy knowing that on the flip of a dime, you could change your mind and move forward with your threats to that animal. Don't you see, Jack? I have to protect my family, even from you, if necessary. There's no question in my mind that you don't love Nicolette and would do anything to protect her and safeguard her happiness. That's what scares me, Jack. I walk into your bar, and it

feels like something out of 'Goodfellas.' You say you left that life years ago for a new one with Sara, and I believed you. I was proud of you, respected you, and trusted you. For a long time before we found our loves, all you and I had was each other. I will never forget all that you did for me, but I have to put some distance between us. I can no longer live under the black cloud of fear when it comes to what you may or may not do. He won't be in prison for much longer, and I don't know how much time is left on that promise. I'm sorry, Giovanni, but after today, I'm walking away and taking Nicolette with me."

"That will never happen, Massimo. No matter what you do, you will never be able to turn her against me."

"You're right, Jack. Probably not, because you will do that all on your own without any help from me. We have two very different views on the world and how we choose to live in it. You are not a bad man, Jack. There's good in you. But I also know that you've carried a heavy burden on your shoulders for far too long now and resent me for it. I just can't be part of this and neither can Nicolette. As long as you still have this thirst for revenge and carry this anger with you, we can have no place in your life. You can have today with our daughter, but we are leaving tonight. And I am asking you to either let your vendetta go, or her, because you cannot have both."

I slumped back into my chair and watched my brother walk out of my office and possibly my life. He was wrong. I hadn't gone back on my word to anyone, and damn him for not trusting me. That animal was still walking around and breathing air. I'd done everything in my power to protect Nicolette, and I would not apologize for it. I couldn't predict what the future held, but for now, I had honored my word.

He thought it was so easy for me to fall back into my old life, just flip-flop back and forth without any consequence. That's not how it worked. Johnny Carlucci set me free when I asked him. He knew that what happened with Mikey Marino changed me. I could no longer be this fierce presence for him on the streets after that act of brutality. I was never the same, but he didn't judge me for it either. He said he always loved me as a son and would always take care of me if I needed any help.

For years after we parted ways in business, Johnny was still there for me in friendship, promising to always be there for me if needed. When word got out about Nicolette, he came to me and asked me what I needed. I knew what he was indirectly asking me, but I respectively declined. He hugged me with all of his strength and left me on my own. I never acted on what I wanted to do, but yet it still was not good enough for my brother.

When Johnny died, I was there holding his hand, and he promised me that I would always have the support of the family if I should need them for anything. Even in his death that promise would not change. I kissed Johnny's hand and said goodbye. He whispered that he loved me and called me his son. His eyes were proud as they slowly closed. My eyes burned with tears watching him slip away from me.

I was so lost in my thoughts that I didn't hear the irritating alert sounding off from my dashboard.

"What the hell? I'm running out of gas?"

I didn't even know where the hell I was. I had been driving since I left Max, not paying too much attention to where I was going. Thankfully, I was still able to go about another few miles up the road. There was not too much around until I noticed a small gas station with only two pumps. The sign was flashing open, and I was thankful for it. I parked my car almost right in front of the pump before it finally sputtered out. I noticed a sign on the pump that said "No Self-Service."

I took off my jacket and tossed it into the back seat. I looked around and waited for someone to come out from the office. After a few minutes, I finally beeped the horn.

Another minute later, a young girl looking to be no more than sixteen years old came running out. She looked scared and flustered, almost tripping over her own feet. Then I saw someone running out immediately behind her. Maybe a mechanic? I wasn't sure. But he seemed focused on the girl, and when he saw me, he stopped running and tried to fix his shirt. His hands were filthy. He spat out what appeared to be chewing tobacco, and then walked up to me and stood in front of the girl.

"You lost pal?" he asked as he spat out more tobacco.

"No, I just need some gas. Fill it up, and check the oil while you're at it."

"We only take cash. You got any?"

"Just fill the damn tank."

Well, that shut him up. I walked up to the building, where there was a soda vending machine. It appeared to be in working order. I put my money in, but nothing came out. I hit the Change Return button, but nothing came out. I was about to curse under my breath when the young girl offered me assistance.

"What kind do you want?" she asked in almost a whisper.

"Coke."

"That button is broken, but there's a trick to it. If you hit the Sprite button, the Coke comes out. Try it?" she said with a hint of a smile.

I hit the button, and sure enough, my soda slid down the shoot.

"Thank you, um...?"

"Sara, my name is Sara."

The sound of her soft voice shot a pain right through my heart, making me miss my wife. She had only left a couple of days ago. It didn't matter to me, though, because it felt like a lifetime already.

I took a sip of my drink and thanked her for her help.

"Sara is my wife's name. Are you okay, Sara? Are you in danger? Blink once for yes, twice for no."

On her small face, her big eyes blinked once, and I instantly felt this fierce need to protect her. She looked nervously over my shoulder to alert me that we were not alone. I didn't know this girl, but there was something familiar about her. It wasn't just her name, but she had an innocence about her. I could have just paid for my gas and went on my way, but Jack Vanelle wasn't that guy.

"Sara! Get back inside, now!" the man with the filthy hands screamed out.

A tear fell down her face. Her body tensed up. She looked like she was about to wet her pants. What had this man done to her? I gave her a reassuring look that seemed to calm her. He shouted again, but this time she didn't move.

"What the fuck, Sara!?! I said get your ass back inside!"

I said to her, "Would you mind holding this for me?"

She nodded as I handed her my drink. My look told her everything she needed to know. This fucker was going down. This was going to be fun.

He started walking towards us as he said to me, "Hey, pal, I don't know who the hell you are, or where you came from, but if you don't want to be coughing up your teeth, it's best that you get back into your car."

He couldn't say another word before I grabbed him by his skinny throat and easily lifted him off the ground. His two hands were trying to grab hold of my one to let him go, but he was unsuccessful. I shoved him back toward the building, where he smashed into the window, shattering it with his backside.

"You motherfucker! You're going to pay for this!" he cried out.

I almost laughed. He came running toward me when I landed a punch to his gut, toppling him backwards onto the dirt. I then placed my heavy foot on his throat while he struggled to breathe. I was successfully cutting off his airway. Blood vessels were beginning to emerge on his cheeks. I removed my foot from his throat. He then turned over onto his hands and knees and coughed to try to get some breath back into his lungs.

I said, "Now that I have your attention…the girl…who is she to you?"

"She's…she's nobody…just works here."

"Wrong answer. She's somebody. She's someone's daughter, sister, and friend. And you, *pal*, are not treating her very nice. What did you say about me eating my teeth? Hmm?"

I picked him up so he was back on his feet, held his throat once again, and punched him directly on his right jaw. He let out a shrieking sound as his jaw was crushed. He spat out a mouthful of blood but didn't move.

"How's that feel? Did you swallow any?"

I knew he couldn't talk after that, but his hearing was still intact.

"Now, you piece of shit, listen to me, because I'm only going to say this once. If you ever put those grimy hands on Sara again, or any other girl for that matter, I will come back here and not so gently remove your lungs with a fucking spoon. Blink once for yes, because you don't have any other choices."

His eyes, which were now red and welling with tears, blinked once.

"Very good, scum bag."

I gave him a stern kick to his ribs just to make sure he was listening. Meanwhile, Sara was crying behind me. Dammit! I had frightened her. I slowly turned around with softer eyes to show her that she wasn't in any danger from me. She threw the soda to the ground and rushed into my arms.

"Thank you, mister. Thank you."

I calmly told her that she was safe.

"Can you give me a ride? I don't belong here."

I didn't even know where I was, but I had a full tank of gas, so I hurried her to my car. We only drove about ten miles from the gas station, and she directed me to drop her off at what looked like a boarding house of some sort.

"Thank you, mister, for saving me. That guy Stevie is an asshole, but thanks to you, I don't think he will be bothering me again."

"You're welcome, Sara. May I ask you a question?"

"Sure, anything."

"Are you hurt? Did he do…anything…to you?"

I couldn't bring myself to say the words, so I carefully tiptoed around it until she understood my question. She let out a sigh, and then answered me.

"He didn't. He tried, but we got interrupted when you arrived and beeped your horn. You saved me."

More tears fell down her cheeks. I was seething with anger and could easily drive back to finish what I started. I reigned in my temper and then handed her my handkerchief. She smiled and accepted it, wiping her eyes. I looked out to the building we were parked in front of.

"Will you be alright? What is this place?"

"I live here with some other girls. It's a half-way house, but not for druggies or drunks. It's more of a home for displaced teens. I've been on my own now for almost a year. My parents are dead, and my grandma couldn't take care of me anymore."

"And the job at the gas station? Have you worked there long? How old are you?"

"You ask a lot of questions, mister, but since you saved me, I'll tell you. I'm seventeen. I have one more year here before they cut me loose at this house. I only took that job about a month ago. That guy Stevie has been trying to get me alone since I started working there. The other mechanic had left before you pulled up, and that meant he finally had me alone."

She wrung out her hands in her lap, which made my heart hurt more for her. I then pulled out my wallet and handed her some money.

"A thousand dollars? Oh my God! I can't take this."

I stopped her from returning it to me.

"Take it, Sara, just please don't go back to that job. Clearly, you weren't safe there."

"I don't know how to thank you. I don't even know the name of my white knight."

"I'm no one's knight, sweet girl, but thank you."

"Are you okay, mister? You look so sad."

"I'm fine. You just remind me of someone who was in a similar situation, and I couldn't do anything about it then. But I have to be on my way. Will you be okay?"

"I'm better now, thanks to you. And in case you were wondering, the interstate is about three miles that way," she said as she pointed behind me. "That will take you back to where you need to be."

She leaned over and gave me a quick hug of thanks and stepped out of my car.

"Thanks again, whoever you are."

I smiled and put the car into drive. My head was spinning with all that had happened in the last few hours. She reminded me of Nicolette, of course she did, with those big brown eyes staring back at me. That poor girl was in danger. I didn't even want to think what could have happened to her if I hadn't stopped for gas. The thought sickened my insides. I couldn't protect my girl when she was hurt, but I was there for this one.

Massimo was right when he said I was carrying a heavy burden, the pain of knowing that I could not protect her from him still haunted me, even in my dreams. I saw Nicolette surrounded by light, and then St. Clair would appear and cloak her in darkness. I wasn't there when she needed me. My brother didn't understand how I felt, when he of all people should. He was too clean cut to ever cross the line, whereas I wouldn't give it a second thought.

I found my way back to the interstate. It had been weeks since I had spoken to my brother. After he left my office, I joined him upstairs with the rest of our family. He had seemed more subdued after our conversation. Christina was wrapped around him and laughing along with Nicolette and Simon. Sara walked over to me to ask what was wrong. I lied and told her I was just a little tired. She knew better but didn't press on.

I pushed aside my feelings and contempt for my brother to enjoy the day I had left with Nicolette. After our dinner, she and Simon stood to get our attention. We were all clinking our glasses, just like we did at their wedding. Simon swept his love into a swooping kiss and then announced her pregnancy. The great news made us all smile and cheer. She was going to make a great mom. Just looking at her so happy brought tears to my eyes. I was fully aware that my brother was staring at me. *Contrary to what he believes, I do have a heart, and it's hurting right now.*

I hadn't decided how long I would remain here in California. I needed a hot shower, good meal, and some rest to clear my head from this mindfuck of a day. I checked in to the Beverly Wilshire Four Seasons Hotel. I had no plan here at all, but if something were to take place, then at least I was visible enough and out in the open. Max had left multiple messages on my voicemail, and I ignored all of them.

After my shower, I stepped out into the opulent hotel room and wished Sara was here with me. We hadn't taken a vacation for more years than I can remember. We put all of our time into our restaurant and then Sara had her volunteer work that kept her busy.

I missed her terribly and wanted her to come home. I knew she was angry with me, but to just walk out without talking to me was not like her. She was my heart. I needed her to breathe, and I didn't know what I was going to do if she decided that she'd had enough.

My cell went off again, and this time I answered it. It was Max telling me that he was back home in Chicago and was surprised that I didn't follow.

"What are you doing, Jack? When are you coming home?"

"What's with the twenty questions, Max? No need to worry about me, so do yourself a favor and back the hell off."

"But I do worry, my friend, and you know why that is. Come home, Jack, and don't do anything that you can't take back."

"Goodbye, Max."

He called out for me, but I had already hung up on him.

It had been nearly two months since I talked to my brother, and I missed him, even after all that happened between us. He was all I had, and I needed him. I knew I couldn't visit with Nicolette, feeling the way I did at the moment. I was torn between what I knew to do, what I wanted to do, and the after effects of what would happen if I chose wrong.

I phoned down to the concierge and ordered up a bottle of my favorite bourbon. He cleared his throat when he said how much this vintage would cost me.

I told him, "Yeah, I know. Send it up."

I didn't have my Sara. I didn't have my brother. I had never felt more alone in all of my life, so I decided to drink a little. Then a little turned into a lot.

Catholicism wasn't lost to me. I kept that part of my life separate from the others. I could hear mama now...

"Giovanni, my sweet boy. Pray with me. We say a passage from St. Francis. Oh, my sweet boy! You need peace of mind. You worry too much for me when it's my job to care for you."

She recited the prayer by memory, and then kissed my forehead.

"I love you, my son. Now, you sleep."

My heavy eyelids closed, and I did what I remembered to do...I prayed for peace.

CHAPTER Fifteen

PUSHED...

The shrill of my phone was beckoning my eyes to open. My head was pounding, and my mouth tasted like cotton. *I'm too old for this shit!* I had been drinking too much since Sara left me, and my body was feeling the effects from it. I rolled over and squinted at the clock. Who was calling me at seven am? I reached for it, nearly knocking over the lamp that was next to it. I slid my finger across the screen to hear Max calling out my name.

"Jack, where are you? I've been calling you all night. Madonne'! What the fuck?"

I dropped the phone to my bed while Max continued to yell at me in English, Italian, and whatever other languages he would choose when he had reached his limit. I sat up leaning against the headboard and gathered my bearings. When I picked up the phone, he was still cursing.

"Basta! You said what you had to say, so now shut the hell up, Max. What's got you so upset? The sun has barely risen out here and I'm not awake yet, so you better have a damn good reason for calling me at this hour."

"What do you want me to say, Jack? You refused to come back

with me, and then when I call you last night, you barely say two words to me. I've seen you like this before, which makes you very dangerous. You are unprotected out there. You need to get back to Chicago."

"I can take care of myself, Max. I'm over this conversation already. I'll call you when I get back."

"And when might that be? Come on, my friend! Give me something."

"I don't know."

I ended the call and then turned my phone off. Scrubbing my face with my hands, trying to shake off yesterday, my mind drifted back to my dreams. I saw my mother. She was speaking to me in Italian, and we were praying. She looked worried for me and wanted to make it all go away so I could sleep in peace.

When mama was dying, I held her hand to comfort her. She knew her time was coming and was only strong enough to talk in short turns. She would tire easily, and I didn't want to put her through that stress. Massimo and I told her over and over again how much we loved her. We promised to always be together and work hard every day to make her proud. She smiled because she was already so proud of both her boys.

On the eve of her passing, Massimo said his goodbyes to our mother. He wanted to be left alone in his grieving.

She was a wise woman whose eyes could read through a man's soul. So when it was my turn, that's kind of how she looked at me. Did she know my sins? I almost wanted to look away from her, but I kept my eyes on her. She held her beloved rosary tightly in her hands, whispering her prayers, and kissing the beads. Mama held my hands and turned them over to place her rosary in them, folding my fingers to clutch them. She could see the uneasiness in me when I held them. It felt wrong to hold something so beautiful and precious, when I had committed so much ugliness and caused harm to others. It almost felt like it was burning my skin.

With all of her strength and goodness, she whispered a blessing to me in Italian and then told me that I was a good man, I would find my way in time, and love would bless me.

"My Gio, my son," she whispered before closing her eyes forever, "you are a good man, my son."

I pulled her lifeless body to my chest. I had never cried so much in all of my life. I was the head of our family now. I knew I had to do better, make mama and papa proud, and show them from Heaven that her prayers and hopes were not lost on me.

Opening my wallet, I retrieved a small tattered picture of my mother. She was smiling with a lace veil that covered her long brown hair. She would always wear it on Sundays for mass. My eyes filled with tears.

"Oh, mama! I miss you so much. You knew, didn't you? And you never judged me for my sins. You just prayed for me and hoped I would find love in my life and be happy. You were right about the love part. I did find it, and she has been the best part of my life, next to sharing a daughter with Massimo. You would have been so proud to know our daughter was blessed with a piece of you. Massimo always loved your middle name, so when it came time to name his child, he could think of no greater name than Nicolette."

I let out some calming breaths and secured my mother's picture back in my wallet. It wasn't often that I lost myself to remembering the past, but lately, that was all I seemed to do.

Max was right. I should get on the next plane and go home, but I wanted to see my Nickel, hold her in my arms, and tell her that I love her. I could easily slip in and out without my brother discovering I was here. Hell! I'm not even registered under my real name here at the hotel.

"Fuck it! She's my daughter too, and if I want to spend some time with her, then to hell with my brother. He hasn't talked to me since Thanksgiving, and who knows when the next time will be? I don't have to explain my actions to anyone. The decision has been made: I will see Nicolette today!"

After my shower, I ordered up some breakfast with some espresso. Nicolette shared my love of Italian things like coffee, Italian pastries, art, and music. Actually, they were the same things Massimo enjoyed too. Damn! I missed my brother, but I was just not ready to talk to him yet.

I drove my rental out to the CALI Center, my daughter's foundation that she started for women. I parked out front and contemplated going in. This was stupid, and I didn't understand why I was putting myself through this bullshit. My Nickel was right inside, and I was sitting out here in a car staring at her place of work.

After another agonizing ten minutes sitting in the car, I finally got out. I had only been here once on the day of the grand opening.

I sat in a packed room surrounded by our family, friends, and women from all walks of life that were there to celebrate the opening of the center and to hear Nicolette speak. She walked out to the podium feeling a little nervous, then took one look over to where Simon was standing, and all was right with her world. She spoke eloquently about her personal story and then shared a few more with us. The only sound in the room was the sound of her voice. All eyes were on my girl. I was so proud of her and the accomplishment she had achieved.

"Sir, may I help you?" I blinked to see a young woman holding a tablet in her hand.

"Um, no thank you, I'm okay. I'm actually here to see Nicolette Paulson. Is she here?"

The woman smiled and laughed.

"She's always here. This is her home away from home."

Now that made me smile, knowing my daughter was happy.

"She's in a meeting right now, but if you tell me your name, I can step in to tell her you're here waiting for her."

"That's okay. I'll just go take a seat in the reception area, and when she's through with her meeting, come find me."

"Very good, sir. Help yourself to a refreshment. We have cookies too, courtesy of the boss. She's become quite the baker since she announced her pregnancy. Wow! Listen to me go on and on. I don't even know your name, and here I am telling you personal information about my boss. I hope you're not a serial killer or anything."

I like this girl! Any second guessing coming here today was now gone after talking to her for a few minutes. I had to hold my stomach on account of how much I was laughing. I needed this laugh in more ways than I could ever explain.

I smiled back and said to her, "Not today, I'm not a killer. You're safe with me. I'm Nicolette's Uncle Jack."

She smiled and turned to go back to her desk.

I was waiting close to an hour when her assistant stepped out to tell me that it shouldn't be too much longer. I waved her off and went back to checking my phone.

I had not heard a word from Sara. I missed her so much and needed her back home with me. But then again, I wasn't home either. It was against my better judgment to yield to anyone, but this was Sara. She gets a free pass. I dialed her number and of course got her voicemail. I wasn't great at expressing my feelings to her in person, let alone pouring my heart out over a phone message.

"Hi, Sara. I miss you so much. Come back to me. I need to tell you so much more than time will allow me on this phone, so come home so I can say the words to your beautiful face. I'm just a shell of a man without you baby, and every day you're gone, I die a little bit more. I'm sorry I hurt you, but you hurt me too, and we need to talk about that. Don't call me back, just come home. I love you."

A few minutes later, I saw Nicolette walking out with a group of men and women. They were all carrying laptop bags, looking like whatever their meeting was about was successful. She shook their hands and then turned back to her assistant, who pointed in my direction.

Nicolette finally noticed me, and a smile graced her beautiful face. She practically ran toward me, but I put my hands out for her to slow her down. She was wearing very high heels, and I didn't want her to fall. Two more strides, and she was in my arms.

"Uncle Jack! What a wonderful surprise. I'm so happy to see

you! Is Aunt Sara with you?"

"Not this trip, love. I'm only here for the day. Can you get out of here for a little while?"

"Say no more. Of course I can. This is my place, and I can do anything I want."

She looked down to her watch and then turned to her assistant, who I now knew as Patty. The remaining appointments on her calendar today were not as pressing as her earlier one, so Patty cancelled the rest of her day.

This was her city, not mine, so Nicolette was my guide. We went down to the beach club and had lunch out on the patio that overlooked the marina down below. All through lunch she talked about her plans for the New Year. She was feeling great with her pregnancy and was soon leaving for a trip with Simon. He was going on a research trip and would be taking Nicolette with him.

I tried very hard to keep up with the animated conversation, but I couldn't ignore the fact at where we were dining. After lunch, we kicked off our shoes and took a walk down the beach.

"Are you okay, Uncle Jack? You were pretty quiet at lunch. Did I talk too much? I'm sorry for monopolizing the conversation. I swear, it's this pregnancy. I am so hyper, I feel like I could do an hour of spin class and then Zumba too!"

"You are so adorable, my sweet girl. I love you so much, and any time I get to hear your voice is welcomed. You can talk my ear off all you want. Remember, I came to you this time."

"So you did! Now, talk to me. You look tired, Uncle Jack. I can see it all over your face, and it saddens me to know that you may be hurting. Please let me in and help you. You've always been there for me when I needed you, so now it's my turn for you."

"I wasn't there every time, Nicolette."

The words were out of my mouth before I could stop myself. She blinked, not understanding what I meant, but she didn't have to. I dropped my chin to my chest and just let it out, all my tears, pain, and deprecating thoughts I had running through my mind and heart.

It all came at me like a freaking speeding train with no breaks.

"Oh, Uncle Jack! Where is this coming from? You were so happy at Thanksgiving. What's happened to change all of that?"

I wiped away my tears and picked up a few shells to throw back into the ocean. She waited for me to answer her question.

"Nicolette, why did you bring me here today? Of all the places here in Los Angeles, you pick the place that you were ra…"

"It's okay, you can finish that sentence. To where I was… raped? Is that what you were going to say?"

"Yes, dammit! That's exactly what I was going to say. Why, Nicolette? Why this place? This beach? This marina? Tell me why!"

My anger was boiling over, and taking it out on her was the last thing I wanted to do.

"Walk with me?" she asked as she held out her hand.

"I'm so sorry for yelling, sweet girl."

She said nothing but nodded. We joined our hands and walked down the beach.

"I'm happy, Uncle Jack, and I eat at the beach club because I like the food. I like to walk around the marina, because it makes me smile to see the fishermen come in with the catch of the day. And I love this beach, because it's the same beach where I fell in love with Simon. I have so many memories here spent with Simon, our friends, and even you, when you flew out here to surprise me for my eighteenth birthday. Simon still drives up and down this coast on his Harley with me hanging on tight. From watching him surf those waves out there, to down that stretch of beach playing volleyball with our friends, I cherish the moments I spent here, and when I returned home from Switzerland to win back Simon's heart, I made a promise to myself almost right where we are standing. God healed me. I survived Michael and what he did to me. Why would I give him power to take away all my happy memories of this place with just one bad one? I have been blessed with so much in my life. I have Simon, who's an amazing husband, friend, and soon will be a father to our twins."

"Twins!?! That's fantastic. When did you find out?"

"Just recently, but I was keeping it private until reaching a safe point in my pregnancy. After everything we've been through, we didn't want to take anything to chance."

"But you're okay, right?"

"Better than okay! I'm wonderful, and my babies are growing every day. Uncle Jack, you just made a new memory, right here on this beach. Now you will always remember this as the place I told you that I'm carrying twins. You see…it's a happy place! And he can never take that away from me. This is why I brought you here today, to show you that I am okay and that he didn't break me. I took that one bad memory, and I turned it into strength. I tell that to every single woman that walks through my door seeking help."

"I would have been there for you had I known. I'm so sorry I wasn't, sweet girl."

"You have nothing to be sorry for. I chose not to tell my parents, or you, and even Simon. I thought I could handle him on my own and no one would ever know, but I was wrong. Does that make it my fault for what happened to me? No, it doesn't. Michael made that decision to hurt me, and something inside of him just drove him to believe in an unreal fantasy. I made my peace with what happened, and after I watched him get led away, I found my closure. He cried for what he did to me. He said all the right things, but it's not for me to know if he was truthful or not. He will be judged someday; it just won't be by me. That part of my life is over, and it should be over for you too."

"Please, Uncle Jack, for your own peace of mind, let Michael St. Clair go, and never think of him again. Mend your fences with my father, and just be happy with Aunt Sara. Don't even try to defend what I just said, because then you would be lying. I saw you with my father and how you treated each other. It broke my heart to witness that much tension between you. He loves and misses you. He just doesn't understand you, but who cares! Just be brothers again."

"Nicolette, you are amazing, our greatest gift. I would do anything for you without question, but my love, there are just some things in my life that I will never explain to you. I've done things in my life that I'm not proud of but accepted them a very long time ago. I know what I am, and what still rages on through my mind. I am not the man you think I am, and for that, I am truly sorry for ever disappointing you. I love you, but some things in life just can't be undone."

"That's not true!" she said as she held my hands. "You are a good man. You're my hero, remember? Please, Uncle Jack, promise me you will stay true to your heart. It's a good one. Trust it with everything you have, and when you're ready, close the door to the darkness. The light is bright, welcoming, and can shine a thousand colors on you. That's what you deserve."

"I love you, Nickel. Next to Sara, you are my moral compass. I know I made many promises back then that I have tried very hard to keep, but things have changed, and it doesn't leave me in a great place. All I can say is that I will try, but please don't hold me to any more promises."

"Okay. A girl can hope, right?"

"You always need that."

I gave my girl a big swooping hug, and then we drove back in silence to her office.

"When will we see you?"

"I'm always here for you, Nickel, and I'm not going anywhere."

"It was really good seeing you, Uncle Jack. I can't wait to tell Simon."

"Sweetheart, I would never ask you to keep anything from your husband, but I really don't want anyone to know I was here."

"How about I tell Simon but not mention it to my father. Is that okay?"

"Yeah, that's fine. I have to go, Nicolette. I'm so proud of you. Take care of those babies."

She tried to smile, but I saw some tears threatening to fall.

"What is it sweet girl? Why the tears?"

"Why do I get the feeling that this was goodbye? You seem like you are a thousand miles away. Please, Uncle Jack, forget about Michael St. Clair. No matter what happens, he can't hurt me anymore. I let him go a long time ago, so you need to do the same. I have never asked you about your past, nor do I believe you owed me any explanation. Your past is yours to own. We've all made choices that we have had to live with, and I know firsthand what that feels like. I have never asked you for anything, but I'm asking now. Forget him. Go back to Chicago, and be happy knowing that I'm okay. Can you do that for me?"

Her honesty wrecked me. Did she know how I dreamed every night of ending the life of the monster that hurt her? To make him bleed just like he made her? To cause him pain and show no mercy like he did for her? How could I possibly walk away knowing he was still a threat? I had to protect her at all costs. But to look into her beautiful eyes was slaying me to my core. I had to tell her what she wanted to hear to ease her mind. She was trying in earnest to be strong and not cry. God! I couldn't take it to see one more tear fall from my beautiful girl.

I pulled her into my arms and held her until she was reassured. Kissing the top of her head and brushing away her hair from her eyes, I gave her what she needed.

"I promise. Now, no more tears. No matter what happens, Nickel, you never have to worry about not seeing me again. I will always watch over you and will never let anyone hurt you again."

That was all the reassurance I was capable of giving, even if it was a half-truth. It wasn't a lie yet, because I hadn't decided what Michael's fate would be.

Max was calling me non-stop. I ignored every call. I packed up my things and checked out of the hotel, barely arriving on time to catch my flight to Chicago.

After I was settled in on the plane, my mind drifted to Sara. I missed her so much and wanted her home with me. I would make it my mission to find her once I was home.

I called Tommy to pick me up at the airport and gave him strict instructions not to alert anyone of my homecoming, especially Max. His heart was in the right place, but mine was not right now and I refused to be backed into a corner. He was thinking that my actions would compromise the family, but he was wrong. I would never do anything to risk exposure for anyone of them.

"Hey, boss, welcome home."

Hearing him say "home" made me silently ache for Sara. It had been days and no word from her.

Tommy extended his hand to me and grabbed my bag. I remained quiet while he drove me back to my bar. I had him drive around to the side where I wouldn't be seen. Knowing Max, he probably had eyes on me. I knew I couldn't avoid him forever and would deal with his baseless fears tomorrow.

Climbing the stairs to my empty home was torture knowing Sara wouldn't be waiting for me in our bed. My heart was breaking. My mind was tormented. No peace would come to me tonight or any night until Sara was home and Michael St. Clair was dead.

CHAPTER Sixteen

PROOF...

Today was the day Michael St. Clair would pay for his sins. Justice would never truly be served until I silenced him, banished him straight to hell, where he could never hurt Nicolette again. All his time spent in prison, had he even learned redemption? His cell had been flipped and his hidden obsessions had been revealed. His intent was clear. He wanted Nicolette and would seek her out once he was free, but not if I had anything to say about it.

I knew what line I was crossing and what I would lose if caught, but it was a risk worth taking. I would never second guess myself once all was in place to carry out what I should have done years ago. Against Max's warnings, I cashed in all the chips that were owed to me for this favor. I had only one chance to make this happen, and today was the day.

He was on laundry detail. The room was located on the lower floors of the prison, surrounded by loud sounds of the industrial machines. He was taken and bound to a chair with his mouth stuffed with a rag to silence his screams. Nestled out of sight in a dark corner of the room, I slowly crept in and approached him. His eyes were red from the cowardly tears that fell down his cheeks. He was moaning and begging for his life.

I leaned in to his ear and whispered, "Do you remember me?"

He shakily nodded his head. I took in several deep breaths and began my speech, "I could have ended your life that day in the hospital, but I didn't. Every day, Michael, I think about that...I could have, but I didn't. I watched you in the courtroom as you sat there, confidently believing that you would live out your sentence and be free one day. Did you think that, Michael?"

He sat there with no emotion and just listened to me. I circled around him, and he didn't move.

"You made my girl bleed, you PIG. Do you remember what I said to you? Hmm...? **Pigs get slaughtered!** You preyed upon an innocent girl, infected her with your seed, and caused her undeniable pain. You robbed her...YOU BROKE HER! I can't let you live one more day knowing that a free life awaits you outside of these walls, because it doesn't."

I removed his gag and asked him one last question, "Do you have anything to say before death comes for you?"

He looked directly into my eyes and said, "Do it! I can't have her...I'm already in hell."

I plunged my blade into his heart with one strong thrust. I stared into his eyes and watched as his life left his pathetic body. He gasped as his eyes slowly closed. I watched as he bled out, and I let out the breath that I was holding. I swore I would never return to this life again. But after what happened to Nicolette, there was no way I could ever live with knowing that the animal that hurt her still had breath in his lungs.

"Nicolette!" I called out, but no one was here.

I was alone. I was in my bed in Chicago, not covered in blood in a California prison. I spent hour after hour believing that what I saw was real, but I realized that it wasn't. It was a fantasy created by me since the day I found out my precious Nicolette had been raped. It was all I thought about, and it was what made Sara leave me.

I needed her to come back to me. She was the only one that could save me from myself. I pushed up against the headboard and banged my head in frustration. *What are you doing?*—the four words that I could not find the answer to. Could I let him go? Trust that he wouldn't go after my girl again? She was protected out in California, unbeknownst to her, or anyone in Nicolette's circle. Not even my brother knew the lengths I had gone through to watch over her.

Had I known sooner about the photographer, he would have been dealt with, but then again, if we hadn't discovered him, then we wouldn't have known about Michael's proof of his stalking. It was so fucked up, I still couldn't wrap my mind around it. The fact that this sick motherfucker was still obsessed with my daughter made me see red. Clearly, prison had taught him nothing, leaving me with some tough choices to make.

I scrubbed my hands down my three-day beard. I was drained to the point of exhaustion. I was alone with just my nightmares to keep me company. No one knew I was home except for Tommy, best to leave it that way for now. I turned over and forced my eyes to close and begged for sleep to takeover.

Eight hours later, my grumbling stomach forced me to wake up. I lost track to when I ate last. Was it at the marina with Nickel? My legs were wobbly as I finally managed to get up and out of bed. My head didn't feel any better. Looking out from my window, it was dark again, proof that I missed another day while losing myself to my pain and loss.

After a shower, I took my private path down to my office. No one could gain access to me upstairs in my home nor my office without me knowing it. It was a safeguard I had put in place when I designed this place. My family was my first priority to protect, and although I wasn't present on the streets, I still had enemies from my years spent there. My reputation spoke for itself, which stopped would-be assholes for even contemplating striking against me, but there was always a first time for someone believing they could.

I pulled out my bottle of Hirsch and poured myself a drink. Not the greatest decision I could make, knowing I hadn't eaten in a while. I called Tommy on the private line upstairs in the bar, and he answered immediately. I asked him to bring me some food, although I wasn't sure if I could even eat it. The alcohol numbed my pain, and it made it easier to forget the realities of my life.

After listening to one too many voicemails from Max, I deleted the rest. I scrolled down the numbers to see if Sara had called, but she didn't. The picture of Sara that graced my desk was staring back at me. This one was taken on the day she was declared cancer-free.

I could have taken Sara anywhere in the world to celebrate, but she was simple and had chosen a picnic in the park. We spread out our blanket and took in the gorgeous sunny day in Lincoln Park where the Chicago skyline was our view. The warmth from the sun felt like heaven on my face.

It had been a long time that I allowed myself to feel any joy since her diagnosis, but today was different. She never gave up on her faith and knew that she would be okay. The doctors had caught it early enough, but I never allowed myself to believe in a positive outcome. Anytime you hear the word cancer, it sounds like a death sentence, no matter how many ways you spin it.

Sara made me believe that we would make it, and once again she was right. She was leaning back on her elbows, basking in the sun. Her floppy hat was moving with the wind, and she never looked more beautiful. I took a couple of pictures of her before she covered her face with her hat. She always blushed and had that natural rosiness to her cheeks. I never wanted her to hide, especially around me. She was my angel, and I would never want anyone else.

"Please come back to me baby, please."

The knock at my door was my saving grace.

"Come in," I called out as I placed her picture back in its rightful place. "Oh, fuck! Not today, Max."

"I'm sorry, boss. He followed me down here," Tommy said regretfully. I waved him off to go back to the bar while I watched Max enter and place down my food tray.

"Where the fuck have you been?" he shouted as he slammed the door behind Tommy.

"Excuse me? Be careful, Max. You don't want to go there with me."

"Yeah, I do my friend. I'm already there and have been since you left for California. You've been gone for days and with no word to me. Get it together, Jackie, and pull yourself out of this hole that you are drowning in."

"I'm trying, Max."

"Well, try harder, because you are doing a piss poor job at convincing me that you are okay. You can't be going off the grid like this, Jack! Not one person other than your boy upstairs knew where you were. How the hell did you get back here without me seeing you?"

"Don't worry about it. I'm here now, so calm the fuck down and let me eat in peace."

"Fine! I'll wait. You look like shit by the way."

I said nothing in return and silently ate my steak. I took my time and savored every bite. Once I was done, I opened the Chianti that Tommy had chosen to accompany my meal. It was my favorite wine that I always enjoyed sharing with Sara, but I wasn't going there at the moment, not when I had Max staring me down. I swear this guy can pass for a statue. His eyes weren't even moving.

"Okay, Max, say your peace and then get the hell out."

"I won't be dismissed again, Jack, so maybe you should watch your tone. When did you get back into town?" he asked with a calmer but stern tone.

"A couple of nights ago. Why do you care?"

"Because I care about you, Jack, and I can't protect you if I don't know where the hell you are."

"Protect me from what? There is nothing I can't handle, Max. I've traveled down the darkest paths of hell and have come out the other side. I can handle things on my own, so drop it."

"No, you can't, Jack! And you haven't been able to in a long time. You proved that with the photographer you let go. Your judgment is clouded. You are not thinking clearly and are putting yourself in an unsafe position, so I took care of it."

I grabbed hold of my desk, nearly white knuckling it and leaned toward Max.

"What did you take care of?"

"Something that should have been done years ago. Your world is righted again, my friend, and now you will sleep easier knowing that justice has finally been served."

"No! Please tell me you didn't do what I think you did."

"Not me personally, but it is done, Jack. He was a threat and needed to be silenced once and for all. Here, take it. The proof is all there in black and white."

I took the folder that Max handed to me and crashed back down into my chair. Prison statuses on Michael St. Clair. Although he was denied parole requests at the time of his sentencing, his father and new lawyer had that overturned. A scheduled meeting was to take place next month. I flipped through more papers, and that's when my eyes focused on two sheets of phone transcripts, prison calls to his father all detailing his manic delusions about Nicolette. The first one read:

```
    "I'll be free soon, father, and then I will
go to her."
    "Michael, please, you must stop this now.
You never had a future with Nicolette, and you
never will. For years I have begged you to
stop this madness, but yet you continue to
darken your thoughts, which will only lead to
more heartache for you."
    "You're wrong father. I've had time to re-
flect these last years, and it doesn't matter
what she said to me that day in the courtroom.
I forgive her. We will begin again far away
```

from Simon, her family, and all who have stood in our way from being together. She will have my child again inside of her body, and then I will know that she will never leave me again."

"Michael, I can't help you anymore. I've done all I can and yet you still won't listen to me. I'm finished here, and you are on your own, my son."

There were several more pages with conversations like this one with his father, and then all communication with his father dropped off. The last transcription I read was between Michael, and his lawyer:

"I will join you at your hearing, but your father will not be in attendance. If, by the grace of God, you are released, then you will be remanded to a private facility in Europe where your father has made arrangements for you to get well. Is this clear to you?"

"Crystal, but I thought I was cut off? Now the old man wants to help me? He just can't decide when it's convenient for him to be a father to me and when it's not. I am a grown man, and I don't need his help. I will be fine on my own."

"And I guess that goes without saying that you will also be fine without his money? Because it's his financial support that pays my retainer, Michael, and without your father's support and mine, then you don't have a chance in hell at making it on the outside if you are released."

"Wrong again. I will survive, because I

will have Nicolette back where she belongs...
with me! Once I have her, you will never have
to worry about me again, and you can tell that
to my father."

That was the last of the conversation transcripts. I was right. I
had been all along, and not one person believed me. He never
changed or even tried to reform into a better man. He spent all this
time plotting his way back to my girl, and I had the proof sitting here
in my hands.

Max was silently looking at me, waiting for a reaction. I was
numb again, and it wasn't from alcohol. The pounding from my
heart was making my chest hurt. He didn't say the words, but at that
moment looking at Max, I knew...Michael St. Clair was dead.

"Max, I..."

"It's done, Jack. Let's leave sleeping dogs where they lie."

"NO!" I screamed.

I knocked over my desk, sending everything on it, including
Sara's picture, to smash on the floor. Max toppled over in shock as I
lunged for him.

"You sonofabitch! You took my choice away from me, and you
can tell me that it's over? It's just beginning, Max. How the hell
could you betray me like this? You knew above anyone else how
much I have been tortured over him, and I was prevaricating the in-
evitable. He was never to be touched by anyone but me! And you
took that away from me! How could you, Max?"

My hands were fisted on his collar as he tried to break free, but
he was no match against me. I released him with a shove to the wall.
He slumped down to catch his breath.

"Jackie, please understand what position you placed the family
in. We knew we had to have your back and still protect not just you,
but the family. If something were to happen to you, like getting
caught murdering someone in prison, then the legacies of Johnny
Carlucci would have never let any one of us live. He loved you like a

son, and this is why you are feared to this day on the streets—not just because of who you are, but because of what you meant to him. Even in death, he is still looking out for you."

"Fuck that, Max! I didn't ask him to. And you don't know anything about my relationship with Johnny, so don't even try. What I did for him has cost me in more ways than you can ever imagine. My wounds are still bleeding and will never heal. The one act I could have control over, you took away from me. Michael St. Clair was mine to deal with, not yours."

"Then you should have taken him out when you had the chance, but you let your brother, your wife, and the love you have for your daughter manipulate you, control you, and change you. We still respected you, Jack, but hell if we understood you! This is over. A promise has been fulfilled, and now it's up to you how you move forward. But whatever you do, stay the hell out of California. You need to stay here. Just be seen, and we will take care of the rest."

I had no words left to say to Max. I turned away and leaned against the wall with my palms flat to the surface. He was behind me and stuffed a piece of paper in my pocket. And then the door closed. I took the paper and read the words that were written on them:

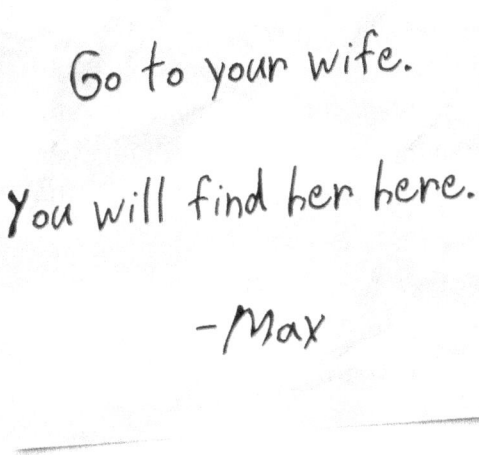

Go to your wife.

You will find her here.

−Max

Another thing he had done for me. Max located Sara, and all I had to do was bring her home. My stomach flipped, and I grabbed the wastebasket, where I vomited everything that was in my stomach, booze and all, until I had nothing left.

Some time had passed and another knock was at my door. Tommy came in and told me the bar was now closed. He easily picked up my desk and began picking everything up from the floor. After removing the jagged pieces of glass from the frame, he handed me my picture of Sara and helped me up.

"What else can I do, boss?"

Another person in my life that wanted to help me, no matter how much I protested to it.

"You know, don't you?" I asked Tommy as he handed me the papers that marked the beginning of the end of Michael St. Clair.

"Yes."

"And? You agree with the decision that was made?"

"I do, and I believe that once you get some rest, you will come to the same conclusion. It's over, boss. It's over."

I got up and took a look around to make sure nothing was missed, and then I turned to leave my office with Tommy following. He was wrong. Max was wrong. I may have not been the one to deliver the fatal stab wound to Michael's heart, but I am far from being absolved.

What I set in motion all those years ago had led me here to this moment. I couldn't undo what had happened, nor did I want to. I had thirsted for this and wanted nothing else. Now that it had happened, though, I didn't feel any better. I was still mentally in the same place I was before Max walked through my door. I still didn't feel satisfied knowing that his reign of terror was over.

It would just be a matter of time before my phone rings, and it would be Massimo thinking that I did it and telling me that I was dead to him, or even worse, Nicolette. How would she ever believe that I didn't break my promise when I had all intent to do just that?

I packed a bag and left instructions with Tommy to take care of the bar in my absence. I had complete trust in him to keep everything in order and running smoothly. I knew I had to get to Sara before the news of this murder would hit the papers. I would not lose her or my family over that piece of shit. He was where he deserved to be…in hell.

Max and the family could rest easy knowing that they carried out a promise I had made. They justified every decision and always had an answer for everything. They never worried about the consequences or the damage they left in their wake. In their eyes, they were protecting me and righting a wrong that should have never happened.

Everything was strategically planned to the very last detail, and all that had to be done was to carry it out. I would never know who did it, because that would be information Max would take to the grave. I also knew that he went against my wishes and had the photographer Eddie Valdez chopped up and used for shark chum in the Pacific Ocean.

Max was wrong. I didn't lose my perspective. My intentions were always clear, but I also knew that I would have never resurrected that part of me had Nicolette never been attacked.

I vowed to be better for not only myself, but for Sara, Nicolette, and the memory of my parents. I swore on their graves, and on all my past sins that I would be better, and I was…until Michael St. Clair came into our lives and wreaked havoc on all of us.

Only two hours from our home is where Sara retreated to. In her letter, she led me to believe that she was leaving to parts unknown, where I could not find her until she wanted to be found. I believed every word, because I wasn't thinking clearly and drank myself into episodes of blacking out. I never thought that she would leave and shatter me. It was easy to lose yourself to the darkness when you had nothing else to live for.

But she didn't go far. She was here at our cabin, not too far from Rock Lodge. We spent many great summers up here with Nicolette, Massimo, and Christina. We had albums filled with pictures of the beautiful memories we shared here, so it would only make sense that Sara now used it as a place to feel safe in and get away from me.

I parked my car down the path so I wouldn't surprise her. It was freezing up here with the grounds covered in fresh snow. Smoke was coming from the chimney. Sara was in there, probably in front of the fireplace reading her favorite book that I had given her. It was a collection of poetry from the greats. From John Keats to William Shakespeare, the book was priceless to her. I would hold her in my arms and just read to her until she fell asleep. I had given it to her when she was first sick, and I promised her that I would add our love story to this collection and never forget what she had given me.

Her love brought me back to life when I didn't think I would ever be deserving of it. I had to prove to Sara that I was that same man that gave her that book. I loved her with all of my heart, and she could have it if she came home with me. I would do anything to make that happen.

CHAPTER Seventeen

HERE'S MY HEART...IT'S YOURS

What the hell am I doing standing out here in the middle of the damn woods freezing my balls off? I stood there and stared at the cabin, willing my feet to move forward, but I was unsure and a little afraid. I didn't want Sara to run any further away. Still, I'd had enough with arguing with myself over remaining out here and watching her or just confronting and fighting with her inside where it was warm.

As I was about to walk up and knock, the front door opened, and Sara appeared on the front porch wearing my Parka jacket. Even though she was mad at me, she kept me close in some small way. At the sight of my beautiful wife standing only a mere few feet away from me, I just wanted to run to her, and that's exactly what I did, but a little slower so not to startle her.

She saw me first, and I froze where I was standing. I remained where I was and gave her time to choose. She would either turn and go back into the cabin, or run straight into my arms, arms that would hold her and never let her go again.

She was silent, and I could hear the sound of my own beating heart. *Come on baby, please show me that I haven't lost you.* Just when I thought all hope was lost, tears began to fall down her cheeks, and she slowly walked over to me. I stepped, she stepped, and then two more strides and she was in my arms crying out the hurt I had caused her.

"Shhh baby, please don't cry. What was our deal? No more crying in this lifetime or the next." I lifted her chin with my finger and locked eyes on her. "I love you, Sara. Please come home."

She tried to step out from my hold, but there was no chance I was allowing that to happen. She wiped her eyes and let out a breath. It was so cold out here, it looked like smoke.

"Can we go inside before we freeze to death?" she said.

I smiled and said yes. I grabbed a few logs for the fire and followed behind Sara. She kicked off her boots but kept my jacket on, curling up on the wingback chair we kept near the fireplace for when I read to her. Sure enough, her book was right beside it.

I threw the logs into the fire and said, "Give it a few minutes, and the room should be toasty warm."

"Thank you, Jack."

"No need to thank me, Sara. I'm just a man that is taking care of his wife, someone he loves very much."

"Keep sweet-talking me like that, and I may let you take me to bed. It's been cold without you, especially at night."

This woman is going to kill me, because if I know Sara, then this is phase one at reminding me what an ass I've been.

"And you don't think our bed at home is not cold without you to lay beside me? As much as I love this game baby, we must not forget the reality of why you are hiding out in our cabin and I'm back in Chicago. You left me, Sara, and I was stripped down and torn apart, night after night without my wife. What do you have to say for yourself?"

"I'm not a child, Jack."

"Stop acting like one then. You ran from me. Do you even have a clue as to how much you hurt me? Baby, I had my apology all planned out driving up here. It was perfect. But now I don't want to say even half of it. I have shared every fiber of my being with you, all of me, even the parts that were too ugly to say, but I did it for you. For years, I was on my own, even when my parents were alive, and I never felt like I fit anywhere but on the streets. For a long time after they died, I just felt abandoned. So when we got married, you promised me that you would never leave me. We would never go to bed angry. We would stay and talk it out no matter how much it hurt, and then we would kiss and make-up. That, my love, was our deal, and you leaving for parts unknown shattered that agreement. So if you want honesty, then there it is. I'm fucking mad at you!"

"Well, I'm fucking mad at you too! That's right, I said it. Don't look at me, Jack, like you are surprised. You know I have been there for you every second of every day we have been together, but I'm tired, and like I told you back home, I want off this ride."

"What are you saying, Sara? You want a divorce? Is that what you are telling me? Because if that's what you want, then you will never get it. I will never break my marital vows to you. You are my wife, and we will never part, even in death. I believe God negotiates."

Her stance had softened, and she looked regretful.

"I don't want a divorce, Jack. I just want my husband back. The man that I married. The man I promised to love forever. The man I promised to never leave even when we fight, who I promised to always kiss good night. I've seen many sides to you, baby, but you've changed over the last few years, and we both know why. Why does everyone else get to move on with their lives, but you, Jack Vanelle, remain frozen in time? The past is slowly choking you to the point where you cannot breathe, and it breaks my heart to watch it. I can't do this anymore. I want my husband back."

"You have me, Sara. I'm right here."

"No, Jack. You are a million miles away from me. I'm so sorry for what I said about Nicolette, but come on, Jack…she's happily married to Simon and finally pregnant. All their dreams are coming true, and they have never allowed her past to hurt their present or future. Why can't you just follow their lead, move on, and be happy too?"

"I will be, baby. I swear it. Just please give me some more time, understanding, and most of all, your love. I need you, want you, and can't breathe without you. Please, Sara, come home."

"…Okay."

"Thank you, Sara, I promise that I will not hurt you again. I'll do better, I swear it."

"I believe you, Jack, and I promise that I will not hurt you again too. I'll do better, I swear it."

Her words gutted me deeper than I ever imagined they would. All the years we've been together, she never hurt me, not ever. She had every right to voice her feelings with me. I always demanded honesty from Sara and would never accept anything less. She had reached her limit—deep down I saw it coming—and yet I made it about me…again. This was what I was most sorry for, because I should have fought harder and apologized until my throat muscles burned with regret.

I knew I had to come clean and tell Sara about St. Clair, but I just got her back. Still, if she found out by anyone other than me, then her trust in me would be irrevocably broken.

"Sara, I have to tell you something."

"Not now, Jack. I need you. Please make love to me?"

Would she hate me later after she gave her body to me? Would I disgust her? Would telling Sara about Michael be what would drive her away from me forever? I didn't want to even think about losing Sara ever again, and now she was asking her husband to make love to her. How could I deny my wife?

"Jack, are you okay?"

"I'm better than okay. I have my wife back."

"Then make love to me like a husband should, and let's put these suffering days behind us."

"Your wish is my command. Now, lose the Parka."

"I love this coat. It kept me warm when we were apart. I missed you."

"I'm here now, and you never have to worry about missing me again, because I'm not going anywhere."

"Promise?"

"Always and forever."

We made love for hours until either one of us couldn't move. I insisted on running a bath for her before we slept. I gave her a massage and lulled my beautiful wife into sleep. Her muscles were tight, especially in her neck, evidence of falling asleep in front of the fireplace. I knew my Sara well enough to know that she didn't sleep much when we were apart. I only prayed that she would give me time to explain everything I had discovered about Michael and his death.

The family made a move without my knowledge, and now it was my turn to protect them. I had no way of knowing what kind of fallout I would face once the news of his murder made national news. I wasn't the one who killed him, but that didn't mean I was innocent either.

The bar cabinet was fully stocked. I knew I shouldn't drink, but I needed one to calm my nerves. I couldn't be next to her with these thoughts, so I sat in her chair and just watched her sleep. After days of not being close with her, it would be easy for me to take her again, but I held back with great restraint. I can't fuck my wife into submission no more than I can make her stay if she wishes to leave after I reveal more of my sins.

Some time had passed, and I was feeling the effects from my bourbon numbing my anxiety. I slipped back into bed with Sara and pulled her close to me. I quickly fell asleep, only to dream the nightmare once again.

"Who the hell are you," asked Michael, "and where is my guard?"

I placed a piece of tape over his mouth to silence him. I didn't need to alert anyone of my presence. Michael was bound to the bedrail by his cuff and now silenced by the tape over his mouth. He was trapped by a stranger who was now hovering over him. We were about to get better acquainted. What a coward! A blind man could see the fear in his eyes.

"Now that I have your attention, asking me who I am is not relevant. Do you think you could just rape my beautiful girl and not expect to be punished for it? You are a pig. And do you want to know what happens to pigs?" I said, taunting Michael, as I pulled a blade from my pocket and wielded it in front of him.

"Pigs get slaughtered. Do you think you can hide behind your daddy or his money and still feel safe? You are lucky to still be breathing. Had I known about you sooner, you wouldn't be."

Grabbing Michael by the throat, I squeezed my fingers as tight as I could around his neck. Gliding the shiny steel blade across his cheek, I said, "You will suffer for what you did, but not today."

"Massimo, I will keep my word and not harm Michael St. Clair for now. I will trust that he will be held accountable for his crimes against our daughter. If that happens, then I will never go back on my word. Having said that, brother, if this fucker walks, then all bets are off. I will not hesitate to call my boys in and keep the promises I made to you today. You need to agree with what I have just told you, and I need to hear the words, Massimo. Do you agree?"

"I agree with you, Jack."

"It's over. It's over. It's over."

My body shot up in a frenzied state. I was drenched in sweat, my stomach felt nauseated, and what was worse was Sara awake and watching me wake from a torturous nightmare.

She was never going to understand. She would hate me. She would leave me. I couldn't do it. I wouldn't do it. Honesty between us was never an issue, but when it came to this, there were just some things I had to protect her from. Telling her about Michael would be one of those things.

"Jack, are you okay? What has you so upset? You were screaming out in your sleep, and repeating over and over again, 'It's over.' Oh my love, we are not over. Please don't ever worry about that again. We are here together now and will go home together, I promise. I love you, Jack."

I was still coming down from my nightmare and didn't say anything further about it. Sara kissed me and left to turn the shower on.

I took that opportunity to call Max and asked him if anything had surfaced yet. He told me no and not to worry. He knew where I was and advised me to stay there for the next few days. I hated to use Sara as an alibi to protect myself, but it was a means to an end.

Max and Tommy were right, he was a threat and wanted to hurt Nicolette again. He needed to be stopped. I knew I had to let my past go and stop blaming myself for not being there for Nicolette. I knew better this time around, and as long as my daughter was safe, then any sin was justified.

"Jack, are you joining me?" Sara called out to me from the bathroom.

I shut my phone off and joined her in the shower. She soothingly washed me with an oversized sponge, running it up and down my chest. We always had this intimacy between us, even when she was mad at me. Our intensity for one another could never be denied. I had to believe that I would survive Michael St. Clair, just as my daughter did. For the blissful days that followed, I only thought of Sara, and every moment we shared was cherished, just loving each other.

CHAPTER Eighteen

NOTHING HURTS IF YOU DON'T LET IT...

After I loaded our bags into the car, I took one last look around the cabin and committed to memory all that we shared here over the last few days. We were back on solid ground, and that was what scared me the most. I knew I was living on borrowed time. As soon as we'd get back to our home, Sara would see the news or paper and find out about Michael. My gut was telling me that she would immediately assume it was me, and everything we repaired in our relationship would be destroyed with this bombshell.

I couldn't allow myself to go there right now. She was happy, we were happy. If and when she confronted me with her questions, I would simply deny it, because although I had murderous intentions, I wasn't the one that did it. The question will be: "Did you murder Michael St. Clair?" And I will firmly state "No" as my answer. But if the questions were to shift to asking me if I was privy to it, or know the person or persons responsible, then I feared she would see right through me.

"Hey, what are you thinking about?" she asked as she wrapped her arms around my waist. "Daydreaming of last night in front of the fireplace? Yeah, I enjoyed that immensely, but it's time to burst our bubble and go home to reality. I miss our home, and I've been up here so long, I don't even know what games are on this weekend?"

"That's my girl, always thinking of the restaurant first."

I kissed her hands, but she pulled away.

"I hope that's not what you really think of me. My first and only priority is you, my love, but we do have a business to return to."

"I'm sorry. I didn't mean it the way it sounded. Of course I know the difference. I just wanted to stay in the bubble a little longer."

"I want that too, Jack, and we will come back soon, I promise."

"Okay, I will hold you to that."

She smiled and put her coat on, totally oblivious to my doubts.

"Sara," I whispered.

She turned around and looked up at me.

"I will never forget this time here with you. It has meant so much. No matter what happens beyond these doors, know I will love you forever, and you are the only one that guides me through every piece of my life. Only you, Sara, only you. You have my heart."

"I love you too, Jack. Now, stop making me cry, and bring us home."

The drive home took a bit longer than expected due to the fresh snow that had fallen the night before. I would have loved to stay a few extra days, but Sara was excited to go home. How could I say no when the smile on her face brightened up a room? She spent the last hour on the phone talking to the kitchen staff, going over the current menu and planning a new one.

When we arrived back home, Sara practically sprinted toward her kitchen. She was the boss back there, and we mere mortals who just followed her lead.

I had Tommy collect all the delivered papers and stow them away in my office to go over. I was looking for anything on Michael, but at the moment, there were no reports on his death. It was business as usual for life in prison. To most, it was just another inmate that got shanked, but this wasn't just anyone. I knew not to be too confident. Max was monitoring the chatter, and we were covered here in Chicago. My trip to California was well-documented to some degree, but also my time in Chicago was too. I made sure I was seen, and the one place I was not was near that prison.

"Knock, knock. Are you coming upstairs? The restaurant is starting to get busy, and the bar is already there."

"Come here, baby."

I patted my lap and gestured to my beautiful wife, who already had specks of flour on her cheeks from baking. God! I loved this woman. She came over, sat down, and got as close as she could with my arms holding her tight. I never wanted to let her go. The days without her had worn heavy on my soul.

"I see you've been busy in the kitchen. How about I carry you upstairs, and we get busy in our bedroom? Like…right now."

"What has gotten into you, Jack Vanelle? Maybe I should go away more often if this is what I'm going to get when I get home?"

My hold on Sara instinctively tightened around her. Even joking around, I never wanted her to leave me again.

"I'm sorry, Jack. That was insensitive of me. I didn't mean to bring up something that hurt us both. Forgive me?"

"It's okay, I overreacted." I shifted her off of me to where she was sitting on my desk. I stood over her and held her face in my hands and said, "Sara, I don't know if I will ever be able to explain the depth of my feelings for you. How much I love you. How much I would do anything for you. I will give you anything you ask for, but the only thing I have ever needed was your love in return. Please, Sara, don't ever leave me again. I will not lose you."

"Jack, you scare me when you talk like this. I know how much you love me, because I love you just as much. Why do you think I fought so hard through my cancer? It was not for myself, but for you, my love. Do you remember the night that I woke up, and you were holding my hand?"

"Of course I do. You came back to me."

"I did, and I heard every word you said to me while I was sleeping. You loved me then as much as you love me now. Believe me when I say this to you: even when I am mad at you, I love you. I left to clear my head and give you some time to work some things through. You came for me, and now we are back home together. No more sad eyes, okay?"

"I was desperate for you, Sara. I was out of my mind with worry, and I didn't know if you were coming back. I should have had more faith in you, and in us. You were so angry with me."

"Jack, why are we rehashing this?"

The words were there, but I couldn't say it. I swallowed hard and tried again to tell Sara about Michael, and then Tommy was at my office door.

"Hey, boss, we have a late delivery upstairs for you to look over. It's the wine you had special ordered."

"I'll be right there."

He closed the door behind him. I kissed Sara and took her hand to follow me out, but she pulled back.

"What?" I asked.

"Seriously, Jack? What the hell is going on with you? What has changed in just a few hours since we've been home?"

"Forgive me, Sara, for being a little off now that we are home. I'm sorry if I keep bringing it up, but the last memory I have of you is when you left me. Maybe I wasn't ready to come back here yet."

She softened with my truth and walked over to me. She placed one arm around my waist and the other on my heart.

She said, "I love you. I'm sorry for leaving you. Please forgive me for my anger and silence."

I was drained and didn't have the strength to say one more sorry, so I said it with my actions. I kissed Sara until we were breathless. The storm that was raging inside of me had calmed with her soothing touch. I wasn't going to think or give *him* anymore of my energy tonight.

We walked together upstairs to a very crowded bar and restaurant. My old friend Geno was here with his sons playing pool. Sara kissed me and walked back into the kitchen, and I joined the guys for a game.

The days that followed our blissful reunion were all about falling back into the steady rhythm of our routines. I was a constant presence in my bar, greeting my customers, having hearty conversations with the old timers who had been with me since opening day, playing a round of pool with friends.

I told myself that I wasn't going to hide and fear the unknown aspects of my fate. Assurances were made to me that the nightmare I was living was over and could finally be laid to rest, but a guy like me knew better. Secrets and sins never stayed buried, no matter how hard you tried to believe that. There was always that one person who had a score to settle or was hell-bent on digging up the truth, no matter what it cost them.

Max texted me to meet him at one of the secured safe houses the Carlucci family used when they needed to disappear for a while. I refused Max's request and asked him to come to the bar instead. My office was ironclad secure, and it was the one place I had 100% control in. Even safe houses had been known to be compromised by the FBI from time to time, and I wasn't going to take any chances.

After I assisted Tommy with the morning deliveries and had lunch with Sara, I excused myself and explained to Sara that I had some work to do and calls to make. She accepted my answer with a kiss and left me to be on my own. I hated more than anything to keep things from her, but this was for her own protection.

Max had arrived about an hour later and stepped into my office wearing an expression I could only regard as grave.

"Skip the pleasantries and just tell me," I said as I gestured to him to sit and get on with it. I wasn't in the mood for his hysterics.

"It's hit the papers. Here, look for yourself."

He dropped *The Los Angeles Times* on my desk with the headline: "Death toll rising in America's prisons." I read the beginning, finding nothing too damaging until I reached the second paragraph:

Michael St. Clair, son of former Paramount Studios President, Clayton St. Clair, was found dead in his Los Angeles County prison cell early Wednesday morning. Prison guards were called to inspect his cell after he was not in attendance for the morning roll-call. Prison officials have stated this is an ongoing active investigation which has been turned over to the FBI, where officials from the Los Angeles sector have now taken over the case. Director Timothy Wade declined comment at the time of this report going to print, but his office did release the following statement: "A specialized team has been assigned to oversee and bring to justice the person or persons responsible for the murder of Michael St. Clair."

An unprecedented number of prison murders have been investigated and gone unsolved. The numbers are on the rise where most cases go unsolved and considered closed and filed as a cold case. Their office further stated that they are confident that this investigation will be handled diligently and professionally by their best agents.

I let out a deep sigh and laid my head back on my chair. I was relatively calm after reading the article. This didn't come as a surprise to me. I knew it was coming. What I didn't know was who was leading the charge. I was thankful that there was no mention of Nicolette, but that didn't mean it wouldn't appear later or even be aired on national news outlets. When news of her attack broke through the gag order the prosecutor had in place, Nicolette completely broke down and had to be hospitalized. I couldn't even imagine how she would react to this news now while she was in a critical phase in her pregnancy.

Max was silent and waiting for some kind of reaction from me. What could I do? It was out, and now I just had to wait for any possible fallout. I leaned my folded hands on my chin and only asked one question, "What do we know that is not written in this article?"

By the look on his face, I knew it wasn't good.

"We heard some chatter down the wire from one of our sources in California, and it was confirmed by another in New York. At first we thought the family was being targeted and investigated—what else is new, right? But this is not your typical wiretapping or trying to pinch one of us for the usual bullshit they always hit us with. This is different."

"And? Spit it out already," I demanded as I slammed my hand down to my desk.

"One of the guys in charge, this agent, is not unknown to you, Jackie. In fact, he has a pretty deep connection to your past. He's dirty, ruthless, and is hell-bent on bringing you down. He's been waiting for this golden opportunity, and now with St. Clair getting clipped in prison, he's going to use all he has in his arsenal to get what he wants."

"It was so much more than just a routine hit, wasn't it Max? I didn't ask you for the details, but now I am. What did the contract say? And how gruesome was it? Tell me now, or the years of our friendship will not matter when I rip your fucking heart out!"

"Jackie, come on. You're talking crazy again. I'm your friend, your oldest friend. I did what I had to do to protect you and the family you walked away from—but a family that would kill for you if asked."

I was seething with anger toward my friend. I may have believed his justifications a week ago, but not anymore. He took my choice away from me, and now I would have to deal with the ramifications of his actions.

"I won't ask again, Max. Tell me what the contract stated."

"To make him suffer painfully, but swiftly. It was a clean job, Jack. I know you imagined something greater than what we delivered, but he's gone and will never be able to hurt your daughter again."

"You're wrong, Max. She can still get hurt. Even the dead have the ability to speak. Now answer me this: Who's the agent behind the badge willing to take down the Big Bad Wolf?"

He handed me a photo. I thought I was looking at a ghost. An uncanny resemblance to the boy I once knew. This guy was slightly different, though. He had a coldness to his eyes. I had never seen him before in my life, but something told me that I knew him. After staring at the photo for a few minutes, I looked back to Max.

"Like I said, Jack, he's connected to your past. Meet Agent Dante Marino, the older brother to Mikey Marino. It spooked me too when I first saw the photo."

"Mikey had a brother? How did I not know this? And now he's a federal agent who has been assigned to prosecute me for the murder of Michael St. Clair? Where the fuck has this guy been?"

"From what we have found out so far, they lived together for only a short time, and then the parents split, taking one son each. He soon became a cop after Mikey's death. He's had a promising career climbing the ranks, making a name for himself in Boston and New York before joining the FBI."

"So, what now…come at me and seek revenge for his brother's death by using his position at the FBI? Why now after all of these years? It's not like I've been in hiding. He must know where I've been and who I am? This doesn't make sense at all. Too many years have gone by for him to still be raging war against me, unless he's gutless and knew no other way until now. I guess I now understand why you wanted me out of California so badly. Dammit, Max! You should have come clean with me then and at least given me some heads up, so I could have watched my own back! But you took matters into your own hands, and now I'm fucked seven ways to Sunday. You left me open, Max! The one fear you say you were afraid I was going to do to the family, and now I'm the one exposed."

"I'm so sorry, Jack. You will never know how much. We will do everything in our power to help you."

"You've done quite enough already, Max. If it's all the same to you, I'll take it from here. Please leave, and don't come back here unless I call or send for you."

My dismissal gutted my friend, but his betrayal gutted me. Good intentions don't always play out the way you envision them to be. I would eventually forgive Max, but I needed time to work through my feelings about it and hoped that his actions didn't put my family and all that I valued in jeopardy.

I knew I had a little time left before Sara would discover this news. I left shortly after Max did and left word for Sara that I had some errands to run. She was so busy, I doubt she would notice me gone but didn't want her to worry.

I had some cards to play—I always did—and it was time to roll the dice and hope I wouldn't be denied my request. I had my own black book of contacts and sources I could call on if I ever needed things taken care of.

My hands were shaking to the point where I had to tighten my fists. Tommy had driven me to the scheduled meeting place after I received the message telling me the time and location. I recognized the estate immediately. It was the family home of the late Johnny Carlucci. I was met at the door by his men, who proceeded to pat me down and then cleared me for entrance. Tommy stayed behind but was also searched.

I took a seat in the library and waited for my meeting. I took time to peruse all the pictures that were aligned perfectly with each other. I was even in a few of them. One picture that I recognized immediately was of Johnny, sitting beside me at his table in front of the bakery. This was his favorite place in the neighborhood, he always said, and he asked me to join him for espresso. As I stared at the photo, my memory went back to that day.

"You want something, Jack. I know my boy. Ask me." he said as

he sipped his coffee and lit a cigar.

What would he say when I asked him to do what no one had ever dared to?

"Johnny, please let me go."

He looked at me over his cup and then placed it back down to the table.

Inhaling a few puffs of his cigar, he then answered my request, "Why now, Jack? Why ask for your freedom now? I know why, and it is not of importance to you. Do you even know how much this saddens me that you sit here and easily ask me to cut ties with the man I see and love as my own son? Why, Jack? Why do you hurt me like this?"

I was sick to my stomach over what I did to that poor kid. I knew the days of living this life were over for me, and I just wanted out. I needed to be out before I lost any more of my soul.

"Johnny, I mean no disrespect. You have been very good to me and to my family, but I'm asking for you to let me go and to allow me to live my life without harm coming to my family for my walking away from your 'family.'"

"You know, Jack, no man has ever confronted me and lived to tell about it. You are special, I always knew this. I also always knew this day would come for us, and I would have to make a decision, one that would probably hurt me very much in the end. I meant what I said to you. I love you like a son because you have proven your loyalty to me and to this family, and for that Jack...you are free. But you will always be a Carlucci where it matters most, and I pray you never forget who has your back in all areas of your life today, tomorrow, and all that will follow after that. Are we understood?"

I nodded my answer, but he surprised me by standing up and taking me into his arms. This was the highest display of respect a Don like Johnny Carlucci could give. He had a tear in his eye, but it never fell.

He stood tall and snapped his fingers for more espresso. Just like that, he had flipped his switch, and it was back to business as usual.

Our friendship sustained all of the years that followed our con-versation. I could never change my past but only live with my choic-es and grow to accept them. I refuted when he treated me better than his own sons that were born to him. I couldn't refuse him, nor could I ever ask him not to address me in any other way. I accepted his term of endearment and tried with great effort not to allow it to hurt my father. My father was a proud man, hard working until the day he died. To disgrace his memory by calling another man "father" would have destroyed him. I vowed to never call him anything but Johnny and always viewed him as a loyal friend.

Although at times my soul was tortured for what I was asked to do for him, I also knew what I signed up for the day he shook my hand and welcomed me into his circle of trust. My story had a differ-ent ending than Mikey's, but he also knew what it meant to be part of the family and the consequences of betraying it.

"I hope you are at peace, my friend. It's all I ever wanted for the both of us," I said out loud not realizing I was no longer alone with my expressive thoughts.

"So poetic, but unnecessary, my friend. We both know he's burning in the deepest realm of hell, don't we, Jack?"

"Dominick," I greeted him.

He carried the same build and look of his late father, but he would never live up to the man himself, and he knew it.

"Formal, and again, not necessary. Do you greet all your friends like that? Or is the curt tone reserved just for me? You called me, Jack, not the other way around."

"My apologies, Dominick. I have some things weighing heavily on my mind."

"I don't disagree with you there. Michael St. Clair, yes?"

"The very one."

"The one that raped and brutalized your daughter. That pig should have been slaughtered and hung out by his balls in a field where vultures could pick at him until there was nothing left of him.

Why, after all this time that has gone by, is your revenge carried out now? You always were the complicated one, weren't you, Jack? I never understood you like my father did. Maybe he was the only one that could. Did you know how it distressed him to know that you wouldn't seek retribution upon hearing about your girl? But of course, in his eyes, you could do no wrong. The sun had risen and set upon you. The prince who never accepted the throne even when offered by the king himself. A pity, Jack, it really is, but that's the past, right? You're here now and back where you belong. Father would be so proud."

"Knock it off, Dominick, and enough with the jabs about the past and *your* father. He's gone now, rest his soul. Don't stand before me and disgrace his memory with your bitterness. It is not my fault you were never regarded in the manner you expected to be. You have it all now anyway, so let's not revisit the past again. You know why I'm here, so let's get down to it."

"Oh, Jack, always hostile. Lucky for me, you were searched at the door, or I would have to worry about that famous temper of yours. Have a seat, fix yourself a drink, and help yourself to a cigar. It may help you take the edge off a bit."

"I'm fine."

"Have it your way. You called for this meeting, so talk."

"Dominick, I know we haven't always agreed, but I always knew you to be fair and never to act in haste. Only a handful of men knew why I had chosen to not take the path you all expected me to after my Nicolette was attacked. I had my reasons, and they were explained in detail to your father. I knew that if ever there was a time I needed help, it would be given to me freely. So I need your help with this. Tell me: why was permission granted for the contract to go out on St. Clair without my knowledge? This is what I demand to know."

CHAPTER
Nineteen

DANCE WITH THE DEVIL...

"You *demand*? How dare you come here and utter those words to me after all I have done for you—what this family has done for you. You can be a self-serving sonofabitch sometimes. It really amazes me how soon they forget."

"I never asked you to do anything for me, Dominick, nor did I use any of my friendships to get what I wanted. I was doing just fine on my own, and there was an end date. I just wasn't there yet."

"Bullshit! You were never going to get there, Jack, because you were bullied into a corner by all who claim to love you. Like your weak and pitiful brother who didn't have the balls to take out that piece of shit when his daughter, his precious princess he vowed to always care for, got hurt. He failed her! And he failed and broke his promise to you. That was your first mistake: to believe him and allow him to just take her away from you. Your next mistake was allowing yourself to be manipulated by your wife. You don't have to tell me what she means to you, because I have it myself with my Talia. But, my friend, my love also knows that she can't push me into doing something I don't believe in. To go against everything I am would be destructive to our marriage, and to me as a man. And lastly, your daughter. You made unrealistic promises to an eighteen-year-old girl that you would always be her knight in shining armor."

"You were bullied, Jack. Backed up against the wall, and it has cost you in more ways than they could ever know. They don't want to see the real you, but we do, Jack. This family has always been here for you, even when you turned your back on us and walked away. My father was an old fool, but I am not. So when Max asked me to set in motion what you already had in place, I freely gave him my blessing."

"It wasn't Max's or your call to make. It was mine."

"The hell it wasn't. If you truly believed that, Jack, then why the call to us? Why bring us into your confidence and then expect us to not have an opinion about it? But again, my father did what you asked of him and respected your wishes. I, on the other hand, owe you nothing. Your wishes were respected for far too long, and when Max brought me up to speed and told me everything that was happening, how could I sit back and do nothing? Don't you understand? That sick fuck was never going to leave your daughter to her life once he got out. Oh yes, my friend, it's right there in that file if you cared to read it. He was set to be paroled, free to come and go as he pleased, and his first stop—which is clearly depicted here—was your daughter! I am the head of this family, and I will do as I wish. And to hell with what you agree with."

Same old Dominick. He never beat around the bush. He didn't have to. His mouth had gotten him into trouble more times than I could count. Half the time, I had to bail him out and reason with Johnny on his behalf. Nothing was given to him, he had to take it once his father had passed. He was the first born and was the heir apparent to the fortunes and businesses that Johnny built from nothing. Dominick was more progressive than his father. Modern at times, and aggressive in acquiring the knowledge to keep bringing his family into the new way of thinking and not being defined by the past.

"You are too quiet, Jack. Penny for your thoughts? Did I hit a nerve?"

"You always do, Dominick. You have that way about you."

"What can I say, Jack? It's a gift. I'm growing tired of this conversation. Let's move on. You want to know what happens next. Well, the feds have the case, and they are running full speed ahead with it. Let them search all they want, but they will never be able to tie this murder to you or this family. All our bases were covered by ten layers of cement. On the record, this was just another inmate who got clipped in prison, but to one Federal Agent Dante Marino, it's a way to get to you. Don't look so surprised, Jack. Yes, I am well aware of Marino and his unsuccessful attempts to bring down the Carlucci family. He's tried before and has failed. I am not worried, nor should you be. But there is another agent involved, and one that is new to the mix."

"And who might that be?"

"Let me show you, if you please."

With a few keystrokes, Dominick pulled up the other member of Marino's team.

"Oh, fuck!" I said.

"Recognize him?"

"I do. That's Jacob, Jacob Paulson. My niece's brother-in-law."

"Oh, the plot thickens. So is he also not to be touched, Jack? The list is so long, I lose track sometimes."

"He's family."

"Not my family. He's a cop, and you know how we feel about that."

"Dominick, leave Jacob Paulson to me."

"Okay. For now, I will. Make no mistake, Jack, if he proves to be a problem, he will be dealt with. A long time ago, a message was delivered to him in the cruelest of ways. I would hate to have to do it again. I so detest violence. I'm a business man, Jack, and in business, I have to protect what's mine. An associate of ours working out of Boston did not adhere to the bounds of an agreement that was made between our family. I'm a generous man, but my patience wore thin, and like I said, a message was delivered. It was kind of like the one you sent to Dante's kid brother all those years ago, but this time around, the imminent death wasn't dragged out."

My head was spinning. I felt like it was going to explode with every word that was coming from his mouth. Dominick was getting off on torturing me with these past secrets that were now mine to keep.

"What message?" I asked with my head hung low.

I needed air. This was a mistake on huge proportions. I shouldn't be here.

"Your boy, Jacob, has quite the colorful resume. How does a professional football player go from winning a Super Bowl to becoming an FBI agent? It's quite an interesting read. He wasn't always with the FBI; he was NYPD for a few years. He was also engaged to a fellow cop. She was too beautiful for that, but to each his own, right? Her gene pool is full of law abiding police officers, but there's always one that's not so good in the litter. Care to guess who that is?"

"Stop playing, Dom, and just tell me."

"Watch your tone, Jack, or I won't finish my story. Papa LaRocha himself. Police chief Joseph LaRocha was in bed with us, can you imagine that? All those service medals and pretty symbols he wore on his uniform, and in reality…just another dirty cop on our payroll. Wait, wait…let me rephrase. We *are* trying to stay with the times now. He was expanding his opportunities—some worked out and some he failed at. But it's always the eager ones, the greedy ones that never get enough of the pie, who always want more. So what do we do? We give more, and in return, we expect our requests to be granted."

"Here, Jack, it's all in the file. Chief LaRocha was not a good man. He was perfect at deceiving his family, but we knew the real man who hid behind his badge and fake persona. He was into us for over $700,000 large, and it was going up day by day. He tried to bargain with us, and we countered. More bad choices on his part followed, and then my hands were tied, Jack. I saw no other way to handle him and bring him back into the fold."

The bile was rising up my throat. I was thanking my good luck that we were in the library where I had access to the outside. I nearly broke down the French doors to the patio and puked my guts up to the point of emptying my stomach.

I knew what Dominick had ordered. *He did not detest violence. Liar!* There was nothing he wouldn't do for the brass ring. And if he had a police chief in his back pocket, then there would be no way of letting him go.

He walked out beside me and threw a handkerchief at my feet.

"Here, take this. You are a mess, Jack. Pull yourself together and come back inside."

I wiped my mouth and took a bottle of water off the side bar table. I gulped it down and took another. He was forcing my hand, and I had no choice but to listen.

"May I continue now? Or will I run the risk of you spewing all over my Tabriz carpet?"

"Come again?"

"A Tabriz carpet. I just acquired it through Sotheby's for a selling price of $68,500 dollars. A small fortune to pay for the best. It does go lovely in this room, wouldn't you agree? Oh, I forgot your lack of design. You are more of a baseball pennant tacked to a wall guy."

"Fuck you, Dom, and get on with it."

I was about to punch him in his throat.

"After several attempts at reasoning with Chief LaRocha, he really left us with no choice. At the time, young and eager Detective Paulson was also working the streets and infiltrating many mob owned businesses. All legal of course, but you know this generation. Always looking to bring down who they believe are the bad guys, when in reality, I'm just trying to make a living like the next guy. To provide for my family and the generations that will follow me. Paulson was becoming a thorn in our side, but for the most part, we were always a few steps ahead of him. He was a good cop, but we were better at working the system. You never know who is connected with the other. You see, Jack, let's map out the players in the mix, shall we? The very corrupt police chief Joseph LaRocha was in bed with us. His daughter was involved with Detective Paulson, who is connected with you by your daughter, Nicolette. We needed to show the chief what happens when he refused to follow our orders time and time again. Paulson was becoming a problem, but so was LaRocha. What to do, what to do? Imagine my surprise when I was told that not only our issues with LaRocha were now handled, but the grieving Detective Paulson was not so focused on our ventures anymore."

"You are one sick and twisted fuck, Dominick. How could you take out a hit on an innocent woman? We don't hurt women...not ever!"

"A means to an end. Call it collateral damage if that helps you sleep better at night."

"It doesn't, Dom. It will never be okay to justify what you did. And if your father was alive, he would have never allowed you to be so reckless."

"Well, it's a good thing that he's dead."

"You asshole!"

I grabbed him by his designer suit and wailed on him with all I had. His men broke through the library doors, but he stopped them. The interruption distracted me and Dominick landed a punch to my stomach and a hit to my jaw. I jumped back up to see a gun on me.

"You pull a gun on me, you pussy? Your father is rolling over in his grave right now. Put it down, Dom, and fight me like a man."

He placed the gun on the desk and wiped his split lip.

"Forgive me, Jack. You took me by surprise. I didn't think a man with your legacy would be so sensitive to this subject matter. It must bring up old wounds for you."

"This was a mistake, Dominick. I was wrong to come here, and from this moment on, I will take care of myself without your 'assistance,' thank you very much."

"We will always be here for you, Jack, make no mistake about that. A wrong needed to be righted, and it is now finished. As for Detective Paulson's fiancée, well that was unfortunate, and we have learned from that mistake. And Marino? Well he's never been the most restrained individual. He's a player on both sides. Whatever suits his purpose he tends to show loyalty to. For now, it's the shield because he thinks he can use it to bring you down, but how wrong he is. We won't let that happen, rest assured. You have my word I will not touch Paulson, but do expect a visit from him soon. I expect he is making his way to Chicago any day now. We will monitor from our end and keep you updated with what we find out. I am not your enemy, Jack, and I never want to be. Take this olive branch that I am extending to you as a sign of a promise my father made to you many years ago."

"Call me what you want, Jack, I don't care. You had your relationship with my father, and I had mine. They were different, but not less complicated. I will always put this family first. At the end of the day…will you? I guess time will tell, my friend. Always a pleasure chatting with you, Jack. I believe you know the way out."

And with his impeccable manners, he bid his goodbye to me, and I was left standing in his father's library, feeling like I was about to sink down in quicksand. I was trapped between two families, and at this point I didn't have a side I was on. I was on the outside looking in, feeling completely alone.

Don't give up on me...

All through the drive back into Chicago, I was trying to wrap my mind around all that Dominick revealed to me today. What the fuck was I supposed to do with this keg bomb I was sitting on? That poor girl was gunned down for the sole purpose to gain leverage over her father. I wasn't a fan of cops, but I did like Jacob. Their entire family were amazing people.

It was easy to see how Nicolette fell for Simon. He treated her like gold, and I had no doubt that his brothers were any different with the women in their lives. That girl didn't deserve to be gunned down on a street. I would never agree with Dominick's animalistic nature to do what he did. She's dead because of her father's foolish choices and Dominick's greed for power.

I had blood on my hands, I never tried to deny that. I couldn't live with myself after what I did to Mikey, and that was why I asked to be let go. To this day, I was still regarded as the muscle behind the king. I never wanted any of that. All I wanted was to help my family, and with that, I'd been paying for it for years. After learning about Nicolette, it was like second nature to reach out to Johnny. After all, I still deemed him as my friend. Sara never understood it but kept her judgments to herself. It wasn't like our bar and restaurant was a mob front. Sure, I had some guys from the neighborhood that frequented our place on occasion, but we were legitimate and hard-working people. I left it all behind and never looked back, but did they? I'm not so sure now after listening to Dominick.

And what the hell am I going to do about Jacob? How will I explain it to Sara, let alone Massimo? And most of all to my beautiful Nickel? She could never know this part of me...not ever. I would surely lose her trust and faith in me.

Maybe they were all right. If I truly wanted Michael St. Clair dead, then I would have followed through with my plan to end his life that day in the hospital or shortly after he was sentenced. You don't wait the time I did and still do nothing.

I'd never forget my conversation with my brother that day in the hospital. He begged me to be better for Sara. He told me he loved me. I believed then that I still had humanity within my soul. I couldn't be the man for Sara, and for Nicolette, if it didn't exist. I'd wasted so much of my life obsessing. Massimo was right all along. I should have been better and not allow the devil back in. Sins didn't stay buried forever, and they were all about to come crashing back into my life.

I sent Tommy home after he dropped me off at my bar. I knew shit was going to hit the fan once I walked through the door and faced Sara's wrath. I ignored all of her calls and hadn't been in touch for hours. The bar was dark and appeared to be closed, raising all my alarms to something not right.

I charged up the stairs to our home, taking two stairs at a time. I called out for Sara, but I was alone. Where the hell was she? Just then, I heard a knock to my door. I flung it open to see Ramone, her assistant chef.

"Where's Sara? Why is the place shut down?" I was shouting at the top of my lungs.

He looked like he was about to wet his pants. This was a side of me they never saw if I could help it.

"She's at the hospital, Mr. Jack. We tried to reach you. We didn't know what to do, so we called an ambulance."

He was twisting his cap and keeping his head down. I grabbed him by the shoulders and demanded answers.

"What hospital? Where is my wife?"

"Northwestern Memorial," he nervously answered me.

I shoved him out of my way, grabbing my keys, and flying down the stairs. I put my truck into gear and hit the gas pedal as hard as I could. I had never driven so fast in my life and was surprised I wasn't pulled over in the process. I left my truck in emergency and threw my keys to an attendant working the parking.

"Sir, you can't leave your car here," he called out.

I didn't give a fuck about the valet or where I could or could not park my truck. I was desperate to get to my wife. *Please let her be alright.* I wasn't paying attention to where I was going and somehow got lost. When I finally reached the ER information desk, I was breathless.

"Sara Vanelle, is she here?"

The nurse handed me a cup of water, but I waved her off.

"My wife? I was told she was brought here by ambulance."

She began typing on her tablet, and then I watched her eyes scan whatever she was reading.

"If you wait here, Mr. Vanelle, I will get the doctor on call who is assigned to your wife's care tonight."

She began to walk away from me, and I gently pulled on her arm.

"Please, just tell me. Is my wife alive?"

"I'm sorry, sir. I will be right back."

I fell to my knees and began punching the floor until my knuckles bled. *Where is my Sara?* I began to shake uncontrollably when the nurse was back with the doctor she mentioned.

"Oh my God! Mr. Vanelle, are you okay? Your hands are bleeding."

She went to tend to me as if I cared about my hands. I just wanted answers about Sara.

"Mr. Vanelle, I'm Dr. Phan. Your wife is resting and already in a private room."

"She's not dead?" I questioned him. My tears were falling hard, and to hell with me trying to stop them.

"Sir, she is very much alive and stable. Please follow me into an exam space where my nurse here, Nicole, can bandage your hands. I will explain your wife's condition to you."

I silently agreed and followed the two into the next room.

"Your name is Nicole?" I asked the nurse who was smiling and being kind to me.

"It is, but my friends call me Nikki. Dr. Phan over here insists on calling me by my full name. I don't even correct him anymore."

"My daughter's name is Nicolette."

"That's a lovely name, sir. Okay, all done. No more punching things, okay?"

I didn't even feel the burn from the antibiotic solution. I was numb from hearing about Sara. I may have been in shock.

"Mr. Vanelle, are you with me?" Dr. Phan asked as he began flashing a light into my eyes.

"Yes. How's my wife? Can I see her?"

"All in good time, sir. Let me check you first. Your heart is racing, probably due to a blood pressure increase," he said as he began to wrap a cuff around my arm, and I just snapped.

"I'm fine. Back the fuck off, and just tell me about my wife or I will wrap this cuff around your neck."

"Sir, there's no need to threaten me. I was just trying to help you. Please calm down, or I will have you removed by security, and then where will that leave you?"

I looked at him with daggers in my eyes. Oh, the good doctor doesn't want to test my limits of control when it comes to my wife. I took a breath and counted to five silently. If he didn't tell me by the time I had reached five, then down he would go. Lucky for him, it didn't get to that point.

"Mr. Vanelle, your wife was brought in earlier this evening with severe cramping and side pain. We ruled out appendicitis, and then did further testing by performing an ultrasound. Your wife experienced an ovarian cyst rupture that led to blood and pus in her abdomen. We immediately brought her into surgery. We removed the infected tissue and confirmed she had no others to speak of. She was very lucky, sir, especially with her health history. I can assure you this does not compromise her remission. This was an isolated incident, and to air on the side of caution, we will keep her admitted for the next couple of days to monitor her recovery."

"Can I see her?" I asked again and again.

I knew what I was hearing but would not believe anything until I saw her, touched her, and felt her heart beating next to mine. He closed his tablet and gestured to me to follow him. I nodded my thanks, and I walked into her room.

She looked pale almost white as a ghost. Beads of sweat were lining her forehead. She looked very sick. This was my fault. I wasn't with her when I should have been. I was out chasing my demons when my angel at home needed me. I held her small hands in mine, she was so delicate.

"Please, God, I know I'm a bastard and deserve no mercy, but please, your grace, don't take my Sara away from me. She's the only good I have in my life. She's the only one I will ever need. Please hear me, and don't take her away from me."

I raised her hands to my lips and kissed them ever so gently. I then rose to kiss her lips, which felt like ice to me. I didn't understand how she could look this way. I hit the call button, and Dr. Phan came in right away.

"Something is wrong. Her head is hot and clammy, but her lips are cold."

He called for his nurse, and she began checking her bags of medicine. Sara was spiking a fever, but it was normal with the infection she had in her body. They added another medicine to her IV line and placed cool ice packs to her forehead.

I was incapacitated by my fear. All my memories were coming back to me from when she was sick with her cancer. She was older now but looked like she did then.

"Sir, she's stable. Her body needs time to heal. The next twelve hours may be a little rough on her. She may even wake up and begin vomiting. I am the charge nurse tonight, and I promise to make sure she's as comfortable as she can be. I will call for a cot to be brought in here so you can be close to her."

"Thank you, but I don't need anything. I'll balance all night on my knees if I have to."

"That won't be necessary, sir. Please let me know if you need anything."

"I just need my wife to get well."

"She's in good hands, sir. I promise."

Another promise? I hate that word. It was overused in too many areas of my life.

At this point, the restaurant was very low on my priority list, but Sara would be pissed if I neglected the one place she loved most. I stepped out to call Ramone. He looked wrecked when I left. He was very close with Sara, and they had worked together side-by-side for nearly ten years now. He thanked me profusely for letting him know about Sara. I could hear his wife praying out loud for her in the background. I then called Tommy to let him know where to find me.

My hands were beginning to throb. They weren't broken, only cut up and bruised. *Good move, Jack, once again proving how you act first, think later.*

After I was prescribed a pain pill for my hands, I walked back in to be with Sara. She was sleeping soundly. The cooling packs seemed to be helping with her fever. I kissed her again on her lips and finally felt some warmth.

"Thank you, God," I whispered.

"Jack..." I heard in a faint tone.

I didn't raise my head until I heard my name again, this time sounding louder and trying a bit harder to get my attention. When I realized where it was coming from, I sat up straight and looked to Sara, who was trying to smile at me.

"I'm sorry," she whispered as tears were falling from her face, which just about made me break in half.

"Sorry? For what, my love? I'm the one that should be sorry. I can't believe I wasn't there when this happened. Please, Sara, forgive me for not taking care of you like I should have."

"Jack, you had no way of knowing this was going to happen to me. I didn't even know it. One minute I was standing on a step ladder reaching for my spices, and next I knew, I was in Ramone's arms. He caught me as I was falling from the sharp pain through my abdomen. I didn't understand what was happening to me. My stomach turned, and then I was vomiting all over my clean floors. It was a mess. The entire kitchen staff including Ramone were in complete panic and thought I was dying. I heard Ramone praying as he was calling 911 for me. I then passed out and woke up in the emergency room."

"I'll say sorry for the rest of my life, and it still won't be enough. You must have been so scared."

"I was, but I knew I would be okay. They took me into surgery, where I dreamed of you. We were back at the cabin, but it was summertime and the entire family was with us, including Nicolette and her baby son. Can you believe I'm already dreaming about what she is going to have?"

"Twins. She's pregnant with twins. She just told me her news."

"Oh, my sweet lord! Double the blessing! I am so happy for her and Simon. And when were you going to tell me?" She smiled and pinched my arm.

"Ouch! Easy there, angel. I'm sorry, baby, I forgot. With finding you and then the time we shared at the cabin, the only thing that was on my mind was making you happy again."

"You always make me happy, Jack, even when I'm mad at you."

"I have so much to tell you, Sara, but not here, and not now. I just want you to get well and never leave me."

"You have me for life, Jack, you know that. Now, I'm exhausted and need rest to heal, but our conversation is not over. When I wake up, I fully expect you to tell me about your bandaged hands."

She then slowly closed her eyes and fell back to sleep. *Oh, my sweet Sara. I pray that is true. I would rather die than lose you to the ugliness of my past.*

She slept soundly for the next few hours and then was awakened by Nicole. She had about an hour left of her shift and wanted to check in with us before she left.

"Her vitals are good, Mr. Vanelle. I don't see why she won't be able to go home tomorrow, but I will let Dr. Phan confirm that."

"Thank you, Nicole, for everything. I'm sorry I was so crazy last night. I'm sure this frightened you," I said, as I raised my bandaged hands.

"Working in an ER, nothing surprises me, sir. You take care of yourself now and your wife."

That I can do, always and forever.

Sara said to me, "You look so tired. Jack, why don't you go home and take a shower, get some food into your system, and please rest. I'll be fine."

"If you believe for a second that I am leaving you here on your own, then you don't know me at all, woman."

I leaned in to kiss her as gently as I could.

"Okay, caveman, have it your way. But can you at least call Tommy to bring you some fresh clothes?"

"What? Do I smell?"

"Yeah, a little bit," she said as she winked.

"You are so lucky I can't throw you over my shoulder and take you to bed. I would so kiss you madly and make love to you for hours."

"I love you, Jack."

"I love you more, so much more than a guy like me deserves. One day you will believe it, love."

Tommy stopped by a bit later with some flowers for Sara and clothes and food for me. I was hungrier than I let on to Sara, but she probably knew.

After a quick shower, I walked down the hall to speak with Tommy. He told me Max had been around when he found about Sara. He wanted to know if he could visit her, but I told him no on the account we would be home tomorrow. Sara had to stay three full days to rule out any complications from her surgery. I had called her oncologist after Dr. Phan had told me about the rupture. Dr. Diamante consulted through video chat with Dr. Phan to discuss the latest test results and scan. He agreed with Dr. Phan, and we were all assured Sara would make a full recovery. It was the best news I could receive. The black cloud that was hanging over my head still posed a threat. With the scare we just got through, I didn't have time to think of anything else.

I was tempted to call my brother and Christina to let them know about Sara but decided against it. They loved Sara but hadn't really talked to me since Thanksgiving. Sara being Sara, she called Christina and chatted with her for an hour on the phone. They usually scheduled a weekly call, but when Sara missed it this week, Christina was worried. I was in the background, trying not to eavesdrop. I was wondering if Massimo would want to speak with me, but Sara just said he sends his love. I knew she was lying for my benefit, but then I received his text.

"HI, JACK. I'M SORRY TO HEAR ABOUT SARA. THANK GOD SHE'S GOING TO BE ALRIGHT. I'M SURE YOU WERE PROBABLY OUT OF YOUR MIND WITH WORRY. KEEPING YOU BOTH IN OUR PRAYERS."

— MASON VANELLE, CEO, VANELLE RECORDS AND MANAGEMENT.

I had almost believed his sincerity until I saw the automated signature. Some things never changed. Sara told me that Nicolette and Simon were out of town on some research trip. I was a bit alarmed that in her condition she had been out on the water, but Sara already calmed me down by telling me they were being well taken care of. I would always worry about Nicolette.

We were going home today. Sara was in the shower when I checked all the morning news programs and the papers. I didn't read anything else on Michael, but I still had Tommy double check as well. I knew I had to come clean with her today, despite all that happened to us the last few days. Yesterday, I sidestepped the onslaught of questions when a huge arrangement of roses arrived for Sara. The card was signed personally by Dominick with well wishes of a speedy recovery. Although they were beautiful, Sara declined to accept them and gave them to the nurses' station instead. She didn't like to be reminded of my past, and Dominick was just that. She liked Max, and even Geno, but kept everyone else at a safe distance.

When we pulled into our space, we couldn't miss the welcome home signs in the windows, and the huge banner inside that read "Welcome Home, Boss Lady." She smiled brightly and clapped her hands in delight. Ramone was the first to greet her, and he gave her a single red rose and a rosary to pray on. She kissed his cheek, which made him turn three shades of red, and accepted her gifts. I quickly ushered her through the welcoming committee and carried her up the stairs.

"Jack, put me down. I'm not so fragile that I can't walk on my own two legs."

"I'll be the judge of that, woman! Don't argue with me."

There was a hint of a warning to my tone. She'd scared the hell out of me since the moment I found out she was rushed to the hospital. I was exhausted and in no mood to have my wife test my limits. All I wanted her to do was rest. She knew better than to counter and just let me do my thing.

Her prescriptions were delivered, along with Ramone's special chicken chili that she loved so much. His wife made a loaf of honey-sweet bread to accompany the chili. I made her eat a huge portion, and then I finished the rest.

"I'm full, Jack, no more," she said as she pushed her tray away.

"Okay, I believe you. Take your pill and then get some rest."

"Will you be here when I wake up?"

My heart dropped.

"Baby, what kind of question is that? Of course I'll be here! I'm just going to go downstairs to check on things and do some work."

"I'm sorry, Jack. I didn't mean to upset you. I just didn't want to be alone."

"You are never alone, and I will not be too far away. Here's your phone. If I'm not here when you wake, then just hit the speed dial and I will be up here in a flash. I love you. Go to sleep."

I kissed her forehead, and when I raised my lips off of her, she was already down for the count. Nothing like a homemade meal to knock you out. Ramone would be getting a raise!

For the most part, the restaurant was pretty quiet. Tommy had everything under control. I phoned Max to stop by sometime this afternoon. He didn't second guess my invitation and came right over.

We took a booth closer to the back, where it was quieter to talk. I declined going down to my office. I didn't want to be too far away from Sara. I checked on her before sitting down with Max, and to my surprise, she was still asleep. I felt her forehead for a fever, but she was fine. Dr. Phan explained that getting extra rest would be needed. I was happy to see that she not only was following her doctor's orders, but mine as well. I left very little room for discussion when it came to Sara. I had been that way since her cancer, and even the slightest change in her health always sent me into a panic. This scare was enough to last me a lifetime.

"So Jackie, how have you been...besides the obvious elephant in the room?" Max nervously asked me.

"As long as Sara is okay, I'm okay."

"I'm sorry, Jack, about everything. I know about your meeting with Dominick. He can be a real prick."

"You don't know the half of it, my friend, but I can't really get into all of that now. Any new developments coming in?"

"Nothing on our end. We're keeping an eye on the guy you told us about. Surprisingly, we've come up short on Marino. The guy seems to be off the grid."

"Keep your ears low to the ground and your eyes wide open. I need this guy located."

"You can count on me, Jack. I won't let you down, not ever again."

I believed my friend with every fiber of my being. He did what he had to do for me and the family he had pledged his allegiance to. I wasn't going to question his loyalty. I knew I had it always, and I was the one that was sorry for ever questioning it.

"I trust you, Max, and thank you for always having my back. You may be the only one."

I said my goodbyes to Max and ordered Tommy to close early tonight and post a sign to be closed tomorrow. I needed some quiet time and no interruptions when I finally talked to Sara.

She had slept the day away with little pain and discomfort. She was eating better and taking her medicine, which pleased me to no end. I would take tonight to hold her and then speak with her in the morning.

I had already negotiated with God for Sara's survival. I was pushing my good fortune by asking for more, but I had to try. I held the rosary that was given to Sara. It had been years since I knew what to do with this, but I recited the prayers in the order that was on the prayer card. Then I spoke from the heart.

"Please, God, if tonight is my last night shared with my angel, then please watch over her tomorrow when we part. She will need your strength to get her though all the pain I will have caused her by my lies and deception. I don't deserve her forgiveness, but I will ask for it anyway."

I then remembered mama and her praying to St. Francis for me. She was another angel in my life that I didn't deserve but who loved me anyway.

Climbing onto our bed and pulling Sara as close as I could, I whispered "I love you's" softly into her ear and drifted off into sleep with the calming sounds of her heart beating next to mine.

"Be a better man for Sara, Jack! You are my brother. I didn't understand you when I was younger, but I do now, and I love you for all you did for me. Please, Jack, don't go down that dark road again, not even for our daughter."

"I love you, Uncle Jack. You are my hero. I'm asking you to let him go, be happy again, and smile. I'm going to need you when these babies are born. They are going to love you just as much as I do."

"I'm not leaving you, Jack, but I am taking a break. I need some time to myself to think some things through, and I can't do that here with you. I'm sorry."

"If you were so sorry, then you would stay and talk to me."

"And say what? You are an island, Jack, tucked away somewhere off the coast of nowhere, and I'm not invited to visit. I have tried, but you stopped me at every turn, so I'm going to go to my own island for a while and take a long vacation from our life…or at least what it used to be before Nicolette was raped."

"Jack! Wake up! Come on, baby. Please come back to me. You need to wake up!"

I was startled and sat up quickly, banging my head against the headboard. I screamed, "Dammit! Fuck! I can't do this anymore."

She looked terrified. I couldn't believe we were here again. I kept hurting my wife over and over again, and her look was always the same.

"I'm sorry, Sara. It was a nightmare."

What else could I say? It was the truth. It had been all my life.

"Yes, I know. You were thrashing your body all over the bed. I slipped out to bring you breakfast and found you like this. We need some help, Jack. Don't you think it's time you talk to someone about these nightmares and terrors? You are choking on them and struggling to breathe. I see it, Jack. I live it with you, and I hurt for you. Please, I want nothing more than to understand you. Will you finally talk to me?"

"Yes, I think I have to."

I couldn't eat even if I wanted to. I left her to wait for me in bed while I scolded my skin in the shower. The hot water was nothing compared to the stinging pain of the words forever imprinted on my heart: *Nicolette was raped...I need a favor Jack...You did good...The message you sent, he will never forget...Who are you?...My son would be here with me, and not with the likes of him.*

Just as I expected, Sara was right where I left her. She looked beautiful. She patted the spot next to her and invited me over. I climbed into our bed and found solace in her arms.

"Sara, I need to tell you something, but before I do, I need to ask you to please hear me out completely before you make any judgments or decisions based on what I'm about to reveal. Can you do that for me?"

"I will do anything for you, Jack. You know that."

"Does that include to stay with me forever? To not walk out our door? To fight for what we have together? To see the man before you who has loved you since I was a boy who didn't know any better, but tried to be better for you? This is what I'm asking you, Sara. Can you do that?"

"I will not leave you, Jack, no matter what you tell me."

"You've done it before."

"That was different, and you know why I left."

I did know, but I still pushed her to challenge me.

"Michael St. Clair is dead."

There, I said it. Now I had to wait. She didn't say a word. Not a blink of her eyes, no tears fell, and she made no move to leave my arms. I moved slightly to touch her, and again, she didn't pull away and, taking me by surprise, she leaned in to kiss me on my forehead.

"Thank you, Jack, for telling me."

What?

"You knew? All this time, and you knew about Michael?" I asked.

"I did."

"And you didn't talk to me about it. Why? I've been in hell over this. My greatest fear in life is to lose you, and I've been trying to tell you but I just couldn't. And then you got sick, and all I wanted to do was take care of you."

"I know, Jack, and I'm sorry you had to go through that, but it wasn't my place to confront you with it. It was yours. This has been our problem all along. You close yourself off to everyone around you, including me. You hide behind the walls you put up in the name of protecting me from harm. The only one that can truly hurt me is you, Jack, and it will be by you pushing me away. That reason—and only that reason—is why I left you. That's why I compared you to an island, because that is exactly who you are and what you are. I can't be that person anymore who fights for every crumb you decide to throw at me when the mood strikes. Either we are in this together— and I mean all-in with no walls between us—or we part ways, and I will love you forever, just not *with* you."

"I'll never let you go, Sara, so don't even try. I will tell you any- thing you want to know if it means keeping you here with me. Please just ask what you've been wondering all along."

"I don't have to, Jack, because I trust you and believe you."

"You shouldn't, Sara. I don't deserve you. I invited an angel to the devil's bed a long time ago, and I've been trying every day since then to live up to the man you need me to be."

"You are everything I need. I am not perfect, Jack, and I am far from being an angel. Please don't break yourself down anymore. You are a good man, the man that I love more than anything else in this world. If you had a choice to believe just one thing I have ever said to you, then please believe that I love you."

"You still didn't ask me," I said.

"Do you need me to say it?"

"I do."

"Did you murder Michael St. Clair?"

"No."

"Did you have him killed?"

"No."

"Did you want to?"

"Yes."

She exhaled and left our bed, grabbing her robe and tying it tightly around her as if it was a shield to protect her. Sara walked over to our window and stared out to the city we loved so much. I knew better not to go to her. This was Sara working out all that was revealed to her. My fingers were itching to touch her, but I feared I would be rejected. She would be repulsed by me. I didn't kill him, but I'm just as responsible for his death…his blood was all over me.

I couldn't wait any longer. Her silence was deafening. I threw on my pajama bottoms and walked over to her.

"Please, Sara, talk to me. Say anything."

She turned to look at me with her arms crossed over her chest and said, "You've been tortured and tormented for so long now, Jack, and I've remained by your side doing everything humanly possible to comfort you. I'm not so naïve in believing that I wasn't aware of your past and who I was marrying. I knew, and I loved you despite of it."

"Sara, I…"

"No, Jack, let me say this."

"Can I touch you?"

"No, you may not. Not yet."

"I wish I could have given you children. You will never know how much it devastated me when I was told I couldn't."

"That didn't matter, Sara, not to me. As long as I had you, then I was okay."

"Jack! Let me talk. We should have tried harder for children. We could have adopted. We could have gone back to Italy where you were born. Orphanages all over the world have unwanted children for couples like us to love. You chose me, Jack, above your desire to be a father. I knew what that cost you inside, but yet I didn't do anything to convince you to try. Then you did the most unselfish act of kindness. You gave your brother a chance to have what you desired most: to be a father and have a child with his wife who he loved with all of his heart. Don't you see, Jack? Nicolette being born saved you in more ways than I ever could. That precious girl broke down your walls and found a place in your heart and forever changed you. It was beautiful to experience that blessing with you."

She continued, "You never believed you deserved anything for yourself: not love, not peace, and certainly not forgiveness. Your past is your past, and you have owned up to every sin you say you have committed. You pray to St. Francis when you don't think any-one is close enough to hear you. Well, I have, Jack, and even when I was sleeping, I heard you pray for me but never for yourself."

At that moment of listening to my Sara bare her soul to me, I collapsed to the floor and wept. I just had no strength left to hold on-to. I needed to release this pain once and for all. All of it that had been wrapped around my heart like jagged chains, piercing me every time I tried to break free from it.

Sara's love and honesty had broken through, and I was finally able to come up for air. She kneeled beside me, wrapping her arms around me. I welcomed her touch and felt safe in her arms.

"I didn't do it, Sara. I didn't hurt anybody. I won't sit here and deny that I didn't wish him dead every single day, because I did. I wanted to be the one. I wanted my revenge. I wanted him to bleed and suffer until he took his last breath. I wanted all of that, Sara. What kind of monster does that make me? I'm no better than him."

"That's not true, Jack! Wanting and doing are two very different things. What he did to Nicolette was unimaginable, a brutal act of violence that no woman should ever have to go through. It was never up to you to make him pay for what he did to Nicolette. You must know this, and that fact has been the one constant in your life. It has controlled you all of these years, and it forced you to push all of us away. It is not your fault what happened to her. You are not God, not this invincible force to control every little thing. No one has that power…no one. Your life is *unfinished* and defined by your past. Change it, Jack. Hold my hand, and walk into the light and free yourself once and for all."

"Jack, forgive yourself for your parents. For Mason. For me. For Nicolette, and even for Michael St. Clair. He too was someone's child, and there is someone in the world grieving over him. We are not meant to understand why people do what they do in this short life. All I know is what we have right here now. Forgive yourself, Jack, and together we will handle everything else waiting for us beyond our doors. No more hiding from me. No more running."

"You just don't know what you are saying, Sara. There is so much more to my life than what was said here today. You will leave if you know the truth."

"No, I won't. Dammit, Jack!"

I didn't see it coming, but I certainly felt the sting of her slap against my cheek.

"Ow! My hand. Your face is like a brick wall. Dammit, Jack, that hurt."

And just like that, the black clouds that were above me parted, and there was warmth. The sun was shining down on me, and I allowed myself to feel. Laughter burst from deep inside of me, and the sound of it resonated throughout our entire home.

"Do you think this is funny? I need ice. Ugh! I can't believe you. Men! Here I am, pouring my heart out to you, and you are laughing at me. Stop that!"

She couldn't help herself and began laughing along with me. I needed to feel and believe all that Sara had said to me. She had no reason to lie to me. She was the best thing that ever happened to me, and I would make new promises to her today. I did it once, and I would do it again. I would break free of my past and stay in the sun with Sara.

"I love you, Sara."

"I love you too, Jack. Sorry for slapping you, but you deserved it."

"I did, and it was just what I needed."

We went back to our bed and held each other for the rest of the morning. We were both drained and needed sleep. She was still here after I revealed my darkest secrets to her.

"Jack, are you awake?" she asked.

I didn't answer with my words. I kissed her in return. We couldn't make love, because she was still recovering. So this was the next best thing, just holding her and keeping her body close to mine.

"Jack, what happens now? Are you in danger?"

That woke me up, and I had to bite my lip before answering.

"How do you want me to answer that? Because no matter what I say will hurt you to some degree."

"I believe I have proved I can handle it Jack, so please just say it."

"Very well. As of right now, I'm under investigation by the FBI. The lead agent is someone I have never met but I'm connected to from my past. I'm told he is out for blood and will not rest until I am prosecuted for Michael's murder and the rest of my sins. Shall I go on?"

"Yes."

"His partner is not a stranger to me, as we consider him to be family. Simon's brother, Jacob, is the other agent assigned to the investigation."

"Oh shit! Shall we contact our lawyer?"

"I don't think Sal specializes in capital murder cases."

"That's not funny, Jack!"

"I wasn't trying to make light of it, Sara, but I need a defense lawyer on standby in case this gets bad and I get charged."

"You're not going to be. You didn't do it."

"But I was out in California during the time of his murder."

"What? When did you go?"

"After you left me."

"Oh my God! We always end up back there, don't we? If I hadn't left, then you wouldn't have gone to California. This is my fault!"

"The hell it is! Stop it right now with this foolish talk, and don't you dare cry! We will find a way out of this nightmare, and we will be okay. After everything we've been through to get us here, I will not settle for anything less. Please wait here, I have to show you something."

I threw some clothes on and ran downstairs to my office safe. I found what I needed and went back to our bedroom. This would be hard to relive with Sara, but I vowed to be honest and not hide anything from her. She made some coffee for us and asked me to eat with her. I declined food, but I did accept the coffee.

"What is this?" she asked after I slid the envelope to her.

"It's an outline, a very descriptive blueprint of Michael St. Clair's intentions for Nicolette once he was released from prison."

"No, after all this time he was still obsessing over her?"

"I'm afraid so. I'm sure this isn't all of it, but it's what we have been able to obtain from his cell. I don't know what the FBI has on me, or Michael, for that matter. What this file contains proves beyond a reasonable doubt that it was not over for Michael and his obsession with my daughter. It also can prove that I had the intent to murder him or have him killed."

I watched Sara shakily open the envelope and begin flipping through the stack of letters, surveillance photos, and newspaper clippings, all of Nicolette. She covered her hand with her mouth and began crying.

"This is sick, Jack. How was he able to get away with this? He never stopped stalking her, even from the confined walls of that prison. He never intended to let her go. He was coming after her, wasn't he?"

I put my head down and stayed silent.

"Wasn't he?" she repeated. "Answer me, Jack."

"Yes. He was coming for her."

"And you stopped him?"

"Indirectly, yes."

"Does Nicolette know any of this? Have you told anyone besides me?"

234

"No, she doesn't know. This is why I flew out to California. I needed to see her and make sure she was safe. We talked for hours, and like you, she knew I was struggling. She asked me to let him go and move on with my life. I wanted to believe that I could. I came home to Chicago, and then Max told me about Michael, and then where to find you. I left the next morning, and you know the rest."

"He can't hurt her anymore, Jack. He can't hurt anyone. I'm so sorry you ever had to go through this on your own. I'm here now, and I am not going anywhere. Whatever happens, we will face together."

The next few days, I stayed home with Sara. She finally convinced me to open the bar, which made our customers very happy. The big games would be on this weekend, and it would always be a full house.

Sara's health was doing better, and although I didn't like it, she went back to working in her kitchen. Ramone was the happiest to have his *jefa* back, which meant boss lady in Spanish. She always laughed when he called her that. I didn't mind, because I got to hear her beautiful laugh.

I also made a bold move and called my brother. He was guarded at first, and then we were able to talk respectfully with each other. Of course he knew about Michael, and at the time upon hearing the news, Nicolette and Simon were still away. I was never more thankful to hear that. I hadn't spoken to Nicolette since my trip to California. I expected I would soon. I apologized to him and to his wife, who I asked to listen in when I apologized to my brother. Our disagreements had strained our relationship, and I had to make amends to his wife. Christina and I were always close. She cried happy tears that we were finally able to move past our anger.

Massimo and I didn't resolve everything. We would need many days to accomplish that feat. He never once asked me about Michael and if I had any involvement. All he said was that he was happy he still had a brother in his life, and he would try very hard to make amends with me. The conversation didn't go beyond that, and we ended our call.

Max was my liaison with Dominick. It was better to keep our distance from each other and my connection to the Carlucci family. I couldn't completely cut my ties to them, as it would be almost impossible. I explained all of my reasons to Sara the best way I could. She said she understood, but I knew she was also frightened for us.

Then there was Jacob, and what I now knew about his fiancée's murder. I could never disclose what I knew fully to him without incriminating the family. Her own father's actions led to her death. How could Chief LaRocha look himself in the mirror every day and not want to shove a gun down his own throat?

Tommy seemed a bit off today, kind of restless. I noticed as I walked up behind the bar.

"What's up boss? Can I get the usual for you?"

"You tell me, Tommy. And no thank you to the drink."

"Boss? I'm not sure what you mean?"

"Sure you do, now spill it. You've been cleaning that damn counter for over an hour. It's clean already. You haven't taken your eyes off the front windows, and you are dropping more glasses quicker than I can replace. Answer my question. What's up?"

"I'm sorry, Jack. I'm just worried, and I'm not doing a great job at hiding it. I've seen a black sedan pass the bar every day this week. The plates are unmarked, and I think it's the feds. They have to be watching the building and keeping tabs on you."

"Let them. I have nothing to hide. I run a legal establishment here, and I am very well known in the community. I am living my life out in the open, so let the chips fall where they may. Keep yourself in check Tommy, and don't get overzealous. Capisce?"

"I hear what you're saying, boss, but I don't want no cops up in here."

"Yeah, that makes two of us."

I left Tommy to take care of the rest of the lunch rush. I needed to clear my head and took a walk down to the park. Walking by the waterfront always did me good. Sara was at the Farmer's Market with Ramone, picking up all she needed for her weekend game menu.

On my walk home, I stopped at Geno's place to get a trim and shave. He was old school and still used the blade to get the most precise shave. It felt like home here, just old friends drinking their espresso and telling stories. He welcomed me in with his robust laugh and took care of me.

"You see, Jack, not a spill of blood," he said as he waved the shiny blade in front of my eyes.

"Not today my friend, and hopefully never again."

He patted me on my back and understood the meaning behind my words.

Max met me at the bakery and joined me the rest of the way back to the bar.

"What do we know?" I asked as we walked and braved the cold temps of Chicago.

"Paulson is here, Jack. His flight landed, and I would bet he's making his way to you."

"Very well. I look forward to speaking to Agent Paulson. Any word on Marino?"

"Not yet. He can't hide forever, but we will find him."

"Yes, he can, but Max, if I have taught you anything, it's to know everything about your enemy. Maybe even know them better than they know themselves. He's out there somewhere, quite possibly watching us right now. He's waited a very long time to settle the score. He's smart but dangerous at the same time. He's led by a haunting past that he didn't have control over. He blames me for his brother's death but hates himself more because he couldn't prevent it. I will meet Marino again, I have no doubt about that, but first let's see what the dutiful Agent Paulson has to say."

I arrived back at the bar with Max beside me. I took the back entrance in and then quickly entered my office so I could view the cameras. Sure enough, Jacob was present upstairs in my bar. It appeared he had ruffled Tommy's feathers and needed to be pulled back.

"How do you want to play this, Jack?" Max asked me as he looked at the monitor.

"Let's go back out and enter through the main entrance. Vito is up in the dining room today. You walk in first and pull him aside. I'm not sure what to expect when I get in there, but stay close and out of the way until I signal you otherwise, okay?"

"You got it. Be careful Jack, he's not your family today, he's your enemy."

"I'll be fine, Max. Go on now. I'm right behind you."

I took a deep breath and a shot of my favorite whiskey before making my way up through my restaurant. No sins stayed buried forever, I knew that to be true beyond a shadow of a doubt.

Jacob Paulson was now leading the brigade to take me down. He was a good man, that Jacob. He'd seen enough pain firsthand to last him a lifetime. He was honest like his father and Simon. Honorable to the very core of their existence. He was Nicolette's family. I couldn't hurt him, nor did I want to. I took another shot of liquid courage and left my office to come face-to-face with Jacob.

Just as I expected, Tommy had lost his cool and was now crying out in pain in the middle of my bar. Jacob was helping himself to my beer. *That's balls, I'll give him that.*

I hung my coat and greeted some of my patrons who were watching the scene go down. I gestured to Max. He knew what I needed him to do. I called for a free round of drinks for all to enjoy and then made my way over to the hunched-over Tommy and Jacob. I signaled to Max and Vito.

"Take Tommy to the ER, and get him fixed up."

Max nodded at me, and left with Tommy. I took a seat at the bar and looked back to Jacob, who was breathing fire. Let's hope the beer he helped himself to would calm him down.

"Help yourself, Jacob. We're family, after all. What's mine is yours."

"Really, Jack? Does your guy, Tommy, know that? Judging how

I received such a warm welcome, I wasn't sure he received the memo."

"You never can be too careful nowadays...So Jacob, welcome to Chicago! It's been a long time. What can I do for you?" I asked him while lighting up a cigar, never taking my eyes off of him.

"I think you know, Jack. You seem to have eyes and ears everywhere."

"Nothing wrong with that, son. I protect what's mine. That's no crime."

"Answer me this, Jack: what lengths would you go to *protect* what you say is yours?"

"Seriously, Jacob? That's your big question? Come on, boy! You can do better than that," I said as I blew out a few puffs of my cigar and tapped the ashes into the ashtray before answering him.

I wasn't a man to be fucked with, and when it came to my family, I'd already proven I would do anything for them. It was very easy to flip the switch on my personality and go dark when I needed to. I could not back down to him, show any weakness, or be over-confident with my tone.

I simply said, "What wouldn't I do? Ask any family man that same question, and I would bet everything I own that the answer would be the same. There's no greater thing on this earth than family. I love mine more than anything else in this world, and from what I know of yours, we are cut from the same cloth."

I watched him shift in his seat and grip the edge of the bar. He was clearly strong and easily had a couple of inches on me. I had no doubt that he would have shattered the glass he was holding if he hadn't placed it back down to the bar.

He finally answered, "I don't think so, Jack. We are miles apart."

Short answers. Exactly what I expected from him. He was feeling me out, like what you would do with your opponent in a chess match. I could play this game quite well, in fact. I placed my cigar into the ashtray and looked directly into his eyes.

"Do you have something to say to me, Jacob, or are we going to continue this dance?"

I watched him finish off his mug of beer before slamming it onto my bar. It appeared Agent Paulson had a temper. That's good. Better to have one when taking me on. He got off his bar stool and looked me directly in the eye.

He said the words I expected him to say: "Michael St. Clair."

PART
Three

Jack Vanelle and Jacob Paulson

Two men
Two pasts
Two goals
One connection
One has made a promise of revenge
The other...an oath of justice
Which rival will prevail?

CHAPTER Twenty-One

LET THE GAMES BEGIN...

Jacob

I watched for a reaction from him when I said Michael's name. He was emotionless and not giving anything away. Nicolette wore the same expression when I told her about Michael's murder. He inhaled another puff of his cigar and then placed it down in the ashtray. Jack remained stoic and walked behind his bar. I watched him carefully as he opened up a bottom cabinet and pulled out a bottle of bourbon. Taking two shot glasses from the rack, he filled the glasses and handed me one to take.

"To Michael St. Clair, may he have a long reign in hell," he said as he downed his shot, whereas mine remained untouched. "This is my favorite drink, and it doesn't come cheap, my friend. Don't waste a gift that's been given to you."

"I hardly consider a shot of bourbon a gift, Jack. Thank you, but I will pass."

"Suit yourself, Jacob," he said as he downed my shot and then went back to his cigar. "How long has it been? I would say a few years at least. We missed you over Thanksgiving."

"I was working."

"Are you working now?"

"I believe you know the answer to that question, Jack. Do you wish to continue this conversation here or somewhere more private?"

"Jacob, I have nothing to hide, and anything I say doesn't have to be said behind a closed door. You obviously have come a long way to speak with me, so get on with it. Why should I give a fuck about Michael St. Clair being dead?"

"Don't you, Jack? After all, he is the one who raped your daughter, and a short prison sentence didn't seem long enough at all for him to pay for it. An eye for an eye...isn't that how it goes? But yet, he had been able to do his time without so much as breaking a nail. Did you know that his original sentence was overturned, and he was scheduled to be released next month?"

I waited for another reaction, but Jack was too cool to react to my questions. I needed to draw him out and push him to where he was dying to go.

"Tell me something, Jacob. Is it so easy for you to sit here in my bar and question me about past events that nearly destroyed my daughter? There's no need to deny that fact of her parentage. I'm not sure how you knew this piece of information, but it's irrelevant to me. My brother may have claimed her as his own, but she is just as much mine as she is his. You speak of what happened to her so flippantly that it makes me sick. Where's your loyalty, Jacob? And your compassion for the person you claim to love and have welcomed into your family? Because from where I am sitting right now, you have no regard at all for her feelings and what she endured at the hands of that animal."

"Jack, we seem to be going off course. My feelings for Nicolette are genuine. I love her like a sister and would never willingly hurt her, but personal feelings aside, I have a murder to investigate. One that many of my superiors believe you had some involvement in. This is why I am here. I am not her brother-in-law today. I'm a cop, and I have a job to do. Now if you please, answer my question."

"Since you have made it perfectly clear that this is not a social visit, I will kindly ask you to leave my bar. I will not answer any questions without my lawyers present, and Jacob, if you ever lay your hands on one of my staff again, I will see it as a threat and use whatever is necessary to take you down."

"You do realize you just threatened a federal agent with violence? And here I thought we would be able to have a civil conversation."

"I don't know what gave you that impression. *I* came in to my place of business. *You* were trespassing by going behind *my* bar, and *you* attacked a member of *my* staff who was doing his job. You didn't flash a badge or state your business. You're just a guy in a suit that asked me a question. I will say what I fucking please in my bar, and I don't care how you perceive it. Nice talking to you, but I have a business to run, and you've taken up enough of my time for one afternoon."

"This is not over, Jack. I will be back."

"Yeah, it is, Jacob. You want to come at me with that shiny badge of yours, be my guest. But know this: the next time you come through my door, you better have a warrant. Until then, get the fuck out of my bar, because you are not welcomed here."

I had eyes on me from all directions of the bar. Jack was still cool with his demeanor, but the look in his eyes shifted to ice.

I grabbed my coat and made my leave but not before turning back to him and saying, "You have a day to work-out whatever is going through your mind right now. I will see you tomorrow, Jack, and we can try again at the conversation I intended to have with you."

He was pissed. I knew I had touched a nerve when I mentioned Nicolette. It didn't sit well with me that I had to go there, but I also needed to test the waters with him. It is clear to me that he knows something about Michael's death. I had to re-think how I would have this go the next time we talk.

I didn't want to come in with guns blazing, but his guy Tommy had set me off, and it just went to shit from there. Just a few months ago, my family broke bread with him, and now here I was, questioning if he was a murderer or not.

After I left Jack to brood about what we discussed, I checked into my room at the Drake Hotel. I also had to status with Wade and put a call in to my father and Duffy. It was nearing dinnertime, and the sky was dark. I hardly accomplished anything today with talking to Jack, only to further anger him with my questions. It was still early back in California, and no time like the present to listen to Wade chew my ass out for insubordination due to my recent actions. It would not sit well with him knowing I was spending my time in a grandiose hotel, but I didn't care. It was my dime that was paying for it.

Wade wasn't as reprimanding as I thought he would be. He actually sounded more frustrated with Marino than me. Wade told me that he hadn't been in touch with Marino since we were both in his office. He said Marino was totally off the grid, which is not like him to do, and it violated about ten codes of misconduct on his part. He instructed me to take the lead on the investigation, and when Marino decided to resurface, he would handle him as such. I scoffed with the change of command, because I had already made it perfectly clear that I was working this case without Marino's help.

Wade had a choice to make. He could remove me and assign the case to another agent or let me do what I do best. No matter what his decision would have been, I still would have worked it and would not care what the FBI had to say about it.

Contrary to what Jack believed, I cared deeply for Nicolette and only want to protect her from harm. It was a risk playing that hand so early in the game, but I needed a reaction from him, and his silence was it. He was knee deep in it, and I could give him my hand to pull him out or let him go down in flames. I was hoping for choice one. I needed Jack Vanelle in more ways than I had time to explain to him. I had to try to get what I needed for my case but also for what I was seeking personally.

Marino opened up the door to my past, and no matter what it cost me, I had to find the truth behind Minela's murder and bring down the person who was responsible for it. My next call was to Duffy.

"How's Chicago? Have you made contact with Jack yet?" he asked.

"I have, and it didn't go well."

"Jacob, you have to be smart when talking to a guy like that. You can't lose your shit, and always remember he will be prepared for anything you confront him with. He's been in the game for a long time, and he understands how it's played. If you lose sight of that, then he will always be a few steps ahead of you and that will not be good for you in the end."

"Duff, that's one of my issues with this entire investigation. Jack Vanelle doesn't strike me as fitting the usual MO we profile. You all portray him as this mob enforcer who has a pile of bodies buried somewhere and that the business, wife, and family are all just a front to who he truly is."

"Jake, there was a time he actively ran with the Carlucci family. There is no hiding that fact. We have years of documented proof that can attest to that. He's never been charged with any serious crimes, but that doesn't mean he's not guilty for some either. He was very young when he ran with the crews. We do know from sources that he did maintain a close bond to the patriarch of the Carlucci family, long after he left that life. It was documented up to Johnny's death back in 2009. He died a very old man in his bed with only one person by his side…not his first born, Dominick, nor his other sons, and no advisors. Just one man, and that was Jack Vanelle."

We also can place Johnny at his bar shortly after he returned home to Chicago following your sister-in-law's attack. Now Jacob, care to figure out what they were talking about? I would bet my shield and everything I own that it was how to even the score with Michael St. Clair."

"That may be true, but there is so much more to Jack Vanelle than what your file says. He's like no one I have ever met before, and I've investigated and locked up many made guys. Jack is different."

"How so?"

"I've spent some time with him and witnessed firsthand how he is around Nicolette and our family. He doesn't come off as this ice cold killer. He's devoted to his family, that's obvious, but it goes deeper than that. I can't really explain it all right now. I just know there's more to him than what you believe to be true."

"Well, it's a good thing you're in charge, my friend, because any other agent would have him burned at the stake by now."

"You mean like Marino?"

"That would be exactly who I mean. And before you ask, we've got nothing on him yet."

"What about his wife? Kids? He's got to be talking to someone. He just can't disappear without informing someone he's close to."

"We did reach out to his wife, and all she said was he was on an out of town assignment. His kids are up at school, so I doubt he would make contact with them. He's made no use of his credit cards, and the last place we can place him was at the pier with you."

"Yeah, that was a good time. The bastard pulled a gun on me."

"Yeah, we know. It's all documented in the file. We have your back on this, Jacob. Marino is a loose wire right now, and he's in a whole lot of trouble. You do what you have to do, and I will cover it from my end. I do believe Wade has seen the light when it comes to Marino. He won't hang you out to dry, and neither will I."

"I guess that's good to know, not just about you, Duff, but Wade. I have to go. I'll be in touch."

"Jacob, I know that sound to your voice, and I don't like it."

"I'm fine, Duff. Leave it alone."

"I can't, Jake. You mean too much to me not to be concerned

for you. I know what she meant to you and how her death nearly destroyed you. Get out of your head space now and concentrate on why you are in Chicago. Jake, are you still there?"

"Yeah, I'm fine. I have to go. Talk to you soon."

I heard him shout my name again before I disconnected the call. I didn't need Duffy of all people taking me down memory lane right now. I never allowed myself to forget Minela or what we went through the night she was gunned down in the street.

That bastard Marino knew the truth—all of it—and I needed to find him. He couldn't hide forever from me. Sooner or later, he would resurface with his demands of me. Then I would be ready.

A shower helped me clear my head, and right about now I was wishing I had some of Jack's bourbon to drink. I knew it was high quality and probably would have taken the edge off, but I was smart to decline the shot.

I looked at my phone as I plugged it into the charger. No missed calls or even a text from Zoey. Where was she? And why hadn't she been in touch? I was weak when it came to Zoey Steele. I had this reminiscent need for her, but who the hell knew where she was? She was another one that had fallen out of plain sight.

CHAPTER
Twenty-Two

LEVERAGE...

Jack

No sooner after Jacob had left my bar, Sara and Ramone returned from their afternoon of shopping. She looked happy despite all that I had revealed to her in the days following her release from the hospital. I declined telling her about Jacob's visit or Tommy's "accident" with his knee.

Tommy came back hours later on crutches and in a foul mood. I had given him the time he would need off so he could rest his leg and recover. He argued with me until I finally had to threaten force with breaking his other knee cap. The scene he caused with Jacob was unnecessary, not that I was happy he was hurt, but he could have used better judgment. We had just had this discussion, and then he disregarded my instructions and got a broken knee as a result of it.

Sara bought the story of Tommy slipping behind the bar. Another lie I so easily told, but after all the shit we'd been through the past few days, this lie was a small one compared to the others I revealed. The bar was covered, and so was the restaurant if I would be called away for any reason. I certainly didn't want to involve handcuffs or my wife see me get arrested for Michael's murder.

We sat down to breakfast, and I noticed how tired Sara looked.

"Are you okay, baby? Do you think you overexerted yourself yesterday while shopping? That marketplace is huge, and I have no doubt that you didn't walk the entire square."

"Very funny, Jack. Did I not choose the best vegetables you have ever seen? Those beefsteak tomatoes were huge. I can't wait to make the Calabrese salad with that olive oil that just came in from Italy."

"Sara, you will not deter me from what I'm really asking by talking about food. You know me better than that, so please just tell me what's troubling you."

She let out a sigh, which always told me that I was right to be concerned.

"Jack, why didn't you tell me that Jacob had visited you yesterday while I was out?"

"I didn't want to worry you."

"So you lied instead? Yeah, that always works better than the truth."

"Sara, it's not like that. I said and did everything wrong while he was here, and I didn't want to make matters worse by upsetting you. He will be back. He's made that perfectly clear. If I may ask you a question?"

"Go ahead. You know I don't keep things from you."

Ouch! Just like Sara to hit me where it hurts…my heart.

"Okay, smartass! How did you know about Jacob visiting the bar?"

"I didn't until you just told me. You see, Jack, I too know how to play the game. You've taught me well enough over the years, and I always know when you are keeping things from me. It's not something I'm proud of, but it is what it is. I can't help you if you shut me out. We've talked about this more than once, and I thought we agreed to be completely open with one another."

"We did, baby, but subject matter like murder is not something we can just chat over coffee now, can we? This is not about me and you, so please stop making it out to be. This began with Nicolette and how I chose to handle what happened to her. I made a thousand mistakes on how I behaved, and now I need to fix that. I have Dominick breathing down my neck, which is enough to handle on any given day. Please Sara, not you too. Trust me to take care of you and to protect what we have. I swear it on the memory of my parents that I will not hurt you again. And if I am forced to keep you in the dark, then you must believe it is for your best interest to safeguard, and not to hurt you. Agreed?" I asked with hopefulness.

I reached over to raise her chin so she would look at me. Oh, she was stubborn but knew deep down I was right.

"Agreed, but I don't like it."

"I didn't think you would, but thank you anyway. I have to run now, so can you give me a smile before I go?"

I would only give her to the count of three before I crushed my lips to hers. She looked up at me, smiled, and then kissed me as she placed her forehead against mine.

"Please be careful, Jack. I need you to come back to me."

"I'll be fine, baby. Please don't worry. I love you so much. We will never be separated in this life or the next one we share."

My phone was buzzing in my pocket. That was Max alerting me of his arrival.

"I have to go. Please rest today and don't push yourself. I will call you later."

I kissed her once more and then quickly made my way down to see Max. I couldn't stay one more minute in her proximity without being tempted to take her back to bed. There would be time for that when this was over.

"Hey, boss, where to?" Max questioned.

"Move over. I'll drive today."

He moved to the passenger seat, and I took over.

"Care to tell me where we are going?" he asked.

"You'll see when we get there."

He didn't ask any more questions and just remained silent until we arrived at our destination. While Sara slept last night, I did some work in my office and reached out to a few contacts who could help me locate Marino. He was sly and wouldn't do something unexpected unless he was pushed to do so.

Dominick confirmed that Marino hadn't been seen since leaving New York for Los Angeles, so that would place him last with Jacob, which got me thinking. This guy was hell-bent on nailing me for Michael's murder, but he just upped and disappeared in the middle of an investigation? He was absolutely brilliant at playing both sides, but I needed to gain the upper hand on this guy before he made another move.

There were many players in this game, one being Dominick, who could change everything completely with just a phone call. I knew I could not push him any further than I did when we last talked. He wouldn't care who got caught in the crossfire if it came down to protecting the family and his interests. He'd already proven that when taking out LaRocha's daughter. I had in my possession what Jacob desired most and would be willing to use it for my freedom if it came down to it. Somehow Marino was also privy to this information, and that's what he was using for leverage on Jacob.

No matter what Jacob's message was that he was trying to convey yesterday, his actions were perfectly clear to me. He was acting under the pretense of the FBI, but I was also confident in knowing that if I disclosed what I knew about his dead fiancée, then the subject of Michael St. Clair's murder would be the last thing on Jacob's mind.

Finally reaching our destination, I pulled the car over in a back alley.

"We're here."

"And where's here? The stench in this alley is going to make me hurl my breakfast," Max said as he held his nose getting out of the car.

I took a look at the old decrepit building before me. It had the year 1939 on the side of it. These buildings were mostly used for drug houses and squatters, but it was the memory of this place that brought me here today.

"Okay, Jack, I'm going to break the door down, and you wait for me on the fire escape. He will make a run for it as soon as I take the door down, okay?"

"Yeah, yeah, Carmine, I got it."

"Oh, I know you do, Jack. Don't let the boss down, okay?"

I did what Carmine instructed me to do and waited. Sure enough, he was right, as Mikey Marino tried to flee via the fire escape. He had nowhere to run, and once I was done with him, he couldn't if he tried.

"Jack, where are we?" Max asked again.

"The burial place."

"What the hell are you talking about?"

"Nothing. Just stay close and follow me."

This building only had four floors to it. I was careful where to step and had Max follow my lead. This place was unstable and should have been torn down years ago, but it was to be sold off by the city for development. I never returned to this place after that night with Carmine and Mikey. I wasn't too sure why I was here now, but when I had a feeling, I just couldn't ignore it. I remembered the apartment like it was yesterday. The door had been replaced since then, but the apartment was the same.

I quietly opened the connecting door to apartment 4G and peered in through the crack. It was empty, as I suspected. Once I knew no one was here, I opened the door and stepped inside to where I had been nearly thirty years ago.

"Jackie, why are we here? This place is a hole. Let's get out of here before we fall in."

"Max, quiet! I'm trying to think."

The one room apartment had a mattress on the floor and a chair in the corner. The small bathroom also looked better than it should have. I took a closer look at the mattress, and it appeared to be clean, definitely not one that had been here for a long time. It was recently placed here. It was obvious that someone had planned to be here very soon, or had been already. My gut was pointing me to Marino. He was just sick enough to return to the very place once used by his brother. Mikey took his life in prison, but it was here where his life changed forever by my hands.

It made perfect sense why he was off the grid. Jacob refused him, so now he changed the game and would come at me directly, but who would he use as bait?

The hairs on the back of my neck stood on end. *No. He wouldn't.*

"Let's go, Max. I have to get back to Sara."

We followed the same path we used to get into the building, passing a few less than desirable guys along the way. One was smoking a crack pipe and his friend was ready to introduce himself to us. We didn't exactly look like we belonged here, but Max wasn't playing and opened his jacket, where his gun was on full display. The guy raised his hands up and began backing up. Max wouldn't hesitate to put a bullet in his brain if necessary. Thankfully it didn't come to that, and we safely returned to our car, which was still in one piece.

"Care to explain what the hell this trip was for? Fuck, Jack! That place should be burned to the ground."

"I don't disagree with you, Max. I was acting on a feeling I had about Mikey and his brother. Dante has disappeared, or at least that's what he wants everyone including the FBI to believe. I think his plan to use Jacob to get to me failed, and now he's upped his game. He's hiding in plain sight, and I have a feeling I will soon hear from him."

"He can't touch you, Jack. You know that, right? We will never allow him to get that close enough."

"I know that, Max, but this is not just about me. It involves Jacob too. When I visited with Dominick, he revealed the circumstances surrounding the murder of Jacob's fiancée. The family was involved with the contract that took her out, and it was her father's screw over with the family that made Dominick react and send a message. At the time, Jacob was working some cases that directly involved some Carlucci interests. By taking out the girl, that indirectly stopped Jacob's investigations and brought the police chief back under the family's control. But eventually, that didn't pan out to their satisfaction. After his daughter's death, Joseph LaRocha suffered a complete breakdown and resigned from the force, leaving Dominick with no one on his payroll."

"Shit! You mean to tell me that he sacrificed his own daughter for the mighty green? He should be rotting in a grave beside her."

"Yes, he should. The information I have in my possession is what I plan to use as my 'Get out of jail free card' with Jacob. I will make sure not to implicate the family and instead point all the evidence back to LaRocha. It will be Jacob's call on how to use it from there. I've been where he is, Max, and he will never rest until he sees the person responsible for her death pay for it. To suffer like he has, yeah…I've definitely been there. He's a good man, and from what I know, a good cop, but I would bet everything I own that Agent Jacob Paulson would forget he's a cop to find his own brand of justice. Every man is capable of stepping outside of their comfort zone with the right motivation. Handing Jacob her killer on a silver platter would do just that. Only time will tell if I'm right about him."

CHAPTER
Twenty-Three

HISTORY REPEATS ITSELF...

Jacob

It had been two days since I met with Jack. I took the extra day to investigate the alleged crime family he was connected to. Johnny Carlucci, who they called "King" on the streets, was feared by all men. A man in his position was never challenged, and if you had the courage to go up against him, you had better be prepared for the consequences if you lost. He had great power and was considered to be merciless at times. Sending a young Jack Vanelle to break a boy's back was proof enough of his ruthless character.

This kid was going nowhere fast with the record he already had by seventeen. What made him think that he could ever cross a man like Carlucci and live to tell about it? He probably would have suffered the same fate as Michael St. Clair in prison had he not taken his own life instead.

With Marino still MIA, Wade released all his personal files to me to look into. This was how I discovered that they were split up as children and raised by only one parent each. Dante got the better parent out of the deal. He was older than Mikey and was given a better chance at a future. He graduated high school with honors. He then graduated in the top ten percent of his class from Boston University, then went on to receive his master's in criminal justice. With his accomplishments, it was no wonder how he landed the position he held with the FBI. To head up an entire division was a big deal, but now with his disappearance, he had put all of that in jeopardy.

And for what…to even the score with Jack over what happened with his brother? It was a sad story, I didn't disagree, but trying to blackmail me into being his bitch was not the way to get the justice he sought. I understood what it was to be loyal to your brothers—I had three of my own. I would do anything for them and knew they would return the favor. But this was different. Dante must have felt an incredible amount of guilt for leaving his brother and then eventually learning what had become of him. But to carry this heavy burden on his shoulders, no matter what he'd accomplished, seemed to be just a waste of time.

I meant what I said to Marino back on that beach. Nothing could ever bring his brother back, not even pinning a crime on Jack Vanelle that I'm pretty sure he did not do. It would take an incredible amount of effort to succeed in taking Michael out, and then making a clean escape from a secured prison without going unnoticed. This was clearly an inside job, a very orchestrated one. I would be a fool to believe Jack didn't know about it completely, but for him to be the one to actually commit the crime? No way.

I wouldn't blindside Jack this time. I would call him and ask to meet. If he refused, then he would have left me with no choice but to use my badge and position to get what I needed. After carefully going over my first encounter with him, I now know that was a mistake on my part.

I'd been fucked up in my brain since California. So much information had since been revealed to me, and I felt as if I had been backed into a corner with no escape. I had to gain the upper hand on

Marino, but I needed to find him first.

I secured all my files in my room safe, then proceeded to call Jack, but was stopped with a knock at my door. With my gun in hand, I peered through the peep hole and saw no one there. I slowly opened the door to find an unmarked envelope. I dragged it into my room with my foot until I could put my gloves on, so my prints would not be on the mystery envelope.

I re-locked my door and secured my gun. It was just a plain yellow envelope with no writing on it. I lifted the clasp to see that it wasn't sealed with the usual glue. I was hoping I could lift a print or DNA off this, but whoever left it for me probably covered their bases.

When I opened the envelope, I quickly realized that I didn't have to search hard for Marino. He already knew where I was. And I also understood why I hadn't received any texts or calls from Zoey.

He had her.

I was horrified with what I was seeing: graphic images of Zoey gagged and bound to a mattress. Her eyes were covered with a blindfold, but I could still recognize her beautiful face despite the mascara streaks running down.

That piece of shit had gone mad and taken Zoey to get to me. Why didn't I figure this out sooner? This was why he'd been off the fucking grid, because he was holed up somewhere with my woman, and God knows what he was doing to her.

My woman? Hell yeah, she's mine! And I was going to get her back and make him pay for ever thinking that he could touch her and get away with it. I would not lose her like I did Minela.

Gripping the sides to the table, I wanted to scream out my fury, but I had to get myself in check and think. *Think, Jacob, think!*

He must have been holding her where no one would ever consider looking. I examined the picture closely and saw nothing that stood out. Just a mattress in a corner with nothing around it but a fast food bag. If I could enlarge the picture somehow, maybe I could get a location of the restaurant and map out the area. I called Duffy right away.

"Come on, Duff, pick up."

"Duffy."

"Duff, he has her, man! He fucking grabbed her right from under me!"

"Slow down Jake, and tell me everything. Who are you talking about...Jack Vanelle?"

"Marino! Fucking Dante Marino has kidnapped my girlfriend, Zoey. I just received an envelope of pictures of her bound and gagged and sprawled out on a mattress. I have to find her."

"Okay, Jake, calm down. We will get her back. What do you need me to do?"

"I'm going to send you the pictures he sent me. One has a fast food bag in the background. I need the name of the restaurant."

"Okay, hang tight, and I will call you back."

I was about to explode when my phone rang with Duffy calling me back.

"What do you have for me?" I practically shouted.

"It looks like it's from a local place. It came up on the south side, Wallace Street."

"Thanks, man. I'm on my way."

"Jake! Listen to me."

"What?"

"You're not thinking clearly right now. Girlfriend? I didn't even know you had one, and now you're going to go in unprotected. Jake, you don't know what you are going to find. Are you just assuming that this is Marino? It could be Jack and his mafia contacts. Let me call some agents in to help you."

"No, Duff, they have a code against hurting women. I have a better idea, and now I know exactly who can help me. You keep this off the radar for now, okay?"

"For how long?"

"Until I call you back."

"Jacob Paulson, you be Goddamned careful! You hear me?"

"Always."

I quickly undressed, put on my bulletproof vest, and then retrieved my other guns. I held my shield in my hand and ran my fingers over my badge number. For so long, this piece of metal made me whole again. It was my saving grace after my football career ended. I was at a crossroads and wasn't sure what path to take. Joining the force was almost a calling. It pulled me in, and I felt like I was home. I convinced myself it was all I had after Minela's death, but I was wrong. I had so much more than I ever dreamed was possible. I had a devoted family that had never left my side, when at times I pushed them away. I found something again that I never thought this heart of mine would ever experience again…love. I found it with Zoey. I knew from the moment we met that she was the one that could save me. Now it was my turn to save her. Looking at her picture on my phone, my heart seized with emotion.

"I'm coming, baby, hang on."

I made my way into Jack's restaurant, looking around for him. I immediately took notice of a guy on crutches off to the side of the bar talking to a few of the customers. He saw me and gestured over to another who stepped out from the corner. *Not today, motherfuckers*. I gritted my teeth and bypassed him to get to the bar.

"I need to see, Jack, right now!"

"He's not here, pig."

I was already over this conversation. I pinned Tommy to the bar and shoved my gun in his mouth with my hand on the safety.

"Now listen to me very carefully. I need to see Jack, and if you don't tell me where he is in the next five seconds, then you are not going to be happy with what I do next."

"Jacob! What are you doing?" a woman's voice called out to me, one that was familiar to me.

By now, most of the customers had run out and only Jack's guys were surrounding me. I held onto Tommy and then looked over my shoulder to see Jack's wife, Sara.

"I'm sorry, Sara, but I need to see Jack."

"He's not here, Jacob. I'm telling you the truth. But he should be back any minute. Please pull back your gun and let Tommy go."

I immediately pulled my gun back and shoved him. He stumbled back and fell to the floor, causing him to cry out with his casted knee.

"You asshole! You did it again."

I didn't pay him any attention, and still holding my gun, I heard a very angry Jack enter the bar.

"What the hell is going on here? You!" he screamed as he dropped his bags and charged at me like a freaking bull. "What the fuck, Jacob? You come in my bar and pull a gun in front of my wife?"

Sara placed herself in-between us, stopping Jack with her hands to his chest.

"Jack, he didn't hurt me. He came here to talk to you, and Tommy got into it with him. Please, Jack, look at me."

He was shooting daggers toward me, and his eyes were en-flamed with anger. It took him a minute to hear Sara's pleas, and then he came back to her. He cupped her face, looked at her, and then pulled her to where she was in back of him, securing her in place. He walked over to Tommy next.

"Did you not hear me? Were my instructions not clear to you? This is not a fucking war zone, Tommy, but you've made it one with your hatred toward him," Jack said, as he aimed his finger towards me. "You just can't lose your shit every time a fucking cop walks through my door, and he's just not anyone, he's family. Now get the hell out of my sight before I break your other leg."

I watched Tommy grab his crutches, scramble to his feet, and leave through the back. Jack let out a deep sigh and then held his head for a moment. Sara wrapped her arms around his waist to calm him down. They walked over to the side, where she whispered some-thing in his ear. He looked more composed after that, and then he finally made his way back to me.

Jack once again called his staff to offer the patrons a free round on him, and then it was back to business as usual. The chaos that erupted in the bar a few moments earlier was already forgotten by the customers who remained at their tables. Clearly, by looking at Jack, he could quickly regain his control and command the room with a simple look.

"My office, downstairs," he said as he walked by me, gesturing me to follow him.

I stayed behind to make my apologies to Sara, who dismissed me quickly. She patted my shoulder and walked back into her kitchen. Something told me that Sara had seen a lot being married to Jack.

He tore his coat and scarf off and tossed them both onto a chair. He was clearly pissed off at me for my actions upstairs in his bar. It was the pitbull inside him that once again came at me.

Running his fingers through his hair, he grabbed a bottle from his desk drawer and slammed two glasses down to his desk.

"Drink it this time. It looks like you need one."

He downed his shot and dared me not to take it. I downed the bourbon, and surprisingly it did not burn my throat. He poured another and pushed it toward me.

"Got a warrant? Because I believe I asked you to have one the next time you wreak havoc in my bar. What the fuck were you thinking pulling a gun in my place?"

"Jack, that wasn't my plan to do that, but if your guy Tommy didn't come at me again, I wouldn't have done that. I came here for you because I need your help, and I believe you are the only one that can."

"Two days ago, I was your lead suspect in a murder case, and now what...I'm magically cleared? Come on, Jacob, what kind of game are you playing at?"

"No game, Jack, and for the record you are still a suspect in the Michael St. Clair investigation, but I'm not here as a cop. Please, Jack? I need your help. Don't make me ask again."

He swirled the amber liquid in his glass before downing his third shot.

"What do you need?"

I tossed a pair of gloves to Jack to put on, and then I handed him the photos of Zoey.

"Christ almighty," he said as he examined the photos. His eyes told me that he knew what he was looking at.

"He's taken her."

"Marino?"

"Yes."

"Your girl?"

"Yes."

He handed me back the photos and leaned back into his chair.

"Jacob, before we take this any further, I need you to clarify some things for me, or all bets are off."

"Go on."

"You can't choose what side you're on just to suit your purpose. Two days ago, you came here as a cop, and now, you're a man in love that will move heaven and earth to find his girl. Even asking his enemy for help to do it."

"Jack..."

"Let me finish. I didn't kill Michael St. Clair, and whatever evidence you have on me has probably been fabricated by a very clearly deranged Agent Marino. He's sick and will have no problem going beyond his authority to bring me down. Clearly by these photos, he has now targeted you as well."

"Jack, I can't get into everything I could say right now. I need to find Zoey before he hurts her."

"How do you know he hasn't already?"

"He wouldn't risk losing his leverage over me, not until I give him what he wants first."

"And what would that be, Jacob...me? That's not going to happen."

"Jack, help me find Zoey, and once she is safe, we will continue this conversation."

He hesitated at first, and then silently nodded in agreement. This case had gone beyond what I ever expected. The players were the same, but the game had definitely changed.

I was now joining forces with the man I was sent to build a case against. Marino played his card early, and now because I wouldn't go along with what he had planned for Jack, he snapped and kidnapped Zoey.

I knew that once we walked out this door, there would be no coming back to where my life was yesterday. I was quite possibly making a career-ending decision by trusting Jack, but I had no choice.

Zoey had been taken. My girl was in danger. I was not going to allow history to repeat itself twice in one lifetime.

CHAPTER
Twenty-Four

I'M HERE...COME OUT AND PLAY

Jack

Before leaving the bar, I called Max and filled him in on everything that had gone down the last hour. He was giving me the lecture about Jacob and to watch my back, but after what we talked about in my office, I believed I could trust Jacob to honor our agreement. Max wanted to inform Dominick of what was about to go down, but I wasn't in any position to order Max not to. I understood his loyalties were divided between me and his pledged allegiance to the family. I just wanted him to assure Dominick that I had the situation under control, and I would meet with him as soon as I could.

Max called me back and told me that I wouldn't be going in alone. Dominick refused to play nice, especially now, knowing that I was partnering with the FBI, so to speak. He ordered Max and members from his crew to cover me if it deemed necessary. Most of the time Dominick was a prick, and at times resented the hell out of me,

266

but he would never let me fall if he could prevent it.

I could handle myself against Dante. It was Jacob who I worried for. He was stepping outside of himself and getting angrier by the minute. He'd been here before, and now his limits were being tested once more.

My phone buzzed in my pocket, probably Max telling me everything was in place. I hit the button on my dash, and he was now on speaker.

"Hey, Max, I'm about twenty minutes out."

"That's good, Jack, really good. Just enough time for what I have planned for Sleeping Beauty tied to my bed."

Motherfucker! It was Marino!

Jacob turned red and was gripping my dashboard with such force, I heard a crackling sound. I raised my hand to silence him.

"Hello, Agent Paulson. Did you miss me? You're too quiet. Our usual conversations are always so entertaining to have. Maybe it's because you haven't gotten laid in a while. But no worries, Paulson, and I have taken really good care of your girl. She can be quite loud when she wants to be."

"You sick, motherfucker! I am going to kill you! If you hurt one hair on her head, I'm going to rip your throat out!"

"Well, which is it? Are you going to rip my throat out? Or kill me? It didn't have to be this way, Jacob. Don't say I didn't give you every opportunity to take down the very man you are now trusting to help you. It's her funeral."

The line went dead, and so did Jacob. He screamed at me to pull the car over. He jumped out and began vomiting all over the side of the road. The screams coming from deep inside of him were his rage and his desire to kill Marino. Every man could be pushed to his limits, and Jacob Paulson was no different than the rest of us.

"Drive," he commanded.

"Jacob, he's trying to get a rise out of you, and you've played right into his hands. We are almost there. You must keep yourself in check. Stay focused on rescuing Zoey. That's all you need to do. We

267

don't know what we are going to find once we enter that building. He's crazed, but he is not too delusional to not have a back-up plan, so be careful."

"Jack, whatever happens in there, he's mine. Do you understand me?"

"More than you will ever know."

I parked in the same location where Max and I were last time. I scanned my eyes around to the surrounding buildings and suspected where Max and his guys would be.

Jacob was armed and ready to take Marino out. I was carrying, but nothing compared to what Jacob had. He looked as if he was going to war. He probably was already there in his mind and heart.

It felt like deja vu all over again. Another Marino was behind the door of apartment 4G, only I would be the one to break down the door this time around. Jacob had secured himself on the adjoining fire escape, where he could charge in when the time was right.

I slowly walked down the hallway that would bring me face-to-face with Dante.

"Okay, coward, I'm here! Now show yourself."

No sound came from the inside of the apartment. I opened the door slightly, and immediately the mattress came into view. And just like he said, Zoey was tied down on it. She was on her back with ropes going across her nearly naked body. She only had a thin sheath covering her. Her eyes were covered, and tape was over her mouth.

Jacob is totally gonna kill him. He's so dead.

Looking at this poor girl brought me back to my conversation with Dominick: *"We don't hurt women. Not ever!"*

I knew at that moment that I had to save her and take my chances walking into this trap he had set for me. There weren't too many places to hide in this place. I pulled out my gun and broke down the doors. I checked the closet, it was empty. The bathroom was also clear. Where the hell was he hiding?

I was about to go to Zoey when Jacob crashed through the window, making me pull my gun on him. He had one in each hand and was ready to shoot.

"Jacob! It's me, Jack. He's not here. Marino is gone."

His eyes were glazed over, almost catatonic. I stepped over to him, lowered his hands, and forced him to look at me.

"Jacob…" I said again, and he was back in the room with me. The killer in him calmed down.

He rushed over to Zoey and began cutting the ropes. I tried as gently as I could to remove the tape from her mouth without hurting her. I felt her wrists. Her pulse was weak, but she was alive. Her wrists and ankles were raw and sliced open. She had a bruise on the side of her cheek and scratches along her arm. But this girl was a fighter, just like my Nickel.

"Zoey, baby, can you hear me?" He was crying over her still body.

No response. He picked her up and held her close to his chest, begging her to wake up.

"We have to get out of here, Jack. I need to get Zoey to a hospital."

"Any sign of Marino?" I asked.

"No, I checked the entire fourth floor. He's running again."

"We will get him, Jacob. I swear it on my life."

"Yeah, Jack, that makes two of us."

He carried her ever so gently down all four flights of stairs. I was looking all around for any sign of Marino, but the area was vacant with no one around. Jacob climbed in the back of my car with Zoey still in his arms, while I drove us to the nearest hospital. I called Max, and he told me that the building was covered. He could see everything from where they were positioned, and there was never a sign of Marino.

"Where is he then?"

We were close to Northwestern Memorial, the same hospital I kept bedside vigil with Sara only a short time ago. I hated to go back in there, but I couldn't just leave Jacob and not know what the night would bring for him or Zoey.

Jacob called ahead and demanded we be met with a trauma team at the emergency room doors. He fired off a list of orders to whoever was on the other end of his call. He was in full police mode now. His phone rang again. All I heard him say was that he had her. I pulled up in front, and a team rushed the car with a stretcher to assess Zoey's condition. Jacob ran alongside her as they got further into the hospital.

Max pulled up not a minute later. He looked beside himself.

"What the fuck Jack? Where is this guy? We had the building surrounded."

He kicked the ground, and then it hit me.

"He wanted me there, but not to find him, but to distract me."

"What are you saying, Jack?"

"He's playing us, Max, has been all along. He knew that once Jacob made contact with me, I would begin to piece it all together. He had no way of knowing what Jacob would or wouldn't say to me, so he probably counted on Jacob revealing his duplicitous side, and change direction. It was clear he had taken Zoey, but he only brought her there today to the apartment. She was being held somewhere else until he made the call to me today. Something didn't seem right when we were first in the apartment. It appeared to be staged to look as if someone was hiding out there, but he wasn't."

"Why would he go through all of this trouble of snatching this girl, and then disappear? Don't you think he would want to settle the score with you once and for all, like an eye for an eye?"

An eye for an eye? I repeated over and over in my head until it became clear. The hairs on the back of my neck stood on end again. *No. He wouldn't.*

"We have to go, Max, right now!"

I jumped into my car and made my way to my bar with Max close behind me. I quickly called Sara, and got her voicemail. No one was picking up at the restaurant either.

"Where the hell is everybody?"

I banged my fist on the steering wheel. I called again and again, and no answer. By the time I got to the restaurant, the bar was closed. Something was very wrong. Sara wouldn't have closed this early, unless she was forced to.

"Jack, what's going on? Why is the place shut down?"

"Something is wrong, Max. No one is answering the bar line, or their cell phones."

"You don't think that crazy fuck came here now? Do you?"

"That's exactly what I think. He's in there waiting for me, and holding my Sara and restaurant hostage."

"Jack, you have one piece on you, and so do I. It's two against one. We can take him."

"No, Max. We have to be smart about this. I can access the camera feed from my phone. If I can see where he is inside, then maybe I can get a jump on him while you grab Sara."

I opened up the app on my phone to view the live feed from all the cameras that cover the bar, dining room, kitchen, and corridors. Everything looked in order with no sign of Marino…or Sara. Dammit! The place was empty, which could only mean one thing: he was upstairs in my house…with my wife.

"I'm going in, Max."

"Jack, the guys are on their way. You can't go in there on your own. You don't know what is going through his mind right now."

"I have to get to Sara. Did you see what he did to that poor girl back at that apartment? I can't wait, Max. I've had enough of this shit. If he's hurt one hair on her head, he's not coming out alive."

I entered our home as quietly as I could. The entire first floor was an open floor plan. There would be nowhere you could hide here, which means they had to be upstairs. I crept up the stairs in slow motion until I reached the top, where our bedroom was located. Gun in hand, I opened the door to find the room empty.

"What the hell?"

I searched the entire room, including the closets, and no one was here.

"Sara!" I called out for her. I continued to scream her name until

I made it back downstairs, and that's when Max ran in.

"Jack, you hear the chopper out there? He's on the roof, and he's got Sara with him. Your boy, Jacob, must have called it in. The place is surrounded."

"Fuck! Marino has nowhere to go now but down. He's just that crazy to take Sara with him. I have to get up there."

"Jack, those cops out there are not going to let you on that roof."

"Max, how do you think he got up there in the first place? Use your head. The top floor leads to the roof where Sara has her garden up there."

"Shit! I forgot. I feel like freaking Spiderman today with climbing fire escapes and shit."

"I have to call Jacob, and then I'm heading up to the roof."

I called his cell twice before he finally picked up. His girl was whisked away by doctors, and he was still waiting to hear news. He had called the Chicago FBI Field Office after we left the apartment. He had Marino on tape, and his threat was heard by not only Chicago, but by Wade himself. He was the one that authorized the takedown of Agent Dante Marino by any means of force. What no one anticipated was Marino grabbing my wife to use as his fucking shield.

He was cornered with nowhere to go. I reached the entrance to the roof with bright helicopter lights shining down on me. Jacob was put through to the field commander on the ground and ordered them to hold their fire and not take me out as one of the potential threats. I didn't care what happened to me, though, as long as Sara wasn't caught in the crossfire.

The helicopter pulled back and scanned its lights on another area of the roof. I called out for Marino and then realized where he was holding Sara. We had a small greenhouse to one side and then a rooftop patio that covered the rest. Up here was where Sara came up with the Rooftop Burger. It was the best thing we had on our menu.

"Oh please, God, let her be alright."

There was a strong smell of gasoline. The odor was stronger as I

272

got closer to the greenhouse, and that's when I saw Sara inside, bound to a chair, and surrounded by unlit candles. Standing by the door was Marino, who was holding a flare.

"*Jack be nimble. Jack be quick. Is Jack quick enough to get my candlestick?* I used to love that nursery rhyme. I read it to my brother when he was little. When I was taken away from him, I left the book with him…you know, to remember me by until I could come for him. He was a good kid, Jack. Just fell into the wrong crowd. I tried to help him, but I was young and could only do so much. By the time I was able to, it was too late for my kid brother. He wouldn't get off the streets, Jack. He said he was part of a family that didn't abandon him like I did."

"That destroyed me, Jack. He wouldn't listen to me, and I had no choice but to leave. But I promised to come back for him when I could take care of us both. I didn't get a second chance with Mikey, because of you…Jack. You hurt my brother and made sure he would suffer for the rest of his life. But he didn't have a long life, because of you…Jack. He had nothing left, so he sliced his fucking wrists to bleed out in a dirty, lonely jail cell. They didn't find him until the next morning. He had no blood left in his body, because he bled out and died alone in his bed…because of you…Jack."

"I was already a cop by then, Jack, and I was powerless against you and your precious family. You mobbed up guys think you own the streets, and you have complete control over everything and everyone, but you're wrong, because I'm the one that has all the power now, and will be the one to decide your fate."

He twirled the flare around his fingers, taunting me with it. All he had to do to release it would be to pull it, and my roof would go up into flames, with all of us on it. I slowly took a step closer, and he screamed for me to stay back.

I looked over to Sara. She was so brave, not even one tear fell. He saw me and circled around her.

"She's so pretty, Jack, and her skin is so soft."

"Don't you touch her!"

273

I took a few more steps closer, and he pulled his gun on me.

"And why not, Jack? You took my brother away from me, I see it's only fair for you to lose someone too. I wonder if she would be appealing to you if I burn her face off. Let's see."

He dragged the unlit flare across her cheeks and then her fore-head. He tapped on the cap with his thumb, pretending to flick it open and activate it. Sara didn't make a move and kept her eyes on me.

"Please don't hurt her. She's done nothing to you. It's me that you want, and I'm here Dante. You knew I would come for her, and now I'm here. So let's do this. There is no way out for you. The only way you are leaving is in a body bag."

"Then I'm taking your precious wife with me! And the last memory you will have of her is burning with her flesh melting away and the piercing sounds of her cries."

"I don't think so!"

I charged at him with every bit of strength that I had to seize the flare away from him. The flare was knocked out of his hand, and we both struggled for the gun. I gained the upper hand on him and land-ed punches to his face repeatedly with my both of my hands until my now healed knuckles began to bleed again.

There was movement on the roof, startling us both. He took ad-vantage of the chaos and landed a kick to my head. By that time, Max had freed Sara and got her away from the greenhouse. I was disoriented from the blow, and that's when he delivered another one with his steel tipped boot.

"You're going to die, Jack! My brother, Mikey, will finally be avenged! See you in hell!"

The lights from the helicopter above flashed brightly down on us, and I made my move.

"Not if I see you there first, Marino!"

I grabbed him by his ankles to knock him down and regain my control. I was a street fighter since I could walk. There was no way I was going to be taken out by a spineless fuck who used the threat of fire to fight his battles for him. He would die by my hands tonight for ever thinking he could touch my wife and come at me. With one last punch to his gut, he fell backwards into the greenhouse, shattering the glass all around him. He was covered in glass, blood everywhere, and still taunted me.

"Is that the best you got, Jack?" he said as he spat blood from his mouth.

"No, Marino. I always have an Ace up my sleeve. I win."

The roof was filled with Chicago PD and FBI agents with guns raised and pointed directly at us.

"I guess you lose, Jack."

His laugh was maniacal, but he quickly stopped when he saw what I bent down to pick up. I lit the flare.

"No, Marino. I never lose. Tell your brother hello from me…in hell."

His eyes widened as I dropped the flare in the greenhouse, causing an inferno all around him. I flung my body to the nearest cover, when the entire structure burned with Marino trapped around a billowing wall of flames.

CHAPTER Twenty-Five

OPEN YOUR EYES...

Jacob

She felt weightless in my arms when I carried her out of that hell hole Marino was keeping her in. Her one side was bruised, along with her wrists and ankles. What did he do to her? Thanks to Jack, Marino is now truly burning in hell, taking his knowledge of what happened to Minela with him.

Thank God they reached Sara in time before Marino could hurt another innocent woman. Jack was confident when he set the greenhouse up in flames. He knew the design of it and how it was built. The fire only affected the structure and took out whatever was near it. The rest of the building had been secured. He took a huge chance by throwing down the flare, not igniting the gasoline cans that were nearby.

I guess he thought he would never be free of Marino, had he not done what he did. He acted in self-defense, and other than the destruction of his own property, I doubt Jack will be held accountable for his death, not after all the evidence we had against Marino.

I hadn't spoken to my father since I left California, and on every channel in the waiting room was the scene from Jack's restaurant. It hit the airwaves the minute the FBI was called in.

"Thank you, Duffy, for always having my back."

He made the call before I could and got our boys down there. I reassured my father that I was safe, and when I could, I would call him back to explain all that happened. Simon and Nicolette were okay. They were laying low at their home, taking care of each other. My father said media reports surrounding Michael had only been aired a couple of times on the networks. Wade and his office were remaining tightlipped about the investigation and simply stated that it was ongoing.

Thinking about work was the last thing on my mind. I knew where I needed to be, and that was here with Zoey. The waiting was killing me. I needed to know that she would be alright. I had so much to say to her. I needed to tell her that I loved her and wanted to be with her for the rest of my life. It was right. Every nerve ending in my body was telling me so. She just had to wake up, so I could let her in on my plans to make her my wife.

As I ended my call with my father, two doctors were walking up to me. They looked conflicted, and my heart just sank. Please...not again.

"Hello, Agent Paulson, I'm Doctor Evermore, and this is my colleague, Dr. Witt, who specializes in poisonous cases. Please, let's take a seat."

"Is she alive? Just tell me."

"She is but is in critical condition at this time. We ran blood and took a toxicology panel. She had a high dose of Rohypnol in her system with a combination of Ketamine. Ketamine by itself can prove to be lethal. If she wakes up, she may experience complete memory loss or have difficulty communicating with you. The next twelve hours will be crucial. If she makes it through, then we have some hope. I'm very sorry."

"*If* she wakes up? You're wrong, she will wake up. That girl in there fought for her life to survive. She's strong and will come back to me."

I grabbed the doctor by his collar and said, "You don't give up on her, you got that? You save her and bring her back to me."

I let him go with a slight shove and demanded to see her. He composed himself and showed me to her room.

"Oh shit!" I shouted loudly.

She was hooked up to a machine helping her breathe, tubes everywhere, and bags of medicine hanging above her. Her head had been bandaged, along with her wrists and ankles. Purplish coloring marred her beautiful porcelain skin. Her plump, ruby lips were not touched by that animal. They were still perfect. I leaned down, kissed her gently, and begged her to fight.

"Please come back to me, Zoey. I love you."

Hours turned into three days, and my beautiful girl was still sleeping. Memories of the nights that we shared were a constant presence in my memory. I had no choice but to call Tenley and tell her about her friend. She then called her parents who flew out from New York to be by their daughter's bedside. You can imagine how awkward it was for me meeting them under these circumstances. They knew nothing about me, and when I introduced myself as her boyfriend, they were clearly taken aback.

Her father, Raymond, remembered me from working the Bornarelli case with Tenley. He was cordial with me but still guarded to why his daughter was with me in the first place. I'd seen worse and stricter fathers, so I could handle this teddy bear with no problem. I had a feeling she had him wrapped around her finger, and what Zoey wanted, Zoey got. I only prayed she would still want me when she woke up from her sleep.

As expected, my entire family flew out to join me, all except Simon. Nicolette wasn't cleared to fly, and he would not leave her side for anything in the world. I understood that more than he knew. Tenley and Jagger also flew out to lend their support for Zoey and me. I was so thankful to have family and friends with me. I had hurt them so much in the past with my distance, and I promised my father that I would never push them away again. They were my people who loved me as much as I loved them back. They would welcome Zoey into the fold the minute she awakened. It would probably be overwhelming for her, but once you were loved by a Paulson, you were loved for life.

"Jacob, you look so tired. Why don't you take a walk just to clear your head. I promise I will not leave her," Tenley said, trying her best to get me to move, but I refused.

"Would you leave him if the roles were reversed?" I gestured over to Jagger, who heard what I said and smiled at his wife when she looked over her shoulder.

"No, I wouldn't. Wild horses couldn't drive me away. I'm sorry for pushing you. I'm just so worried for you, and for my best friend. She should be awake by now, right?"

"Every case is different. Don't lose faith, okay?"

"Never."

Jagger held his wife in his arms, as I continued to pray that I would be able to have that kind of affection again with Zoey.

Eight excruciating days had gone by, and still no change. Her parents remained in Chicago, taking a suite at a hotel nearby. My brothers needed to return to their teams, and I didn't stop them. My parents also had to return home but called me every day in hopes I would have some good news soon.

Duffy arrived late last night to lend support and to also update me on the Marino/Vanelle/St. Clair investigation.

"I won't leave her side!" I practically shouted at my friend.

"Look, Jake, take a walk with me. That's an order. You need to get out of this room, because what I have to say has to be said in private."

Duffy wasn't backing down, I had no choice but to go with him. Her nurse promised me that she would not leave Zoey until I returned.

"Make it quick, Duff. I need to get back to her."

"Jake, please take a breath. I love you like a son, you know that, and it's breaking my heart to see you like this."

"I'm fine, Duff, and if that's what you needed to say, then you said it. I heard all the cautionary tales from my father already. I don't need another lecture. I have to go back."

"Stop! Sit down, and I mean right fucking now. If you don't take a breath, then you are going to collapse. We should all be so wise like your father. If you would take a beat and just count to ten, you may still have a shot at living a long life. Damn, Jake, I've never seen you this way before, and we've been friends for a long time now. You need to start talking, and right now."

"Ugh! I'm sorry, Duff. I'm just out of my mind. I can't believe I'm here again. She has to pull through. She just has to. I don't think I can go through that amount of pain again. Yes, we have been friends for a long time now, and you have seen me at my worst, but this is different, man. I don't know how to explain what I'm feeling."

"Try."

"Duff, not everyone has what my brother has with Nicolette, that fairytale love story that you allow yourself into believing is possible. You hand over your heart to the one person you've chosen to spend your life with. And without even blinking, she's gunned down and dies in your arms. I have carried the weight of that death for far too long now, and I just want to be free of the nightmares that replay in my mind night after night. I was completely dead inside, and when I met Zoey, her zest for life was like a defibrillator to my heart. She's the one, Duff, and I need her to survive what that crazy fuck Marino, did to her."

"Jake, I hate to ask, but was she, you know, sexually assaulted?"

"No, and thank God. She suffered enough just being injected with those drugs and tied down like an animal. I've been racking my brain trying to figure out how he was able to get his hands on her in the first place? The last time I saw Zoey was in my hotel room. She was going to shower and then leave for the condo she was staying at. After that, all communication was cut-off between us."

"Come sit with me. I have some things here you need to know."

He looked too serious, which put my overactive imagination into a deeper spiral. I sat down, and Duffy opened up a file on Marino. Pictures of Zoey, coming and going from my hotel room. An address to the condo, and picture of her getting into her rental car. *Fuck!* He was totally sick and out of his mind.

I said, "He admitted to me when we talked in Wade's office that he knew about Zoey, and I flipped out and told him to cut the surveillance on me. I had no idea that he was going after Zoey. Now it all makes sense, because the day I left her at my hotel room was the same day I had my confrontation with him down at the pier. I refused him, Duff, and then he retaliated by taking Zoey. This is my fault, all of it. I pushed him over the edge by not going along with his plan."

"That's bullshit, and you know it. This guy was drowning in his own madness and doing a superb job at hiding it. Your instincts about him were dead-on from the very beginning. I'm just sorry that we didn't see it until it was too late. There's more Jake, much more. You know when he was taunting you about Minela? Well, that wasn't him just messing with you. It was the real deal. He really knew who was responsible for her murder."

"What are you saying? Did he leave the evidence behind? Is it in this file?"

"I'm sorry, Jake, it's not. His home has been flipped by our team in New York. His office has been searched, as well as his hotel room back in LA. We found nothing but this letter to you." He handed me the unopened envelope, where my name was scrawled on the front.

"I can't do it, Duff. This is Marino still trying to pull the strings. He's probably laughing at me from hell."

"Read it, Jake. Maybe he grew a conscience and told you in this letter."

"I doubt that very much, but let's see what he has to say."

Dear Agent Paulson,

I'm dead! I don't know how exactly I went out, but if this letter ends up in your hands, then I have failed at what I set out to accomplish, and that is to get revenge on Jack Vanelle for what he did to my brother.

You have to give it to Duffy for actually being a good cop and finding this letter to give to you. I only wrote one, so feel privileged.

Here's the real reason why I chose you to help me bring Jack Vanelle down to his knees: you are the lone ranger. Tragedy has made you fearless, cold, and dark. Those three attributes drive you to take out anyone in your way, and I thought you would be that guy, but I was wrong. You saw right through me, and even when I manipulated you with allegedly what I knew about your fiancées murder, you still did not yield, which frustrated the shit out of me.

So why the letter? Because I'm a bastard, but I never pretended to be anything else. I was never going to give up the person responsible for your girl's death, because that would prove to be detrimental for my family if something would happen to me. But I wasn't always so self-serving. There was a time when I actually had a heart, and I cared, but when you lose someone whom you love more than yourself, it changes you to the point that you don't recognize yourself in the mirror. If you and I ever had anything in common, then that would be it.

Here's a few breadcrumbs for you to begin the walk to her murderer's doorstep: you weren't the first man in her life she loved. There was another before you, and after her death, he was never whole again.

You are a smart man, Jacob Paulson, I have no doubt you will figure this out. He's waiting for you.

DM...

"Jake, are you alright?"

I couldn't breathe, and I sure as hell wasn't alright. I handed the letter to Duffy to read, and he didn't look any better after he finished.

"We will keep looking, Jake. On her memory, I swear we will find out who is responsible for taking her away from you."

"It's been years, Duff, and we are no closer today than we were back then. Just let her rest in peace. It's over man, it's just over. I think I'm done."

"What are you saying, Jake?"

I couldn't say the words, so I did the next best thing.

"Here. I don't want this anymore."

I placed my gun and my shield down to the table in front of Duffy.

"No, Jake, not like this. You're not thinking clearly. You just read the final rantings of a self-destructive, crazy man and are letting it cloud your judgement. Give yourself some time. Take all the time you need, and then we will talk."

"Whatever, Duff. I have to get back to Zoey."

I secured my gun back into my holster, and clipped my badge back to my belt. These two objects now felt like weights pulling me down, and I just wanted to be free of them and this life I lost myself to. We began to walk out when Zoey's nurse came rushing toward me.

"Agent Paulson, thank goodness I found you."

Oh my God! No, she cannot be dead!

"She's awake. Ms. Steele has opened her eyes, and her doctors are with her now."

I was paralyzed. I couldn't move, and my mind was trying to register what she was telling me. *Zoey's alive?* She made it through and has come back to me, but why can't I move? Will she remember me?

"Jake, didn't you hear her? Let's go see your girl," Duffy said as he tried to coax me to move, but I was paralyzed by my fear.

"Come on, son. It's going to be okay. I've got you."

And then I was walking, with my friend pulling me along.

This would be our defining moment. Zoey's eyes would tell me what I knew I needed to see to believe. Then her touch would come next. I loved the feel of her skin next to mine. Her response would help me believe that her body remembered me. And then I would kiss her and pray she would share my love for her. My desire to make her mine. To love her forever.

Please, baby, show me all of those things.

CHAPTER

Twenty-Six

You have my past...but I need my future

Jack

"What a freaking mess you have up there. No worries, Jackie. You will be up and running in no time," Max said after talking with my contractor. I just nodded at my friend for trying to put my mind at ease.

Burned up buildings can be replaced, not people. To say I was playing with fire was an understatement. I wasn't going to set another predator free to come at me one day and strike again. Marino was deranged in thinking he could ever best me. He never knew how much regret I have carried with me over what I did to his brother, and now he would never know. After he made the decision to take my Sara, all bets were off and my guilt ended.

After the damage was no longer visible to see, the scars of what we went through would still be there, but I hoped in time that we could forget and make new memories here at our place.

I hadn't seen or talked with Jacob since the night we rescued the women we loved. She still hadn't woken up yet from her coma, and I only hoped he would get a second chance with her. The key to his past had been weighing heavily on my mind since Dominick revealed the truth to me. Jacob deserved the truth, and I had to tell him. What he decided to do with it was on him, but I didn't think I could ever look at Nicolette again, knowing what I knew. If this were me, I would want to know.

Dominick had been calling, and wanted a sit down with me. I hadn't allowed Sara out of my sight, but she ordered me out before she went crazy with my hovering.

That was when I made up my mind to go to him and once again ask to be let go. Max drove with me, and the car ride was completely met with silence. He knew what I was about to do. When Johnny agreed to let me go all those years ago, I thought I could still have a piece of them with me, but I was wrong. Mikey Marino and even St. Clair showed me how my past was controlling my life. All the hurt I suffered over Nicolette, and what she went through, I made it my own and allowed it to take over my life.

I had justified my choices, my actions, and what I believed to be right all of my life. What happened to Nicolette was a tragedy. What happened to Michael St. Clair was justice. Sara could find the hope in the hopeless, but not even for her would I ever grieve for him. I held my wife in my arms and watched our dream restaurant nearly burn to the ground, along with all my sins. I set myself free that night and vowed to never think of them again. Today would prove if I could actually do it.

"You okay, Jack?" Max asked as I stared at the mansion before me. It looked almost haunted with the ghosts all around it.

"Yeah, I'm fine. Wait here, okay? I need to talk to Dominick on my own."

"Sure thing, Jack. It's going to be alright. He's an asshole, we know this, but he's not so naïve in his thinking that he can ever gain the upper hand on you. Remember that."

I entered the foyer and was greeted by Dominick. I looked around and saw no one else.

"No guards? No pat-down?"

"I didn't think they were necessary, unless you are planning to kill me. Are you, Jack? If that's the case, then it will only prove that I was fooled by the bounds of our friendship."

"I'm not here to kill you, Dominick. That would be the last thing on my mind."

"Very well. Follow me, friend, and let's have a drink. Hirsch Reserve, is that still your choice of drink? I keep several bottles on hand, just for you."

"Yes, thank you."

"You always preferred the very best or nothing at all. Why the long face, Jack? I would think you would be on cloud nine after Marino's untimely death. That was brilliant, by the way. The boys haven't stopped talking about it. That took balls to burn him alive and in front of the world to see. One for the books, Jack. We are in awe of you."

"I don't take any pleasure in that, Dominick. He took my wife and used her to get to me. I had no choice."

"Oh, my friend, that's where you are wrong. We always have a choice. It's deciding if we were right in the end, but in your case, you were. If it wasn't you, then he would have been dealt with eventually. Another mistake on my father's part. Marino should have been handled back in Boston, but he got to live and cause more damage. But that's over now. The investigation of Michael St. Clair's murder has been closed, another unsolved to be filed away. I told you, Jack, we had your back, and there was nothing to be worried about."

"With Marino coming unhinged when he did, he practically handed you your freedom on a silver platter. He was a liability for us and for the FBI. As most agencies tend to do, he will slowly be faded out until completely forgotten, and they will move on and forget he ever existed. Now, I do hope your lovely Sara, received my gifts."

"She did. The flowers brightened her day, and the wine was delicious."

All lies, by the way. She was too gracious to throw away something so beautiful, so she once again gave her flowers away to make someone smile. She didn't want any tokens of affection from Dominick Carlucci. Just her name off his tongue pissed me off. The case of wine was divided up with the kitchen staff. It was an amazing vintage, but Sara ordered it to be gone, and I wasn't going to refuse her requests. It was part of breaking off from the past. That was why I was here today.

"That makes me very happy, Jack. Now, what's on your mind?" he asked as he handed me a cigar, looking quite relaxed in his father's chair. Like a king on his throne. His arrogance made the room stink.

"Dominick, I will never forget my loyalties to this family, the bonds of friendship that were formed and still are strong to this day. I would never do anything to betray the trust you have in me, nor bring harm to this dynasty that your father built. You were right when you said I was bullied into making a decision that I knew I couldn't live with. You lifted that burden off my shoulders, and set me free by doing so. I need you do that once again for me, today. I need my freedom from the ties that bind me to you and to this family. For whatever time I have left to spend on this earth, I want to live them in the light with my wife and my family, the family I was born into, my brother for one. Your family chose me, but I don't belong here anymore. I am Giovanni Vanelli. I am my father's son, not yours. It took almost losing myself to the same madness and promises of revenge, as it did to Marino."

I said my peace and waited for Dominick to say his. He rubbed his fingers over his chin, and then filled our glasses with the drink of our choice.

"Drink up, Jack. It looks like you could use one." He downed his with one gulp and steadied his elbows on his father's desk. "The devotion you hold for our family and for your own is admirable, and

I truly respect you for it. I always have, Jack. You've always been the better man, and it's no wonder why father was so fond of you. To be asked to be free would mean you never left, and we know better now, don't we Jack? I welcomed you back with open arms when we talked last, but you refused me. I didn't believe your denials then, and I don't believe you now, but that's my problem, not yours. You don't get to have it both ways, Jack. Either you are with us, or you are against us. Choose wisely, my friend, because once you say the words, I will never allow you to take them back. I will shove them down your throat and make you choke on them."

He wore a look of betrayal in his eyes. This was not how I intended this meeting to go.

"Dominick, there are hundreds of Jacks you have under your reign of power. You do not need me for anything anymore. My time with this family has been over for years, and please do not mistake the friendships I have held onto as my unwavering allegiance to you. You can't relive history and leave out the parts you easily have forgotten. It doesn't work that way Dominick, and for me, it never will. What you say you did for *me* was done to serve your purpose, not mine. I would think twice before ever threatening me again. I have no issues with you, Dominick, nor do I want to. I only wish to leave here with an amicable agreement."

"Fine! I will give you what you desire most, but we are never too far away. You remember that, my friend."

"There's one more thing, Dominick."

"Are you fucking serious? Have you not been given enough? You want more from me? Not ten minutes ago, you asked for freedom. I've granted that request, and now you dare to ask for more? You have balls the size of Texas. You never stop surprising me, Jack, with your arrogance and what you feel you are entitled to."

"Are you finished? Enough already, Dominick. Please save the superior leadership-in-your-face tactics for your men, not me. Now…Joseph LaRocha."

"What about him?"

"Without implicating the family, I intend to tell Jacob Paulson the truth behind his fiancées death."

"When hell freezes over! If you cross that line, Jack, I swear there will be no coming back from it. He's a fucking cop—a federal agent I might add—who can take down this house, brick by brick with the knowledge you have. I was a fool to ever tell you."

"You are far from being a fool, and no lines will ever be crossed, because you know me better than that. I just want to lead him in the right direction. He never needs to know the details. Please, Dominick, I can't in good conscience keep this from him. He needs to find closure in losing her, and if his second chance survives what Marino has done to her, he will have that. And maybe, just maybe, I'll have some closure of my own. Forgiveness is the first step to redemption. I've finally been able to get mine. Don't deny him the same chance, Dominick. Her blood is on your hands, just as much as it is on her father's."

I might almost agree to a hot branding iron down my throat for this conversation. Dominick was relentless and unwilling to bend. I couldn't say any more than I already had to him. The next move had to be his.

"It should have been you sitting behind this desk, and not me. That realization comes to mind after every conversation I have with you. I can't rewrite history, Jack, as you so eloquently remind me. I will give you my consent and trust that whatever you choose to tell Agent Paulson will never come back to this house and to me. Do you understand?"

"I do, Dominick, and thank you."

"You're welcome Jack."

He rounded his desk and took my face in his hands to kiss both sides of my cheeks. He took a step back and said, "Hold out your right hand, palm up."

I did what he asked without knowing what he would do. In less than a second, his intentions were clear. He pulled a double edged blade from his pocket and sliced a line down my palm, reopening my first blood line to the family. It hurt like hell, but I would not show him my pain. I understood why he did it and honored the rare, time-old tradition with my acceptance and silence.

"Now, my friend, you are truly free."

He said nothing more and left me on my own. I knew the second he drew my blood, he would never lay his eyes upon me again. I left that house and never looked back.

I would never share my true past with my family. Massimo made his peace with me, and we found a new beginning as brothers. I knew what I had with Nicolette, and I would never question my role in her life. I'd always been there where it mattered the most, and it had taken me years to finally realize that. My life with Sara was all that I needed. I would spend my days making her happy and my nights holding her in my arms. To the ones that believed a guy like me didn't deserve the life I had and the blessings I was fortunate to receive...well, maybe they're right, but I have it. On the memory of my parents, I made new promises to my family, ones I would honor all the days of my life that remained.

After I received word that Jacob's girlfriend had awakened and was on her way to making a full recovery, I knew I could no longer sit on the information I had in my possession. It was time to give Jacob the truth. What he would do with it once he had it would solely be on him. This was not my sin I carried, but in some way, I still felt this overwhelming sense of responsibility to help him. I was taking a big risk sharing with Jacob what I knew, but if me doing so gave him peace, then it would have been worth it in the end.

CHAPTER
Twenty-Seven

YOU BROUGHT ME BACK TO LIFE...

Jacob

W hen the nurse told me that Zoey was finally awake, I didn't believe it and couldn't move. It was what I had been praying for since the night I rescued her. Once I regained the ability to move my legs, I took off running back to her room with Duffy trailing behind me.

I got to her room, held onto the door frame, and just listened to the sound of her voice. It was raspy but clear. She was telling her father how much she loved him. Tenley was crying happy tears with her husband by her side. All that was missing was me. When Zoey finally saw me, her eyes were my invitation to come closer. This time, my legs moved.

Leave it to me to ask something stupid, "Do you know who I am?"

Tenley stopped crying, and her tears were replaced with laughter. Jagger looked at me like I was nuts, and her parents just looked confused. Give me a break! For days I'd been reading the side effects of what she may experience after the drugs were out of her system. I didn't know what to expect, so I asked the only question that came to mind.

She gave me a sexy wink and then smiled as brightly as the night sky.

"Aren't you the hot FBI Agent that handcuffed me to your bed and had your way with me?"

Oh hell no! She didn't just say that, and in front of her father, who was about to deck me one. I cleared my throat and just went for it.

"Yeah, that would be me, handcuffs and all."

"No, I've never seen you before. Who are you again?"

Wise-ass! She began to laugh, and I knew she would be okay.

"Hi, Jake, I've missed you."

"Not as much as I've missed you. Don't ever scare me like that again. Zoey, I know you are probably going to think I am completely insane, and we haven't known each other all that long, but I love you. I have from the minute I laid my eyes on you. I want you in my life, sparkle girl. I love you."

The laughter ceased, and the entire room went on lockdown after my very bold declaration of love for Zoey. *Please say something, baby. Don't leave me hanging.*

"What took you so long? I love you too!" Zoey replied.

"Yes!" shouted Tenley. I couldn't help smiling, and then I looked over my shoulder to her father. Zoey was his only child, and I knew that he loved and fiercely protected her.

"Well, go on, son. Kiss her, for crying out loud."

"Thank you, sir."

She was giggling again with that precious laugh of hers. I couldn't kiss her the way I wanted to, so I went in for gentle, but she wasn't having it. Zoey pulled me down and crushed her ruby lips to mine. I was so lost in her kiss, I felt dizzy.

With one kiss, she had my complete submission. In that moment

I knew I would do anything for her. Tenley hit me on my shoulder to give me a hug, and then hugged her friend. Jagger shook my hand and said his goodbyes to Zoey. Next to leave were her parents, and then Duffy made his discreet exit.

Her doctor examined her before I arrived in her room. The drugs were completely out of her system, and all she would need now was rest to recover. While she was sleeping, her bruises were slowly fading, and all her scans came back clean. She was anxious to be released and return home. The bigger question would be: where to…home to New York, or to my home with me in Colorado?

I knew in my heart that I wasn't going to change my mind about walking away from the FBI. Having to relive Minela's death and to be taunted by that sick bastard, Marino, I then realized I had seen my fair share of ugliness to last me a lifetime. I only wanted a fresh start, and I hoped Zoey would want to share her life with me. If her kiss was the first clue showing me that she wanted the same thing, then I was on the right track of making her mine.

After we were left on our own, I got as close as I could to Zoey without disturbing the IV lines that were attached to her. The sight of them made my stomach turn, and my heart hurt more.

"I was so scared. I thought I lost you before we even began. Zoey, I meant every word I said to you. I love you…so much, and all I see is you for my future."

Tears were beginning to form in her beautiful eyes, and she raised her hand to touch my face. Just her touching me made me feel whole again. I would do everything in my power to hold onto this feeling.

"Jake, maybe it's time we have that conversation."

And with that, I felt like I had crashed and burned. With just a few words, the future I was envisioning with Zoey had come to a crashing halt. *She didn't feel the same way?*

"Jake, stop. Whatever you are thinking, stop it now. I'm sorry, I didn't mean to upset you. Please allow me to explain?"

And then she gave me hope. Of course I would listen. She guts me to my core with just one look, and damn if her touch doesn't make my dick crush hard against my zipper.

"Soon, baby. Soon," she said to me.

"What?" I tried to hide my obvious physical reaction to her.

"You know what I mean, lover, and like I said, soon. As I was saying, let's talk."

"No, I believe you were staring at a certain body part I possess. You are practically drooling."

"Okay, now I am officially distracted. Take off your pants," she said.

She laughed. And I broke out into laughter to the point I had tears in my eyes. It felt good to laugh, to feel anything other than the worry I'd been through this past week and then some. I kissed her again, and she moved over so I could slide in next to her. She was so small, she easily fit perfectly to my body. I put my arm over her and pulled her as close as her IV lines would allow. I was home.

"Jake, I meant what I said too. I love you. I've kissed a lot of frogs, and now I have found my prince. Before I woke up, I was dreaming about being back in New York when you were working the case with Tenley. She actually thought I was crushing on Shane, the other cowboy in her life."

Just the mention of the possibility of Zoey liking someone else made me see red. I hadn't introduced my jealous side yet, but knowing Zoey, it probably would turn her on.

"The entire time Tenley was speaking, all I kept thinking about was you. You kind of took my breath away, and then after the night we shared, I knew you probably ruined me for other men. I know it's been a whirlwind flash romance, but it just feels right, you know? When I left New York, I swear at that very moment, I was just setting out for an adventure, not knowing what I would find once I got out there. I worked too much and had no life. I never realized how lonely I was until I saw what Tenley had with Jagger. I wanted what she had, and when we met, I actually believed I could have it…with you. Does that scare the shit out of you, or what? I know I must sound like a lovesick girl, but I swear to you, Jake, I've never wanted anyone as much as I want you."

How is she real? I thought as I wrapped my arms around her tighter.

"Are you okay, Jake? Do you want to run for the hills?"

"I'm better than okay, baby. I'm perfect. I'm just screaming in my head right now and fist pumping in the air to the fact that you are here with me. I love you. Zoey, and I want exactly what you want."

She wiggled in my arms to give her some room. She turned over and placed her head on my chest, where she stayed for the remainder of the night. She slept soundly, and I didn't care how my neck would hurt in the morning. As long as she was okay, all was right in my world.

My phone vibrated in my pocket several times. I ignored whoever was calling me and tried not to disturb Zoey. When I finally opened my eyes, she wasn't in bed with me. I jumped out and called out for her.

"I'm here, Jake," she called out, walking slowly out from the bathroom and pushing her IV pole that she was still connected to.

"How did you get out of bed without me knowing it? You need to get back in bed, now."

"Hey, caveman! Just because I said I loved you, that doesn't mean you get to boss me around. Okay, I take that back. You may only boss me around in bed. Any other areas are off limits."

"Very funny, sexy girl, but I'm serious, Zoey. Get back into bed. And just so you know, I fully intend to dominate every inch of your tempting body."

"I never doubted you for a second," she replied. "I can't wait to get these IV's out. They are always in the way."

I leaned down, scooped her into my arms, and gently placed her back in her bed.

"This I know. Zoey, there is so much I want to share with you. I need to tell you parts of my past that I've shared with no one. It needs to be said, but this is not the place to do it."

"It's okay, Jake, we have all the time in the world."

Yes, we do.

"I would like to talk to you about one thing if I may?" I asked.

"Of course, you know you can."

"Bringing up your ordeal is the last thing I want to do, but I need to know. The last morning we were together, you told me you were going back to the condo where you were staying. How did you end up here in Chicago?"

She began to tremble, and I immediately got back into bed to hold her.

"I'm sorry, Zoey. You're not ready to talk about it. This could wait until you are feeling better."

"I'm okay, Jake. I just need to breathe. After you left for work, I took a shower, ate breakfast, and then walked down to the parking garage. I was unlocking my door, and then I was grabbed from behind with a rag being placed over my mouth. The next thing I remember, I was on a private plane. I was dizzy and disoriented. I tried to focus on the man sitting in front of me, but I couldn't. I was seat belted but my hands were tied in front of me. I didn't know where I was when the plane landed, and then I felt a stick to my arm, and I was out again. The next time I woke up, I was in that room. I tried to fight back, Jake, I really did, but I didn't even know who was holding me prisoner. He hit me hard against my face, and I fell back to the mattress. He was on top of me, ripping my clothes off. I thought he was going to rape me or kill me right there. He hit me again, and then it went dark. I was beginning to wake, and that's when I felt the tight ropes crisscrossed over my body. I couldn't move. He kept saying over and over again that it would soon be over, and his nightmare was just beginning. I was foolish to scream because it only angered him, and then he covered my mouth. The pungent stench of urine was filling my nostrils. I was then wishing to be knocked out again so I would forget where I was. I didn't have to wish for long, because he injected me again. And then I woke up almost nine days later. You rescued me, my hero."

"I was terrified and just wanted you to wake up and see me, but you barely had a pulse. I'm so sorry he hurt you because of me."

"It's not your fault, Jake, and I swear he didn't take anything from me. The bruises will fade, and I will heal."

To experience that day was hard enough, but to hear it again with Zoey reliving all that he did to her was just slicing my heart to ribbons. I wanted that motherfucker's heart ripped out from his chest. Too bad I didn't get the chance. Jack had all the fun, making sure Marino got what he deserved.

"Hey, caveman, you are crushing my bones. Have you forgotten that you are over six feet in height and feel like a brick wall?"

"Oh my God! I'm sorry, Zoey. Did I hurt you?"

"No, I stopped you just in time. Jake, it's over. I'm okay, and I'm safe. He's gone, so please stop reliving it in your mind. Once was enough for me."

"Dammit! It's my phone again."

"You've ignored it all night and a few times this morning. Don't you think you should answer it?"

"Nothing gets past you now, does it?"

"I'm a bad ass lawyer from New York City, so what do you think?"

"Point taken," I responded to her as I picked up my phone. "This is Paulson. Yeah, hi, Jack."

I detangled myself from Zoey, mouthed to her that I would be right back, and took the call outside.

"Yeah, I can meet today, but you have to come here to the hospital. I'm not ready to leave Zoey. Okay, I'll see you in an hour."

"You know, caveman, I'm not some fragile piece of glass that will shatter at any moment. I'm fine. You need to get out of here for a while and take some time for yourself. At least go grab a hot shower and some food."

"I appreciate the concern, but I'm fine. I have showered, and Tenley has made me eat."

"Okay, sue me for caring," she said, trying to look hurt, but she couldn't if she tried.

"Your pout is freaking adorable. Please do that again when we are in bed, and I promise you, I will not let you leave it for a week."

"Oh, lover, I am going to hold you to that."

"I would expect nothing less."

I loved the easiness I had with Zoey. It brought me back to a time I shared with Minela, but these two women were so different in many ways. There was no comparison.

Tenley and Jagger said their goodbyes to Zoey and me. They needed to get back to their ranch, and after all, they were still newlyweds. I was so thankful for her friendship. Jagger was slowly warming up to the idea of being friends with me, but I think he was still a little pissed at me for trying to one up him back in Wyoming.

The girls promised to see each other soon, wherever that may be. I still hadn't had the chance to really talk with Zoey, but that would happen as soon as she was released. Her father couldn't convince her to return to their family home. Zoey made it clear she was an adult and could take care of herself. She was still on leave from the firm and mentioned no plans of returning to her life in New York.

We finished our breakfast, and then my phone buzzed again. It was Jack telling me he was waiting for me downstairs in the lobby.

"I have to go, baby. Will you be okay on your own?"

"Of course I will. Go, and don't worry about me. I'm being sprung from all these wires today. When you were in the shower, Dr. Witt came in with my labs. I've been completely cleared and should be released later tonight."

"Zoey, we haven't even talked about our plans, or your plans."

"We will. Do you have a hotel room?"

"I do. I'm staying at the Drake."

"Then no worries. That's where I'll be."

God! I loved this woman. After leaving Zoey, I practically skipped all the way down to the lobby. I even took the stairs, I was so high on Zoey, and I needed to release some energy. The needy side of my manhood couldn't wait to be buried inside of her again.

Jack was waiting for me by the revolving doors.

"Hey, Jack, thanks for coming down."

I shook his hand, and then he pulled me into a hug, which totally caught me off guard. It wasn't like we were close or anything, he only showed that sign of affection toward Simon.

I said to him, "Hey, big guy, we don't have to hug if it's all the same to you. Just last week, I was the bad guy, remember?"

"You were never the bad guy, Jacob, and I'm very sorry for how Tommy and I treated you. You are family, and I knew you had a job to do."

"Thank you for that, Jack, but no apologies necessary. I'm just happy we got through it."

"I'm sure you are. Thank God your girl is okay."

"And your wife? How is she feeling?"

"She's great, never better."

"And the Neighborhood Bar & Grille? Has it risen from the ashes?"

"It's coming along. Sara will have it up and running in no time."

"Good. I miss the burgers."

After sharing a lighter moment, Jack's mood shifted to a more serious one.

"Jake, we need to talk, and it can't be here. I have a car outside. Can we talk in private?"

He didn't look like he would take no for an answer, so I followed him outside.

"Okay, Jack, what's on your mind?"

"About Michael St. Clair…?"

I stopped him right there and said, "Jack, I'm not at liberty to discuss Michael St. Clair with you, not ever. As I was told by my superiors back in LA and in New York, the investigation to his death has been closed. His father filed a wrongful death lawsuit against the prison, and I'm sure a settlement will be reached quickly. The obvious and only suspect was you. That was quickly determined after

Marino dropped off the grid and the events that followed. Whatever my personal relationship with you is, does not, and will never convince me that you were blameless in this crime. You know it, and I know it, so talking about burgers is not going to make me forget that simple fact. You got away with murder, Jack, and if knowing that helps you sleep better at night, then good for you. Now, if it's all the same to you, I have a beautiful woman waiting for me upstairs."

"Jacob, I have much more to say to you, and I'm asking you to listen."

I looked at my watch.

"You've got five minutes."

"I think I'm going to need more than that, Jake. I'm just asking you to hear me out. You need to hear this."

"Okay, Jack, I'm listening."

"For the record, I don't sleep well at night because of so much weighing me down, but after what I have to tell you, maybe I will. Years ago, I sealed my fate with Dante Marino when I broke the back of his kid brother. He never got over Mikey's death and blamed me for three decades and vowed revenge."

"Jack, I know all this. It's ancient history."

"Not for me, Jake. I am the very reason why Dante Marino came into your life, and just recently discovered the part he played in your fiancée's death."

"You mean murder, right? Isn't that what you should have said? I've been down this road already, Jack, every fucking day I was with him. The secrets of Minela's death died with him in that fire on your damn roof."

"You're wrong, Jake. His secrets are right here in this file."

Not again! I couldn't do this again, not with Jack fucking Vanelle. All he did was lie. I would be a fool to trust him, especially about anything to do with Minela.

"Jacob, please look at it. It's all in there."

I grabbed the file from his hands and began reading it. I couldn't believe what I was seeing. Copies of ledger accounts dating back almost ten years ago and ending one year after Minela was killed. This couldn't be happening, not him. Then my mind went back to Marino's letter to me.

Here's a few breadcrumbs to begin the walk to her murderer's doorstep: you weren't the first man in her life she loved. There was another before you, and after her death, he was never whole again. You are a smart man, Jacob Paulson, I have no doubt you will not figure this out. He's waiting for you.

"This is all about her father? Joseph LaRocha was a dirty cop on the take? Is that what you are fucking telling me, Jack?"

I threw the file back at him. His face said it all.

"Yes, that's exactly what I'm saying."

"I don't believe it, Jack. It can't be true. He treated his daughter like a queen. He would never sacrifice his own daughter for fucking money."

"Well, that's exactly what he did, Jacob! Wake up! Listen to me! Do you honestly believe that I would be so cruel to make this up? What would I have to gain to rain down this hell on you? He was dirty and way in over his head. He had a gambling addiction and could not stop burying himself deeper into the hole. He used his position as a way to get out, but then he would go back and sink lower and owe more money. He mortgaged everything he owned, and it still wasn't enough to pay back his loans. More favors were granted, but the debt would never be fully paid because he fucked his benefactors over, and that's when they had enough."

"Who did it Jack? You fucking tell me, right now!"

"It was a contract hit. One for you, and one for her. They got her first, and then you checked out for a while after her death, and the cases you were working on that affected their business got lost and buried under a thousand other cases. They didn't feel you needed to be taken out after that, so you were left to grieve on your own, and it was back to business as usual. LaRocha remained on the payroll, but his purpose to them was short-lived. You know the rest, Jake. He had a breakdown and lost everything."

302

"No, Jack, he lost everything the minute the daughter he claimed to love took a bullet for him! That bastard made me sweat for his fucking blessing to marry her! Oh, Jesus! He knew all this time and let me believe that I was responsible for it all, because I wasn't willing to pull back on the cases I was working. Oh God! My beautiful girl, gunned down in the middle of the fucking street like she was nothing, while he sat in the comfort of his fucking house on the hill. He knew, he fucking knew and did…nothing!"

I couldn't hold it any longer. I was screaming at the top of my lungs, punching the shit out of his car. This was what Marino knew. He worked the Boston area and was just as dirty as LaRocha was. They all had blood on their hands, my girl's blood.

"Jacob, I am so sorry."

"Fuck you, Jack. As far as I'm concerned, you can join Marino in hell. No matter how many ways you spin it and declare you are a changed man—a better fucking man—you are fooling yourself. Stay the hell away from me, or I swear on the life that those motherfucker's took, that I will kill you where you stand."

I got out of his car and nearly collapsed to my knees. I couldn't breathe. I didn't know where to go. My head was spinning, and my world went dark. I was being pulled to the darkest moment in my life.

She was dying in my arms, and I could do nothing to save her. I was screaming for help, but it was too late…she was gone.

My head was pounding, and my eyes felt heavy to open. I moved my head and felt a sharp pain to the back of my skull. When I finally came to, I was in a hospital bed, and Jack was here.

"I guess I didn't make myself clear earlier about never wanting to see you again."

"You were, Jacob. I heard every word you said, and I don't blame you. I'm so sorry, man. I swear if I could change this for you, I would. No matter what you believe, I was never that lost to ever condone violence against an innocent woman."

"So? Just what I need, a former mob enforcer with a fucking

heart."

"Yes. That heart still feels Jacob, and it mourns your loss. I'm so sorry."

I turned away from him and blocked him out until he left. A nurse came in after him and explained the bump on my head. The emergency room doctor was behind her.

"Hello, Agent Paulson, I'm Dr. Phan. You're going to have quite the headache, but your CT scan looks good. The gentleman who brought you in said you passed out and hit your head on the sidewalk. This time of year, the walks out there are snow-covered, and layers of ice are under it. You got lucky."

"I have to get out of here," I said as I began to pull the IV line from my arm, causing it to sting.

"Sir, you are in no shape to go anywhere."

"Back the fuck off! I'm a grown-ass man, and I am perfectly capable of taking care of myself. Give me something to sign, so I can be on my way."

"You need to be monitored, Agent Paulson."

"I'm fine, you said it yourself. Believe me, doc, I've seen worse."

Holy shit! It had been nearly four hours since I said goodbye to Zoey, and she had to be wondering what happened to me. I quietly opened the door to her room and found her sleeping. I shut the door without waking her and called Duffy. I told him to meet me in Boston no later than noon tomorrow.

Time to pay a visit to my almost father-in-law. You bet your ass he's waiting for me.

CHAPTER Twenty-Eight

A NEW DAY...AFTER THE STORM

Jack

I did the right thing, I know I did, so why did it hurt so much to tell the truth? Jacob was livid. I thought he was going to rip my throat out. In the heat of the moment, he hit the sheet of ice and went down for the count. His head was bleeding all over the sidewalk, and I had to rush through the doors of the ER to get help.

I knew I was the last person he wanted to see, but I had to wait until he woke up. I even sent a message to his girl, letting her know not to worry. She hadn't been released yet and was waiting on Jacob to return. He blindsided me with his anger. I knew he would be upset, but maybe there was hope in me to believe he would actually be grateful for my truth. But he wasn't. Just the opposite, in fact.

I was done putting myself through this torment. I followed through with telling Jacob the truth, it may have been ugly and hard to hear, but it was the truth. He deserved to know who was responsible for taking his love away from him. How could he ever move on with his life without it? I would want to know if I were him. Maybe it wasn't my choice to make, but this was actually one I could live with.

When I got back to the bar, I inspected all that was accomplished today. The roof looked like there was never a fire. I had to hand it to my girl, who was working around the clock to give us back our place.

She left me a note telling me that she was taking a girls' night out. I was happy to hear she was giving herself a much needed break. Sara didn't ask for this shit storm to fall down on her, and I would do anything to make her forget all that she'd been through.

Tommy was back behind the bar, happy as ever. The scowl he was wearing since Jacob arrived was now gone, and he was back to working the bar and chatting it up with the customers. There was no need to ever have a re-opening since we never closed in the first place. The damage upstairs was contained to one area, and the rest of the structure was sound. I took a seat, and as he began to pour me my usual, I raised my hands and declined. He put the bottle back on the shelf and looked like he wanted to say something.

"I'm sorry," he said.

"For?"

"For not being here for Sara when that maniac showed up. I'm always here, Jack, and the one time I was needed most, I split because I was pissed off at you. If anything would have happened to her…"

He trailed off and couldn't finish his sentence. He was choked up, and gripping the bar.

"Look, Tommy, it wasn't your responsibility to protect Sara, although I appreciate it. It's my job to look out for my wife. It's not your fault that asshole grabbed her. It's mine, and it is something I will live with for the rest of my life."

"He's gone now, boss, so don't waste one more second on that piece of shit. And the next time I see that guy, Jacob, I will make things right with him. I know he's family, and I want to make peace if he should ever come here again. Again, I was just looking out for the bar and you. I wasn't thinking when I should have. And now I have a banged up knee to show for it."

"I wouldn't worry about seeing Jacob anytime soon, maybe not ever. I'll take that drink now."

I leaned down onto the bar and rested my throbbing head. So much for my brand new start, I've royally fucked things up. Some of the guys came in to play pool, including Max, who immediately spotted me.

"Hey, Jackie, how's it going?"

"I'm fine," I said with a guarded tone. "You seem to be in a good mood Max, what gives?"

"Can't a guy be happy? Come on, Jack, you need to loosen up a little."

"I'll take it under advisement. Nice seeing you, Max."

He pulled my arm back, and I turned to give him the one look that made him release his hold on me.

"Sorry, Jack, I just wanted to check on you. We're still friends, right?"

"Yeah, Max, we are."

I gave him a half hug, and then I walked upstairs and didn't look back to my friend, who I knew was hoping I would stay and talk. I was spent and pulled in so many directions. I just wanted to crawl under the covers with Sara and not get out of bed for a week. After the renovation was complete, maybe I could convince her to go up to the cabin again or even take a trip to warmer climates.

I took a shower, and re-heated some dinner Sara had left for me. Grabbing a beer, I took a seat by our window to look out to the city below. I flipped over my palm and ran my finger over the reminder of my past life. Dominick showed no mercy when he slashed my palm. The wound needed stitches on account of how he went deeper than the first time I received this mark. He poured all of his anger into the force of forever reminding me how much I had disgraced the family by walking away from them. He put up a convincing front that he was New Age, all about business, and making the mighty green, but behind the façade, he was a traditionalist. He carried what he learned from his father and grandfather before him. He did what he felt he had to, and I wasn't going to challenge what he believed to be right.

Sara never questioned me about it. Some things were better left unsaid. I walked over to the counter, where my wallet was, and pulled out my St. Francis card. Closing my eyes and holding the card to my heart, I prayed for Jacob and hoped he would find peace in whatever he decided to do about what he had learned. And because I'm a selfish bastard, I said a prayer for myself. The lightning bolts hadn't taken me out yet, so I took my chances with the saint that mama always prayed to when she worried for me.

These last few years, I had prayed for more absolution that I ever had in my entire life. I didn't know if I was forgiven for any of my sins, but I had to believe that I was, at least in some small way. Nicolette always told me that God didn't work that way. He forgave all who hurt us, even the ones we felt didn't deserve it. I knew who she was referring to, and I always gnashed my teeth together so I wouldn't say anything to hurt her.

I was about to turn in, when my phone began to ring. I picked it up to see it was Dominick calling me. Cold chills ran up my spine, and I instantly felt pain in my hand. Why in the hell was he calling me?

"Dominick."

"Good evening, Jack. I trust you're well."

"I'm fine, Dominick. Why the call?"

"Is your television on?"

"No, why?"

"Turn it on, and find out. I'll wait."

What the hell was he playing at now? I got up in a huff and grabbed the remote. He told me to turn on channel seven, as a breaking report was about to go live.

I could hear the clinking of ice in a glass, as I waited for the news to come on. And then I couldn't believe my eyes at what I was watching. I turned up the volume so I could hear the report.

"Good evening. We are interrupting your regular scheduled program to bring you breaking news out of Boston. The former city police chief, Joseph LaRocha, was found dead in his home earlier this evening from a self-inflicted gunshot wound. His body was found by his son, patrolman Paolo LaRocha of the 47th precinct."

"Chief LaRocha, since retiring from his position with the Boston Police Department, has rarely been seen out in public. This report coming from a once-close neighbor and friend to the family. You may remember the violent crime back in 2012, when his only daughter, Detective Minela LaRocha, was gunned down in cold blood while walking home with her then fiancée, former NFL player and current Federal Agent, Jacob Paulson. Her murder has never been solved."

"Are you still there, Jack?"

"I'm here," I coldly replied.

"I guess you followed through with your promise of…what did you call it? Righting a wrong and helping poor Agent Paulson find some closure? I guess he did get that closure after all? Too bad the news report got it wrong. Her murder has been solved, you saw to that Jack, when you grew a conscience and sang like a fucking bird. I'm sure Agent Paulson feels great right about now. Anyhow, I thought you would like to know. Sleep well, Jack."

The line went dead, and it took all my self-control not to bust up my phone that I was gripping with all of my strength. He actually did it, didn't he? It had to be Jacob who confronted LaRocha with what he knew, and being the coward that LaRocha is, he took his own life. That fucker should have killed himself a long time ago!

If confronting LaRocha was something Jacob needed to do to breathe again, then he did the right thing. I did the right thing. I didn't have too many things in my life where I could say that and it would be true. Freeing Jacob from his past felt right, and I would never be sorry for it. I was only sorry for the pain it caused him to hear it.

We all make promises to the people we love and to ourselves. We do what we believe we can live with. I believed Jacob knew that before ever deciding to confront LaRocha, as I knew when telling him the truth.

This was over. The last piece to the puzzle had been solved. The dark would turn to light, and the nightmares would fade away, never to be thought of again. It was truly over, and I could breathe again.

CHAPTER Twenty-Nine

TRUTH DOESN'T ALWAYS SET YOU FREE...

Jacob

My phone call to Duffy took longer than I expected it to. He wanted to know every last detail of my conversation with Jack, but I pushed it off until I could meet with him tomorrow in Boston. My head was killing me with a slow pounding at the base of my skull. Making my way back to Zoey's room, I entered to find her missing from her bed. I called out to her before checking the bathroom, and that too was empty.

A sudden panic began to rise within me. *She wouldn't have just checked out without telling me? Stop it, Paulson, you're just twisted in your head over Jack right now. Your girl is here. You just have to find her.*

I took a few calming breaths, and then my next call was to Janice, the goddess of all travel agents. She was able to arrange a private jet to take me to Boston. The plane was being prepped before I even hung up with her. This was another perk of having banked millions from my football days, along with my inheritance. I'd invested wisely, and I was financially sound to just spend the rest of my days lazing around on a beach if I wanted to, but only if Zoey was by my side.

I never flaunted my wealth to any of my buddies on the force, or even at the FBI. They all knew who I was but accepted me just the same. I did use my contacts for good sometimes, like getting Duffy season pass tickets for the New York Giants. He'd been a good friend, and I owed him a lot.

Speaking of him, no sooner after hanging up with Janice, Duffy was calling me and tried with great effort to talk me out of flying to Boston. I didn't want to hear it, and my mind had been made up.

"For the last time, I'm fine, and I know what I am doing. I leave in about an hour. I just have to gather Zoey, and then I will call you when I land. Goodbye, Duffy."

"And just where, Agent Paulson, are you taking me to?"

Just the sight of Zoey set my soul on fire. She looked lovely in the clothes that Tenley had bought for her. Her hair was pulled back in a messy ponytail, and for make-up, she was only wearing lip gloss, which I was about to kiss off.

"Good evening, Ms. Steele. You are gorgeous!"

I placed my hands onto the armrests of her wheelchair and kissed her plump lips. I had meant to be gentle, but my kiss soon turned aggressive, as I demanded entrance to her mouth. Our tongues tangled with each other, and Zoey whimpered a soft moan that just about made me come. It had been a long time since we'd been together, and all I wanted was to make love to her. It was a need that caused me to lose my mind.

"That's quite a welcome, Agent Paulson! Shall I leave and come back in again?"

"Just try it, and I will take you over my knee and turn your skin to a lovely shade of pink."

"How about I just stay, and you do that anyway."

My girl wanted to play!

"As inviting as that sounds, you are still healing, and I am not going to touch you the way I want to until I know you are one hundred percent recovered. It still pains me to look at your bruises."

"Oh, Jake, I am better. And maybe I need a different kind of healing, one where you bury that big cock of yours inside of me and ride me so hard that I'm hoarse from screaming your name. Yeah, that kind of medicine is exactly what I need."

"Thank you, beautiful girl. Now I have to go commando, because my boxers are filled with come."

"Are they really?" she was actually smiling.

"I was just joking, but I am close, so please stop playing with my emotions."

"Okay, then let me just play with your dick, and we will call it even. She pulled on my belt and would have had my pants down if it wasn't for the nurse walking in with her discharge papers. I quickly refastened my pants, while Zoey smiled wickedly at me. *She is so getting spanked.*

She was laughing to the point where her cheeks were turning shades of red. I kissed her sensually on her lips, and then I was the one moaning. We needed to be on our way, and I still needed to explain to Zoey my sudden change of plans.

"As much as I would love to continue this game of wills with you, we need to leave for the airport."

"Where are we going? I thought we would be going back to the Drake Hotel?"

"That was my original plan, where we would really talk, but this afternoon when I met with Jack Vanelle, everything changed. Please trust me, Zoey, and just come with me. I will have more time to talk to you once we are up in the air and on our own with no interruption. The doctors have cleared you to fly, so what's it going to be?"

"Seriously, Jake? A little finesse wouldn't kill you. Fine! I will go to…?"

"Boston, we are going to Boston."

"I will go to Boston with you, but you need to start talking, and don't try to stall me with that sexy mouth of yours, because you know I will cave. I'm so weak when you are in touching distance. I lose my mind over you."

"You took the words right out of my mouth, because baby, that's exactly how I feel about you. I love you, and thank you."

She smiled and wiped a tear from her eyes. I grabbed her bag, and we left for the airport. I wish I was taking Zoey back to my ranch in Colorado. It was the one place that I felt most at home. I had designed the house of my dreams and watched it get built, brick by brick. It was heaven on earth. I would return home every chance I had when I wasn't playing football. During the off-season, I never left the ranch. I had my horses and the beautiful Rocky Mountains as my view. I missed that place so much.

I never had an opportunity to show Minela what I loved and hoped to share it with her. She was a city girl, and I knew when the time came, it would take some convincing on my part. I never brought a woman to my home, or to my bed, and now being with Zoey, that's all I want to do. That dream would have to wait until I finished my business with Joseph LaRocha. I knew I could never find the closure I so desperately wanted until I made him see how his selfishness and greed got his daughter killed.

We boarded the plane and took our seats. We would be airborne in a few minutes, and then I would brace myself for one hell of a conversation with Zoey. She wanted answers, and deserved them, but I just got her back and didn't want to risk losing her over someone from my past. She held my hand as we began our take-off. She was adorable with her eyes closed and one little hand squeezing my own.

"You don't like take-offs?"

"No, I don't. I always get really nervous, but once we level out, I'm fine."

"It's okay, baby. I've got you."

"You certainly do, Agent Paulson, but did you bring the handcuffs?"

That's my sweet temptress. I was getting more lost in her beautiful eyes as I continued to stare at her, and thank God she made it. I don't know how I got so lucky to meet Zoey when I did, but I would never question it again. She was here with me now, and if I had my way, she would be forever.

"Well?" she asked. "You never answered my question: did you pack them?"

"I never leave home without them," I winked back at her.

Once we were at cruising altitude, we unbuckled our seatbelts and moved over to the leather sofa. Janice went all out with the accommodations. She knew what I liked when I traveled. The jet had a private bedroom, but with Zoey just being released from the hospital, I wasn't ready to introduce her to the mile-high club yet. We needed to talk first, and the conversation I needed to have with her could no longer wait.

She sensed my apprehension but gave me room to breathe and waited until I was ready. I stretched my legs and invited Zoey to sit in between them with my arms around her, a perfect position for me to lay kisses down onto her head. If it became too much for her to hear, I would let her go to find safe haven in the bedroom. I never talked about my past, not ever, and it was very hard for me to find the words, but I started with the reason why we were going to Boston. I started with *her.*

"Her name was Minela LaRocha, and she was to be my wife, but our love story ended the night she was gunned down and died in my arms." I immediately felt Zoey shiver, but I held her so I could continue with my story. "She was beautiful, smart, tough, and a damn good cop. When we met, it was like oil and water. I was adamant about not wanting another partner, but she soon changed my mind. She challenged me to get to know her better, and at the end of the day, that's all I wanted to do. Our working relationship eventually turned personal, and I was in love for the very first time in my life."

"She was his only daughter, the pride and joy of his life. She was one of five children, the first four all boys, and all cops. She defied her father's wishes and joined the force. I met her when she transferred from Boston to New York. We were both detectives, and Duffy, who you met, warned me off from the very first day."

"Why would he do that?" she asked, turning to look up at me.

"Duffy wasn't being a jerk or anything, but he knew me better than most. He gave me her stats and experience, and I wasn't really interested in all of that because I was stubborn and wanted to work alone. As I left his office, he told me not to fall in love with her, which of course, I scoffed at the notion. What was he, crazy? You don't fall in love with the person who has your back on the streets! But after spending one afternoon with her, I was pretty much eating my words."

"I fell in love, and I fell hard. All I wanted was to have what my brother had with his wife. What my parents share and still have today after years of being together. It was time for me to man up and tell her how I felt, and I didn't really have to do much convincing, because she felt the same way. We dove into the big pool of love, moved into a shoe box of an apartment, and were happy. Losing Minela made me lose parts of myself. I drove my family away and used my work as my refuge. I was just…dead…inside, and I didn't really care."

I let out a deep sigh, and closed my eyes to fight back the tears, but it was too late. They were falling, and Zoey turned and held me close to her.

"Shhh, it's okay Jake. I'm here, and I love you."

I wanted to make love to this amazing woman holding me in her arms. Skin on skin was all I could think about. She could talk dirty to me all day long, but what I was craving most was intimacy with her. I needed her, and she needed me too. She moved off of me and extended her hand out for me to take.

"When did you know that you wanted to be with me?" I asked her as we lay in bed wrapped up in each other, very naked.

"There is something about you, Jake, that I can't even articulate into words. I knew I had to have you, but you were so guarded with everyone around you. I don't even believe I saw your teeth until you smiled at Tenley's wedding. You were so hot in your suit, and I was fantasizing fucking you with you only wearing that blue tie that matched your eyes. I know you must be thinking I'm absolutely crazy with my wild thoughts, but guys have been doing it for years! Girls are entitled to some hot one night stands too."

"Is that all you wanted when we went back to my hotel room?"

I hated to ask, but I wanted to know.

"Yes, but I kind of had the feeling you did too. Am I wrong?"

"No, you're not, but then it was so much…"

"More?"

"Yeah, something like that. I tried to convince myself that it was a one-time thing, and we would go our separate ways, but then after I found your note, I wasn't so convinced."

"That was fun. I had never done anything like that before, but something about you just excited me, and I wanted to see if what I was feeling was real. You know the rest of the story."

"Zoey, it can have a perfect ending if it's me who you really want, not just the fantasy. I'm looking for more in my life. I want to get married, have a family. I want it all, and I'm asking you if you feel the same way?"

She suddenly was quiet, too quiet, and I didn't like it. I know I just dropped a lot of baggage from my past on her, but I needed her to communicate with me, not shut down every time I showed her my heart. I was chastising myself for pushing her. I understood that I came off strong, as patience was never one of my strong suits. I wanted her, it was that simple. I could work with some hesitation, knowing how much fun it would be to convince her to give us a chance.

"Hey, are you still with me?" I finally asked.

"I am, just deep in thought."

"Anything I can help you with?"

"No, you've given me enough to think about, and I mean that in

317

a good way. Jacob, why are you so sure about me?"

Finally! She was talking, and now don't fuck it up Paulson. Simply tell her without scaring the shit out of her. I shifted our bodies and pulled her right on top of me. I wanted to hold her face and look in her eyes when I told her my answer.

"Zoey, I wasn't looking for you when we met. I was not an easy man to be around. Most times I came off as cold and pretty much a dick. Just ask Jagger. I'm sure he won't hold back on how we met."

She laughed and said, "I've heard about the pissing contest, go on."

"I won't give you every detail about the women in my little black book, but one did exist, and it was filled with women I dated, had random hook-ups with, and some I called friends. But never one that I could actually say I was in love with, until Minela. She was my first love, and one I will never forget. Losing her in the manner I did, just broke me. I was walking, talking, breathing, but I wasn't living. I gave up on ever finding love again, and then one day...there was you. You just took my breath away with your sassy mouth, pink streaks in your hair, and that gorgeous ass of yours that made my heart skip a beat or two. And after the night we shared, I was scared to death on how I was feeling. It was strong, Zoey, and I almost didn't believe it. That's why it was so easy to believe that it was a one-time thing and nothing more, but then you came to me, and I knew I was just fooling myself. You came at me with such a force, you knocked me on my ass, and then all I wanted was to mark you and make you mine."

"You. Brought. Me. Back. To. Life. And I've never felt more alive than when I am with you. I don't believe I can explain it any other way. This right here—you and me—just feels right. I haven't had this in a very long time, and I want to just hold onto you with all my strength. You are not just a reason to forget my past. You, Zoey Steele, are my second chance."

"Thank you for telling me," she said as she leaned in to kiss me.

"So you don't think I'm totally crazy?"

"I totally think you are crazy, but if you want to be crazy in love with me, then that's the best way to be."

"I want to make love to you, beautiful girl, but I just can't...not here, and not before I tell you the reason why we are going to Boston."

"I'm listening."

"My meeting with Jack, wasn't like anything I expected it to be. He shared some information with me about Minela's murder and who was responsible for it. I didn't want to believe it, but the proof was placed in my hands. I was so angry that I didn't trust myself in the car with Jack, I wanted to just make him hurt for showing me the proof. I got out of the car and was raging inside, and that's when I fell and hit my head on the ice. That's why I was gone for so freaking long, because I was getting my head stitched up, and my heart torn out...again. The end of the nightmare I've been living is in Boston, and I have to face it once and for all, or all the dreams I am imagining with you will never happen if I don't close the door to my past."

"Okay."

"Zoey, you must have questions, something to ask me."

"Jake, I see the conflict in your eyes. You are not that great at hiding your pain as well as you think you are. I see it, baby, and if I could take it away, I would, but that's up to you. You do what you have to do, and when it's over, I will be here waiting for you."

After our talk, we stayed in bed in each other's arms, and just listening to Zoey's heart made me feel complete. She was amazing, supportive, and so accepting of my past. I knew what I would be facing once I stepped off this plane and went to LaRocha with what I knew. After hearing Jack's story, there was no way I could ever let this go, not even for Minela. She loved her father more than anything and would not want her family hurt, but I owed him nothing. He took her away from me, and I wanted him to tell me why.

By the time we arrived at Boston Logan Airport, it was after midnight. We settled into our suite at the Ritz-Carlton. I drew a bath for Zoey, and then gave her a massage. She endured so much because of Marino, and now I had her flying cross-country to join me on my path of revenge toward LaRocha. After my personal attention to her sweet body, she was asleep before her head hit the pillow. I wanted nothing more than to crawl into bed with her, but I needed to call Duffy and prepare for tomorrow.

"Wake up, beautiful girl."

I started kissing her on her neck, and then down her naked back. She shifted slightly, but she couldn't fool me. She was awake and enjoying my morning wake-up call. When I finally reached her delectable mouth, she opened her eyes, and I swear I saw my reflection staring back at me. They were beautiful and sparkling with light.

"God, I love you."

"How about loving on me for a while?" she sassily asked, knowing I knew she was naked underneath the sheet.

"I wish I could, but I have business to take care of. The sooner I end this, the sooner I can come back for you, and we will begin the first day to the rest of our lives. How does that sound?"

"It sounds perfect. Hurry back."

"I will, I promise."

And then I noticed her look slightly unsure. I lifted her chin with my finger to make her look at me.

"Zoey, I can't leave here until I know you are okay. What's going on in your mind right now?"

"I'm fine. It's just the last time you left me in a hotel room…"

She turned away and began to cry. The sight of her crying gutted me. I pulled her onto my lap, where she was straddling me.

"I swear to you, baby, that I am coming back for you. You are perfectly safe here and have nothing to worry about." She crushed her body to mine, and I could feel her slowly calming down. I needed to finish this with LaRocha and get Zoey out of this fucking city. This was the last place I wanted to be, but there was no turning back now.

An hour later, I was sitting in an unmarked car in front of the

LaRocha family home. This would be my first and last time I would ever lay eyes on this house.

"One last time, Jake. Are you sure you want to do this?"

"Duffy, I've never been surer in all of my life. You've seen the evidence. That motherfucker in there is responsible for his own daughter's murder. He needs to say it, Duff, and I need to hear it."

"Jake, we will never be able to charge him for her murder or involvement in her murder. I just don't see what good can come from this. This knowledge that you now have is from a former mob enforcer that we just cleared in a murder investigation. How the fuck can you even believe this to be true?"

"I see the doubt. Duff, and you have the right to your opinion, but Jack had no reason to lie to me. Why would he? It serves no purpose. I'm not looking to bring him to the justice we have promised to serve to. You can join me in there and show him whatever you want, but I'm not a cop today. This is personal."

He sat there for a minute, rubbed his fingers through his balding hair, and then let out a deep sigh.

"I'm with you, Jake. You do what you have to do, but know I will step in if I have to. You have suffered enough, and I'm not going to allow you to go down one more dark road, you hear me?"

"I do, and thank you."

I took a deep breath before I knocked on the door to the brick home. This was an upscale neighborhood in Boston's Beacon Hill. I looked down the street. All the homes were surrounded by snow-covered landscaping that probably came to life in the spring. Luxury cars were in the driveways, and I just shook my head at it all. No cop would ever be able to afford a home like this on their salary, but a no good, dirty one on the take easily could.

"Jake? Are we doing this?" Duffy asked as he tapped me on my shoulder, bringing me back to the reason why I was here.

"Yeah, we are."

I knocked hard a couple of times, and a housekeeper answered the door. She wouldn't know me, and I chose to skip the pleasantries. I showed her my badge, and then Duffy followed suit. She opened the door wider and let us in. The house was disturbingly quiet. I asked if anyone else was in the home, and she said only Mr. LaRocha, who never left his study.

His wife was in a private care facility after suffering a stroke that left her incapacitated. After losing her only daughter, she was never the same, slowly becoming a shell of the once full of life woman. *Fucker!* He lived in this pretentious home with no warmth left to it. This was what blood money buys.

The housekeeper knocked on the study door, and he yelled out for her to go away. I told her to leave us. She turned and scurried off.

I opened the door, and he shouted again, "What are you deaf? I told you to go away!"

He remained in his chair, staring out the window, until he heard my voice. He turned around in shock. The last time we were together was the day we buried Minela.

"Jacob?" He said my name as if he didn't believe I was real and standing just a few feet away from him. "What...what are you doing here? We haven't seen or heard from you since..."

"Since...your daughter's funeral? Where I watched my beautiful fiancée get lowered down into the cold earth."

"I'm not doing this with you, Jacob. I don't know why you are here, but you need to get the hell out, right now," he bellowed back at me.

"I'm afraid I can't do that, Joe."

"I have nothing to say to you, or your mute friend standing behind you."

"Well, I have a few things to say to you, and I am not leaving until I do. So shut the hell up, and don't interrupt me."

Duffy took a few steps back and gave me the room I needed. As I looked around the room, my eyes found a picture of Minela in her Boston PD uniform. It looked like it was taken on her graduation day from the academy. She was surrounded by her brothers and parents. She looked so proud of her accomplishment.

"So tell me, Joe, how much blood money paid for this house? The fancy cars? That fucking Rolex on your wrist? I know what you did, and I just want to know why? Why was the once-respected police chief of Boston in bed with the fucking mob? The same dirty business you owed nearly a million dollars to, and when you wouldn't pay back your debts, they settled another way, right, Joe?"

"Get out! Just leave me alone. How can you come into my home and spew lies about me? I loved her. She was my daughter!"

He threw his glass and slammed his fists down to his desk.

"A daughter that was sacrificed for your fucking gambling addiction! A daughter that was gunned down in the middle of the street, who died in my arms, you cold sonofabitch! I loved her. We were going to be married and would be today if you hadn't been such a coward. You let her be killed, and then allowed me to believe that somehow it was my fault. How do you live with yourself knowing you are responsible for taking a life, a precious life who had everything to live for, but took the bullet that should have been for you?"

"How do you live with yourself? You tell me why you did this! How could you?" Answer me, dammit! You can't, can you? Because you are still a coward. You lost your daughter. Your wife is not your wife anymore. She's nothing but an empty shell. Was it worth it? You get to sit here, day in and day out, drinking your scotch. You don't get to feel sorry for yourself when she is rotting in the fucking ground because of you. You should be the one, not her."

He replied, "Don't you think I would if I could? My beautiful girl…they took her from me."

"No, you did this. Your greed and damn ambition got her killed. You. Took. Her. Away. From. Me. You took away a living angel! And you never even said you were sorry. I dreamed of this moment since the night she died. I would never stop looking for the person responsible for taking away my precious girl. I knew what I wanted to do but also knew I would have to follow the law and bring her killer to justice. That day never came for me…until today. I have a file full of evidence I could use to bring you down and send you to prison for the rest of your miserable life, but even that would be too good for you. The only justice I could ever live with is to see you dead, but I won't do it. She loved you. She only wanted you to be proud of her and give us your blessing for our marriage."

"Stop it, please. I can't hear no more, please," he pleaded. He was broken and weak.

I watched him open a locked drawer to his desk. He pulled out a Glock 22 from the side drawer and placed it down in front of him. Duffy's hand went to his service weapon. I put my hand up to him to keep him at bay. LaRocha shoved the gun closer to me.

Looking directly into my eyes, he said, "Do it! I have nothing to live for. My daughter is dead, and I want to be with her. Do it, Jacob! Have your justice, so I can be with her again. Do it!"

I stepped closer but didn't touch the gun.

"You will never see Minela again, and do you want to know why that is? Because you are a living form of the devil, and you belong in hell. My beautiful girl's soul is in heaven, and I pray every single day that she is at peace. And then I thank God for her not being here to see her poor excuse for a father. You are nothing. You deserve nothing. You belong in hell."

"That's just it, Jacob, I'm already there," he said, sobbing.

"Then the next step should be easy. Let's go, Duffy. We're done here."

Duffy looked around the room in confusion and debated silently if we should leave him like this. I was done, and there would be no changing my mind. I had nothing left to say to him and wished never to lay eyes on him again.

I turned away from LaRocha, where he still remained in his chair, behind his desk, staring down to his gun. I walked out first, and then Duffy hesitated once more, but then joined me.

The housekeeper reappeared and showed us out. We were back in my car, and I drove us back to the city. My hands were shaking the whole time.

"Jake, talk to me. Are you okay? That was intense back there."

"Yeah, it was, but it's over, Duffy. I meant what I said. I wasn't going to end his life and give him the peace he was seeking. He lived his life like a coward and will die as a coward. It just won't be by my hands."

One week later, I was standing before a review committee, answering questions pertaining to Joseph LaRocha's fatal suicide. When I left his home, he was alive. His housekeeper stated that when questioned. I explained that I was there for a personal matter and not under the guise of the FBI. I never compromised the position I held or the oath I took. What led me to his door has now been destroyed, and I, along with Duffy, will take it to our graves.

Afterwards, Duffy asked me into his office to have the conversation he had pushed aside in hopes I would change my mind. The answer was clear to me the moment I saw Zoey and the condition she was in. I just wanted out of this life, which was why I was there now. I had already filed my official resignation with my New York field director, and now it was time to say it to Duffy. I placed my badge and my service weapon down on his desk and stepped back with my hands folded behind my back.

"Are you sure about this?" Duffy asked. He had been my mentor since I came up from the NYPD, and he taught me everything I knew about being a cop. He would always be a cop and probably would have to be shoved out the door when his time was up. For me, that time was now.

"Yes, I am. I don't want this life anymore. It's ugly, and it holds too many memories that I wish to forget."

"You had some good ones too, Jake."

"I know, but it's not enough for me to stay."

"You know, Jake, I may have not done what you did back in Boston, but I understand why, and I am so sorry you ever had to go through that. You are my friend, and I will always have your back in any decision you make. Just know that I'm here if you should ever change your mind."

He walked around the desk to take me into his arms, slap me on my back, and grab onto my coat. He was a good friend. He wiped a tear from his eye. "Tough guys don't cry," he once said to me, but here he was doing just that. I didn't razz him about it, and just smiled at the memory of one of many of our great conversations. I grabbed my box of personal items and made my way to his door.

He kicked his feet up and said, "Fine, go be stupid. Marry that girl before she gets away."

I couldn't hold in my laughter if I wanted to, not this time. I wanted this more than anything in the world, and I would soon have it.

"I fully intend to, my friend. Happily ever after is waiting for me, and her name is Zoey Steele. But soon she will be Mrs. Jacob Paulson…forever."

CHAPTER *Thirty*

ONE YEAR LATER...

Jack

We were invited to spend Christmas in California with Simon, Nicolette, and their beautiful children, Kai and Cali. They were born at the end of June via cesarean section for Nicolette. She carried her babies to nearly full-term, and they weighed in at over four pounds each.

I was so proud of her. She was a mother, and her dream had finally come true. Everything she had gone through had led to this defining moment. Considering my actions over the past year, I was lucky I was here at all. The smoke had cleared, and I was rebuilding my life, one without my past weighing me down. I kept my promise to move forward with my life and spend it happily with my family. Our restaurant was restored to its original glory and once again frequented by our close-knit community. Max still came in from time to time for a game of pool or to chat it up with Tommy, but it was never the same since I cut my ties to the other family in my life that owned my past.

We had chosen different paths in life, and when it came down to it, we just didn't fit in each other's world...not anymore. I wanted to prove to Sara, Massimo, and especially to Nicolette that I was worthy of their love and trust. I wanted to be Uncle Jack to her children, and watch them grow up as I did with my Nickel.

As for Jacob, he kept to his word and never spoke to me again. How could he, after I revealed what I knew about the most horrific tragedy in his past? I hadn't seen him in nearly a year after our meeting. Even when I visited the babies, he made sure not to be there. Seeing me again would only serve as a reminder to what he had lost. I wasn't directly involved, but I knew who was.

Simon explained this to me one day as we walked the beach near their home. He would always respect me because I was important to Nicolette, but he had to put his family first. He never said the words aloud, but I believed he knew the truth about Michael's demise, the role I played in it, and how it ultimately affected his brother's life. When it came to family, lines should never be drawn out in the sand, but Simon would always choose Jacob before me. This I knew and came to terms with. I had no choice if I wanted to be in their lives. I was welcomed, but also kept at a safe distance.

I heard Jacob left the FBI, got married, and was now living a quieter life on his ranch in Colorado. I had no right to know anything about him, but it gave me peace when Nicolette shared the news with me.

Christmas would be my first time in the same room with him. Out of loyalty to his brother, Jacob shared an afternoon with me but stayed as far away as he could. He protectively held his wife close to his side, every once in a while finding me in the room. When our eyes did connect, they were cold and unforgiving. I reconciled that rather quickly and went on to enjoy the holiday with my new great nephew and niece.

The babies each carried traits from both their father and mother.

Cali would be a beauty like Nicolette. Her hair was her color of dark brown, whereas Kai had lighter tones like Simon. I waited patiently for my turn to hold them, but I was last on the long line. The women cooed and awed over the babies, while I watched with tears in my eyes. This was their happy moment, and I once again was lucky enough to witness it.

Nicolette continued to look over where I was seated. I was alone, watching the celebration before me. I was invited, but somehow I knew I really wasn't included. Simon stayed close to his parents and brothers. They were laughing and sharing what was sure to be good memories.

Although we had made peace with one another, I still felt on the outside looking in around Massimo, doing my best to smile and not take anything too personal. What did I expect? I was here due to Nicolette's kind invitation. I would accept anything they offered.

When it was my turn with the babies, Nicolette asked me to follow her down to their nursery where we could have privacy. Sara gave me a sweet smile and blew me a kiss. She was my rock. A small sofa was centered in front of the window to look out to the ocean. With the love of the ocean flowing through their genes, I had no doubt that these babies would be surfers like their father. Their names were unique and special just like their parents' love story. Kai's name meant the sea, chosen by Simon, who dedicated his life to preserving oceans all over the world. Nicolette chose Cali's name. She once told me that she wanted her daughter to be empowered one day, to always have courage, to inspire ones that have lost hope, and to find true love in the hearts of many. Nicolette did that every day with the women who walked through her foundation. Her daughter would be strong and change the world just like her beautiful mother before her.

I was nervous to hold them. They had turned six months old on Christmas Day and were wearing outfits with the number six on them. She handed me Kai first, then Cali. My tears were unstoppable just at the sight of these angels in my arms. I was blessed with so much in my life, and it was still a battle of will to believe I deserved what I was generously given. The only ones that never judged me were Sara and Nicolette. I was only better because of them, and I would continue to be better for these two miracles nestled sweetly in my arms.

"They will love you, Uncle Jack. I will make sure of it…I promise."

"You don't need to say that, Nicolette, not to me. I will never forget this gift you have given me today. I love you, Nickel, and I always will."

"Uncle Jack, if I have learned anything in this life, it is to not give up on the ones that love me. You are my hero, remember? That was our deal a long time ago, and I expect you to be one for my children. Thank you, Uncle Jack, for protecting me and keeping me safe. I love you. Please never forget that."

She leaned down to kiss me and gave me some time with Kai and Cali. Without saying the actual words, I knew and understood what Nicolette so desperately wanted me to believe.

More tears fell down as I held them. Kai looked so much like Simon. Every once in a while, Cali would pucker her little lips, reminding me of Nicolette when she was born. They looked peaceful and content. What could they be dreaming about that makes them smile in their sleep? I shared a story with them about their great grandparents, and how much they would have loved them.

"Oh, precious ones, you are tiny angels sent from above. You've come to fill our hearts with joy. May your life always be filled with love and peace. Uncle Jack loves you, little ones."

Nicolette and Simon returned to the nursery. I could tell Nicolette heard what I said to her children. She wiped away her tears and took her daughter from my arms, but not before, I placed a kiss to her head. I did the same for Kai before Simon took his son.

I left their home that day with Sara's hand in mine. I always wore my heart on my sleeve when it came to my family. I fiercely loved and protected them. It was time for them to stand on their own and allow me to do the same.

My life went on, and it was spent loving Sara and tending to my bar. I never stopped walking through the city I loved, along the sidewalks and among the businesses that people like mama and papa worked so hard to build. My past would forever be bound to these streets, where I fought, survived, and finally broke free from.

As I got closer to my bar from one of those walks, I could hear the cheers of excitement coming from the inside. Denver was winning, and my place was packed with happy customers. I waved to Tommy, who was behind the bar, chatting it up with the customers. I took a glance through the window of the kitchen and saw Sara busy at work, smiling doing what she loved most. Of course, she always sensed when I was near and looked up to wink at me. I made my way up the stairs to my home, but not before looking down to the crowd below.

My life was far from being finished, but my past was. I would continue to live in the now, and never look back to the man I once was.

Not every story has the perfect ending. Right here, right now, if this was mine, then my happily ever after was more than I ever dreamed possible.

CHAPTER Thirty-One

ONE YEAR LATER...

Jacob

Zoey never asked me about what happened on that fateful day with LaRocha. I would never keep anything from her, but I also needed time to process all that had happened, especially after I watched the news and confirmed what I knew he would do in the end.

The same gun he retrieved from his desk was the one he used to end his life. He went out quietly with no note left behind. He put that gun to the base of his neck and blew a hole right through his body. He instantly died in his own pool of blood. He was found by his son, Paolo, who would never know the truth to why I was there on the last day of his father's life.

Maybe they knew? I would never know because I never saw or spoke to any one of the LaRocha men since her funeral. They went about their lives, as I did with mine. I thought I would be forever connected with them because of Minela and the love we had for her, but no.

She would want me to be free, to find happiness once again, and to love again. As it pained me to do so, I left my heart in that house along with everything I had ever felt for his daughter.

Before leaving Boston, I did make my first and only trip to her grave. I hadn't been there since she was laid to rest. I cursed at myself when I had forgotten where she was in the cemetery. I needed to ask where she was, so I could pay my respects. I felt ashamed for not remembering.

When I finally found her resting place throughout rows and rows of memorials, I knelt down to the snow-covered ground and spent a few minutes with the girl I once dreamed of sharing my life with. I was not alone, though. Zoey was there with me. I needed her more than my next breath. She gave me the time I needed, but also gave me comfort in knowing that she was close and I wasn't alone…not anymore.

I brushed off the snow that was covering her name with my glove. Running my fingers over the inscription made me feel chills throughout my body, and it wasn't from the cold. Would she hate me for what I did to her father? I wasn't sure if I would ever be ready for that answer, so I prayed for peace…peace in knowing that this nightmare was truly over, and I could get on with my life. Parts of my past would never be forgotten. It was impossible to ever think otherwise, because that would mean that she, and the love I felt for her, never existed.

Knowing Zoey could probably hear my words, I recited them in silence for only Minela to hear:

"I love you, beautiful girl. You showed me what it is to love and to feel how it is when you are loved back. Our time together was short, but it was a time that was magical. I would give anything to have you here with me, but we both know that's not how it is written in our story. Please don't hate me for what I've done. If angels do have the power to watch from up above, then you know I had no other choice. I'll never be sorry for it, but only sorry for you. Rest in

peace, Minela."

As I rose to my feet, Zoey was there to hold me. I cupped her face and kissed her lips.

"Let's go home. I love you."

"Lead the way, my love."

No one in my family was surprised about the announcement I made about my plans to marry Zoey. The Paulson's, in their amazing way, welcomed Zoey into our family with open arms, and plenty of bone crushing hugs followed.

As for Simon and Nicolette, they had survived once again a potential threat to their happiness. After my confrontation with Jack, I received an anonymous package. The unmarked envelope was stuffed with pictures and an outline of intent meant for Nicolette, planned out from Michael St. Clair once he was to be released on parole. I was sickened by what I saw and felt relief knowing he was dead and could no longer hurt her. I knew who had sent the envelope to me and his reasoning behind it. Guilt comes in many shapes and sizes, and he was trying to justify the choices he made…choices that brought Marino into my life, forcing me to come to terms with Minela's murder.

His truth ripped me open, and I would need thousands of stitches to put me back together again. I hated Jack Vanelle on sight, and I hated the world he came from. I had already closed one door to my past with Chief LaRocha; I would not go down this road again with Jack. When our paths crossed, I swore to uphold the law to the best of my ability and to bring to justice those who threatened to break what I vowed to protect. He had a criminal past, tied to one of the most powerful mafia families in Chicago. For all the time I had known him, he was just Nicolette's Uncle Jack and a bar owner. I soon learned the realities of the real Jack Vanelle, and one I wish to never speak of again.

I was taking the procedural measures of leaving the FBI, and I had a choice to make. I could hand over what landed in my hands, or destroy it like before with LaRocha. St. Clair was dead and the investigation had been closed. Nicolette deserved to be happy and live a wonderful blessed life with Simon.

After we celebrated Zoey's welcoming into our family, I was left on my own with Simon. We walked along the same beach we reunited on months ago when I first arrived in California. I promised him that I would always protect him and Nicolette. No one would ever hurt them again, especially me. The first time was hard enough for me to hear his words. I could never go through that again with him. He meant too much to me.

I asked his advice first and gave him the time to answer me. He knew it was like opening Pandora's Box, and once he made the decision of looking inside, he would always have the knowledge of the secrets that I was holding in my hand. He reached out his hand, and I knew he needed this to move forward. He looked at everything the file contained. I watched him take in several deep breaths, probably to calm himself down from what he was feeling. He then simply said to me, "Destroy it, and let's never speak of this again." We never did.

As for Jack, Simon was the one that was connected to him through Nicolette. I would never ask him to choose, already knowing my brother would be loyal to me. He respected my wishes, and he would do his best not to have my path ever cross with Jack's. If it were ever to be unavoidable, then I would respectively keep my distance. He served as a reminder of bad things, and I didn't need any more of those. My life was centered on Zoey and the future we would have together.

That day came on a sunny day in October. We were married on our ranch in front of only our closest friends and family. My new nephew and niece served as mini ring bearer and flower girl. They stole the show with their grand entrance. Baby Cali wore a miniature version of a wedding dress. The top was cotton like an onesie, and the bottom was a puffy skirt with ruffled tights underneath. And the little man, Kai, wore a one-piece cotton tuxedo and had a tiny pillow attached to his wrist. Simon carried his son, while Nicolette carried their daughter down the aisle. My mother was crying. Zoey's mother was crying. Every woman in attendance was crying. Babies had a way of doing that to you.

Then it was the moment I had been waiting for. Zoey arrived on a white stallion, on loan from my neighbor who bred horses. The horse was called Snow, and she was covered in flowers with the most beautiful beauty sitting on her and then being brought down to me. The horse stopped at the entrance to the aisle, and her father took it from there. He held out his hands to help Zoey off the horse. He kissed her cheek and walked his daughter down the aisle. Once she was close enough to touch, our hands connected, and we both mouthed the words "I love you."

Her father gave the minister his blessing, and then we said our vows. They were simple. I thanked Zoey for giving me the best gift, I could ever receive, and that was simply her unconditional love, friendship, and soon her promise of children. She brought me back to life when I had all but given up on ever finding love again. I was in tears by the time I slipped the ring onto her finger. My brothers all patted me on my back in support.

When it was time for Zoey to say her vows to me, she too kept it simple. She thanked her matron of honor and best friend, Tenley, for going back home. If it wasn't for Tenley finding the road back to her heart, then Zoey would have never found me. She told me that she never found love with anyone before me. She was happy that she waited for God to bring her the prince she was wishing for.

We were pronounced husband and wife as the sun set over the Rocky Mountains. It was as if the sunset was meant just for my new bride and me. I looked up to heaven and whispered a silent thank you.

After our wedding, life was perfect. We had made a home in the house I had built. We planned our life in this home. My goal was to get her pregnant as soon as possible. I was right when I knew Zoey would want children right away, especially after spending time with Kai and Cali. I left the FBI behind, and Zoey was on a permanent leave from her law practice. She loved the law, but it no longer gave her the satisfaction it once did. I was okay with whatever she decided, but I was a selfish man and wanted her all to myself. *Yeah...this marriage thing is awesome.*

Ten months later, we welcomed our first child, a son. He was strong with fierce lungs. He was the loudest baby in the nursery. We named him Christopher Michael Paulson, and our family was complete.

As I held my son in my arms, I knew the life I had in this moment was perfect, one that had no darkness, pain, or loss. It was filled with light, warmth, and love. I no longer carried broken pieces of my life that were unfinished. I was whole again. My heart was full of love for my beautiful wife and son, who had changed my life. I no longer lived with the past that nearly destroyed me.

You can never know where you're going until you know where you've been. I understood that better than anyone. After the rain, the clouds parted, and there was sun. Zoey found a place in my heart and changed my life. It was a blessed one, and I was exactly where I was meant to be.

Other Books by Mary A. Wasowski

A Changed Life **(standalone)**

Forever Series:

Forever: Book One
Second Chance at Forever: Book Two
Our Forever Promise: Book Three

All Roads Lead Home **(standalone)**

About the Author

Mary A. Wasowski is a Best Selling Author who writes adult contemporary romance. Best known for her *Forever Series*. This is her sixth publication.

A romantic at heart. She is an avid reader when she's not writing. Her Kindle goes everywhere with her! Born and raised in New Jersey, she shares her life with her husband, Henry, and three sons. She now lives in North Carolina, and works as a full-time writer.

Stay in touch

I would love to hear from you.
Please stay connected wherever you are.

EMAIL:
AuthorMaryAWasowski@gmail.com

FACEBOOK:
https://www.facebook.com/pages/Author-Mary-A-Wasowski

TWITTER:
https://twitter.com/wasow6

INSTAGRAM:
https://instagram.com/authormaryawasowski/

WEBSITE:
http://authormaryawasowski.com/

GOODREADS:
https://www.goodreads.com/author/show/6949510.Mary_A_Wasowski

GOOGLE +:
https://plus.google.com/+MaryWasowski

TSU:
http://www.tsu.co/authormaryawasowski

www.ingramcontent.com/pod-product-compliance
Lightning Source LLC
Chambersburg PA
CBHW071247250626
47163CB00002B/363